# ❧ SHELTER

BOOKS BY
JAYNE ANNE PHILLIPS

Black Tickets

Machine Dreams

Fast Lanes

Shelter

LIMITED EDITIONS

The Secret Country

How Mickey Made It

Counting

Sweethearts

# SHELTER

JAYNE ANNE PHILLIPS

Houghton Mifflin / Seymour Lawrence

BOSTON    NEW YORK

FOR SAM

Library of Congress Cataloging-in-Publication Data

Phillips, Jayne Anne, date.
    Shelter / Jayne Anne Phillips.
            p.    cm.
    ISBN 0-395-48890-7
    I. Title.
    PS3566.H479S48    1994
    813'.54 — dc20    94-8391    CIP

Printed in the United States of America

BP 10 9 8 7 6 5 4 3

Book design by Anne Chalmers

Portions of this book have appeared, in different form, in *Esquire, Granta,* and *Listening to Ourselves: More Stories from "The Sound of Writing"* (Anchor Books,
1994). The quotation on pages 192 and 193 is taken from *Uncle Arthur's Bedtime
Stories,* by Arthur S. Maxwell (Review and Herald Publishing, 1950).

*Author's note:* The rhyme "Up the Airy Mountain" was found in my mother's papers, written in her hand as a six-year-old, 1931. The source of the rhyme is unknown. I wish to thank the National Endowment for the Arts, the Guggenheim
Foundation, and the MacDowell Colony for generous support during the writing of
this work. I'm grateful to Joe Kanon, Camille Hykes, and Larry Cooper for sensitive
editing. And I continue to thank Sam Lawrence, the angel of my writing life, in every
word.

# ❈ WHO THEY ARE

## IN GAITHER

Audrey and Wes Swenson, the parents
Lenny and Alma, the sisters

Mina and Nickel Campbell, the parents
Delia and Johnny, the children
Aunt Bird, Mina's sister

Henry and Catherine Briarley
Cap (Catherine), the daughter
Juanita, their housekeeper

## IN THE COUNTRY

Carmody and Hilda Carmody, his wife
Buddy, her little boy

Parson
His legion

Mrs. Thompson-Warner, widow, camp directress

Frank, camp employee

McAdams and Pearlie, camp employees

The workmen by the river

Mud River

Turtle Hole

And I saw an angel come down from heaven,
having the key of the bottomless pit and a
great chain in his hand. And he laid hold on
the dragon, that old serpent, which is the
Devil . . . and bound him a thousand years,
And cast him into the bottomless pit, and
shut him up, and set a seal upon him, that he
should deceive the nations no more, till the
thousand years should be fulfilled: and after
that he must be loosed a little season.

—Revelation 20:1–3


Every angel is terrifying.

—Rilke, *Duino Elegies*

LATE JULY, 1963

SHELTER COUNTY,
WEST VIRGINIA

*Concede the heat of noon in summer camps. The quarters waver-*
*ing in bottled heat, cots lined up in the big dark rooms that are*
*pitch black if you walk in out of the sun. Black, quiet, empty, and*
*the screen door banging shut three times behind you. Allowed in*
*alone only if you are faint. Perhaps the heat has come over you,*
*settled in from above and sucked your insides until you must lie*
*down to sleep in the empty cabin while the rest are at hiking or*
*canoes or archery. Now you lie there sleeping and the room is*
*heavy and warm, but cooler than noon, the rough wooden walls*
*exuding shade. The cots are precisely mute. Identical and differ-*
*ent in olive-green blankets, each pulled tight and tucked. In your*
*mind, you see the bodies lying there, each in its own future. You*
*are frightened because it is you here with the future. And they are*
*scattered along Mud River walk, obscured by dense leaves, their*
*occasional cries no louder than the sounds of the invisible birds.*
*Or they are standing in line before bright targets stretched across*
*baled hay. They are holding taut bows straight out, pulling back*
*on the strings with all their strength.*

# ❧ LENNY: HIGHER AND HIGHEST

The sky burned white to blond to powder to an almighty blue; the sun fell unobstructed. The girls wore heavy green shorts that were too long and short-sleeved white blouses embroidered in a clover silhouette above the right breast. The blouses were all too big; only the older girls with larger breasts looked strangely seductive in them. The dark shorts were forest-green gabardine, fluted with fine yellow braid on two deep pockets. In Charleston, the state headquarters of Girl Guides did not concede the heat of the Appalachian summer; they recommended knee socks with garters, neckerchiefs with a gold pin at the throat, wool berets. But Camp Shelter was newly reopened, the cabins were in shored-up disrepair, the cots themselves castoffs from a Boy Scout camp in the Panhandle. The county was low income, the mines, statewide, laid off. Only the shorts and blouses were regulation; girls on Supplement or Full Supplement wore secondhand uniforms and got away with rolling up their sleeves.

The upper sites had no cabins at all, just tents donated by the Veterans of Foreign Wars. The tents were war surplus, army olive, weathered, alight on squat frames that were new and rough. Each frame seemed the unfinished skeleton of some more ambitious structure. A row of pale two-by-fours angled out from the wooden platforms that served as floors; like rows of awkward elbows, each held a lashed knot tight and the square form of the tent remained uncomfortably aloft. The raised front flaps were tied back, revealing olive interiors so completely plain that the metal cots with their blue-striped mattresses looked direly ornamental. The plank floors tilted and some were supported by posts in front or behind. Lenny and Cap were in the last row of Highest; beyond the rear wall of their tent, the world dropped off. Tattered in the descending bank, brush and flowers grew waist high. Lenny had stood there, looking up. From behind, the tents seemed temporary and strange. Like the dwellings of nomads in flight from floods, they perched on the hillsides in ascending order. Enclaves meant to be A, B, and C camps were soon dubbed High, Higher, and Highest: Girl Guides were rotated ever higher, the better to experience lashing in the wild and long hikes to flag raising. Seniors at Highest camp walked provisions up every morning after early swim in Mud River, and were never seen except at breakfast and at seven A.M. formation. Lenny and Cap stood then in a single line with the rest, just round the flag, looking hard and scratched in their dark, wrinkled Bermudas as the Juniors struggled out of the woods. The Seniors wore slouchy beige or white hats and terry-cloth wristbands: marks of combat with the insects and the heat, and the mist they were already walking through when reveille sounded far below at the quad. The dew-slick windings that were the trails from Highest were a jungle unto themselves and smelled of melons and snakes. Lenny was a Senior with the Seniors. What did they do up there all day? *A million things,* Lenny had lied to her sister, Alma, who was only a Junior and slept in a civilized cabin off the quad. At night the Seniors sang. Lenny knew they were made to sing. From below, their fires would appear as haphazard orange winks in the dark, and their voices must carry as vague chants that lifted and dropped: *Come by here, my Lord.* Lenny thought they were probably praying.

After cooking and mess duty and campfire close, they finally went to their tents, each one a canvas bunker whose sides and drooping roof held the heat of the day. Lenny and Cap were on the side of the mountain; if they tied up the front and rear flaps, air moved through the tent like a blessing. At ten and eleven they were still awake, indolent, murmuring, lying on narrow cots with the sheets still tucked. Cap wore her underwear but Lenny took off everything, relieved to be rid at last of the blouse that buttoned to the neck, the heavy shorts that covered her to her knees. She lay on her bed, legs spread, arms out, her blond hair flung over her face. Her hair, weighty, dense, released from its binding elastic, smelled of woodsmoke but felt cool; she imagined its light color made it cool in the dark of night on Highest. Even the lanterns were out. The counselors were sleeping, having made up chore lists for tomorrow; in these hours, Lenny was free. She felt her body borne up and slowly spinning, spun free by the cooling air, the blackness, the night sounds that grew louder and louder as she concentrated on each one: crickets emitting their pierced warbles, the woods owls hooting like they were trying to get breath, the grasses moving ever so slightly, crack of a twig. Though she complained, Lenny liked camp; she liked being dirty, dousing a change of uniform in the stream, throwing it over a rope line to dry, and putting it on still damp. She liked how the river slid, brown and flat, just a stretch of woods from Turtle Hole, the swimming pond whose mysterious depths were forbidden. She liked being with girls and the fact there were no boys, just Buddy, the cook's little kid, who followed them everywhere like the plague, and Frank, the good-looking bugler, perhaps a year older than they, safely observed from a distance. There were four or five county workmen, faceless in khaki clothes, but their river colony of ditches and pipes seemed unreal as home.

Walking was real. Lenny liked the endless walking that was by now automatic, the meaningless, inarguable up and down of the mountain. The routine, the common movements of the group, were oddly pleasant: nothing to be thought of, nothing to be decided, only this chore or that chore, all of them alike, really, the cleaning of objects, the storage of objects, the carrying up and down the mountain of objects. Even food seemed a series of objects, peeled and cut and cooked into mash, even the water to cook it hauled from somewhere. All day Lenny carried this or that — apples, potatoes, buckets, wood — through shimmering heat, conscious sometimes of the heat as a nearly liquid element, as though they were all kept upright, forced to move by what oppressed them. They struggled against it as swimmers struggle, cutting through, buoyed up.

The days were long. When dark descended, Lenny felt cooled and numb. She thought of the glass of beer in her father's hand: she felt as translucent and dense. He would be drinking beer now, on the dark porch at home, in the absolute quiet of Alma's and Lenny's absence, Audrey a canceled zero somewhere in the workings of the house. Lenny couldn't imagine her mother except in the context of Alma and herself; her father she saw clearly. Wes existed apart from them, always — that was Audrey's constant reproach. Home nights, Lenny often walked outside with a paper cup and Wes would pour her part of his beer; she drank it down in slow swallows and it spread through her. At night in Camp Shelter, protected by Cap and dozens of sleeping strangers, she imagined the beer pouring into her and over her, thick and golden like cold, syrupy lava, poured from her father's glass in a Technicolor dream. She wasn't here with Cap, she wasn't anywhere. In the emptiness, full, she nearly slept but didn't sleep, and floated.

## ※ PARSON: IN THE SHACK AT NIGHT

At night the shack was darker even than the night beyond it, and when he first lay down on his pallet he felt himself cosseted within some creature whose existence he had always suspected. He seemed to be in utter darkness, the dark that is in the inner guts of living things, and he listened for a heartbeat and heard it, a pounding on a wall, a wrenching pump pump pump that was wet and sick, and gradually the close, furry dark took on a bit of the light of the open night, the night in the forest. Out there the sky looked paler than the trees, which were so black they had no depth, and palest of all was the glassy surface of Turtle Hole, which he could see through the two windows of the front wall of the shack. A week ago he'd torn down the tar paper covering the cracked glass: Turtle Hole lay forward and to the right. From deep in the overhanging trees he glimpsed its opaque light. The water was roundly lopsided like a bowl squashed flat, the water was motionless like night ice that still might tremble if some creature swam beneath the perfect surface, the water scared him mightily and so he lay very still, he lay there and the space of the shack enlarged. Floater, underling, he clung to an udder of charcoal dark and saw the steep pitch of the shack roof above him, weathered gray of the boards pale against tar paper. Someone else had stayed here, stuffed paper between the boards, nailed up a few wood scraps in the corner where the slant was worst. Must have been a chicken coop, with a roosting shelf some tramp had long ago made into a bed. Now the partition boards were gone and the shelf built up with straw, straw he smelt chickens in, an old dust of powder and feathers, he'd sooner bed with rats than chickens, he'd killed rats many a time, shot them with a revolver when he was Preacher's boy. But chickens made him scared, the way they bobbed and pecked, jerking here and there on devilish horned feet, blinking their raw, pink eyes that were stupid and soulless as the eyes of fish. The noise they made, the *bwak bwak* cut and cluck, the *ck ck ck* that stammered and froze his blood, how he used to have to chop their heads off at Proudytown, stand there and hold the bloody hatchet while their headless bodies flopped and staggered like runt machines. They were evil, the way they couldn't die, they might have made him evil too, kitchen matron quarreling at him, go on out there and pick up them birds, big boy like you scared of chickens, you gonna eat it you better be ready to kill it, but he didn't eat it, never did, he didn't want that flesh inside him even when his guts rolled with hunger. Oh, it was dark inside him, he knew he was born dark and he liked to be in the daytime, in the dark he had to lie still and watch.

He told himself everything evil was long gone from here. Summers and winters the shack had been empty, falling down for years, who knew how many, maybe as far back as when he was with Preacher, sermonizing, sixteen years old, cowlick and a swarth of beard, dark kid, *guinea kid,* they taunted him at school, in need of a haircut and clothes, in need of a home, Preacher would say from the pulpit. So he became Preacher's foster son, even preached on Fridays, sweating, Bible in his hand, and while he'd shouted in Preacher's Calvary house, snakes had molted here in this abandoned slant of boards. Parson had found skins, some of them so old they fell to dust when he lifted them out of leaves and dirt. Whatever he found that was good he put beneath his pallet: the dry leaves, an empty honeycomb, the clean bones of small animals rotted and returned to powders, and the snakeskins. There were rags of blankets left by vagrants, men who must have slept here in winter when the camp was closed. And since he'd gotten work on the pipe crew, the directress, a fat redheaded woman white as pink-tinged chalk, had sent him twice to the dump with a truckload of junk. Now he had a metal kitchen chair with a ripped plastic seat, and a cot mattress discolored and torn, softer under him than any bed he remembered. He had magazines. He had a dish with a blue flower on it, and a bucket with no handle he filled at Turtle Hole near dusk. Kneeling to fill it, he saw his own face wavering and broken on the cool surface, sometimes he splattered the image with his hand, with his face, biting water that tasted clean and cut like glass, cold and brilliant, and when he came up sputtering he heard the girls singing in their camps, the sounds vague and high, mesmerizing, every night they sang and he could never hear the words, there were different words from different directions and their nonsensical rise and fall seemed to call and answer, calling him, answering, and he knew he'd come to the right place, he'd followed Carmody and come to a place he was meant to find. It almost didn't matter who he followed, any of them, fallen, vicious in their minds, could lead him to grace.

In prison he'd watched Carmody carefully. Carmody, long and lank, his faded, wheat-colored hair and squinty eyes, his face that was not young with its callow, unfinished look, showing always an edge of the rabbity anger that caused him to hang back, scheming while his cohorts strutted and preened. Carmody moved, not seeming to move, planned while he appeared to sleep: Parson dreamed Carmody was water, an elongated sheen not unlike Turtle Hole in color and brilliance, an oval water that moved along the edges of things like a shade or a ghost, a water that moved up walls, through bars, edged past the warrens of cells along the main corridor of the prison, water that glistened, featureless and flat, probing, searching to take on any shape, any color, anything to get out. For some of them, prison was no worse than what they'd lived through. But prison broke Carmody up, he was wild to finish his time, afraid of the wardens, afraid of the other men. He even seemed afraid of his wife and kid, or afraid to see them, the wife a big woman gone to fat and the kid a pale towhead, quick and thin, darting beside her like a shadow tethered to a string. Before their rare visits Carmody was jumpy. He said his old lady was a nut for God, she and Parson would get on, but Parson wasn't much for women, was he, and Carmody laughed. Parson could smell the fear on him, a bitter vegetable smell like rotted seeds and pulp. For a while they'd shared a cell in D block: Carmody flowed from one side to the other, pacing in the dark, ranting about the block bosses and their gofers until he knelt in the corner and beat at the wall with his fist, a rhythmic pounding punctuated by frantic whispers, I gotta be a good boy, good boy, gotta be a good boy, *kill* them, *fuck* them, until Parson dragged him by the back of his shirt to the bunks and prayed over him. Oh Christ, Carmody would mutter, struggle like a cat in a sack, shut up you crazy loon, they all know you're crazy, why the hell do you think they leave you alone? But the praying always worked and Parson was strong enough to hold Carmody still, hold him in the healing grip of the Heavenly Father and press hard against the evil, press hard and shake the Devil loose.

Now Parson could hear the Devil walk near the shack at night, stalking spirits in the vaporous air. The devil made a scrunching sound in the grasses and leaves and loose dirt, a sound like a creature with tiny feet, and there was the airy, slick whish of the Devil's probing tongue, tasting and wanting, just on the other side of the thin board wall. The mist of Turtle Hole was like wet smoke in the hours before dawn. In those hours Parson had to stay awake to pray, his was a consecrated soul, no matter that the Devil slithered and wandered, sniffing at the corners of the boards, picking away with his bony, glowing fingers at the rotting wood. *Poor devil,* the country people would say of a man in the grip of poverty, disease, dissolution. And that face of the Devil pulled and sucked at Parson, weeping. Wasn't the Devil a fallen child, too hungry to eat, starving, ravenous, alone so long he didn't remember who'd first cast him out, a boy child, abandoned, *lost?* Parson had to pray the old prayers, ones he'd learned when Preacher had first called him Parson Boy and made him kneel to speak. Those prayers were words and more than words, flailing chants that set the air to humming, made it thick, kept the Devil pressed back beyond the boundaries of the Kingdom, back where the Devil moaned and cried, outcast, betrayed, while Preacher rattled on like a man wielding chains and whips. Back then, Parson lay in his bed in the wooden house by the

river in Calvary, not thirty miles from Proudytown and the Indus-
trial School for Boys where he'd spent the last six years. He lay in
bed in his closet room behind the small kitchen and listened to
Preacher pray alone in the parlor furnished with folding chairs,
chairs filled three meetings a week with Christ's pilgrims. Phrases
cut and slashed across Parson's vision like colors and worked their
way into his sleep. *Hear ye, Jerusalem! Cast out your sinners and
entreat your guests, slick with the liquid gold of the Devil's songs
* . . . Parson mouthed the cadences of the lines and forgot what his
name had been before, at the orphanage in Huntington, the city and
the dingy park, at the foster homes where he'd always just arrived
or was preparing to leave until the last, the one where he'd set the
house on fire to get away and old Mr. Harkness had died, stone
drunk on the broken bathroom floor, where he'd staggered from
Parson's bed. Harkness was one of the Devil's weaker servants, but
foster homes for older kids were hard to come by in the coal towns,
and the social workers sometimes placed boys with a widower on a
farm. The caseworker called Harkness, rheumy-eyed and sober, *the
picture of sincerity;* Parson had been there four months, along with
another boy of seven or eight who never talked, just ate his rice and
beans and grits and boiled chicken at Harkness's scarred table without looking up. There was the familiar mud of the country winter
and the hogs and the six goats to milk, and that was all right, the
goats were warm and quick. Their strange vertical pupils scared the
little kid, who tailed along after Parson regardless, eager to be outside because Harkness was in the kitchen, drinking. After dark he
took his Wild Turkey out of the tin cup that hung by the door on a
hook. Even then he didn't hit them; he staggered, cooking suppers,
and reeled around in the downstairs rooms after they'd gone to bed.
Later he came up, crying softly or whimpering, and lay down fully
clothed on their beds. The little boy slept under his bed but Parson
lay wrapped in his blankets, motionless under Harkness's tentative,
cautious touch until the old man fell asleep or stumbled away,
afraid. Now in the shack at night Parson watched the shapely dark
congeal into faces, all their powerful faces, his succession of keepers
and parents. Harkness wasn't the worst of them but he was helpless,
sober all morning at his half-time job as a postal worker, offering
his apologetic grin, seeing their clothes were clean and making a

show of buying new schoolbooks instead of used ones. The night of the fire was cold and Harkness's cold face felt dead to the touch, used and stretched like putty. His mouth and the smell of the whiskey were on Parson's ears and neck. Harkness begged to get into the blankets and did, then walked to the bathroom, fell down. Parson got up and went downstairs. There were still hot coals in the fireplace and he pulled the iron grate across the bricks to the rug, and the rug caught and began to blaze. It was warm quickly and there was a lot of light, and Parson went back up and pulled the kid from under the bed and they went out the bathroom window, walking over Harkness, and as they slid down the roof they could feel it was already hot and smoke came off the shingles. The kid said they'd better get the goats out, since the barn was attached to the house. They did and the goats went off, their hooves crackling over dry leaves in the dark.

The boys watched the fire from the edge of the woods. They weren't even cold, the old place made such flames, and later at the police station there was a Christmas tree on the desk. Parson told them he made the fire but no one believed him, and the kid said nothing. Parson said other things, how the Devil had licked his ears and breathed on him with his sick breath and begged to get warm. Then he was sent to Proudytown and the psychologist found out he couldn't read. He learned, decoding old texts no longer used by the county schools, a few words to a page with pictures of the blond children and the spotted dog. Run, Spot, run! Betty throws the ball! Beyond the brick facade of the school the winter sky was low slung and yellow. Scrub pine edged the hills, gnarled and overgrown, crushed by the weight of the cold, the damp that smelled of decaying straw. Parson read Bible stories from a children's book and went to the prayer meetings run by Preacher Summers, the volunteer revivalist from Calvary. Everyone called him Preacher. In chapel he turned the lights up bright, then snapped them off and prayed in the sudden dark; once in a downpour he opened the windows wide. *Hear the cleansing thunder of the Lord! Among you are souls bound for God, chosen to recognize His enemies and cast them out — the wind may tear the clothes from your backs, the multitude may call you infidel, but the Lord's child never stumbles.*

Here at the camp Parson wore khakis like the others, work

clothes given the pipe crew by the foreman. He was in disguise, just like in prison. In the shack at night Parson saw the dead, the legion of the vapor world, and the shades of the living who were marked for death. Carmody floated near the ceiling, leered his snide joke of a grin, or lounged along the low board wall in prison blues. *Where you from? You from up in my country? What you in for?* He'd laugh, and his laughter was too long and too slow. *Not saying, or don't know, maybe. They say you ought to be locked up with the loons.* Carmody's mocking words were drawn out like the sounds on Preacher's old Victrola. Preacher used to lay his finger on a record to slow the sound of the hymn, distort it to a garbled rumble: *The Devil speaks in many guises, but this is the sound of his dark, sick soul. Never pity those who are sick with evil.* The darkness in the shack swelled a little around Preacher's words, rippled, shivered like the skin of a horse. Carmody rippled too. Along the angled rafters Harkness floated in his ill-kempt blue uniform, whimpered like a dog half froze, kicked with his feet as though he were trying to swim. But the river was a ways through the trees and Turtle Hole was too perfect to admit such desolation. Harkness began a low buzzing like a fly trapped in a screen, and Parson slept.

## ❧ BUDDY CARMODY: BLACK LEAVES

No one was safe at church in the dark, but Buddy knew better than to beg not to go. While Dad was away in Carolina they'd walked down the road to the clapboard building maybe three nights a week, winter and summer, and every Sunday. Now they only went if Dad was asleep, but lately he drank himself into a stupor most nights. Then home was like it used to be. Buddy and Mam could play Crazy 8's and Slapjack at the table, and pop corn on the stove in the covered skillet. Buddy hated going to church when it was already dark, pulling on his long pants and a button-collar shirt in the heat. The clothes stuck to his sweat. At least now he didn't have to take a bath first, or Dad might wake up and get to swearing. Mam only wiped Buddy across the face with a cold cloth and made him scrub his hands. Now she shoved him gently toward the sink, whispering at him to hurry up. He squeezed the yellow soap, a slippery rectangular hunk of Fels Naptha she'd brought home from the camp kitchen. The strong-smelling lather stung his scratches.

Buddy didn't think he remembered Dad from before the prison visits, not really. He remembered someone, but Dad had gone away. Five years he was gone, and now Buddy wondered why he'd come back. It was like he didn't know he'd left jail, the way he woke up in the dark and didn't know where he was, and then went after Mam like a dog that was near starved and loony. When he was like that, she did what he wanted, and he was so loud he woke Buddy up. Fighting sleep to listen, Buddy got nervous and drowsy like he used to sometimes at school; he'd hear things, and then hear the shivery echo of each word or sound, the echoes coming faster and closer until he couldn't keep his eyes open. Sometimes in the morning Buddy didn't know what he'd really heard or what was animals fighting in his dreams, big animals with vast, muffled forms, making sounds that shook the room.

"Buddy? You ready?" Mam nodded toward the door. She had on her church clothes that fast.

He put the soap back on the drainboard and held his hands in cold water, splashed his face. He smelled wild onions on his fingers and wished it were afternoon. During summers when Mam cooked at the camp, he was on his own between meals in the big camp kitchen, wandering back and forth through the woods and along the road, using the house as an outpost he owned in Mam's absence. Now Dad was home, Buddy stayed in the woods and the fields, and walked back with Mam from Camp Shelter after supper. Once they rounded the bend she'd take off her crepe-soled shoes and Buddy would carry them. She'd roll down her nylons that only came to her knees, like socks, and put them in her pocket. My god, she'd tell Buddy, them girls throw away enough food every day to feed us for a month. But she brought supper home to Dad, and she'd found an extra freezer at camp that worked once she plugged it in. Mrs. Thompson-Warner had already told her she could buy it cheap, since it looked like the camp might shut down when the girls left. She was not going to steal food, no, stealing was a sin, but it was all right to freeze leftovers, and when camp closed she hoped she'd get one of the pipe crew to move that big freezer in their truck. Hadn't they said how they liked the lemonade she sent out to them with Frank?

"Come on out here on the porch and dress. Ain't a soul going to see you, it's full dark, and he's not sleeping sound." She leaned toward Buddy, her bulky shape vanilla-scented, her big arms filmy in her white blouse. Then she turned, her broad skirt preceding him out the door like a dark wall. They huddled down, her knees cracking as she knelt to hold his pants, and she pulled on the shirt and buttoned him in before he'd even got his hands through the cuffs.

"Mam, this shirt is hot. I'm sweating to pieces."

"Now, I had to iron it, didn't I? We just get to walking, you'll cool down on the road."

She was talking and they were down the rickety steps and the house was behind them with Dad in it, asleep like a bomb could sleep, Buddy thought, and the moon was up so bright he could see the shoulders of the road looking blond against dark brush. After the dew came up, the road didn't smell dusty, didn't smoke up a tawny veil that could drift and follow him. Now the road lay still, glowy and damp. It was the same road they walked to Camp Shelter, but church was farther on. The stone pillars of the camp entrance were dark shapes all grown over with vines. Honeysuckle licked up and down their height, countless sprays of blossoms emerging luminously ivory and gold against the dark, stacked rocks. The camp was all hidden, Buddy thought: some drunk going along at night, a drunk on foot, a drunk in a car, might not even find it. Like tonight Dad had cursed how he couldn't drive out of this place, had to walk two mile to even get to a paved road. Maybe he knew a little lady who would lend him a car that worked. You get yourself a car from some rip, better you just keep driving, Mam had told him. I'll drive, he'd said. But how could he, he'd only wreck himself. Maybe he'd get a car and not drink so he could drive.

"Mam, is our road two miles out to the highway?"

"No, course not. It's barely a mile. Don't we walk it every day, all winter? We dress warm, why, we're all right." Her breath came in soft, wuffling huffs, a kind of music. "That's why I buy us the best boots I can get, and gloves for inside our mittens, and you got that fur hat I made you."

Buddy wanted her to stay quiet so he could hear her beside him, the sound coming from above and just ahead of him, a sound familiar as his own heartbeat. Sometimes when he was by himself, he'd open his mouth a little and pant slowly, softly, trying to sound like her. In the winter her breath came out of her like furled clouds. Now she went on like a chant or a song.

"Wasn't enough for you a whole coat from that fur. Just pieces of an old muskrat jacket I got at Goodwill. Had I found more, I would have lined your coat . . ."

He stopped listening, aware of sounds beyond her voice. Just here the road was a space with tall, dense walls of foliage on either side. Honeysuckle trailers moved, slight and wafting. The same trembly flowers grew like a tangled webbing all around the frame church, and Buddy thought he could smell them too, like the heady perfume and the church itself and all the voices singing in it were creeping back along the road. Spirit could creep that way. He smelled it coming toward them.

"Listen to me, Buddy." Mam was talking still. "Don't you pay Dad any mind when he rails on like he does. He rants out his head."

"Out his head." Buddy paused. "Why is he like that?"

"Oh, he didn't used to drink so bad. But he never could stand being cooped up. Jail scared him, I reckon, reminded him of things he tries not to think about." She felt for Buddy behind her, and took his hand. "I know it's scary, but maybe the Lord means you to see what drink does to men. Then you know never to put that poison in yourself."

Buddy wanted to say Dad was poison. Instead he asked, "Would we ever get us a car?"

"Couldn't get a car moving on this road in much snow, and takes money to fix cars. They're always breaking down. And it don't hurt people to walk, whatever weather. You know my uncle gave me this house and we own it free and clear." She laughed. "When you were little and starting school, I thought of finding something in town. But those rents were so high! So what I did was get one of those plastic saucer sleds, and I'd pull you all the way down the road to the bus. You had the best time!"

During the school year, she worked in the kitchen at Buddy's school. She was the biggest of all the big women in white uniforms. It was mostly country kids who ate hot lunch, and Mam who stood behind the counter, spooning red beans onto plastic rectangular plates. Town kids got mad if their beans touched their cornbread. Mam shoved the dense yellow wedges to the side, her hand in a see-through glove the kids called monster hand. When she began working at the sink instead, Buddy could eat better, but he wanted her near him; he'd never ridden the bus without her. Last winter, he'd made her stop pulling him on the sled. It started to scare him, how hard she'd be wheezing by the time they got to the bus stop. If she fell down in the snow, he wouldn't be able to move her.

"You think you're too grown up for that stuff now," she said. "Remember how we'd hide that saucer in the pine trees and get on the bus, then pull it out in the afternoon and go on back home?"

"Yeah." He was listening hard. At certain points on the road, he could hear the girls in the upper camp, far up the mountain, singing around their fire. No words, just a windy carrying sound Buddy thought of as Lenny. He thought of the sound as her voice, and he heard it near her even in the daytime, like it wafted off her skin, and nothing could ever touch her or grab her. He'd be safe with Lenny. He was scared at church with Mam. Sitting in the long pews, she was like all the rest, saying amen, nodding, agreeing in a voice Buddy didn't recognize, a voice that was broken, gone soft. He was even scared of the road when they walked to church. It was his road, but at night it led to the church with the round windows that were like eyes. He wanted the sanctuary of the trees, their darkened leaves and layered pewter depths, and he longed to run into the woods where Mam wouldn't follow. He could imagine her standing in the road, looking at the border of the trees as at a surface of unmoving water, shouting his name, but he would have disappeared, vanished. Mam could never track him, no one could, not even Dad. A long time ago he'd learned how to run and move, cleaving sideways and upwards, using roots and vines, using stones in the stream to leave no trail at all. He could be running the stream now, hearing the rattle of the water, flying across and over it to Lenny, but he was here with Mam.

"Will you look at this?" She pulled his hand for him to stop, and they stood seeing the thickly grown trees, how they were all tangled up with glossy piles of rhododendron. The moon shone bright and just here the honeysuckle had broken out in a long gash of whitey yellow that spilled like a waterfall down a length of green. The smell of it washed over them. "Smells like honey cooked to a boil and cooling in the air. No wonder the bees go wild. But we got it to ourselves now the dew is up."

"I figure all that's on this road is ours," Buddy said.

"You do, do you. Even the bees that's thick in the daytime, even that camp where I'm working."

"We're the only house on the road, and there ain't nobody at the camp all winter, all fall, even all spring."

She laughed a warm, pleased laugh and moved her fleshy hand to the back of his neck. "That how it seems to you, why that's fine with me. Used to be a couple more families, back before you remember, but they moved out. Reckon they did better in life."

"Well," Buddy said fiercely, "them old broken houses of theirs don't count. This here is our road."

"And this is our honeysuckle?"

"Sure it is." And he grasped a leggy branch within his reach, bending it to break it off and make her take it.

"Hold on there. You don't pick honeysuckle, why it wilts right off if you pick it. Wilder than you are, and that's saying something." She took the blossoming branch from his fingers and bent to look at the lacy flowers, holding them so they were just near Buddy's face. "You know 'honeysuckle' was one of your first words? Nearly three before you talked, and you come out with a big word like that. I figured you was going to be a late-blooming genius."

"What's a genius?" He ran a finger along a flower, parts so small he couldn't feel them — small like a hair, like an insect's leg.

"Oh, someone who's different from other folks." She straightened up and let go of the flower. "And I reckon you are different, ain't you."

Sometimes she said a question but it wasn't a question. He made the branch nod like a leafy wand. "Is Dad a genius?"

"What? Not likely. No, genius means you know more, out of nowhere, but you might only know about a certain thing." She paused. "Like you know about this road, and the woods around here."

Buddy snapped the end off the long spray he held. "Look, you can wear it to church. It'll last that long, I know it will. I'll fix it on you."

"All right then, Buddy." She bent down till she was his height and he fixed the flower to the top buttonhole of her white blouse, her good one she always ironed for church, and the pale spray curled up around her collar.

"You know there's a Jesus story about honeysuckle?" She pulled off one of the flowers and touched its parts. "These three long petals at the top, they're Jesus' head and arms spread on the cross, and this one petal going down, that's His legs bound together and nailed to the wood. And this long, thin neck of the flower, that's because He was so far from God in His Agony."

Buddy pointed to the delicate threads outflung from the center of the bloom.

"That's the spirit flowing from Him when His soul went up to heaven." She touched the flower to Buddy's mouth.

He tasted an orange dust. Now she was funning with him a little and he wiped his lips and spat the dust away, relieved. He looked into her eyes that were so known to him, her flat hazel eyes with their green flecks like lights shot through them from behind. Like she was hiding in her narrow eyes, behind her white face that was round and smooth as a big bald moon. "Was Dad there when I said that word 'honeysuckle'?"

She kissed his lips a quick hard kiss and stood, then turned to keep walking. "No, he wasn't there."

"Was he in jail then too?"

"No, he just wasn't there. He didn't come to be your dad till after that."

"Well, who was my dad back then?"

"Nobody. Was just you and me then. You and me playing on the road and back of the house and in the stream . . ." She was walking away from him. "Step it up now, we'll be late for service."

But they wouldn't be late. Even this far away, he could hear the

20

singing, the night was so quiet. And the singing always kept on until the preaching started. The songs were mournful from far off, but stronger and scarier as Mam and Buddy got closer. They could see the church in the clearing; like a dead thing come alive, the church could wear different faces. In summer dusk a yellowy, jack-o'-lantern light crept across it and the white building with its whitewashed steps looked illumined against greeny brush and bushes and honeysuckle bloom. By day the windows with their little square panes looked blind and blackened. But inside, light fell amongst the singers like blue smoke, a smoke with no smell, a smoke like the dead would make if they were burning. Now, at night, the cold ice was burning up in there. The different preachers talked about the dead, and how to be safe from burning. Buddy thought the dead would burn in the river, where no one but the dead could catch on fire. They would be burning in Mud River, under the same rattling silver bridge the school bus crossed on the way to Gaither, and Buddy thought they started to burn as Mam walked up the steps to the double doors of the church. Mam's skirt was orange and her haunches moved the whole broad surface of the silky cloth. Black leaves on the cloth moved too, and her feet in their white sandals trod the steps so heavily that Buddy felt the wood shake as he made his own reluctant ascent behind her.

## ❧ ALMA: THE BLACK FIELD

She could hear them falling asleep to the right and left of her, going out like glowlights across the narrow aisle between the cots. The metal springs stopped their minuscule, responsive squeaking. Just at full dark a lone bulb would come on outside with a buzz and a click, shed its umbrella of yellow light into the upper eave of

B wing. The light fell through the high window in bars that stopped and started; Alma knew it was for Delia, who'd cut her lip sleep-walking. Tonight McAdams, their counselor, had looked in on them twice before she left them alone, as though watching them or inter-rupting the dark could stop Delia from getting up. Really, it was Alma who stopped her. Now the bulb outside began to buzz on its gooseneck fixture, five electric instants to which Alma counted by thousands. The light erupted and softened midair, falling across bodies that seemed anonymous, motionless forms; none of the faces showed. Alma pursed her lips to breathe, pretending she sucked the oxygen from the air in a slender column, a shape maybe as wide as the pencil McAdams kept tucked behind her ear during chores.

Boys did that with pencils, and shopkeepers did, women selling fabric, and men did. Wes did sometimes, at the dining room table, his big notebooks laid open in front of him while he smoked a cigarette. He held the cigarette instead of a pencil, squinting as he drew in, holding it in the flat of his thumb and two fingers, not tilted at an angle the way women smoked. Alma couldn't watch him smoke if he knew she was there. If he didn't notice her, she peered at him sideways, and thought of Delia's little brother, John-John. Mina Campbell had nursed Johnny in front of the girls. He'd grab on to Mina and suckle, moving his mouth in a long kiss; his hands would drift aimlessly across her shirt, onto her face. Watching her father smoke, Alma half expected Wes wanted to touch some-one that way. He touched the glossy pictures of the big mining machinery he sold, brushing ashes off his brochures and manuals. Or he yelled out, Audrey! Bring me a Coke! If they were getting along, he wouldn't ask for beer. If he went away, he loaded a suitcase and all those blue manuals into the back seat of the Chevy, and Audrey carried on as though nothing were different, listening for a phone call.

Times were bad, Alma heard everyone say so. Maybe Wes was gone because the mines were laying off and he roamed farther and farther to sell machines, to Kentucky or the Carolinas, maybe north to Maryland, often on tips from Henry Briarley, who owned Consol Coal and knew men everywhere. Audrey said Henry knew everyone and didn't care about anybody. Just your father's type, Audrey would say. But Henry was Cap's father; he must care about Cap, especially since Mrs. Briarley didn't live with them and it was the housekeeper who cooked and cleaned, and drove Cap everywhere. Cap cared about Lenny. She was always wanting Lenny to stay over, stay for dinner, stay the weekend. I'd like to know what that girl's going to do without you next fall at her fancy boarding school, Audrey would say to Lenny, maybe Henry would like to pay for you to go with her. But Lenny never took the bait; she only looked back at her magazine or her TV show. Her favorite was Fractured Fairy Tales; she and Cap did their homework every afternoon in front of Rocky and Bullwinkle. They'd call each other on the phone after the fairy-tale segment and speak in monosyllables, as though cartoons were some big secret. Wasn't Lenny scared because Cap was leaving? She never seemed afraid when Wes disappeared for days, but that was because she didn't know anything; Alma had never told her. At least Mina Campbell would never send Delia away to a school. Audrey said the Campbells were nearly penniless with Delia's father gone; they lived off Mina's sister mostly, money from the beauty salon. Wes could come back but Nickel Campbell never would. He had driven off Mud River Bridge, the same one all the girls from Gaither crossed in cars to get to Camp Shelter. Alma couldn't think of his face anymore; she only saw the murky water moving, at eye level, as though she'd been in the car with him. But she'd been in her mother's car on all those forty-minute drives to Winfield, nearly every Saturday since last summer. She'd never seen Nickel Campbell's car in Winfield, not even the first time at the bus station, when she'd seen Nickel Campbell himself.

Alma heard music. Pearlie, the A-wing counselor, had turned on her pink transistor. She was probably shaving her legs or looking at the hairs in her nose with a hand mirror, wielding her metal tweezers. She was stupid; Alma couldn't read in bed anymore because Pearlie had taken away her flashlight. Alma had a pile of books but there was never any time to lie down and read. Actually they were Delia's books. Delia had given Alma nearly all of them. Every night in the dark at camp, Alma had used them to stay awake late, but now she could only lie and think, imagining the books in her footlocker, gleaming subtly at their edges like chunks of radium. The books themselves and the words in the books were charged with power.

She used to read the books at Delia's house, at Delia's dining room table. Nickel Campbell worked for Henry Briarley at Consol Coal, and he was always gone in the afternoons, but on Alma's occasional overnight visits he sat reading by a bay window. The Campbells' living room looked out on railroad tracks and the overgrown athletic field of Presbyterian College. The small room was lined with bookshelves; books were always scattered and stacked by Nickel Campbell's chair, as though he were studying for a test. Delia and Alma sat in the square dining room where no one dined, where the table supported pots of Mina's lush, crowded spider plants, mail, magazines. Alma read *Huckleberry Finn* or *Kidnapped* while Delia sat tracing whole pages of her comic books onto onionskin typing paper. A Motorola television glittered *The Price Is Right* in a corner, pots rattled in the kitchen. The baby, John-John, not walking yet, visible through the narrow door frame, sat on the linoleum floor and held on to the porcelain leg of an old-fashioned sink. "Delia," Nickel Campbell said without looking at them, "why don't you give Alma those old books. If you ever get interested, maybe she'd lend them back to you."

There were ten books, in a set called Classics, hardbound, with yellowing pages, and "Nickel Thackery Campbell" was written in black ink on the inside back cover of each. Alma thought he must have signed them after he read them, not before; now she did the same to her own books, the ones she'd read, in a cursive script she practiced on a separate sheet. But she'd only brought the Classics books to camp, settled in with her clothes, instead of the boxes of crackers and chips Lenny had packed.

"Alma, why are you still awake?"

McAdams was leaning over her. At night McAdams wore a long T-shirt that came to her knees; it was striped blue the way the mattresses were striped with their sheets off, as though McAdams matched the cots.

"I was just listening, like, to the woods."

"Oh, the woods." McAdams sat on the edge of the cot, gesturing for Alma to shift her legs. "You wouldn't be waiting for me to fall asleep, now, would you?"

"Are you Irish, McAdams?"

"Are you asking? Of course I'm Irish, and I'm Catholic, and I'm tired. Any other questions?"

"But you go to Presbyterian College."

She shrugged. "Financial aid."

"Catholics go to confession, don't they. And they have saints." There really were sounds in the woods. Alma heard the shrill pipings of crickets far away, like they were singing under a cloth. "Who was Saint Patrick, really?" she asked.

"He was the one who drove the snakes out of Ireland. Except he didn't, there just weren't any snakes because Ireland is an island. Can you say that fast three times?"

"Say what?"

"Ireland is an island. It's a joke. You know, a joke." She sighed. "What's up with you, Alma?"

"Delia's father was alive on Saint Patrick's Day. It happened the next day." Alma paused. "Did you drive over Mud River Bridge on your way to camp?"

"No. I came from the other direction. My folks live in Bellington, but you know I go to school in Gaither. I've driven over the bridge hundreds of times. Most people drive over it without any problem. Her dad just had an accident. Right?" She waited for Alma to speak, then went on. "You feel bad for Delia. But Delia's going to be OK. She's lucky to have a true friend like you."

Alma sat up, her hand at her throat. *True.* She thought she might choke on the word, even though she hadn't said it.

"Hey, what's this? You crying?" McAdams moved to put an arm around Alma, but Alma had ducked her head and averted her face. McAdams grabbed her by the shoulders and pulled her closer. "Like the song says, put your head on my shoulder. We gotta talk. Do you know if Delia sleepwalked before her dad died?"

"I don't think so. I never saw her."

"Listen, I want you to stop sleeping with Delia. It's not your job. I'm the counselor and I'm watching out for her. The door of the cabin doesn't lock, but it's latched — she'd never be able to open it in her sleep. There's nowhere she can go. If you see her sleepwalking, don't wake her. Just lead her back to bed, or come and get me. That's all."

"But she hurt herself."

"Only because she got outside and she tripped on the steps. That won't happen now."

Alma was whispering. "I don't want them to send her home. It's better if she's at camp."

"Delia's not going anywhere. Don't worry." She shifted her weight to help Alma lie down, and grimaced. "What *is* this thing under your mattress? Did you bring your own rifle to camp?"

"No, it's my baton."

"Hey, you a twirler?"

"No, I just have a baton. I didn't want to leave it at home."

"How about keeping it *under* your cot? She felt beneath the mattress and pulled the baton free. "Pretty tough, sleeping on batons. I'll show you some moves sometime. Now, go to sleep."

McAdams walked away, disappearing up the aisle between the beds. Even Pearlie's radio was silent. In the quiet cabin, Alma could think about the Winfield bus station, how it smelled like peanuts and dirt. Audrey had said they were going to Souders Department Store to buy Alma a fall jacket, and they did go there, after, but first Audrey bypassed the wide main boulevard of Winfield and pulled into the bus station parking lot. Winfield was the only real city for miles around, a city big enough to have hotels and stores with elevators. Even so, not much came and went through the bus station. Atop the squat, yellow brick building stood a faded representation of a greyhound, a sign nearly as long as the buses parked at the back of the station. It was meant to be the usual sleek, anonymous image, but it was hand painted, transformed, made clumsy and real. The dog had an expression at once cartoonish and melancholy, and its form cast a shadow across the car as Audrey drove slowly past, easing into a space not fully visible from the street. "We'll have lunch here," Audrey said. "Here?" Alma echoed. Audrey regarded her, considering. "I might want to check on a ticket."

Inside, the station was dusty and neglected, and a man slept noisily on one of the iron benches in the waiting area. Alma followed Audrey to the lunch counter, an outpost of booths and tables toward the rear of the building. Nickel Campbell sat at a table by the wall, a wall maybe the height of a man's shoulder, and beyond it was a cafeteria counter with a steam table. Audrey had walked right up to him, holding Alma's hand. He feigned no surprise and gestured to indicate they should sit with him. The chairs were metal, their seats covered with the same yellow vinyl as the Swensons' kitchen chairs at home. For a moment Alma was deeply embarrassed that her family owned and used objects similar to those found in a bus station, but she realized Nickel Campbell wouldn't remember. He'd been to their house only once, and that was to a barbecue, a week ago; Wes and Nickel had been the only men present, and they'd stayed on the porch while the women carried food in and out. People at the bus station got their own food on plastic trays. "Alma," Audrey said, "you must be hungry. Go ahead and get a tray, and I'll pay for your food when I come."

Alma had walked away from them, around the partition of the little wall. People seemed to have appeared suddenly from nowhere, maybe a bus had pulled in, and there was a line of six or seven customers, one of them dragging a recalcitrant toddler. Alma moved along the wall behind them, and realized she could hear Nickel Campbell's voice. He and Audrey were sitting just opposite. The wall was barely tall enough to obscure the top of Alma's head.

"What possessed you to bring Alma?" he said.

And then Audrey's voice: she'd had to, really, what excuse did she have to drive to Winfield on a Saturday or any other day, he mustn't worry, Alma would keep it all to herself.

"What do you mean?" he said. "She's like sisters with Delia."

Yes, but Alma was unusual, Audrey could trust her, she knew it, and there was no other way. Audrey would schedule lessons here for Alma, baton maybe, on Saturdays, Nickel was always in Winfield on Saturdays, wasn't he, on business for Consol?

"Audrey . . ." he'd said in his wise, sad voice, and Alma had moved along the wall, then stared at her feet. She'd moved because the woman behind her was starting to edge past, and her mother had been right, Alma was starved.

She was hungry now, too. Her belly ached with a feathery hurt. At suppers in the dining hall, Juniors were the oldest girls. The Seniors cooked dinner themselves in Highest camp, but Juniors and Primaries filed in at six P.M. to sit in rows at the long white tables, eat family style, and pass the job jar to pick a chore. Alma thought of Lenny then, always, safely above them all in the woods with Cap, while the tumult of the dining hall raged and the platters of spaghetti or fried chicken were passed. Every night, during dessert, a girl from each cabin had to give a two-minute supper speech about freedom and the American way of life. The speeches were supposed to reflect what they'd learned about Democracy and Communism in heritage class. Heritage class was really about secrets, but most of the girls talked about Betsy Ross or Mrs. Jefferson Davis, depending on whether the D.A.R. or the Daughters of the Confederacy had sponsored them. There was an applause vote on which speech was best. Usually the last speaker won; the girls couldn't seem to concentrate much on what was said amidst the clatter of forks. A diaphanous murmur of talk continued despite the counselors' efforts to maintain quiet. But Mrs. Thompson-Warner, the directress, ran heritage class, and she paid close attention; she even took notes on the speeches. There was a rumor that she gave some special, private prize to the girl *she* judged the best each night. Alma hadn't been able to eat much at supper; she'd been elected at noon to give the speech the next day. B wing expected Alma to win because she had a big vocabulary and was one of the few to listen much in heritage class. All the other candidates from their cabin had been A-wing girls, who were thirteen-year-olds. B-wing girls were twelve, but Alma wasn't twelve until next week. She'd almost had to stay in one of the Primary cabins, near the quad. Primaries had noon rest, like babies. Actually Alma liked the idea of noon rest, but she wouldn't be separated from Delia, and some of the younger kids were fourth graders. They gloried in all the rules and were delighted to proceed everywhere in lines. Frank the bugler and little Buddy, the fat cook's son, who was eight, were the only ones in camp who wore no uniforms and obeyed no rules. Frank obeyed reveille and taps; flag circles morning and evening were the only times the girls could count on seeing him. He was a secret too.

Across the aisle, Alma heard Delia turn in her bed. She was asleep; they were all asleep, but McAdams might still be listening for sounds. Alma began to move, shifting her weight by increments to the metal edge of her cot. McAdams had put a towel over Delia's pillow, to keep her from bleeding on her pillowcase; there weren't any extra bed linens. Last night Alma had been so tired from the hike to Highest that she had fallen asleep in her own bed, and Delia had fallen asleep as well, without waking her. Delia always slept like a stone. Sometimes, even during the day, she came back to the cabin and fell asleep. She was allowed because the counselors all knew about her father driving off the bridge, but the counselors didn't know about anything, not really. Alma thought Delia was tired because she had to try so hard not to think. When she was asleep, she couldn't try anymore; Alma had to hold on to her. Now Alma touched the cool wood floor of the cabin with her toes and slid like an otter into the pool of dark around her bed. Crouched, she held still. No sound. And she began to inch forward, swimming the distance on all fours. She would reach Delia and they would both sleep. This part seemed to her the beginning of a journey that lasted the night, and all the night moved in slow motion, coursing through them and over them, an island on Delia's bed. Whatever dreams began in Alma's mind would pass harmlessly into the air.

Alma didn't ever want to leave camp, despite the heat and the chores and the hiking. From the first night, Delia had come and stood over her in the dark. Alma had looked up at her and realized Delia did know: somehow, she knew everything, but she didn't know she knew. Her eyes were open but she didn't see. Suddenly it was as though Alma hadn't really spent all those Saturday mornings wandering alone through Souders Department Store, waiting for her mother to pick her up in three hours at the big revolving door in front. It was like Delia had been with her, the two of them anonymous among cosmetics counters and mirrored displays of bottles, tubes, barrettes. They'd both walked unobtrusively through the five floors of the crowded store, then bought a magazine at the notions department and ordered hot chocolate and toast at the basement lunch counter. And Alma hadn't sat alone, reading something like *Seventeen*, imagining how easily Lenny could step into the glossy pages and be lost to her forever. If Delia had been there, they would have joked about the models and drawn on them with pens. They would have tried on clothes and hats, and requested Top 40 songs in the music department. Alma had done all those things at first, and she'd carried her new baton in a plastic bag with a fancy handle, wishing it had come in a case with a clasp; she wanted to assemble it, break it down, like a flute or a clarinet or a gun. But finally she left it in the car each time, and walked through the store aimlessly, more interested in the salesgirls than in the merchandise. It became her practice to observe them unnoticed, and try to overhear their conversations. She knew the names of her favorites and looked for them each week, to see how they'd worn their hair that day, or whether they looked worried. She learned to keep moving, be nearly invisible. She could read at the lunch counter if she went there just at ten, between the breakfast and lunch rushes; she'd stay nearly an hour and leave a good tip, instead of getting more hot chocolate. And she'd be waiting at the door on the stroke of twelve. Audrey stopped saying where she and Nickel Campbell had been, but she didn't usually drive up from the direction of the bus station. Watching for her, Alma pretended to look for Lenny, as though they were grown and Lenny was coming for her; Lenny was driving something low and beautiful, something fast, and they were on their way together.

"No," Delia said now, and turned in her sleep.

Alma moved soundlessly forward and surfaced at the head of Delia's bed. The shadowy dark seemed to break and eddy on the glint of Delia's hair, on her white shoulders in their camp T-shirt, her long pale back, all of her curved away. She slept on her side, her knees pulled up, as though she were waiting, making room. Alma knelt on the mattress, one knee at a time, in silence, and slid beneath the sheet. She lay with her face on the cool side of the pillow, smelling Delia's curls and the back of Delia's neck, and she fit herself to Delia's shape. She could hold on, one arm under Delia just at the curve of her waist, hands clasped, and they could both drift without moving.

Now they slept, released.

Even Lenny was her sleep self in Alma's vision, a self washed free. There were the night sounds of camp, loud, cacophonous, the cricket warble and soughing of leafy branches and twelve girls breathing, turning, crying out like weepers surprised by dreams, but all those sounds dimmed as Alma continued to negotiate the narrow aisle between the row of beds. She seemed to walk a long time; the aisle went on longer than any cabin until it was the hallway at home, and home was deathly quiet, the woods far away. Dreaming, Alma heard the bathroom faucet dripping and reached out to touch its metal neck, then bent to drink in forbidden fashion, fitting her mouth around its circular lip. She doesn't have to swallow, the water snakes down her throat like contraband, and she is just climbing to get closer, fit her whole body into the oval sink, when she turns to find herself in Lenny's room. Lenny looks cold, but comfortably so, as though she is meant to be cold, like marble or crystal. She sleeps like a nun, fearless and still, on her back, her hands at her sides, her head gently inclined. Her face, expressionless, perfect and smooth, seems a face unconcerned with possibilities, a face waiting to be alive. Her long, loose hair is the color of bleached hay, hay that has weathered in fields. All day her hair is bound in a long blond swatch, a silky blunt-cut ponytail that swings when she moves. Wes, who learned to barber in the army, trims it once a month — and now Lenny is in the kitchen, stalwart in her straight chair, Wes with his sharp scissors and rat-tail comb. Winter howls at the windows as Audrey puts newspapers under them to catch the hair, but Alma steps back into summer and the pale wisps begin to fall into the grass of the yard, take flight on a gust of darkening breeze. Alma looks up into the black field of the night sky and sees Lenny and their father tilting and spinning through space, Lenny seated, their father's hands in her hair.

## ✖ LENNY: TURTLE HOLE

"Lenny, you can hear them." Cap moved on her bed. "They're flying."

"What, the owls?"

"No, there — like whistling rattles, but they zoom close and go away. Bats. They must fly up from down near the river."

"How do you know there are bats?"

"I heard the counselors talking. Bats. They get rabies."

"There aren't bats," Lenny said. "If there was even a chance, the counselors would be wearing protective clothing after dark. Suits of armor."

Cap laughed her gravelly, private laugh. "Lenore, aren't you scared, lying naked like that? What if the bats swarm in and cover you with their rat bodies and their little claws and their crackly wings?" She crawled silently from her bed and lay full length on the plank floor at the rear of the tent, her face at the edge, peering out into darkness. "Last night I thought I saw them, but there was no moon and they vanished too fast. Tonight we'll see them, at the tops of the trees, where the light is strongest."

"What light? All I see is the light of those white underpants of yours."

Lenny thought of crawling quietly onto Cap's back and sleeping on top of her, letting her weight settle in. She had such thoughts; somehow, at camp, Cap had become as familiar, ever present, owned, as Alma at home. There to be touched and jostled and irritated, except it was Cap — not Alma, Cap — who was stronger and a little shorter than Lenny, whose freckled skin smelled of some velvet woods creature, whose breath smelled enticingly of tobacco, who stole cigarettes from purses. They were both fifteen but Cap was older by several months; her face was browned from the sun and her eyes looked lighter now, gray as slate, and hard. Cap, whose father was Mr. Briarley of Consol Coal, lived in Gaither in a big house with a maid. She slept in a canopy bed. Lenny had slept there with her, under a kind of ruffled ceiling. Here in the night-green drab of the tent, in the woods, along the trails, in the institution of the routine, they were a team, cut loose from the safe things that separated them. Lenny teased and held back but Cap smiled, breathing *at your service* or *Queen Lenore the Unconscious*; she shoved and teased and made all the games more fun. She liked baiting Lenny, she dared her to wrestle, she laughed and plotted pranks that were never carried out, just talked about in the dark in wild, interesting words, curses Cap said her father had yelled at her mother. In the dark, she whispered in sibilant tones that sounded like another language, very fast and harsh. She affected a Natasha accent from the Bullwinkle cartoons but made it delicious and threatening, squinting her eyes, moving her hands as though to ward off cobwebs. She was powerful, off on her own in a society she could circumvent, but her power supported Lenny — Lenny could daydream or forget, shirk some chore, and Cap would take up the slack, finish for her, do it for her. She was "of service" but she wanted something back. Lenny was only waiting to find out what it was.

"Lenny, I see them. They're eating the clouds of gnats that come out of the weeds at night. Quick, you can see them." Cap felt for Lenny's arm and pulled.

"All right." Lenny hated to get up when she was floating, but she stood upright and the feeling stayed with her. She was even a little dizzy, getting to her knees, then lying down with her chin at the edge of the flooring. Cap touched Lenny's face, turning her head and pointing down at the crown of the trees below them. Just on the surface of the foliage, shadows fluttered. The shadows rose higher and took form, scraps of black paper, shaken angrily, gaining the air in spasms.

"*Look* at them," Cap whispered.

For an instant, naked, Lenny was paralyzed with surprise. Her skin tingled as though a veil had been pulled across her flesh. The bats moved, their flight inherently terrifying in its speed, its inhuman tremor. The night looked navy blue, round as a deep plate. The bats were soot and remnants, emitting the silent screams of their community. Then pieces of the mosaic dropped suddenly and swooped, lifted, and were gone, flown back over Highest to the north.

Dimly, Lenny heard Cap murmuring and felt her wrist wetted and warmed. Cap held it in her mouth as a dog holds damaged prey, teeth resting on the flesh just hard enough to make an impression. Instinctively, Lenny kicked and swung, felt herself released, Cap's misplaced slap at her face landing on her neck. Cap left her hand there and grasped Lenny's hair. "Take it easy, Lenore, I was joking. They're just bats."

"Well, I never saw them before," Lenny spat back. "I've never seen them, they're not like birds at all, they're horrible."

"OK, OK, forget you saw them. Who said they were like birds? They're vermin."

"Oh, be quiet. Can't you stop showing me things? Leave me alone."

"Sure thing." Cap hissed the words and rose from the floor in one movement. Her bed creaked when she sat, then she sighed, betraying herself.

Listening, Lenny was frightened again. "Let's go, let's go down the mountain. I can't sleep now because of you. You have to come too."

"What?"

"No one will even know we left. We can go down here, right off the edge of the tent, circle around to the woods trail, and go down to Turtle Hole. We can swim and be back in an hour."

"Lenny, I don't want to put my clothes back on and walk all the way down there."

"Yes you do. I can tell you do."

"I'll only do it," Cap said, "if you go just as you are now."

"Don't be dumb. The brush off this way is full of briars."

"All right. But once we get on the trail, you have to take off everything but your shoes." Already, Cap was putting on her clothes, fighting her way into a T-shirt.

Lenny tossed her head defiantly, like at home, even though no one was watching. She found her shorts on the floor and pulled them on. "Fine," she said, "I don't care. There's no one on the trail. But when we get to the water, you have to go in too. Both of us."

"Oh, in that mud bottom," Cap said, "when you can even touch the bottom! You sink to your ankles . . . I'll have to tread water, I can't bear it!" She stage-whispered, her Natasha accent drunkenly precise.

Zippers, tying of laces, double knots at the ends, no slipping in the darkest dark of Highest trail. Cap opened the footlocker to find the flashlight but Lenny shushed her and closed the heavy lid — no light, she signaled, cat's eyes, night vision, see in the tunnel, radar, laser light — anyway, someone would see a flashlight beam, suddenly cutting across the trail.

"You first." Cap motioned toward the edge.

They squatted and Lenny was over first. The slender pole, central support propping the tent floor, smelled of dirt. The rubber soles of Lenny's sneakers slowed her short descent and when she was down, she looked up. Peculiar feeling, like spying under someone's secret room; the board floor with its wide slats showed space between the lengths, as though the ground illuminated upward.

Exhilarated, Lenny turned and ran, lifting her knees high to skirt the briars, plundering the smell and the wetness. Grasses ripped as she moved. Little by little, she could see. She touched with her fingertips the wet umbrellaed tops of Queen Anne's lace, heard the briars catch at her, didn't feel them. Ahead, the furzy towering shapes of the trees sheltered Highest trail, a few hundred feet down from the tents. All the rest were sleeping! And this was better than a dream. Lenny gained the trail and stopped. She took off her heavy green shorts and the blouse she hadn't bothered to button. The dirt she trod in her sneakers seemed softer, more velvet, dew had wet it. The whole world looked softened, night-furred; the depths of the woods were an odd black shot with deep green. She stood at attention, listening with her skin. Years ago, they'd let her go shirtless in the summer, like a boy. It had felt like this, catching the blinkering fireflies in bottles, but not so good. Cap was beside her, breathing as though she'd jumped onto the trail from a high place, dropped down from the limbs of the trees. She picked up Lenny's clothes and threw them to the side of the trail, then shoved. They were running, skip, stub, touch the rock sides of the slanted earth, touching with their shoes each big stone they skirted in daylight. Going down in darkness was fast, unbelievably fast, no sound but their breath, *hut hut hut* as though someone softly punched them as they dropped.

They heard the stream before they saw it; they washed dishes and pots here, dunked their sweaty clothes, gulped handfuls of water so cold it stung. The stream tumbled down the mountain to join Mud River, widened, widened, flattened finally at the bottom of the hill, and grew slow. Just before it joined the river it flowed over its former banks, dammed by a deserted beaver dam and fallen trees. The beaver dam stood sentinel, a dike of branches and crumbling mud. Whatever washed down through the stream came to rest against it; no one walked or swam too close. There were a few cans and bottles, some of them broken, and the occasional desolate bit of clothing: a ladies' glove, a man's shoe. Then there was the river, wide as a three-lane road, and the trail alongside like an afterthought. Now Lenny could make out the swinging bridge, still and elemental in the dark. Moonlight caught one edge and glistened the shape; it hung there like a woman's necklace. Lenny wanted to start across but Cap took her arm and urged her farther up along the boundary of the woods — the opposite bank had been torn up by the workmen laying pipe. At night the scarred ground and dirt piles, the tubular mounds of iron, seemed an abandoned desecration. On this side, farther along the river, the trail split off through the woods to Turtle Hole. Here, at the border of camp property, the county people swam when camp was not in session, diving from a flat boulder that overhung the water. Girl Guides didn't swim there, which was odd, as the water was a perfect silver oval, deep in the center. Maybe there were snapping turtles, or ghosts. How would it look at night? Lenny wanted to see. The bridge moved as though trod upon, and shimmered as they left it behind.

Threading their way along the narrow riverbank, they were scouts or spies, moving as though pursued, scrambling precisely. Cap was first, a certain shield. Lenny consciously echoed her movements, crouching, swooping, standing taller and striding; she felt like a clean white cloth, a rippling slipstream. She saw her own naked legs move reliably over the dark ground and stayed in tandem, Cap's shadow, secret even to herself, invisible. Cap would move fast and go far — Lenny imagined following, unseen, to distant times and places, places most people from Gaither would never go. An understanding struck Lenny wordlessly: Cap had arrived in Gaither only to find Lenny. That's why she was here where she didn't belong. Even now, Lenny felt crowds watching them, rows of silent presence, and she turned her head to see the glower of the trees, row upon row of staggered slender shapes. Second-growth maples, oaks, ash, the trees held upright their densely leaved bouquets. Only the knobby beginnings of branches were visible under the foliage, as though a few thin arms supported these masses of minutely stirred leaves. Lenny moved quickly and her rapidly changing perspective lent the trees a semblance of movement as subtle as the shifting of an eye. The forest was not like rocks or sticks, it was *alive*. She had never really known before.

They had left the river behind and were moving through the woods, almost to Turtle Hole. Cap slowed and crouched down. Lenny was impatient. Now she could see the water, perfect, silver and contained.

"Be quiet," Cap whispered. "There's someone here, up high, on the rock." She lowered herself into the tall reeds along the border of the woods and they both sat, peering through stalks.

"Is it Buddy, wandering around at night?" Lenny saw no one.

"No, he wouldn't be out this late. No, it's a man." Cap sighed intently.

They both moved forward carefully, nearly to the edge of the water. Lenny listened. She heard movement, the quiet clank of something metal. A hunched form sat on the flat slab of boulder that overhung the water. Then the form straightened and pointed an immensely long, thin finger into the night sky. The finger cracked and whistled, flinging an invisible line far out.

"He's fishing," Cap said.

The line had landed and sunk its weighted hook. Soundlessly, concentric echoes widened across the breadth of the water. The surface looked placid and heavy, reflecting dull particles of light. By day Turtle Hole was just the dull green of a turtle's horny flesh; now it was different, and the mute border of the trees was black. The form sat quietly, holding the long pole. He was dressed in dark pants — he wore no shirt but Lenny saw the glint of a belt buckle. He turned and settled, leaning against a large stone. They could make out his staring face, his eyes fixed on the water.

"Frank," Lenny breathed. Here was where he came at night, probably every night. She knew of him suddenly, days at his campsite, sleeping miserably in the drowsy heat, appearing to play reveille and taps, to mow the grassy quad with the old push mower. His wrinkled clothes. Sometimes he wore a billed hat. He noticed none of them. They were beneath his notice because this is where he lived while the rest of them were dead in their swoony sleep. No one told him what to do. He was alone.

Cap touched Lenny and pointed. Not speaking, they inched closer, careful to stay concealed. The grasses smelled pungent and were sharp; Lenny felt them trailing over her skin and knew they tasted sour. Through the reeds, she could see him. He moved his head, not hearing them but sensing an approach. They stopped, perhaps thirty feet to his right.

Lenny knew she would stand and make him see her. She felt dulled, heavy with urgency, like an insect pinned to paper, trying to beat its wings. She heard the low vibrato of crickets and wanted to walk straight toward him. She must have begun to stand.

Cap stopped her with a whisper. "No, let him see me first." She stood silently, waiting for him to find her. Lenny crouched, her head level with Cap's knees. She gazed up the length of Cap's long body and remembered her mother's bare arms in summer, how large Audrey had seemed, a giant at the screen door of the kitchen, how the door whammed shut with a slash, cutting the air like a weapon. The concrete stoop beyond was lit up by the angle of the sun, its nubby surface embedded with shards of glitter. Lenny felt herself momentarily blinded by those dazzling mornings, as though a light were switched on in the dark, but it was night now, and in fact the night sky was pricked with stars far above Cap's shoulders. The stars were endless, faceted and glowing. Like fireworks, they had exploded into the sky and were still receding, falling and burning.

"He saw me," Cap said. She had knelt back into the grass and she was untying Lenny's sneakers. Lenny shifted her weight and the shoes were gently pulled away. The water was close and the ground was damp.

Hidden, Lenny felt powerful and safe. But he had seen them; he had put down the pole and was looking into the dark, empty air above the grasses. No motion, no sound. The feeling would crumble and burn up, like the stars, unless she moved. Whoever, whatever he was, she felt herself hurtling toward him. She held him in her gaze and stood. The air was vast as outer space, and warm. She couldn't read his eyes, his expression, he was only a form, standing, beginning to move. The water, a silver mass, held more light than the night could hold, and she moved toward it. She couldn't feel the ground. Her feet, her legs, were pleasantly numb, tingling, but her hands stung with heat and she opened them. She waded into the water to be held up, but the water, to her waist, to her breasts, was not heavy enough to help. She saw him slip into the pond in his baggy pants, moving toward her, and she only wanted him to hurry. The water broke around him and the sound of its crack and gentle roll seemed delayed, like thunder after mile-high lightning. She had to open her mouth to breathe.

Now he was close, his face, his eyes. He didn't recognize her, he had never seen her before and perhaps didn't see her now; she was safe and she opened her arms to him. He didn't seem like Frank, the boy they'd watched. So near, he was almost a man; his hands were broad and flat, his shoulders squared at her forehead. She stroked him and felt his muscles tense as though her touch was electric. He was ready and he was afraid. His open palms on her nipples were a soft pressure meant to confirm her nakedness but she moved forward and up and made him support her weight. She couldn't stand; she wanted to close her eyes and hold on. Her head was above him now, her face in his hair. He was unbearably fragrant, like flowers and dust, and his thick dry hair was warm. He nuzzled inside, between her breasts, like a vicious baby, pushing, using his mouth. He moved his hands, lifting her against him, sucked at her skin, her throat, tasting until he found her lips. She had never really kissed anyone but her parents and girlfriends; it wasn't what she had thought. It was more like eating, eating something swollen and sweet that you could taste but never swallow, never have. She was feeding him, filling him up, but he couldn't pull her close enough. He pushed deeper with his tongue, slower, pulling her tighter the length of their bodies. His hands grew frantic, moving haphazardly over her; their panic began to pull everything into focus. Lenny felt a core of blurry fear almost coalesce but then Cap was in the water near them, touching them both, circling round them, her mouth on his neck, his ears, as though she were whispering. He was breathing quickly, trying to move them toward the bank, but Cap held Lenny against him, touching the backs of Lenny's thighs, urging her closer so that Lenny opened her legs and clasped his waist. His hands found her hips and she touched the hard buckle of his belt, pressed her hand close under it, inside. When she touched him he froze and made a sound that started a throbbing pain in her. She nearly moved to touch herself but felt a hand hard against her. She felt it probe inside and let her weight rest there, then she clasped him tighter and stopped thinking. His mouth was on hers but she pulled away, gasping; she had to cry out, then she couldn't stop her voice. Shattering, she heard a coarse, continuous moaning as she turned, over and over, tumbling through some pierced and narrow space. She felt a hot rush and knew she was urinating, emptying into the hand that held her. She let that warmth happen and the turning eased. Tears of relief filled her eyes even as he stiffened against her, voicing his own smothered sounds. She wanted to hold him but Cap was between them, urging her back. Lenny remembered the water again as an element separate from herself; she could taste it, smell it. She wanted to sleep in it, let herself sink. Her feet touched the mud bottom and Cap was pulling her away. They moved together, escaping before anything was said, before he heard their voices or truly saw them. They ran, throwing water off their long bodies, forgetting Lenny's shoes in the tall reeds, stumbling until they gained the path. The woods stretched before them, dense, connected shapes surprisingly the same, but the color of the night had altered.

## ❧ PARSON: THE GIRL WHO WAS A FISH

He awakens in witch's light, the light of the Devil's love, night light made luminous by moon glow and mist rising off the water. Now the night is coolest and Turtle Hole, warmed by the sun, drifts a moist, low-lying cloud. Moonsmoke, Preacher had called it, smelling the air in Calvary, where a stream behind the rickety wooden porch of the house charged the air with a similar languid wet on summer nights. Where was Preacher now? Dead and rotted, and Parson wakes at this hour, always, near midnight, rolling up toward consciousness the way words rolled up on the bottom of the plastic 8 ball Preacher had kept at the house. It's how prayer moves, he'd say, cloudy and clear, come and go; waking those years, Parson would often hear him reading aloud, conversing with a heavenly ghost. Later, in prison, Parson woke to nothing, dead air, the men rocked shut in acres of separate cells. Here the air is so alive it tingles, alive with all of them, all the children breathing their milky sleep, pearling the night with their breath. It's a kind of heaven he's found, and the evil that could hurt such innocence was great, it would be an evil unafraid of good, an evil thriving as shadow of every gesture and desire, every future. Time moved that way, and disease, and fire ate that way, catching the edge and burning toward the center. Burning to follow Carmody, find him, Parson had waited a week after Carmody's parole, then walked off a work detail, easily, carefully, overlooked after seven years as a slow and powerful child, content, dementedly religious, afraid of the outside. He'd walked off with just the clothes he wore, his Bible strapped to his stomach under his shirt, walked the first few miles, his prison blues not so different from any laborer's clothes. A trucker at a gas station gave him a ride straight out of Carolina, gave him a map. Parson found a half-familiar cluster of names and marked those names with the cross of the Lord — Winfield, Bellington, Gaither, town names printed smaller and smaller, and the camp, Camp Shelter, set off as a small pastel square, a forest preserve, yes, preserved, in the northern part of the state. Carmody had said he lived at Shelter, hell no, wasn't no town, just a dirt road and a few hicks, each with a couple of acres, and a church full of crazies down the bend. The women yelling and rolling, Carmody had laughed, fuck Jesus blind if they could, and Parson thought, in the jostle and roar of the truck cab, of Jesus, the mystery, taking a woman to Him as Preacher had taken women, sometimes in Parson's little room, on Parson's cot, pious women feverish with guilt or want. Preacher was a big man, heavy, clothed in black and the dark woolen coat he wore in winters; beneath him the women seemed prostrate as he worked over them, performing a sacrament that elicited the heavy breathing of hard labor. Sent out for wood, Parson looked in the window near the foot of the bed and watched, seeing only Preacher's backside and the women's white legs straddling the edges of the narrow cot or flung up over Preacher's behind. He was too big to hold in his bulky clothes and their flimsy, imploring limbs seemed useless. Parson could see nothing, really, the women saw nothing, it was fast and hard and Preacher got inside them without taking off their clothes, without removing his own, then he sat up over them, still panting, pulled them upright and prayed over them. It wasn't the young girls who came around but the older women, thin ones, dried out and wan like something had left them too long in the sun. Left for dead, Preacher would say, and they never told, only never came back, or returned when they couldn't stay away. They needed that punishing comfort, the sharp heat of it, Preacher said, and he was a grievous sinner tempted by need, a sinner as surely as any murderer or thief, he brought sinners to the Crucible because he was a sinner himself. Those needy women were evil. He trusted only the big women, women like Carmody's wife, he said they slept in their bodies, had vanquished the Devil in the fortification of the flesh. They were the ones to whom he delegated the organization of church suppers and revivals, the posting of notices. They brought food to the back porch in baskets, breads and cakes and roasted meats, homemade butter faded and white as the worn complexions of those other women, who stumbled through the door of Parson's low-ceilinged room as though they were faint or sick, who flung themselves down on the narrow cot in the sway of an urge Parson felt, watching them. Like a fire in his guts, sick with burning, and when he told Preacher, the old man said he must spill his seed on barren ground, never in the house or in his bed, seduced by pleasure, he must cleanse himself kneeling and alone where the earth was hard, or in the cold of the river. Throw it in the river, Preacher said, that is the seed of evil. Too late for a man of sixty, but Parson might yet remain clean. He was a big boy, Preacher said, an animal needy as a dog or a horse, a man never mothered by a woman, but he must pour the passion of the body into the work of the Lord, and Parson began to lead prayers at meetings, and to preach. He spoke of evil, having known it, he spoke of smelling its approach and described the smell, he spoke of the Devil's fragrant oils and the swollen itch of the Devil's hunger, of stanching the flow of the Devil's bloody need, for that need was a mortal wound at the ravaged breast of Jesus, who took no woman and no man and was loved by God. Yet the Devil cleaved unto whatever fed him and feasted, drunk with flesh, feasted until he failed to defend his mind from angels. It was then Parson felt himself empowered as a warrior of the Lord, free to suck at the marrow of the Devil's sated bones.

Sitting in the cab of one truck after another on that journey to Shelter, Parson had seen the familiar valleys and hovering brackish mountains, the small encroachable skies of southern West Virginia. The land revealed itself like an old dream as a trucker turned on a gospel station; radio chants of songs Parson had led in prison services broke over him like benedictions. Yes, he'd been right to follow Carmody, whose frightened maniacal anger so readily changed to a lax and satiated evil those nights he traded his wife's mailed parcels of clothes and food to the guards for liquor. Then he ranted about girls and women, crouched beside Parson's bunk to rasp in coarse whispers how he'd ripped into this one or that one with a cock like a wood plank till she screamed and begged for more, then he'd whipped her around and shoved it up before she could pull away, ha, they never wanted to do that, up the behind where it was good and tight, Parson knew, sure, reform school boy, foster kid. Women paid attention too when you turned them over and piled in, you had to hold on and shove till your lights came on and then they couldn't get loose to crawl away, eh? right? better do me, this is your chance, till Parson grabbed him to shut him up, to stop his evil mouth, the cell glowing blue with the Devil's light in the blackout of prison black, like being inside a grave, and Parson punched Carmody onto the floor in the corner and held him down, and Carmody felt silken, tasted sweet, as though his body retained some childish perfume despite the loutish, feline sneak in the man. But the flesh of the Devil seduced and fondled was always sweet, not foul with the stench of death like the Devil betrayed and wandering. Carmody groaned and arched himself and laced his fingers into Parson's thick, dark hair, trying to push Parson's wet mouth lower, harder, and Parson heard the Devil's suckling cries, the Devil's whimpering want, and he raised up to lie full length upon the Devil's form. He balanced himself there and felt his hands at the throat of the Demon, squeezing the sound and the taste, and Carmody began to buck like a horse. Parson released him then, sat up and hit him once, hard in the face, and left him there, motionless, crawled onto his own bunk, arranging his limbs as one would arrange articles on a shelf. He often felt his body to be an object, something to be moved here and there, and he felt most free when he had seen the Devil in some vulnerable guise and subdued him, beat him back with a power he watched himself employ.

That power was a mystery, sudden, unquestioned, full of wind, like flying. All during the trip to Shelter, Parson had felt some remnant of the power just clinging to the edges of his vision, a fuzz along the plane of the highway, a vibration of color where the

43

landscape met the sky. He'd got as far as Bellington with various truckers, then walked out Route 19, past the chair factory, and two construction workers in a pickup stopped to give him a ride. They worked at Camp Shelter, they said, out past Gaither, laying pipe, and said they might use him if he wanted to sign on. Slow work, and hot, digging and hauling, but they hoped to make it last all summer and they could pay him under the table, cash, no stubs or checks. Parson agreed. The Lord continued to provide, just as he'd provided Proudytown and the meeting with Preacher, and the long road, even earlier, of foster keepers tainted with evil, some of the evil seductive and sweet. Then prison after Preacher died, prison a concentration of evil and grace, like being sealed in a concrete tomb, a cave or catacomb, Parson an ancient prophet, alone seven years with only the voice of the Lord to believe. Then the Lord had rolled away the rock as surely as for his Holy Son, and Parson had walked to a deliverance meant for him, for Carmody, for this place, the camp in the trees. Riding all night in the trucks of mercy on lit-up roads, he'd almost forgotten the world, but the world came over him like fever that first morning — close faces of the workmen, empty beer bottles on the dash, day heating up and the dense overhanging trees unstirred, how the metal bridge over the river rattled like a fit and they drove a dirt road, bumping along in dew-moistened dust till they passed through the pillars of the camp entrance, the stones themselves overgrown with kudzu and honeysuckle. He'd gone with them right to the work site, a secluded riverbank in the heart of the world, they'd let him have a worn khaki work shirt and trousers, and he'd worked all day for an advance on his week's wages, given him that evening at a roadhouse where they all had hamburgers and beer. He was passing through, Parson told them, but he reckoned he was meant to work with them awhile. He told stories he'd heard other inmates tell, about working construction in Houston by the canal, how the wetbacks would fall asleep at night in the irrigation ditch and drown when the canal was flushed. Then they were straight and dead as logs, Parson said, though he'd never really seen Houston, but he'd thought at night, alone, for years, of how the bodies might look, floating, buoyed by every motion of the water. He saw the narrow water dark and full like ink, like the black dark of the shack he slept in at night, the forest and the camp crouched all around him, breathing. He too could float like death in this darkness, awake and nearly dreaming.

This night he rises in one effortless movement to look out the window of the shack at Turtle Hole; he feels he has moved by merely imagining movement. The water shines, and the black piece of boulder overhanging one side is darker than the air around it. The boy, Frank, sits fishing, suspended in the dark like an ornament. His bare chest looks unnaturally white, and when he throws his line out Parson can feel the hook rip through resisting water. Mornings at seven, the kid blows reveille on a beat-up trumpet at the quad, a grassy oval near three stone hewn buildings that seem too massive to house the activities of children. Even the workmen down by the river could hear the kid's bugle, the sound was so piercing, breaking on the high notes. Moments later would come the girls' voices pledging allegiance, faint and dreamy. Parson has never seen them, saluting in a circular line; the men were already at work by then, or at least gathered by the river to drink coffee. The other four brought tall thermoses but Parson drank from a plastic cup while the foreman laid plans.

Plans were always the same: dig out earth for ten foot of pipe, set the pipe, and spend afternoon cutting brush for the trail road for the truck. They kept the trail close but wound around stands of trees too near the riverbank. Sometimes they dragged pipe with chains as far as thirty, forty feet, in teams, like horses. Sweating, cursing, they paced themselves with their own insolent complaints while the foreman cursed loudest how he'd only taken the job because the mines had laid him off, goddamn mickey mouse operation. Occasionally the little girls hiked the forested hills across the river. They were led by college-girl counselors and their faces appeared and disappeared far off amongst the trees, their white blouses forming a shifting, patchy mosaic. Sprites, the men called them, as though they were forest spirits, and when they were too high up or far away to be seen, their laughter and their urgent, childish speech carried down bright and tiny, perfectly preserved. The older girls, camping higher in the hills, were subjects of speculation and offhand jokes only because the camp directress had asked the men not to set foot across the river without special permission. They were discouraged from walking through the camp except when they were on their way to or from the work site, as though Girl Guides were somehow threatened by the vision of five men in khakis. They'd said as much to Frank, who was sent out hot afternoons with paper cups and a big jug of cold lemonade, and Frank told them he didn't work for Mrs. Thompson-Warner and Hilda Carmody didn't either, or they wouldn't be getting any lemonade. The place was just rented out to Girl Guides these three weeks; unless there was a church camp coming or the Y-Teens, the camp would be vacant most of August. Probably it would shut down. Figure I could hire on with you men? But the foreman had smiled, his lips wet with the cold sweet liquid. Boy can't do a man's job, you a boy, ain't you? I can dig, Frank had said, and I got my own tent I stay in. I don't think so, kid, but you tell that fat woman she makes good lemonade. Sweet as a baby's tits. Those women you take orders from know how much time you spend spying on the girls up at the top of the hill? I don't go up there, the boy had said, they gotta do everything themselves. And the foreman had joked about *everything*, how that old redheaded dame sure seemed worried about those girls, worried about somebody. Nah, she's worried about Communists, Frank had said.

Yes, she was worried. At night in the shack Parson can feel her think in her sleep, creasing her powdered forehead while the Devil passes in and out her open window. Those white frilly curtains she'd hung rippled each time the Devil moved and his legs were the flayed red color of raw meat, and wet like that, and Parson knows the smell in her room is the smell of blood. Blood smelled of meat, warm rotted meat, sticky, like when Preacher had got shot at the card game and the feel of his blood had stayed on Parson's hands. In the shack at night Parson still smells blood, staggering in his dreams under Preacher's weight on the slippery metal stairs of that hotel fire escape. Snow had turned to rain over all the gray parking lot behind the building as Parson dragged them both to Preacher's old pickup, going through the old man's pockets for the keys as he held the falling bulk of his burden up against the cab of the truck. Preacher was still breathing, a sound like rasps of air through ragged holes, and Parson got him into the truck, his own hands and front bloodied, pulling fast out of the lot as the attendant came to the door of the little booth. Parson didn't think of hospitals, he thought only of getting away, going home, Preacher would want to go home. He had driven several streets, roaring down alleys to cut out toward the highway, trying to hold Preacher upright with one arm, when the girl's startled face and form appeared like an apparition beyond the wet glass of the windshield. There was the dull thud of contact overwhelmed by the scream of the brakes and the girl flew up onto the broad hood of the truck, rolling hard, coming for Parson, flying as though impelled into the windshield, hitting lengthwise across it head to foot, assaulting Parson with her wet yellow hair and wide death gaze. She was like a fish with thin human arms outspread, a fish in a flimsy raincoat with a girl's blue face, slapping so hard on the wet glass that Parson screamed into her broken shape, screamed even after she rolled back along the hood and onto the street. In the shack at night he remembered the trundling sound her body had made rolling away, an object out of its element, because she was a fish, that was clear when the police came and he stood looking down at her in the wet street. This man is shot to death, they'd said about Preacher, and grabbed Parson's arms as though he might run, but they had to drag him away. He wanted to look at her, this fish, the ends of her long yellow hair spiky with moisture, her wet coat open, her limbs pulled close as though she were one long shape and might ripple across the puddled surface of the pavement like an eel. But they covered her up and put him in a squad car and he didn't see her again until he got to the penitentiary in Carolina nearly six months later, and she would swim at night, every night, naked, thin and white, through the darkened main corridor of the cell block. The dark there was green and oily, nearly phosphorescent, and she swam face forward, her wet hair flat to her head, legless, armless, her body one undulating streak.

Now Parson wakens in the shack and sees Frank fishing Turtle Hole, the long bamboo pole barely visible over the glassy surface of the water. He imagines the girl who is a fish, circling deep within that wet bowl, down where the line and hook will never touch. The boy seems to hang suspended against an outcropping of dark rock, pulling his line out again and again only to throw it across to the same spot, raking the surface in slow swaths. He seems to break the water gingerly, stirring it in identical sweeps as though it were volatile. But the water sleeps. Parson sees the two girls long before

Frank knows they are there, he sees them walking across the river trail from the woods, moving carefully and quickly, nearly in tandem. They are not ghosts. One is in white but for her dark pants. The other is more than human. Nude, whiter still, she follows the first as though to restate each gesture and step with longer, thinner limbs, a bound shimmer of pale hair moving behind her. They have no faces, only forms, and the paler, more fluid one swims the air, only seeming to walk. Parson goes to the door of the shack and beyond it, moving soundlessly closer, crouching along the barely discernible trail to the water. He creeps through reeds and lies hidden, watching: no, this girl is different, but she is the same, as though she's a sister to the one in the street, the one who swims still in some dark space, searching for him. And might never find him again, never, until he is a shade himself. Already he sees and hears as a shade, hearing no voices now but feeling himself inside the mind of the girl who might be a fish; he finds himself surrounded by her magnified, sonorous pulse, by a great ruffling of air. She might be capable of flight, there is such wind in her, and electric blue flares that shoot up like fires, and in the dark of her something cracks, loud as the crack of a gun, keeps cracking apart. Parson shakes himself to be outside her again, watching, and in a moment he sees them, the two girls, on their knees at the edge of Turtle Hole. Frank has not seen them, he must be nearly sleeping, staring at the unbroken surface of the water.

See how the water holds still, as though enclosed in glass, sheer as first ice. But the night air is warm, just cooling, and as Parson creeps closer, so close he can see her face, the other girl stands, silent, waiting for Frank to look at her. When he does, she kneels back into the reeds, and the taller one appears, nearly opalescent above the dark grasses. She has a face like stone, stone shaped by hand: the brow, the wide-set eyes, the straight nose and parted lips. In jail in Greensboro, waiting to come to trial, Parson had seen from the high window two stone women tower above the courthouse steps across the street. At night, the street deserted, the building lit so their shadows fell across the broad steps, Parson imagined the end of the world, no people at all but just these buildings, sidewalks, long empty streets, and the statues fallen over. Now he imagines this girl as one of them, the whole white length of her lying not in the depths of Turtle Hole but in the stream, which was shallow and looked so clear, her face washed by water until the regular features and cast of eye are obscured. Until she is smooth as scooped stone, long and tapered in her body, a rock fish, a fish with breasts. Her breasts are like white apples, full and compact, young, not the large breasts men slept in, but breasts men mouthed and tasted, nearly tore with their teeth. The nipples are faint bruises at the centers. Parson sees Frank, unmoving on the rock like a light-blinded animal, so startled at the sudden appearance of her body that he has not really seen her face. He looks, keeps looking, and as he does, she lifts each foot gently, never altering her gaze, so the other girl can remove her shoes. Then she walks into the water as though drawn to its center, as though she would walk until she disappeared, and the boy stands and jumps in. *I threw it in the water,* Parson had told the men in Carolina. They were men in suits but there were no windows in the little room, they took off their jackets and rolled up their sleeves. There was the one who gave Parson cigarettes and called him son, and the one who shoved him from wall to wall while fluorescent tubes buzzed overhead. Parson remembered the heat and how the men had paced like winded dogs, big dogs who could only sweat from their tongues. *Who shot him? Who were the others? Did you shoot him? Where's the gun the gun the gun* . . . but Parson wouldn't answer, wouldn't say. They had come straight for him in the fluid, moving room just as the boy swam for this girl now; Parson dug his fingers into the dirt and watched her lift herself, hold to Frank's shoulders as though she might drink the whole deep bowl of Turtle Hole, drown as Parson had drowned in the cage room that smelled of those men. The girl was a fish, he'd told them, lost from Christ as they were lost, as Preacher was lost, gambling on evil, and the room had circled as the whole sheen of Turtle Hole now begins to circle, stirred to move by their bodies and the silence they make until the other girl wades in, her clothes wet and darkened, her darker hair a black cap. She is the dark one who puts her mouth on them, touches them, she and Frank hold the naked girl between them and the girl cries out. The sound she keeps making freezes Parson's blood, he has to lie down in the reeds and hold himself tight, clutch his ears, but she goes on and he begins to try to crawl away, move backwards like an animal in a narrow space. This is how that other one would have sounded had she opened her mouth and let a sound roll from her long white throat. In all the years he has seen her, navigating dark air like a sea, she has not made this sound from death. The sound goes on, eating its own fear, released and saved, and when it stops Parson cannot remember where he is, all of space seems so empty. But it is night here and the girls move in the water, emerge pouring water from their bodies, the naked one shining, stumbling, and they run then, gain the path and are gone. Parson watches Frank, who calls once to them and follows, just to the edge of the water, then crawls out and lies down, seems to rouse himself, walks back through the woods to where Parson knows he has a tent in the clearing.

Now the night looks blue. There is silence but for a far-off wind just grazing the woods by the river, and the rustling of those leaves is half heard. The moon will lighten the air even more in an hour, two hours, mist will settle above the water, never touching, so that the surface can still be seen and the white smoky vapor might be hung above it from invisible cords. Parson walks to where the girls stood and sees they have left the shoes. He takes them to the shack and feels them all over, looks at them in the glint of the window, then thinks of the flashlight one of the workmen gave him. He takes it from under the corner of his pallet and shines a short, wide beam of light across the shoes. White canvas sneakers with frayed shoestrings. One of them has a cloth decal of Mickey Mouse (Parson remembers the foreman cursing *goddamn mickey mouse operation*) sewn inside. The other has a gummed label on which is written: LENNY.

The night looked bluer now, bruised with moonlight, and Lenny saw that mist had begun to rise from the river. A cool smoke hovered just on the surface, thick and thin in patches, and Lenny felt as though the ground itself were no more substantial than clouds on the water. Her feet touched the path but she couldn't quite tell where she was walking, she didn't care, it didn't matter. Suddenly they were gone from the river, they were high in the woods, leaving the cover of the trees to climb the steep meadow to the tent. Cap shimmied up the pole to the wood floor and Lenny followed her but they said nothing. Lenny's clothes were damp from the trail but her body still glowed and burned, and when she lay down on her cot the feeling was worse. She could turn just so under the sheet, curl up, press her fists between her legs so hard it hurt, and she must have slept, wondering how to find him, how to be with him again, with both of them, dreaming Cap had done something to her, she couldn't find her way out of Cap's hands. She woke and slept and Alma was waiting for her by the river, Alma was looking for her in the river, and the crows were in the meadow at dawn, screeching their hoarse calls. The crows were screaming too loud and he had found her and put his hands over her ears, he read her face with his mouth, kissing her, talking so urgently, making words on her skin with his tongue, his teeth, but she couldn't hear him, there was no sound, he had no voice. She slept, and Highest camp was in a dream, they all overslept until reveille sounded again and again, fast and shrill and far away.

When reveille began the bodies moaned and turned as mosquitoes caught in giant webs above the screens were turning. Alma and Delia rolled, hit weathered floor, grabbed each other. Guttural sounds, push for the door. Tangled in nightgowns, they fell over each other in the foyer where the cabin's wings separated, bones of an arm. Wrapped in arms, sleep-ridden, they lifted the heavy latch of the barn-board door, scraped their ankles on the concrete steps, and ran grabbing hands, hissing, up the gravel trail to where the woods broke by the quadrangle. Reveille built in the blocked light, piercing, staccato, an automatic gun on gold wind.

"Is he there? Is he there?" Alma heard Delia whisper a cadenced repetition, breathing in time and running.

They threw themselves down. Crept to where the woods ended and lay in creepers. But they could never see him, and the sound washed into them from air. Alma moaned. Where was he? Every morning he stood in a different spot, trying to make it interesting for himself, or because it wasn't serious. Alma dug in, stubbed her dark toes on rocks; her long oval face was intent. She searched with her eyes, considering.

Alma was silent. The game was not a game. Where was Frank, really, where? Alma had to find him; Delia said she loved Frank but Alma wondered. She thought Delia wanted to be Frank, wanted to be a son with all her might, so she could have her father inside her and never look for him. Alma squared her body, felt her pelvis find the bowl of the ground. Beside her Delia rustled in vines. Alma tightened arms around her. She felt Delia's weedy presence; she felt the A-line wasp of Delia curling in the brushy cover. Her own stone thighs pressed dark in the rotating dirt. She thought of words she liked to pronounce, words in Nickel Campbell's books, long words with smudged letters. She heard, close to her ears, the whine of bloodsuckers in the grass.

"Alma Swenson, Delia Campbell," Alma said over and over, to counter the mosquitoes, to drift the whisper of their names across the quad. She pulled the grass and crawled up closer; her cocoa irises fixed on a point and held. She wanted to see Frank, study him; she thought she saw a shadow before it lengthened and became the top of the flagpole, knobbed in gold, the long cord snaking down. The flag began to ripple, the rope cord swaying gently in a breeze only the early morning allowed. Frank had to let go to blow reveille again; he held the bugle with one hand and saluted with the other, racing through the shrill assault three times in rapid succession. He was all alone out there; secretly, Alma knew how he looked, exactly how he stood.

Yesterday morning McAdams had taken Alma to the infirmary with Delia before anyone was up; the nurse had to clean Delia's swollen lips with hydrogen peroxide and tape gauze on the cut. Nurse said Delia should give her mouth a rest, don't talk too much today, and keep the bandage moist with salve. Just then, reveille had begun, so near everyone was startled, and Alma ran to stand just beside the door. The infirmary was a tool shed attached to the dining hall; Alma could see Frank from behind. His arms looked skinny. He was scruffy, ramrod straight, held taut by the bleating of the bugle; he was at least fifteen. Beyond him, the open quad, the line of the woods, the paths that led to the cabins lost in trees, looked dewy, already warm, as though steam would rise when the sun hit.

Now Alma's eyes watered. Her face was too near the grass.

"I hate camp," Delia whimpered, twisting a knee into Alma's solid flesh. "Hate it, hate it, but I don't ever want to go home."

"Do your lips hurt much?"

"Frank will go home. At the end of camp, everyone will have to go home."

Alma touched the smear of hard scab at the edge of Delia's mouth. "Did they make you call your mom?"

"Yeah, but I just told her I tripped and got a little cut on my mouth."

"You did?" Alma was amazed, not that Delia lied, but that Mina accepted the lie so easily. If Alma had admitted to any accident at camp, her own mother would have gotten into the car and driven the fifteen miles to see the damage for herself. Audrey believed that scars on a girl's face were serious. Delia already had some scars, little ones, from chickenpox. Audrey had remarked on Delia's scars more than once. *Nothing but negligence on Mina's part. You were four when you had chickenpox. I made you wear gloves. At night I used stringed mittens and knotted them close together. Oh, you hated them, but your complexion is perfect.* Alma knew better than to mention she liked the scars; they were like pretty starbursts at Delia's temple.

"It's all stiff," Delia said, "but at least I won't have to talk to anyone today."

"We don't talk to anyone but each other anyway. Right?"

Delia nodded. "Today is hobby hours. You can make more flower pictures. You can make mine again."

Alma would, though the dust of the dried flowers made her sneeze. At least during hobby hours she could sit at a table like a human being and not be fooling with bows and arrows, or tying knots on a board in the sun. She closed her eyes to hear the bugle's shriek, to concentrate on Frank, see him alone on the dewy quad, but she heard silence, a morning silence dense only with minute sounds.

"Look." Alma nodded into open space, for she saw Frank walking away across the level green, holding the bugle aslant at his hip, the bell of its mouth pressed against him. He walked back toward the dining hall into a glimmer, a trick of the light, and beyond him a pickup truck glided along on the grass, soundless as a boat on a sea.

"It's over," Delia whispered.

The last wind was in the trees. They clambered up, an awkward beetle, running headlong to be back in the cabin before McAdams arrived in B wing with her clipboard.

They were singing from church still, all night they'd kept on. Buddy wanted to watch Frank blow reveille, hear Frank from inside the camp kitchen with Mam. But he slept so hard he couldn't move and there were words in his mind: Mam had sayings she'd taught him to think if his prayers were said and he still couldn't sleep. Sing-songs, she called them, and he liked the one about the woods that had trees, and a lot of soft dark with nothing but wind, because he thought the words at night when he was safe, or he was safe when Mam told him the words: *Up the airy mountain, down the rushy glen.* Rushy glen was like the name of a town or a road, a fork of some road that twisted back through the county, and Arey's Feed Store was the big wooden store near the train tracks in Gaither, but no train stopped there anymore. Mam and Buddy had to take the bus through Gaither and Bellington clear to Winfield to get on the train, and the train was like sleeping too, how it rattled and swayed him in the dark and Mam told him sayings then, the same words that always got him sleeping, *glen, glen, we dare not go a-hunting, for fear of little men.* A dare was a tease kids said to get you into trouble, but little men didn't make trouble, Mam said they were very little, like elves. Elves were afraid of people and people were afraid of them, they stayed away from each other, that sounded good, and his favorite part was *wee folk, good folk, trooping all together, green jacket, red cap, white owl's feather.* The owls in the trees sat hooting in the dark but sunlight was in Buddy's eyes; hunters went out at night with lights that bright and the animals couldn't run, a rabbit could freeze in a car's headlights, miners wore headlights, lights on their hard hats. But down in the tunnels of the deep mines there were no animals, just rock and coal and water rattling, Dad said. Dad had worked in the mines. A long time ago when he worked, Mam said he had a job and made good money and plumbed the house — that meant pipes to carry water. In the trains there were little sinks and metal toilets, how could trains have pipes for water, a saying was words you called to mind and never forgot, you could always find them. He wanted to be like the little men, walk in a line all the same. Hidden away. *Down along the rocky shore, some make their home,* a shore was like a riverbank and

Buddy could live by the river. He could have a tent like Frank's and use all the big pipes that sat along the riverbank, make a fort of branches leaned against them. Mam said the pipes would get buried later when they brought in a bulldozer to cover up the trenches, that would happen when camp closed, a trench was a long ditch, no light in a trench, the pipes would roll in and lie still. Buddy wanted to move but the words came in their singsong to say he was still asleep, he was hungry and sleeping and he should already be awake. *They live on crispy pancakes, of yellow tide foam,* that sounded so good, like sweet cracker, Mam, wouldn't it be? Where was she? In his sleep, he listened for sounds, the rattle of the kettle, her footsteps on a floor. Yellow foam was bubbles and floating, like how the stream got scummy. Runoff from the mines was dirty, but food the little men ate would be clean, full of air like the cotton candy Mam bought him when the carnival set up in Gaither every spring. Dad had been gone when the carnival came in trucks with the metal rides folded up, but Dad was here now. Buddy called him Dad. *Some swim the reeds, of the black mountain lakes* and Dad made the house full of that same deep water. Buddy dreamed the house swam off in strange angles now, stretching so he couldn't see into all the rooms. Things hid *with frogs for their watchdogs, all night awake.* Buddy heard the radio coming from the porch, but Mam never played the radio, they left so early for camp. Something was wrong. He opened his eyes and lay still.

There was the chair and the footstool Mam propped her feet on at night. Down the room a way he couldn't see into the bigger bed. The dark green blanket Mam had hung for a divider was still; no one moved behind it. The woolly cloth was nailed right onto the ceiling but had pulled free in one corner and drooped. The same sunlight that fell almost direct into Buddy's eyes played in panels across it. Mam had left him, gone to cook and left him here asleep. She'd left him sleep because he hadn't waked up in time, and now he'd have to get away without Dad seeing him.

She didn't know about Dad. She didn't know.

He found his clothes at the foot of the bed where Mam always put them, and he got out of his pajamas noiselessly. His bed was a metal cot just like the girls slept in at Camp Shelter; it squeaked something awful every time he moved. Mam had brought it home just before camp started. Borrowed it, she said. Before that, in the first week Dad was back, Buddy had slept on an air mattress on the floor, softer and better; it was like since the bed came, Dad could hear Buddy's every turn or twitch all night, and started to notice him in the days.

Naked, he crouched on the floor beside his cot, got into his pants and shirt. The radio was playing so clear, no static. No other sound, like there were tiny girls singing out there about a boyfriend. *Hey la, hey la, wait and see!* Boom boom! Drums in the plastic box of the transistor. Dad might be in the back and Buddy should go out the front. Or he might be on the porch, just waiting, and Buddy should go out the kitchen door and around by the woods.

He was halfway across the kitchen linoleum. The red and white diamonds were flecked with yellow and Buddy had a charm about keeping his feet exactly within their dimensions and making it out the door.

"Hey there, boy," said a voice. "What about breakfast?"

Dad stood behind the porch screen door, a shape, tensed on the balls of his feet. He was fast, a fast runner, long and skinny. Buddy was nearly as fast. But he didn't want to run into the woods, lead Dad into the trees. He stood still, feeling the cool of the floor move up through his feet, into him.

"Come on out here," Dad said. "Come see what I got parked down here in front of the house." He held the door open.

Buddy moved through it, past him. He went to the far side of the porch, by the railing, and looked down at the car. It was a red car with a dented fender. All the windows were rolled down.

"I got you something too," Dad said.

He held out a blue leather bag in one hand, a pull-string bag open at the mouth. Buddy leaned to look inside and saw marbles, cat's-eyes and a big shooter. He reached out but Dad pulled the bag away, then jumped back on his toes and made as if to throw it. Buddy was supposed to catch, and the leather pouch landed in his cupped hands.

"You know how to shoot? I can teach you. After breakfast." He eased himself into his chair, watching Buddy. "I figured you two were at church last night," he said.

Buddy nodded.

"While you were gone I took me a little walk out to the road. Got a ride into town. Damn if I didn't meet up with a nice little lady, wants me to take care of her car for a while." He tilted back in the chair and propped his feet across the railing. Buddy couldn't get through to the steps unless he ducked under, and if Dad wasn't drunk, his arm could shoot out and grab whatever moved, quick as the flicked tongue of a lizard.

"I don't mind doing a favor," he said now, and cocked an eyebrow at Buddy. "You mind?"

"What's that?"

"You mind doing a favor?"

Buddy shook his head.

"Then put that bag of marbles in your pocket. Go in there and get the tomato juice out of the refrigerator, and my pint of vodka. I'll eat light."

Buddy went back inside. He could get out the back door now, but Dad would only catch up later. He opened the squat icebox and stood staring. For a crazy instant he thought of getting inside, fitting right between the nearly empty metal racks. "Well?" he heard from the porch. "And bring some ice." The tray was so cold it stuck to Buddy's fingers. He had the six-pack of V-8 in one hand and the pint bottle of vodka under his arm and the cold ice tray burning into his fingers; the screen banged as he went out. He wished he had a gun. Beyond the porch there were butterflies, six or seven bright yellow ones, dropping and starting like some little whirlwind had them in a swirl. But the morning was still and hot.

Dad had his shirt off already and he took the ice tray and whammed it against the porch rail near his chair. Splinters of ice flew everywhere and a couple of big chunks skidded along the board floor. "She goes off to cook for a hundred girls and leaves us here to shift for ourselves. You believe 'at?" He smiled up at Buddy, waiting. Then he said softly, "You forgot the glasses, Miss."

But he had them sitting on the floor, under his chair, two plastic tumblers. Buddy leaned over and picked them up.

"Now you got the glasses," Dad said. He put ice into both of them and poured Buddy some juice and himself a pale red mixture. "I been waiting for you to wake up," he told Buddy. "My god, all that religion must have tired you out. Couldn't skittle out the door with her this morning." He drank down the glass and poured another. There were flecks of moisture on his lips. "Bud-eee, Bud-eee," he said, mimicking Mam, saying the name in the drawn-out way she pronounced it when she called Buddy in from the road or the woods. He shook the ice in his glass and the liquid moved, and he drank it then, fast, his Adam's apple moving in his throat. "Chugalug," he said, watching Buddy.

Buddy picked up his own cup and began to drink. He had to just keep drinking the cold, thick juice. He had to drink without stopping.

Dad was drinking too, another glass, then he put in more ice and poured the rest of the pint in, only faintly pink, and he drank it, blinking, and his eyes got wet. He pointed at Buddy. "I'm going to be taking a ride, now I got me a car. Just need me a stake." He laughed. "Maybe I'll take you with me. That would get her goat, wouldn't it."

Buddy stepped back, drinking.

Dad leaned forward, like a bird arching its long neck. "You don't want to come, though, do you. Nah." He took a deep breath, then, in one long motion, heaved the empty bottle into the air, out from the porch. It tumbled end over end, twinkling a little, and fell soundlessly into the brush down the bank, on the other side of the road.

Buddy could hear himself breathing. In. Out.

"You and your Mam," Dad said. "You a couple of girls, ain't you."

Buddy knew not to answer yet. Not to move.

"Well, ain't you? Couple of girls? Or not. Yes or no?"

Buddy nodded. He held out his glass.

Dad put an ice cube in it. "Two girls," he said. "Then do what a girl does."

Buddy put the ice cube in his mouth and held it.

Dad took hold of Buddy's wrist and turned away in his chair, so Buddy stood just behind him. Maybe he would leave the radio on this time. But he turned it off. He breathed a few times, jerked his head hard like he was shaking water off, settled in, opened his fly. "All right then," he said.

Buddy took the big ice cube from his mouth, his jaws aching.

He held it in his free hand and moved it over Dad's head, in his hair, around and around, then down onto Dad's neck. Dad began to breathe like he did, his feet down off the rail, his legs spread out in front of him. He would have hold of himself by now but Buddy kept watch on the solid bank of trees across the road, their foliage level with the porch. Their leaves moved; Buddy strained to hear them, heard them, made the sound big in his ears. A saying in the air, a singsong that stayed awake. He could see the air whisper through the leaves, track its movement, like some form made of air was in the trees, and he kept his eyes on the shape that rippled there. He moved the ice along Dad's white, freckled shoulders but he didn't look at them anymore; he had to move the ice down Dad's chest, onto Dad's flat brown nipples, into the hollow between, exactly right, to get it over with. He had to do just this, the same each time, exactly the same. Buddy could hear Dad slapping, straining, but Dad couldn't make Buddy look; he couldn't see Buddy's eyes. Even someone walking right below couldn't see up on the porch, and there was no one to hear. The trees rustled, their layered foliage ruffling out toward Buddy, then moving backward, pulled in as though what was far behind the trees beckoned, nodding. Buddy had to lean over Dad's shoulder to reach down his belly with the ice, and Dad began to whimper. He tensed until his whole body seemed to vibrate and his grip on Buddy's wrist squeezed like a vise. When he started to talk it was almost over. "Don't do that to me," he would say, the words all run together and his voice high-pitched, shrunken. "Don't do that to me don't do that to me." But he wasn't talking to Buddy. Buddy was supposed to move the ice, not stop. And there was a pent-up squealing, and Dad was finished, and Dad was crying. He let go of Buddy then and Buddy could run, he was supposed to, if he was still there Dad would yell at him, "What are you looking at? You get away from me you leave me alone!"

The first time, Buddy had watched, he had looked, but now he never looked. He ran down the porch steps, across the road and down the bank into the trees. He ran yelling, pouring it all out of himself into the wide woods. Today he threw down the stub of ice and jammed his wet hand in his pocket. The leather bag of marbles clanked into his palm as he ran toward the camp to Mam.

# ❧ PARSON: DUMP RUN

One long, thin swath of cloud drifted above the river's surface as though a ghostly swimmer had metamorphosed and arisen; beyond it the bleat of the kid's bugle erupted its piercing assault three times and stopped, leaving a quiet so dense Parson heard the minute creaks of the swinging bridge above them, a hundred yards to their right. The murmurings of the men over their coffee seemed not language but river sounds, and this space by the low-lying water seemed a forgotten shelf, a location in which they were placed and held. The men referred to themselves as *the dirt platoon,* as though they were soldier remnants of some small castoff army delegated to dig and haul; it was *Private, hump it, for Chrissakes!* or *Sarge, gimme a smoke!* By noon their faces and bodies were powdered and smeared with dirt but in the mornings they looked nearly pale, cursing and grunting, passing Parson a steaming plastic cup. The coffee at his lips was hot and bitter and he thought about the name, *Lenny,* until it was merely a sound, a feeling, a twinge in his guts. He watched the river cloud begin to break up, drift, pieces of white amoebic mist eaten by the air or the warble of the water, and he wondered if any of the others had seen it. The foreman was laughing, nodding at him, going on about how Parson's *assistance was requested* by the front office, that fucking dame and her junk, *dump run,* they'd have to offload this pipe and let him take the truck for an hour. It was a joke and they always made Parson go, since he seldom talked and seemed to do what he was told, and that dame drove everyone up the wall. They made like they were going to start in digging but Parson knew they'd sit on their flats smoking cigarettes, and he took the keys and the others finally rose to begin unloading, two men to a pipe length. To Parson it seemed the others had been here forever, marking time; if they were an army, they fought only the heat of the long days and the weight of the pipe, and there was no commander but the endless whisper of the river. It was the river that spoke and talked, not this crow-voiced foreman who gestured at him now, telling him to *git on,* do his good deed and get the truck back.

Grasshoppers flew up around him, dozens of them, disturbed as

61

he drove along the brush track they'd cut in from the dirt road; he could hear the whir of their wings and one of them lit for a moment on his bare arm, its mandibles frothed with a minuscule globular blob of spit. He jerked his arm away, swerving the truck onto the harder surface of the dirt road, and the insect dropped, smearing his flesh with a brown juice. They were a plague: locusts, gypsy moths, hoppers, any of the creatures that consumed insatiably and moved in droves. He began to sweat, feeling the omen implicit in the stain on his skin, and he considered taking the truck, getting as far as he could before ditching it, but he felt the Devil's pull, a kind of magnetic tension, almost a vibration, strung tight in the air. Parson had to stay here, this country, this ground, waiting for Carmody, waiting to see how the Devil moved or talked, in who, in what. He pulled through the camp entrance and wound around over the grass to the back of the big dining hall. Lines of girls fanned off the front porch and the smell of bacon hung in the air, a smell so tantalizing in the building heat that Parson felt himself salivate like a dog. But the directress approached before the truck even fully stopped, raised her bangled arms, and the sudden violent urge to eat, to fill himself with smoked meat as though meat were the salty taste of all the girls he must never touch, dropped completely from him.

Then he was standing by the truck, though he didn't remember getting out. The directress, close to him, smelled of vanilla, like a cake — some perfume she wore — and she was white as cake and soft and round. No mate for the Demon, no match. But she was empty and evil; she scared Parson because the evil would work through her to get to someone else, many others maybe. She herself would be no prize for the Devil, no barrier to his greed, but the Demon was near her like a shadow, never left her. She knew about evil, she was afraid, he could smell her fear. Frank was there, piling up junk, but she gestured to Parson and began to speak the Devil's names, pointing to the cover of a magazine, top one in a ruffled stack tied with twine.

"There is *Lucifer* in the flesh, there is *Beelzebub*, there is the *Devil* himself," she was saying.

Parson looked at her straight on, amazed, realizing she was somehow kin to the big, lonely women in Preacher's congregations, women who had fanned themselves with folded paper while Parson spoke of evil and retribution. But this one was wealthy, she held herself drawn up and tense, she wanted to be clean.

She pointed to the magazine and the image of a short, fat, bald man whose hairless face seemed swollen, whose tiny, bright eyes were squeezed small like a pig's. "The Democrats are fools to think of a treaty with Khrushchev," she went on. Parson loaded junk, boxes of empty metal cans, broken lengths of wood, spotted linoleum flooring ripped up in irregular pieces. Leaning, bending near her, he smelled again her sugary smell, like a bake shop, yes, a smell suddenly so specific that he felt dizzy, remembering the sweet shop in Greensboro, in the hotel where Preacher had played cards that day. They'd gone to a revival down in Carolina and Preacher had got wind of a high-stakes game. The hotel in town so fancy, and the sweet shop all pink and white like this woman. *"People have to be educated to recognize evil,"* said her voice close his back, a fat, soft, woman's voice. The hoarse whisper of the Demon echoed her every word, hissed in Parson's head. *"Better load that refrigerator now,"* it said, *"or you won't have room."* Straining to lift the empty, doorless cabinet, Parson shut out the sound of her and recited a litany of his own, a litany so fast he never had to speak, just move his lips, sounds meant to shut out the sugar and the sweets and the images of that night in Greensboro when Preacher had got shot.

Parson remembered pieces. The sweet shop where they stand before walking upstairs to the room. The long glass cases holding trays of pastry swans in lines, cookies in the shape of four-leaf clovers, sprinkled with sugar bits. The sugar green as bottle glass, glinting in minute squares. Saint Pat's Day, a day for pagans, but snowing this late in March, a freak storm that will turn to rain. Warm hotel, and the heady sugar smell. Swans made of sweet crust filled with yellow cream, their long necks dipped in chocolate. Parson is nineteen and he has never seen . . . a sugar swan. Kneels. Eye-level flotilla of confections on paper lace. So perfect, made for no reason or use. What sort of children hold these sweets in their palms, even eat them as though they are bread or meat? Children far from the smell of the wind in Calvary, the riverblown smell of wet growth, algae, the greeny water where frogs breed after the thaw, frog eggs a fresh rot smell not so different from the sour yogurt smell of women, the real smell wet inside their fake perfumes.

Preacher urges Parson away, up long stairs of dark oiled wood, dark walls ascending upwards into darkness. Then the upstairs bedroom where the men gamble, smoke in the air, blinds drawn, shirt flung over the lamp so the light is dim. Fire lit in the grate, room too warm. Lines of talk. *Should have seen him,* Preacher laughing, *big grown kid wants a sugar swan,* and how one of the men sends down for a tray of the pastries but Parson won't eat one, only holds it in his hand, looking, and later during the fight the whole tray is thrown into the fire, bitter smell of the burnt sugar pungent as the smell of burning hair. Fire crackles, explodes, or the explosion is in the room, the table goes over, cards in the air a slow arc that rains on Parson's face. Then another crack, loud, like lightning, and the other men are gone, out the window to the metal fire-escape stairs, nearly falling in a jumble, their arms and legs jerking like sticks as they descend against the snow. Smell of human guts like the smell in the den of a beast, and the smell fills the room, smoky, darkening all but the comets that flash as Parson rolls Preacher onto his back like a feed sack in a black suit. Preacher's front slick, smeared, splashing red on the floor, on the window, on the snow that covers the fire escape, and out there in the air, the day is blinding white, whiter and whiter.

"You winded? You want a cold drink?" The directress's powdered face was not even so white, and now she put her face close to Parson, and he could hear the Devil laugh.

"I don't want any drink." Parson stepped away and saw the Devil leering from behind her, a thin wraith of a devil in a shadow cloak wide as this woman. Then the Devil shrank to a gray wrinkle at her side and faded off completely. "Don't want any drink," he said again. He knew his voice sounded strange.

"Well, that's all there is," she said, and lit a cigarette. Two rings flashed on the hand that held the gold lighter. "I do appreciate your assistance, once again."

He nodded, wanted to leave, but the little flame in the cigarette glowed up as she inhaled. The tiny fire held him.

"You live near here?" Her words came out in a slender fume of smoke.

She could make trouble for him, send him away. "I stay with my brother in a house down the road."

"You mean Hilda's family, Hilda Carmody, the cook? They're the only house back in there now, I believe."

Parson nodded, for Carmody was surely his brother; Parson was near him, always, breathing his look and his smell, watching Carmody's big wife arrive every morning at Camp Shelter with the blond kid in tow. He'd seen her pull the boy across the quad like a weightless paper toy on a string. Waiting to go to Carmody, waiting for the moment and the time, Parson could almost see into Carmody's wooden house, into the dirt flat of the backyard, or would the yard be grassy and overgrown, sloping off to the narrow stream that fed the river and rattled through the woods? "I'll be going, got to get the truck back," he told the directress now.

Suddenly she straightened, looked him in the eye, and held out her hand. "I'm Virginia Thompson-Warner, regional secretary of the Daughters of the American Revolution. I certainly have a lot of respect for your sister-in-law, she accomplishes a great deal almost single-handedly." The directress touched him then, grasped his hand, and her hand in his was flat and thick and cool as the raw white breast of a fish.

Parson pulled away, startled. To her right, the sheer curtains of her small room behind the dining hall fluttered just a little in the open window. The long rear of the building was beside them and the sudden *whap whap* of the kitchen screen door sounded, kept sounding.

"Oh, do stop that," said the directress sharply. "Must you kick at the door?"

It was Carmody's kid, peering out at them through the screen.

The directress sighed. "No need to introduce you. You know each other."

"Surely," Parson said. He reminded himself to smile slightly, like a man on a TV show.

The boy continued to regard them as the door swung open and shut, a summertime, scruffier version of the child Parson had last seen close up at the prison. He held a little pouch aslant in one hand and marbles began to drop out, rolling backwards across the kitchen floor behind him. The kid made no move to pick them up. A light came off him, a glow to say he was marked. He began kicking the screen door again. *Whap. Whap.*

"Well then," said the directress, "I won't take his silence personally."

"No, ma'am." Parson turned and he was in the truck and the truck was moving, rolling slowly over the grass toward the road, but the look of the boy's face was in his head. The boy knew him, would know him, and the boy knew Carmody, knew who Carmody was. His round wan face was browned with sun and his hair was even lighter, his eyes lighter, set off in his pinched face. There was a pale corona around him, like an echo of the dark gold that fell across the woods just after dusk. The illumined green of the trees turned dark. The woods were unlit, cast in a warm, still pall. Like a curtain dropping, twilight enveloped the forest in a chorus of insect sound. Parson knew the boy sat then in Carmody's wooden house, listening, dreading night, when his big mother stood as the only bulwark in a long, dark passage. In the shack at night, Parson listened too. The dark wasn't safe, and the dark would leak into day. *Whap.* The time was coming, approaching, and he was tired, he wasn't strong yet, he needed to sleep. He would unload at the dump and return the truck and say he needed to sleep, he had to lie down now.

## 🕷 ALMA: PLASTIC ROSES

McAdams and Pearlie, the A-wing counselor, slept in a small space just off the foyer of the cabin. Their door was never left open but Alma had seen inside their room yesterday. McAdams had discovered Delia outside at dawn; Delia had knocked down some torn window screens propped on the cabin porch and made a clatter when she fell down the steps. Alma heard the noise in her own uneasy sleep, sat straight up in her cot, realized she'd let Delia go. She'd stayed in her own bed and forgotten her migration in the dark to Delia's cot; now the cot was empty. Alma was on the cabin's broad front porch then, and crows were squalling, far away, somewhere up the mountain. The screen door slammed; McAdams and Alma ran down the cabin steps together. There were only three broad ones made of brick, and Delia had not really awakened until McAdams and Alma knelt over her. She lay on her side, her T-shirt pulled up above her hips, eyes closed, blood all over her face. McAdams and Alma picked her up between them. Even then, she didn't open her eyes; she wouldn't look at who or what was carrying her. When she did look, she was propped up with pillows on McAdams's bed. Alma was crying a kind of long, high noise, but no one paid any attention. McAdams peered at Delia, curious, taking her time, before Pearlie rushed in with a wet cloth. McAdams wiped away the blood. Alma heard her say Delia didn't need stitches on her mouth, it was mostly a nosebleed. By then Alma was standing by the door, but Pearlie shut it, then McAdams opened it and let Alma in. McAdams pulled on clothes while Alma kept the wet cloths in place until the nosebleed stopped, so they could go to the infirmary.

Later, Delia was allowed to rest during flag raising and breakfast. Alma was sent back to the cabin with her. Delia really had fallen asleep on her cot — as though sleepwalking weren't sleep and she was making up for lost time. Alone, Alma went into the counselors' room, which was strictly forbidden. She sat eating doughnuts on McAdams's bed, memorizing what she wasn't supposed to see. There was barely room for two cots and a table with a lamp. McAdams and Pearlie kept their clothes piled on a built-in shelf, their notebooks and manuals and clipboards on the dirty sill of the one window. They wore khaki shorts and white blouses, white socks and tennis shoes, and green lanyards around their necks with big silver whistles, in case someone got lost in the woods. They seemed to have lived in the cabin always. Alma couldn't imagine them in any other circumstance, though in fact they'd been in camp only a week longer than their charges, for training session. Alma had watched them suspiciously the first night during introductions. She had wanted camp to be like the army, like her father's photo album of the war in Korea, and Pearlie was a pink blonde with frosted, tousled hair. Alma knew: Pearlie had sat still, wearing a shower cap perforated with dozens of pinholes, while minute strands of her hair were

67

doused in a pungent blue lotion. The lotion stank, and anyone who touched it had to wear gloves.

Delia's Aunt Bird was a beauty operator. Since Nickel Campbell had died in March, Alma had spent hours in Bird's shop with Delia; it was easier than being at home after school with her mother. All that spring, Audrey spent the days in bed, or working in her garden, or driving in the car; she was gone. Mina Campbell was gone too, in the afternoons, taking courses at the college; it fell to Delia and Alma to take care of John-John while Bird worked beside them over this or that customer. There were two other beauticians, young girls just graduated from the Academy in Bellington, but Bird ran the show and the talk. Everyone was safe in this commotion. Gossip and the whir of space heaters blinked on and off under the white noise of the big hair dryers, which were like spaceship versions of barber's chairs. Women sat motionless, reading *Photoplay* or *Reader's Digest*, while the bulbous metallic globes of the dryers were lowered into place over their heads. Delia would abandon John-John to sweep up the feathery hair that littered the linoleum floor, working the big push broom in dreamy, circular motions. Alma was left to entertain Johnny, who was almost two and sat playing with curlers. Bird had bins of the fluorescent corkscrew shapes, all sized by color; John-John liked to mix them up and throw them but Alma was trying to interest him in the fact that the colors had names. She lined up the red, the blue, the purple, whispered words in his ear as women talked over their heads about dentists, doctors, recipes, and slipcovers. John-John's ear, fleshy and pink, delicately whorled as a shell, became a receptacle for secrets; John thought colors were secrets. He had a certain way of glancing up at Alma through his lashes as he surreptitiously nudged a curler into the red pile. She wanted to say to him, very quietly, in the same secretive tone, your dad and my mom, but she didn't let herself. Somehow, deep inside, he might understand. It had to be enough to pretend he was her brother, her baby; somehow, in some way, wasn't he hers?

Alma knew she didn't have Delia in the same way anymore. It had been all right until Nickel Campbell died; Delia had never seemed to notice anything, know anything. But now she seemed eminently puzzled, suspicious, distracted. Alma wondered if everyone knew everything, now that Nickel Campbell was dead, but no.

Audrey had said it was still their secret, hers and Alma's, and she had taken Alma with her at first, on her drives to Winfield and Bellington, back around on the country roads that smelled of hay and soil, as though spring were bursting out of the wet, punished ground. Finally she seemed to realize that Alma was on the point of not getting into the car with her, and she began to stay home and garden. She plowed up the whole lower yard and planted; it was as though she still had Nickel Campbell, his absence, out there in the ground, and she kept it close beside her.

Everyone had someone or something. Lenny had Cap, and Cap had Lenny. Wes had his own plans; he was selling accounts for Henry Briarley now, marketing coal, and he traveled nearly all the time, appearing at home on weekends. Mina Campbell had her course books and practiced dictation with earphones on. Aunt Bird had Mina; she called Mina "my baby sister," but it was hard to believe they were sisters. Bird was skinny and stooped, middle-aged, in her round tortoise-shell glasses and blond Jacqueline bouffant — she had named the hairstyle after Jackie Kennedy, and she had a dark rinse called Bouvier to urge on brunettes who were going gray. Mina's hair was perfectly dark, almost black, and her dark eyes were beautiful. But Delia and John-John had Nickel's eyes, exactly, hazel eyes shot with gold lights. And the lights in Bird's shop seemed golden, warm and goldly pink, no matter the weather or time of day.

Bird called the place Birdy's, even though Bird was her married name. She was widowed or divorced, no one seemed to care which, in another town long ago, and had followed Mina and Nickel to Gaither. She was always remarking, in the girls' hearing, how Mina and the kids ought to sell that little house that leaked and move in here with her — why, she positively rattled around in this big place by herself, with only the bottom floor given over to the shop. And it was a big house, a cupolaed Victorian just across from the post office, built long before the post office, before Main Street extended so far south to the unused railroad tracks. Maybe it wasn't so quiet on the edge of downtown, Bird would say, and no professors for neighbors, but a business had to be centrally located. And besides, how was Mina going to finish her secretarial courses and work, with John-John only two years old? Bird could put a playpen right here in the shop, or give some girl from the country board and room to take

69

care of him. Maybe not forever, Bird would say mysteriously, Mina being a young, healthy woman — here she would glance at Delia, and Delia would glare at her — but there were times family had to pull together until conditions improved. All the women would nod sagely, and coal trucks rattled by on Main Street, shaking the big front window. After all they've been through, Bird would say. If Delia was out of the room, changing Johnny upstairs, she'd go on to say it wasn't as if anyone else was going to help, Nickel's own family not even showing up for the funeral, as though what he'd done was Mina's fault! Here Alma's heart began to pound and her face grew hot. Audrey had told a different story. *They came to this godforsaken town because Mina made such a scandal up north with the drinking, and Nickel with no one to help, since his family had disowned him for marrying her in the first place — but she was pregnant and he did the honorable thing. Honor! He didn't learn honor in those fancy schools, or from his skinflint father. Most men would have kicked her into the gutter, but Nickel married her and then spent every penny he had on fancy hospitals, as though anything but abstinence cures an alcoholic.* Lord, Bird would say, who'd have thought I raised her all those years after our parents died, for her to go and have children who are orphans themselves. She'd nod meaningfully at Alma, whom she thought far more mature than Delia, so quiet and sensible. Respect for the dead, she'd address Alma in a low tone, as though everyone in the shop weren't listening. I don't speak badly of Nickel, she'd say, but he was always, well, inward. My pretty little Mina tried to bring him out of himself, make a life for him. And Bird would shake her head, hearing Delia walk in the room above them.

Alma knew her mother would never set foot in Bird's shop. She said Bird's was a continuous hen party, for hens with below-average IQs. But when Alma heard Delia through the floor, it was as though Audrey were the one walking overhead, looking down on all these women, her voice floating into Alma's thoughts. *Bird is a meddlesome gossip with a past of her own. Nickel was exhausted with Mina's sickness, thinking he could never leave her or she'd drink herself to death, and he was trapped in that job with Henry Briarley, a last favor from Nickel's high-and-mighty father. Some favor! Nickel doing the bidding of a rich man not fit to shine his shoes.*

But Nickel had left Mina, hadn't he? *No, I'll never believe it. He wouldn't have left those kids. My god, how we agonized over all of you.*

Shoes. The women at Bird's shop liked to take their shoes off and warm their feet in front of the little coal stove. The cast-iron front was molded in the shapes of hearts and birds with banners in their beaks, painted white, like everything in the shop, but the paint had turned pale pink in the heat, pink like the pink counters and chairs, the baseboards and window frames, Bird's uniform. Alma thought of the glow in the belly of the squat stove as a kind of heartbeat, the fire racing up and shifting when Bird opened the little door. Up on the third floor, where Bird wanted Mina and the children to live, there was a sleeping porch with a swing. Alma loved to sit there while Delia said how stupid and bossy Bird was. The girls dressed Johnny in his jacket and hood, let him have the swing, while they sat on the floor bundled in their coats and watched traffic move the length of Main Street. Up high the trucks weren't so loud, and the dirt of the coal didn't seem to reach them. The upper rooms were full of strange wallpapers that hung down in strips, and flaked, fuzzy spots on the ceilings that looked like forest lichen. *Delia's right not to want to live with Bird.* Alma would hear her mother's voice float behind Delia's complaints. *Bird is common, just like her sister. Mina's idea of a good time is to go bowling, and have babies one after the other. There were three miscarriages before Johnny, and after every one she'd get to drinking, and he'd send her back to that same expensive hospital. She was always after Nickel to sell the piano, get rid of those boxes of books, go deer hunting with Henry and his cronies. Can you imagine! Nickel out in the woods with Wes and Henry. What would they talk about, Dickens and Beethoven?*

Downstairs, Alma knew the women would be talking about other women, or the change, or stories about teachers at the high school, or sick headaches. There was a warm convivial laughter and the smell of nail polish and hair dyes. Moments at a time, Alma wished her own mother could magically transform into one of Bird's customers, be like the others. This is how women were.

Women like this might finish college, be camp counselors in the summer, but they brought along a set of electric hair curlers and makeup kits well stocked with blushers and lipsticks. Pearlie rolled her frosted hair every day before dinner, and shaved her legs. Her voice was pert and chiming and she was just the kind of girl boys would like — boys with cars, boys like the ones who hung out at the Stardust in Gaither. But Pearlie was from Winfield, which was almost a city, and she probably wouldn't think of talking to high school boys from Gaither. Her name was Colleen, she'd told everyone, but they should call her Pearlie, like her sorority sisters at the university did. Alma imagined a sorority was for rich girls who could pay for nice clothes; the rooms would be like hotel rooms and there would be a maid to do the cleaning. McAdams had stood up then and said she was B-wing counselor.

Tall, lanky, tawny-complected, McAdams wore her dark hair cropped short and straight in a shimmery bowl on her head. Alma recognized her immediately as one of the princes in John-John's *Fantastic Fairy Tales*, the book he insisted Alma and Delia read to him over and over. Alma had read it so often that she no longer heard her own voice enunciate the words. Johnny didn't care; he just wanted someone to provide a chant of accompaniment as he turned pages. Even in the heat of Camp Shelter, Alma could smell the chill of the tunnel staircase in "Twelve Dancing Princesses." Suppose McAdams were the one descending those damp stones, dressed in brilliant clown-like trousers and velvet slippers, carrying a raven and a lamp? The prince, pictured from behind in the illustration, looked broad-shouldered and strong, but slender, and his hair was black.

McAdams would be a junior at Presbyterian, a small private college in Gaither, which meant she'd lived near Delia for two years. Her window might have been one of the small, lit rectangles Alma had glimpsed at night, across the old baseball field from the porch of Delia's house. The Campbells lived in an enclave of one-story frame houses once owned by the college (for faculty, Nickel had said — more likely for groundskeepers, Mina had corrected him over supper — and wasn't it ironic that he lived in a house like the ones his grandparents had built for their employees). The college had sold off the houses long ago, but now they wanted to buy them back and tear them down and build a new student union. But everyone on Fayette Street ignored the college, just as they ignored the old train tracks that ran in front of their string of similar houses. Kids were allowed to play on the unused tracks and the neglected baseball field, but they weren't allowed on the campus itself, a sea of green lawns bordered with clipped hedges, shaded by immense oaks and maples. From Fayette Street, the college seemed a town unto itself, a perfect town of four-story brick buildings with antebellum, white-columned entrances and balconies. Alma's mother, Audrey, had gone to school there, and Delia's mother had too, just for business courses, when the Campbells first moved to Gaither. Now that Nickel was, what, gone, buried, disappeared, Mina went to class every day to finish her degree, so she could support the family. Audrey had told Alma why. *The insurance company is disputing Mina's claim, I know all about it, and Henry Briarley, bless his generous soul, won't pay them any pension because Nickel didn't die at work. Work! My god! Life is work, Alma, and you may as well know it now.*

McAdams didn't know about the funeral, about Delia's house on Fayette Street, about Audrey saying she'd planted sweet corn so she could lie down between the rows in August when it was too hot to move anymore. Alma watched McAdams and felt free. This was a new life. Watching McAdams helped her feel that if this life ever ended and camp was over, they might all return to the old life and find it unchanged. Audrey would never have begun the Saturday trips to Winfield to see Nickel Campbell, Alma would never have seen the Winfield bus station or gotten a baton she could still barely twirl. Bird would again be Delia's maiden aunt who ate with them on holidays and birthdays, the one her dad made jokes about, and Nickel himself would be there, back from the afternoon at Whites-carver's when he'd stayed so still in the box, looking utterly unlike himself, being the first dead man Alma had ever seen. He wouldn't be dead anymore. He would be a little sleepy, that's all, not talka-tive, and he wouldn't remember anything about where he'd been. *No use asking,* Mina would warn Delia and Alma, *you two take Johnny outside and leave your dad be now.*

But wishing nothing had ever happened was like walking around asleep in the dark. Was he bleeding when they found him, when someone pulled him out of the river? No, the water had washed the blood away. He would always be dead. And Delia would move into

Bird's apartment, the one above the beauty shop, where Mina and Johnny were staying right now so Bird could mind him in the mornings while Mina went to class. It all had to do with whether the insurance company paid. Everyone in Gaither, not just Audrey, knew. Alma had heard Mina take the phone into the pantry once at Delia's house, and talk with the door shut, asking in a low, steely voice why her husband would drive off a bridge on purpose, and was that what she was supposed to tell her kids?

She hadn't told them anything, Alma was sure of it. John-John didn't understand anyway, and Mina didn't tell Delia things, woman to woman, the way Audrey told Alma. Delia was lucky, in a crazy way. And Alma was the only kid who knew more than most of the grownups knew, more than Nickel's wife or Nickel's daughter. At camp, with Delia, Alma wanted to stop knowing. Mina had almost kept Delia at home to baby-sit Johnny. She'd tried get the deposit back but the camp wouldn't return it, and thanks to the generosity of a benefactor, would offer Full Supplement toward the balance. So Delia had come to camp with Alma.

Camp was like being asleep, like a long, long dream. Even Delia's fall seemed not to have awakened anyone. Introductions night seemed weeks ago; in fact, this was only the tenth day in Camp Shelter. Time was big here and Alma wanted oceans of it, more and more, so that her past seemed a smaller and smaller island, barely discernible as the sailor looks back from the sea. Now McAdams announced today's schedule and the girls listened, most of them still in their cots. They did look like a rustic version of the dancing-princess story, Alma thought; there were actually twelve cots to a wing, with look-alike worn white sheets and olive-green blankets. There was a footlocker under each rumpled bed, not a shimmery gown and slippers. The girls' faces were indistinct in the early morning light, the blinds of the big windows still drawn in a futile attempt to discourage the migration of mosquitoes through the rusty screens at night. McAdams was the perfect organizer of ignominious royalty; she delivered her pronouncements in a jaunty tone that brooked no argument, yet forgave in advance any clumsiness or fear. She addressed them as a group, captains of industry, little wanderers, B Troop, and she never yelled in high-pitched frustration like Pearlie, only joked, increasingly tongue-in-cheek, as though camp were an elaborate game, and the idea was to increase the intricacy of the game by inventing ever more detailed rules and rituals.

"Arise, group. We now have nine minutes to flag raising and breakfast, then we shall proceed in tandem to hobby hours, since, if you remember, archery was yesterday. Heritage class will serve as a restful interlude before activities, which include a hike to Highest camp and the peak, if we move fast enough to make the peak, I make no promises, and then, after lunch" — a dramatic pause — "canoeing." McAdams consulted her watch as Alma groaned. "Now, now, this is not a transatlantic voyage, merely a serene meander under the bridge to the dock past the turn in the river. Those of you with hives or rashes or other skin ailments" — she pretended to regard them in turn through imaginary pince-nez — "will please not ingest river water, berries, or small pebbles." Laughter from the assemblage. "And you will please not lose your footing, as Frank — yes, Frank — has agreed to assist us, help you to your precarious seats in the aforementioned canoes, since fishing girls out of the drink will only retard our progress and delay the moment when Frank helps you back *out* of said canoes." More laughter. "Eight minutes. Inspection while we're gone. Tuck your bed corners. On to the enchanted forest."

She turned and was gone, taking up her position outside, near the cabin steps. She never watched them carry out her orders but elicited a secretive cooperation. Everyone hurried to comply while McAdams's voice counted down. "Eight minutes . . . seven . . . six minutes, group." To Alma the room resembled nothing so much as a living pinball machine, with girls ricocheting to and from the closet-sized bathroom as though set in motion by pump-action levers. They jumped into wrinkled uniforms, stood on their beds to pull the dingy sheets tight. Alma knelt by her cot, smelling the wool drab of the blanket as she tugged its frayed edges. Close to her face, the scratchy cloth was faintly redolent of wet dog, or of John-John's wool teddy, the one he liked to drop in the sink at Bird's shop. The teddy was a hand-me-down: Johnny was named after President Kennedy's son, Bird liked to say, but he was minus the silver spoon in his mouth. Johnny would be standing now in the playpen at Bird's salon, watching the electric fans turn in the narrow windows, long strings of the yellowed blinds dangling and twirling. In summer the space heaters were put away and the fans swiveled their mechanical necks, stirring the perfumed air into windy ripples. The rings on the window blinds were all decorated with scented artificial roses Bird had ordered from a catalogue. Their bright red plastic weighted the strings and their revolutions seemed measured as a minuet; in motion, the roses resembled tiny faces with pursed mouths. Johnny would be watching them circle and sway, and the air would be full of the machine hum of dryers and fans, the squeaking of the elevated chairs as Bird or her employees worked the foot pumps, the voices of the women a watery murmur punctuated with the shrill dual chimes of laughter and exclamation. Johnny was still there, like a bright raft bobbing on sonorous water. Alma wished he were here instead, at camp with Delia and her, where they could all be proper orphans and walk the trails from one established point to the next. John-John was small for his age, Alma reflected; he could sleep in Delia's cot with them, in the middle between Delia and her, and he wouldn't even need his crib. Delia wouldn't sleepwalk anymore. And they could all live in this green construction until Alma thought of where to go next.

Alma had watched McAdams draw on her clipboard during hobby hours. She knew McAdams drew mazes, elaborate mazes that grew from a central penciled point and expanded in straight, squared lines, perfect angles, all in miniature. Alma imagined wending her way to a new home through one of those graphite maps, discovering as her prize the exact beginning of a world. She wanted to hold Johnny by the hand and keep her arm around Delia, and stay there, the three of them, in the center, watching and waiting in the heart of a fortress. Only someone very wise would ever find them.

The big oven had a silver front. It was like a black box crouching on short legs, and on top there were eight heavy burners shaped like crowns. Mam washed them with the bristly silver wool that stuck in her cuts and scrapes, little iron hairs that sting, don't you touch that scour pad. He wanted to pick up those crowns but if she caught him on the stool he'd get a licking. Sweet jesus Buddy do you want to burn your hands clean off and get me fired in the bargain, get on outside till I can get this breakfast cooked, and when he stood just inside the black screen door and looked out at the trees, everything was silvered by the glisten of warped mesh. The redheaded directress was outside. Frank and the workman with the pickup truck were loading up her junk again. That workman, the darker one, sometimes looked up when Buddy sat on the swinging bridge to watch the men's slow progress, digging and hauling by the river. Now Buddy watched him slant his eyes at the directress's powdered face. Scared of her, maybe. Buddy wasn't, and he kicked the screen door hard with one foot, keeping time. Kitchen bang and clang behind him, and that same radio station playing girl songs. *It's my party.* When the directress tried to talk to Buddy through the screen, he backed up and crouched in the shadowy pantry. He'd rolled the marbles out onto the floor and they were bright glass eyes with the rippled colors burnt clear through. Tilting and spinning, they gleamed off each other like marauders. He heard the pickup drive off and Mam's white, thick-soled shoes appeared beside his hands, what you got out here Buddy, pick them things up before someone breaks their neck. Mam, filling up the small space, opening armfuls of big cans, Honey Bee orange juice smell, sweet tin syrup, brassy and gold. She pushed him a little from behind and her big hands smelled of water and dough, and when the door banged he was outside alone.

The big trees behind the dining hall hung their leafy branches down like waterfalls. He could climb them and sit hidden but he wanted to wait and listen, he could hear the girls walking down the trail, he could hear them talking their bird sounds near and far and see them appear, white blinks that moved behind the covering green. He was running then and he knew all the paths from games he played alone, pretending to hunt and shoot, climbing fast with gangs he made up. Wee folk from Mam's singsong rhyme were sounds in the leaves; soldiers were cracks in the branches. Higher up, soldiers were thunder or wind. Since Dad was back from Carolina Buddy ran faster, creeping and hiding, quieter, silent, walking rocks in the stream like Dad was some animal tracking him, smelling where Buddy had been. But Dad never walked in the forest, he stayed to the house and the road; he wasn't the one Buddy thought about, the one who'd give him a rifle and a hat with earflaps, take him hunting and complain, sternly, *stay with me boy, you creep around in front and behind till I don't know where to shoot that's safe*. From far off the tall girls really were like a line of clumsy deer, shivering the woods. Close up they were loud, talking and laughing, they didn't care who heard them, not like Buddy. He could go along in the bushes and cover like a frog in a hop, a woods mouse sliding over big roots, between the stems and vines and thorny runners. The tall girls never saw until he wanted them to see. How old are you this year, Buddy, and he said eight even if he couldn't write eight or write words, the letters with all their black jumping shapes turned around this way and that. In school he had to sit in the circle with the others but finally the teacher stopped asking him and he only sat holding the book, not seeing it, seeing instead the shoes of the girl beside him, little black shoes that shone and had bows and no laces. If only his shoes had no laces. He didn't care about reading but he wanted to learn to tie his shoes, at home he wanted to but his mother tied them with double knots so they never loosened and he couldn't get them off, they find out you can't tie shoes they might not let you in that school and what will I do with you while I'm at work? In summer there were no shoes and he didn't have to sit anymore, asleep and awake and not moving till he was so pinched and drawn up he had to run at recess, back and forth without stopping, whooping and screaming till the boys followed him and the girls stood watching.

Now he was in the trees, deep in the quiet, silent and loose, ranging up and down the trails and through the woods, I don't know where you come from, boy, Dad would say, you got stones for brains and the woods sense of a she-fox; then Mam would tighten the corners of her mouth and put her big hand on Buddy's head, touch his hair so tender he stood still to feel it. Today his pockets were stuffed with rolls, with the plastic jam cups served at breakfast, and spinach leaves he'd taken from the sink when Mam didn't see. Bait for the trap, trap, trap. He counted his footfalls, not with numbers but with words, a word, he'd get him a rabbit this week, he knew he would, and he'd show it to the girls, keep it hidden here, away from Mam and Dad. Climbing, he remembered the discarded crate outside Great Hall, the one he'd helped Frank open yesterday, Frank tugging and cursing, You know what this is, Buddy? A lectern from some mail-order place, I guess that crazy dame is going to make speeches, and together they'd kicked and shoved the wooden box back against the stone foundation of the hall. It would still be there and Buddy would only have to nail some wire across one end, maybe both ends, Frank would help him for a few beers. Sneak back to the house and get them around noon when Mam was busy with lunch and Dad would be sleeping on the porch, Dad would be sleeping on the broken metal chaise while the flies made their sounds near his face, sleeping on his side with his feet tucked up and his long arms folded over his belly, that's how he'd slept in jail, Buddy knew, on a hard slab like a piece of meat. The old feather tick in the bed felt too soft now and Mam made him nervous, he said. Why, you as big as the side of a barn, like trying to straddle a whale, then his laughter beyond the wall of the blanket tacked between the beds . . . you still feel it though, big as you are, your old hard luck pushing up, like this, this, and her voice all rough like she was tired from walking hard, go on out of here, get away from me, he not even asleep. What you talking about, he's a farm boy, seen it since he's old enough to wiggle, lie back there before I show you how to. In his sleep Buddy could hear them, like they talked all night in the worn, shiny dark, and when Buddy opened his eyes he watched a big mosquito move its tangled legs in a web that bridged a corner of the window. You think we any different than those dogs and chickens and cats, Dad would say, those hogs, those coons you hear scream out by the dump? They did scream, wild women, Dad called them, fighting over garbage they washed in the same stream that moved through Camp Shelter. Buddy had seen them, hunched by the water in moonlight like midget crones, worrying whatever scrap like they were blind and had to find it, dipping their monkeyish hands and pulling back to hiss, screaming warnings, showing the teeth in their masked, bright-eyed faces. Hurtling down the hills of the meadow, through the brush of the trails in the woods, they looked like small bushy bears, trundling at a fast, wobbly roll. Buddy envied them: if they tucked their cat-like heads they could roll like balls. He might have a coon if he could ever find a baby and bring it up, but that was luck, they were mean as snakes and bit, a rabbit was easy to get and if he built a cage in the woods so no one saw, Dad wouldn't kill it, seemed like Dad ate whatever moved. You'd get yourself a job instead of sleeping all day you wouldn't be in such a lather at night, Mam told him, there's men laying pipe right down at the camp. Moving through the trees, Buddy heard their voices played back like whispers, like he must have heard them in the dark while he was dreaming. Let em lay pipe, I got plans. What plans? You get to drinking and fighting again, you can sleep somewhere else. He's old enough to see it now and I don't want him watchin. Dad's cackled laughter. You fixin to kick me out? Won't have to fix nothin, you on parole, they'll come and get you. You not callin nobody, you waited five years for my sorry ass. Her long sigh mixed in with the sough of night breeze and the house seemed to move, eddy like a paper boat on the surface of the stream that was still warbling down by the woods in the dark, and Buddy would dream he was outside in the string hammock between the pines, rocking in the shade where no grass grew, there was only hard bare dirt littered with needles and sticks, dirt black and moist from the old shade of the tilted, pencil-point trees. He remembered when Mam would sweep the ground with a broom on Sundays and they'd spread a blanket and eat blackberries Buddy picked down by the road, when it was all like a long song broken up by the screech of trains, trains they took to the prison in December and April. Shiny lights in the station, gleam of the rows of empty benches on a floor like flat, pearly stone. Big as a church, bigger, the biggest city he'd ever seen and no people except droves that came and went, he might have seen these girls there, the girls from Highest camp at the top of the mountain. They might have been there, unseen by anyone but him, talking and laughing, making a bright space in the center under the big clock, under the statue. The statue was a giant man painted hard and black, holding the clock before him like a shield, and his helmet was fastened on with bolts of lightning. The girls would have stood shining near his naked iron legs, Lenny the tallest, palest one, and when the trains came shuddering in beyond the closed doors to the tracks, she would have touched her face to the lowered sword of the giant and felt the same vibration Buddy felt in his feet and his hands. He heard a whining in his head like when he listened to the rails in the woods, rails where the trains no longer moved, had moved once, lifting the branches of trees on a bellowing roar. And when he and Mam picked up bags and parcels and moved out with the rest, out to where it was dark beyond the doors and the tracks were laid down in long pits and the trains were steaming, the girls would have moved on ahead in the pale-lit twilight of the outdoor lamps. He almost remembered them now, glimmering far ahead. Light shone through them to where the rails emptied in blackness. A train could fall off the edge, falling and falling down like a heavy clanking serpent. What's out there, he'd asked Mam, and she told him those lights were the city, a city stayed lit all night. He remembered when they were going to the jail, she didn't like him to ask her why, for a long time she didn't say Dad got sent there, just that he went. The train rattled through the night and the sound made Buddy sleep but he knew Mam was awake, reading the palm-sized Bible she took traveling. Later, once, they were walking from the motel to the dead stone face of the prison and she said Dad had done a bad wrong and was waiting here to be forgiven. Buddy knew then that Mam was mistaken, she knew even less than Buddy knew, because Dad would not wait to be forgiven, he was only waiting for them to open all the doors and gates, and that would take a long time. The first door didn't want to open at all and Mam had a hard time pulling it while Buddy dragged through the paper sacks of fruitcake and baked chicken and new long underwear, then they were inside where it was no longer cold but it was like night again, with the lights on overhead, and men in uniforms like mail clerks all had circular metal rings of keys. And all the time Buddy walked, burdened with sacks and parcels, he heard the jingling of the keys, their chiming, desolate sound the measure of each man's gait. Before him Mam moved on silently in her long gray coat, the broad rounded wall of her backside wider than any two of the men.

He was safe with Mam, her tilting, gentle lurch the only indication he was where he should be. She walked her slow, considered,

heavy walk and he moved in her wake where there was no resistance, just a cleared path whose view was blocked by her bulk. He
didn't need to see, it was all like blindman's bluff, walking down
the road to the school bus fall, winter, spring, sucked into a tumult
of voices as the bus wheezed and clamped shut its shuddered doors.
Mam rode too, sitting always behind the driver, a woman she knew,
and the kids on the bus first taunted him, your mother is fat, big as
an elephant, a house, and he spat back threats, challenges, shut up
or she'll sit on your belly and crush you dead, she's done it, I've seen
her. What's the ruckus back there? the driver yelled. You kids sit
down, and Mam would turn and fix them all with a silencing look.
When she worked in the lunchroom she wore her hair in a net. If
they went to the grocery or the welfare or the welfare clinic they
walked home or caught a ride with someone who let them off at
their road. Behind her, Buddy didn't care if he saw where they were
going, he could feel by the air and the weighty sound of densely
leaved branches above them that they were on their road, he knew
the ruts and turns and the narrow, broken bridge where the stream
ran under, the stream that bled its sound behind his house, through
Camp Shelter, the stream that went underground in the cave and
fed Turtle Hole. Behind the big rock near the water, a slanted hole
opened like a hideout. Buddy didn't go in the cave; it was too low
and still, and water rattled inside like something in a drawer. At the
prison there'd been no sound but footsteps on cement, the buzzing
of the lights overhead a low drone like insects trapped in glass tubes.
In the prison he'd been glad he couldn't see, he'd wished he didn't
have to see Dad, look across the counter and through the window.
Dad wore pajama clothes and his eyes were burnt. Stand him up
there beside you, let me see if the wise guy has growed. Eh? You
still a wise guy? Mam lifted Buddy before he could run and Buddy
was higher than the half walls of the cubicles. Clusters of huddled
visitors looked up, dark rumpled men opposite them looked up, a
guard started over and Buddy jumped down. He hid then under the
counter while Dad was laughing, Jesus! You think he's gonna storm
the gates? After an instant Mam laughed, polite and quiet, the guard
had sat down again but Buddy stayed hidden. Mam's black boots
were wet and the white flesh above her rolled woolen socks was

veined with blue, like she was too big for her skin. At night in the cold Buddy slept with her and dreamed he was running, running like this in the woods, higher and higher, cleaving sideways and upwards on a loose dirt bank, moving on all fours to grasp roots and vines under the canopy of trees. Make no sound, leave no sign, that was not a rhyme but a song he sung, hearing the girls near him now, above and to the right, *up the airy mountain* all in a column like a green centipede. Buddy knew it all, every move they made: they were marching to breakfast, having raised their own flag at Highest, he could circle round behind and watch, follow them down, find Lenny and Cap near the rear of the line and tell them about the rabbit, promise he'd trap one, they could touch it, he'd let them as a secret, away from the rest. He ran with the promise in mind, sensing at his fingers the loose, thick scruff of the rabbit's neck, its hide like a fluid glove over a clockworks of small hard bones and long pink slides of muscle. He could smell the rabbit, waiting somewhere and looking, its pounding heart like a seed that jumped.

## ▓ LENNY: OFFERINGS

Lenny knelt over a jumble of empty bowls. Her reflection in their empty surfaces wavered back at her. Mess kits were the only mirrors Senior girls ever saw in camp; Lenny thought the ripply mirage of a shape, a face, was better than the real picture, more honest, because, really, nothing was so clear. With the flaps down the tent was still shadowy and dim inside, but light pulsed at each break in the canvas. None of the flaps actually met despite their string ties; daylight fell through in illumined bars. She crouched on her haunches in one of those bright lines, smelling the meadow beneath her through the wide slats of the board floor. A dark smell, still sweet, like clover and soil. Dense, heavy. Safe.

Waking up scared was like sleeping on mirrors, or sitting on reflective ice so thin it might crack if she moved in any direction at all. Some dream had made her cry, and she'd overslept, but before she could begin to worry about having no shoes or seeing Frank at flag raising, standing back in the line to stay hidden, their counselor had appeared in the tent and dumped twelve mess kits onto the floor. They were all still dirty, apparently, and would have to be washed again; Lenny and Cap would have to do the job properly and catch up with the group later. If they wanted breakfast in the dining hall, they'd better hop to it. "*Hop* to it?" Cap had asked, her pillow over her face. "You mean, like a rabbit?" But the counselor had ignored her. Probably they'd all been told to ignore Cap's remarks, since Henry Briarley had helped the camp open, and provided at least one Full Supplement — for Delia Campbell, Alma's friend, whose father had worked in the office at Consol Coal. Wasn't just a car wreck, Cap had said, Nickel Campbell drove into the river on purpose. A big gamble. What if he'd lived and had to answer everyone's questions? Drowning, you always tried to save yourself. It was a reflex. That's why people put rocks in their pockets when they walked into water and didn't plan to walk out. Right?

Lenny glanced over at Cap now. "You know, you could help me with these dishes instead of lying there on your cot like a rich housewife in some soap opera."

"Soap opera. I like that." Cap laughed, stayed prone, and pantomimed a long drag on an imaginary cigarette.

"You don't know what I'm thinking about," Lenny said.

"I don't have to. No matter what you're thinking, I gotta have my cigarette."

"Not likely. There's not a cigarette in this entire campsite, no matter whose tent we searched."

"Then I'll have to make do. Isn't that the term your mother uses, Lenore, 'make do'?" Cap took another long drag out of the air, and exhaled. "It's sad, that term. Don't you think?"

"I guess." Lenny began sorting aluminum forks from spoons, so familiar, so oddly shaped, as though campers shouldn't touch sharp edges. There were no knives in Girl Guide mess kits; the handle of the spoon was to serve a double function, and both implements were meant to be secured by a metal clip inside the larger dish. No rattling in a regulation mess kit.

"On second thought, I don't want to make do. There's got to be a cigarette in this camp. Frank could get them, I bet, from the work crew by the river. They're always sitting around on those pipes, smoking and doing nothing." She sat up. "Those flunkies would give Frank a pack of cigarettes for us. They'd think it was cute."

"You addict."

"Lenny, that's boring." Her feet hit the board floor of the tent and she walked over to stand just beside Lenny. Her ankles and toes were still smeared with the dried mud of Turtle Hole. "How about 'you nasty delinquent,' or 'you fledgling degenerate'?"

"Not so fledgling."

Cap knelt down, her face just opposite Lenny's. "Stick with me, Lenore. We're OK." She smiled. "They can't get us if we're together."

Lenny shoved half the plates and bowls into a confusion of shapes around Cap's dirty feet, and looked into her green eyes. Or not green — emerald, Cap liked to say. There was still a smell of the Chanel No. 5 she sprayed in her hair from a bottle Catherine Briarley had left in her bathroom in Gaither. The bottle now sat incongruously under Cap's bunk beside a sterling silver manicure set that was zipped into a silk pouch.

"Together," Lenny repeated, and let her face nearly touch Cap's. "Are we going to get married and have kids and live in a split-level ranch house?"

Cap sighed. "What am I going to do with you? Ranch houses are never split-level. They're all on one floor, like the ranches of old. Like Ben Cartwright's place on *Bonanza*." She backed off and began to throw the dirty dishes into an empty backpack, then looked up at Lenny. "Is Frank more like Adam or Little Joe? Let's decide."

"I don't want to talk about it. And you might want to put on some clothes. Like that uniform over there in the corner."

"This one?" Cap retrieved a wrinkled mass from beyond the footlockers. "What's the matter? You don't like my clothes? Just because you got yourself dressed under the covers in something nearly clean? How incredibly modest."

"I'm tired. It's like I didn't really sleep." Lenny felt her eyes well up. Startled, she looked away from Cap and began throwing the rest of the metal dishes into a plastic clothes basket they used as a drainer in the stream.

"Ask me to iron my shorts, why don't you. Ask me anything." Cap shook out the Bermudas, held them up. "Mice and spiders, out! We'll do anything to restore Queen Lenore to her former power. Quickly now, the regime could topple, the people could rise up. Ask, ask, and it shall be granted."

"Just get dressed," Lenny answered, then thought she saw a kind of shadow flit across Cap's eyes, or through them, or the shadow was in her voice. Say something harmless, Lenny thought, to keep them from talking. "How did 'Catherine' turn into 'Cap'? Did your mother call you that?"

"Never. I was a baby and my dad called me Cappy, because she forbade 'Cathy,' too ordinary. He did it to aggravate her, then shortened it to Cap. Or I did, maybe."

"Maybe," Lenny answered, turning to leave the tent. She heard Cap behind her, pulling on clothes.

It was true, Lenny thought, she was Cap Briarley to everyone in Gaither. No one but her mother seemed to have ever called her Catherine. Lenny called her Natasha; Natasha was a cartoon spy, an outlaw witch. They pretended they were heroes at school, sometimes at home, righting wrongs with one-liners. They considered Rocky and Bullwinkle to be more real than the Beach Boys or Troy Donahue, whose pictures were plastered on lockers in the basement of the junior high. Cap made fun of movie stars to Lenny, made fun of the other girls, talked back to the boys, bright-eyed, her tongue sharp. Cap and Lenny were together at school, and school was life; home was some afterthought they attended to on the phone, doing algebra while they watched TV. Lenny liked the idea of a flying squirrel with a silk scarf and aviator goggles, and the moose who couldn't keep up, but Cap was nothing like Bullwinkle, except she did take up room, so much room, like a real creature from a cold place, a creature born wet, on the shores of a snow lake. The lake would have a silence around it that was clear, like ice, the air so cold it burned, no one could taste it. Lenny felt Cap hover near her, past her, behind her, to one side or another, pushing her, looking at her. Sometimes there was a point of heat in the back of Lenny's throat, like a hunger. The hunger waited, an old, jagged part of her. Being with Cap reminded Lenny of hunger and noise, of aching.

But when she bent over the stream, she felt empty and clear. It felt good to be so alone in the woods. She could hear Cap's feet on the path, and the clank of the dishes in the backpack. Lenny stacked tin mess plates into sticky piles. If chores weren't done right, the counselors liked to say, Girl Guides could practice doing chores again. Supper last night seemed weeks ago, but it was only last night, and the plates and cups weren't clean enough. It was only because they'd had pancakes. How could you scrub off dried syrup in water this cold? Goofing around last night, she'd lost the plastic scour pad. Well, they could scrub them with rocks. Use more soap, keep rinse water separate, and pour the soapy water on the ground, not in the stream.

Cap knelt beside her, and they set up their system. Dishes. Soap. Bucket of rinse water. Empty clothes basket for clean mess kits. Later, someone else would have to sort everything and reassemble the kits — they'd all laboriously scratched their initials on each important fragment of the whole.

"I love having everyone gone," Lenny said. "It's so quiet. Like a real woods, not a camp."

"They're gone. They'll see him and we won't," Cap said, soaping plates. "He'll be looking at all of them, wondering."

"I'm glad we're staying here. What if he knew who we were?"

"What if he did? You think he's going to tell someone?" Cap reached out to touch Lenny's bare foot. "He's part of the secret, isn't he? He did it too. You think he's going to find your sneakers and read your name inside? He doesn't even know you were wearing shoes. He won't know who we are unless we tell him, unless we find him again."

"I've got to find those sneakers," Lenny said.

"What for?"

"Oh, god. Let's get finished. I'm hungry, I'm so starved. I want to miss flag raising and go to breakfast."

They traded off, tossing collapsed metal cups into the water, setting the clothes basket in the stream itself to receive whatever seemed clean enough to pass muster. Cap was so silent, Lenny could tell she was scared — or not scared, but puzzling it all out. Crossing the meadow to the woods, with Cap behind her, both of them lugging their silly, cumbersome burdens, Lenny had wanted to tell her it was a pact, like other promises they'd made. But once they'd got to the stream, she couldn't get herself to speak. It was like she was awake and Cap wasn't. Like Cap was always teasing her, pushing, but looking for where to move, how far to go. Mornings, Lenny lay in her cot, waiting for Cap to wake up, listening.

Very early, crows fed in the space of tangled weeds and tall grass behind their tent. Just after dawn the ratchety screams began, sounding near and far, overlapping echoes that approached and faded. The racket never seemed to wake Cap. She was a bronze color now and slept outflung, like a golden net. Her auburn hair had lost the distinct salon shape Catherine Briarley had charged Juanita with maintaining at a shop in Winfield twice a month; now it nearly touched her shoulders and curled in the humidity. Lenny would look into a shaft of sun, closing her eyes to peer into that cranberry red behind her lids; the red was luminous, like lit-up blood; she could watch it dapple and break into black spots that revolved like dividing cells. Cap liked to say the bats and the morning birds were Queen Lenore's minions, a joke mythology. But the bats were a night populace, no joke. They whistled in Lenny's dreams, sucking a black juice. The crows were black too, but glossy, bigger than chickens. Floppy when they walked, slightly drunken. But they could swoop and dive, hunt with their feet. Their noise was adoration Cap didn't seem to hear, a raucous threat, a beckoning; Lenny imagined the crows alighting with offerings of mice and bats, and hard-shelled water bugs, marooned on their scarab backs. It was praise Lenny understood, praise she might organize, like the ritual of throwing flowers in the stream, chains of ripped scraps and ragged stems to dress their ankles.

"Look, Cap, the flowers are still here from yesterday." Lenny was standing in the water, pointing to colors in the current.

"Caught on the rocks. It's so shallow." Cap took the bucket from Lenny and dumped the dishes into a tangled clatter on the bank. "You want more flowers? What a glutton. I could throw some at you."

"They do look like food." Lenny bent down to cup water in her

88

palm, and drank it, mincing a scarlet petal between her front teeth. She smiled at Cap, and the red stain was on her lips.

The water gurgled, dappled with flowers that still looked fresh. Pale blue chicory winked and floated, thrown in yesterday by the handful, and the spidery yellow loosestrife bobbed on woody stems. The bee balm were deep red, like wounds in the cold water, and clumps of mountain laurel were the size of snowballs.

"I have a dream about us being in the stream," Lenny told Cap.

It was true. Lenny dreamed about Cap when the bats were flying. She dreamed when the crows screamed. Lenny floated on her back in the dream, and she wore a sequined gown like the dress Cap kept draped in plastic in the back of her closet. Catherine Winthrop had worn the dress as a debutante. She really had been Catherine Winthrop then, Cap said, in Connecticut, her brocade skirt sewn with pearls. In Lenny's dream the heavy bodice of the dress was even more elaborate, an armor of beaded flowers bearing Lenny up, and she couldn't open her eyes. Cap stood over her, gently directing the float of her body with long sticks.

Lenny knew the beaded dress probably still hung in Cap's closet, but Cap's mother was gone. She was turning into Catherine Winthrop again, for real, taking back her maiden name and living in Connecticut with Cap's grandparents. Cap was supposed to be Catherine Briarley now; she was supposed to leave Gaither in the fall and be rewarded with her own sports car. Like Catherine Winthrop of Connecticut, Catherine Briarley was destined to attend a good eastern boarding school and then go on to Barnard, but Catherine Briarley existed nowhere on earth. If she did exist, Cap liked to intone in a vicious hiss, she would be dangerous and vengeful, a desperado implemented to avenge Catherine Winthrop, who likewise did not exist in Gaither, West Virginia.

A long time ago, Cap had learned to curse as her father cursed, voice held in check, the flat, buttery Georgia inflection and the words burned in, branded on the flesh of their intended: *You want I should send her off to some horse-infested snoot school, pay to get her bedded bucked and fucked by some married faculty shit who digs for urns in Turkey and then gives schoolgirls the clap, wasn't that how it went?* Lenny was supposed to join in then, doing Cap's mother's voice, a funny, broken tone, defeated, choked with rage: *You ignorant rube, you like it that she spends her time with kids whose fathers crawl around in that mine of yours. One of these days she'll marry some grease monkey from the Texaco station and then you'll be satisfied, write her a big check when she hasn't got a dime and be the hero.* Now Cap's version of Henry's laughter, picking up words in a mocking interrogative: *Big check? Why, she won't need any big check! She'll have that famous trust fund your daddy will invent any day now! She can marry the fucking janitor out at Consol and fly him to some ritz penthouse?* Then, flatly: *Let her do anything, but don't let her be you — you are done for.* Now an exaggeration of Henry's disappointed, self-mocking chuckle: *You have been done many times. And remember, if you condescend to play golf in Gaither, you'd better be playing with somebody's wife. This is not Westchester County or New Haven, your checkered career is over.*

Their fights had taught Cap the only version she knew of her mother's history, and she'd taught Lenny that history as intimate sport between them. Catherine Briarley was nothing like Lenny's experience of a mother, nothing like Audrey, with her endless stories and harangues. Catherine told her daughter nothing, only said, softly, to Juanita, Henry is a bastard. She said it so Cap heard; she said it for Cap. In Gaither, no friends picked Catherine up in convertibles; she'd had only Juanita. Catherine was gone now but Juanita was still there. Juanita was the maid who wore no uniform because there were no maid's uniforms in Gaither, whose husband dropped her off in the pickup each morning and retrieved her after supper. Last fall, shortly after Catherine Briarley had decamped, Juanita would sit peeling potatoes while Lenny and Cap did their homework at the same kitchen table. She tightened her lips while the girls traded lines, repeated, arms akimbo, giggling, the same words she'd once heard float down from the ceiling in the raised voices of the original speakers. Juanita would click her tongue and watch the kitchen clock. When Cap mouthed some of Henry's more colorful epithets, she'd cross herself and begin to giggle too, darting her eyes at her charge as though half afraid and half delighted. Cap said Juanita was a gypsy from over around Dago Hill. She'd never really been a maid but she was the only one who'd answered the ad. *She's punctual and she doesn't steal,* Lenny was supposed to say when they were alone in Cap's room upstairs. *What the hell would she want that you've got,* Cap would laugh, being Henry. Cap told how they broke glasses quarreling, drinking cocktails, and Juanita would clean up the mess before she left. At night, Henry went to Catherine's room. Juanita had gone home and didn't hear the muffled sounds Cap thought were more fighting until she was old enough to discern the difference.

Now Lenny knew: the sounds were a kind of fighting, a weeping. Last night she herself had cried out and they had all disappeared in the sound. Frank's hands were on her breasts, kneading them like a cat, like he wanted something out of them, and his mouth and his jaw and his teeth were in her neck. Cap and Lenny had played games with their bodies before, but now it was different. The water at night was silky camouflage: Cap had wanted to touch Frank, touch her, move them around like they were blind animals. But she'd got scared. It was scary to watch; maybe she had put her hand on Lenny to keep Frank out. She wanted Frank to show them what people did, and she wanted to keep him out.

"I heard you crying in your sleep. You were dreaming about me then, weren't you?"

"I dreamed about my sister," Lenny said.

"But I'm your sister," Cap said, nudging her. "You're supposed to dream about me, aren't you?"

"You are my sister. You're as bad as Alma."

They had to do the dishes so often that the chore was automatic. They knelt side by side, their knees in the water, one of them scrubbing at the plates with a flat rock, the other dunking them in the bucket to rinse, then back into the stream. They sat like penitents, their shoulders nearly touching.

Cap piled the wet plates bottom up, in little towers that tilted and fell. "If you're asleep and I'm awake, I think of things for you to dream."

"Like what?"

"Things I know, things of mine. Things you could keep for me, so I could forget them. Like when I first moved to Gaither and I just was alone all the time, except for the cats."

She'd lived in Gaither five years. That first summer, Catherine had stayed in Connecticut. Henry and Cap had lived out of suitcases, their clothes laundered but never ironed, the big rooms of the Victorian house emptying off each other like a series of deserted squares. Lenny couldn't believe there was a time when Cap didn't know her: Cap lying on the cool wooden floor of her room after Henry went to the mine office, knowing all she had to do that day was wash the sticky plates from her father's fried eggs. There must have been cicadas starting in the summer trees, lulling Cap back to sleep with their warbled buzzing. Lenny let her wake up when the light had changed, run from room to room, draw the blinds and shut windows to keep the house cool. She ran the narrow back stairs Lenny knew so well, up and down from attic to basement, yelling. At noon she made sandwiches for herself and poured cups of milk for the stray cats that lived in the ruined garden of the house.

"I remember you had cats," Lenny said.

"There were a lot of cats, like eight or nine. The house had been empty for about a year, and all these kittens had grown up wild. I got some of them to let me tie yarn around their necks and I called them by the colors — Red, Blue, Black. They would all hide in the plants when I came out to the garden, but I wouldn't give them any food until they let me touch them. Then my dad found out about them."

"What did he do?"

"He called the dogcatcher and they came with these big nets. But they didn't catch them all. They caught the ones with the collars, the ones I'd tamed. Your parents will always do that to you, won't they."

"Do what?"

"Make you part of some trap they think up."

Lenny laughed. "Remember confirmation class?"

"That was the first day I saw you, at the church. My dad always tried to make me stay at home until he got back from work — we didn't have Juanita then. But one day I left and walked downtown."

Lenny imagined the neighborhood, saw it stretch out as empty as the house; for a block on either side, the expansive Queen Annes with walled yards continued. No cars drove by. No kids — older doctors and dentists, aged professors from the local college, their aged wives who stayed indoors, escaping the heat. The map played out: just before Main Street and a downtown of hardware stores, banks, gas stations, ladies' shops, the three restaurants Cap and her father patronized for supper, was the Baptist church, a red brick edifice whose vast windows were leaded in fantastic shapes. Here Cap first saw Lenny, waiting on the steps of the church while her mother signed her up for girls' confirmation classes. She lay across the steps as though the steps were not hard stone, her pale hair in braids, her face so still Cap thought she was asleep and bent over her, looking. When Lenny opened her eyes and stared, her gaze was empty and calm, like a placid lake. Perhaps she'd seemed the opposite of Catherine Briarley; she'd seemed someone who belonged where she was, like rain on a window.

"You must have walked over a mile," Lenny said. "Didn't we get Cokes at the drugstore? And my mom took you home later. She went on and on at me about your big house."

"I couldn't believe how you were just lying across the steps, like some bewitched Sleeping Beauty —"

"My mother had dragged me to the church and I wouldn't go inside, and it was hot and the stone was cool, and I knew she'd be pissed off when she came out and saw me lying there." Lenny was laughing, and shaking the wet metal cups against rocks in the water. The cups jingled. "But I heard this voice in my face, 'Wake up,' and there you were, like you appeared out of nowhere. You made out to my mother that you'd come to sign up to be a Baptist."

"I did become a Baptist. I guess I'm still a Baptist. I mean, I was never unconfirmed."

They'd sat together in the sanctuary for weeks while the minister lectured them about joining God's flock. A stained-glass *Jesus and the Children* towered over them. Light poured through Jesus' robe, scarlet against the blue sky of that other world. They practiced sitting very still in the pew, pretending to be incarnations of the girl in the massive image, the child whose hand rested on a lamb, whose expectant gaze was the essence of glass.

"Lenny, what happened to the scour pad?"

"I don't know. It disappeared yesterday."

"Lenny, you lose everything. I don't know if I'm going to lend you any shoes."

"Rocks scour the plates just fine. And I'm going to find my own shoes. Who wants to wear pink sneakers, and they won't fit anyway."

"Juanita packed them. She likes pink. My mother has a deal with Juanita to make sure I get all the stuff she sends me from Connecticut."

Lenny sat back on her heels. "Didn't your mother finally move down to Gaither after she found out your dad let you join the church? We wore those white gowns that were barely sewn up the sides. And we gave each other lilies. Remember?" Her eyes widened and she fixed Cap with a look that was nearly startled, like she'd forgotten the flowers and their milky smell.

Together, they'd been confirmed. Henry, amused, had watched from the congregation. Their baptism took place the next morning, privately, in the strange cement pool behind the altar. The pool was a rectangle perhaps five feet deep, hidden behind a heavy velvet curtain. The girls wore white cotton gowns and were barefoot; the pool was filled with water made aquamarine by chlorine drops. Potted lilies lined the border of the cement. The snowy, waxen flowers seemed drowsy. Lenny felt herself submerged in the minister's black-robed arms, her hair swirling in an underwater cloud. She was the only one who'd believed she would float in the act of coming to God, her arms straight in her belled sleeves. When the minister let go and raised his hands to say the words, Lenny opened her eyes, gazing upward as though the roof had lifted from the building. Sinking, she exhaled a Milky Way of tiny bubbles and found Cap within that liquid crescent — she never remembered seeing anyone jump in. She opened her mouth to laugh — suddenly it was all so funny — but the water was big and filled her up when she tried to talk. They grabbed the folds of each other's gowns and struggled to the surface. There they stood gasping, doubly confirmed: it was the first time they'd tried to save anything but themselves.

Waxy rhododendron leaves were cold against his face and neck, they smelled of carrots, cold and sweet, and he pressed them to his mouth, peering through green cover to watch the girls at the stream. The others were sounds receding down the mountain, the soft pounding of their footsteps repeated and repeated. But somehow Lenny and Cap were here, kneeling, their hands in water, jangling and clanking a dank, pretty music. Banging stones, Buddy thought, and he wanted to do it too, then he saw the pile of tin plates and spoons and metal cups they were rinsing in the stream. They were talking and saying words but he didn't hear any words, only the trill and inflection of the words and the laughter, the pour and splash of water, and he could hear their bodies, he thought he could, the way they crouched and knelt and moved on their haunches, their wrinkled blouses white in the clearing by the water. They held out their long creamy arms to each other, handing off piles of plates and stacks of the collapsible metal cups that came in Girl Guide mess kits.

Buddy had a cup like that at home, one he'd found last fall at Highest when the tents were rolled up and stored under a tarp. Then the weathered platforms on stilts sat empty like big scattered pieces of a finished game. Buddy had leapt from one to another, hollering like he was after the Russians because these were army tents, and he pretended he was painted in wobbly, muddy colors like the army used when they wanted to hide in the woods. The Russians in his game had faces like Dad's and like prison men, pinched-up faces and wild, tangled hands, and they wore blue prison uniforms like Dad used to wear. Buddy could see them wherever they were, but they couldn't see him, he was invisible, spotted brown and green like the army guys in comic books.

Now Lenny and Cap looked dappled too, spotted by shade and sun. They really were part of some army, Buddy thought, gold pins on their shirts and braided pockets, but they looked rumpled and their hair was messed. They couldn't win. No matter how old they were, they were only two girls, tall grownup girls, and the Russians would grab them and beat them and put them in prison, and Buddy would make a rescue, yelling special words and fighting with a stick. Russians would get Lenny first because she was the tallest girl in camp, and she would fall asleep in prison from being scared, like Buddy fell asleep sometimes if a bad thing happened. Buddy would make a litter out of sapling sticks and rope with blankets on top, just like he'd seen Mam do once for a big old hound dog lame in two legs. But the dog had been a bundled heap on the litter, crouched low while they pulled him along, and Lenny would stretch out long and thin, sleeping. The dog had stayed on their porch a week before he healed enough to run off, but Buddy would take Lenny to the cave near Turtle Hole and she would never run off: Buddy would tell her how Russians lived in the woods. Russians would look for her but never find her: only Buddy knew about the cave, how it opened like a yawn as tall as him behind bushes and brushy cover, just under the back ledge of the diving rock at Turtle Hole. Lenny could sleep on the mossy rock floor, inside where Buddy was afraid to go, and Buddy would bring food to her; Lenny could wash her metal plates in this same shallow stream as it rattled through the back of the cave in the dark. Lenny would make the same sounds she made now, scouring the plates with stones. Her long pale hair hung loose and dragged in the stream when she bent over. Buddy crept closer and thought her hair would cling to his hands like corn silk damp from the husk.

"Why did you have to lose the scour pad, Lenny? It's stupid to wash them with rocks."

"It's stupid to wash them at all in cold water with hand soap. If we can't get soap in the stream, how do they expect us to rinse dishes?"

Now Buddy picked up pebbles to skitter along the water, to hit the plates they'd stacked, and the pebbles made sounds like rain blown suddenly off leaves. Lenny looked up; he'd known she would, but Cap kept on talking.

"If you'd gotten all the food off your share last night, we wouldn't have to do them over again . . ."

And while she talked Buddy came into the clearing in a skitter, like a deer. Lenny was barefoot like him, her toenails painted with flaking pieces of red, and Buddy crouched across from her with the narrow stream between them and held his head just so, like her, moved his hands, his foot, and when she shook her hair out, he

96

shook his too. She laughed and he made a somersault, rubbed his eyes like his hands were paws, peeked about like an animal waking up.

"Buddy, you found us," Lenny said. "You're always finding us, aren't you. Such a wise guy."

Cap was talking. "This kid is everywhere. Don't you ever stay home, kid? What's he doing now?"

"Well, he was me but now he's a raccoon."

"Great. If he's going to bug us, give him some dishes to wash."

Cap tossed him a few plates that Buddy held up with his wrists to catch the light and show how coons liked shiny things. Then he licked them and sniffed them and trundled round them in a lumpy crawl and banged them together while the girls laughed. When they laughed like that, he was too big to be a raccoon anymore and he had to stand up and jump and do his best handstand, the one where he kept his legs straight until he flipped backwards and landed on his feet. He bunched down in himself, sat on his haunches and twitched his face, scratched his head with his back foot like a rabbit. Finally they clapped for him.

"Shake the water off those dishes, would you?" Lenny threw some of the plates to Buddy.

The metal clanked when the plates banged and he asked Lenny were they going to breakfast, why weren't they going, why not? "I got me some rolls in my pocket," he said, and pulled them free. He didn't want the rolls or even like rolls so much, mostly he liked to hold them in his hands when they were first warm from the pans. But now the bread was squeezed small, and Cap rolled her eyes at him so he threw the rolls high in the air and let them fall for birds. He grabbed the metal plates on his side of the stream, the clean ones that still smelled of the water, and jumped, jumped, jumped their wetness onto his skin, happy to hear Lenny talk, happy the way her voice was low and deep, happy Cap liked her too, made her talk and answer, and the two of them were like two birds flying, gliding up and down and crowing warnings.

"Lenny got us in trouble, Buddy." Cap was smiling, making fun. "She didn't do her housework well enough last night. But she does some things real well if I teach her."

"Oh, shut up," Lenny said. "Really, don't be telling him things."

"Why not? You think he's going to tell his mother?"

Cap snorted and Lenny shoved her so she lost her balance and her foot went in the stream.

"If you want to borrow my sneakers, you better be nice," Cap said.

Lenny made a face before she told Buddy, like he was grown up, "Cap lost my shoes last night and now she wants me to wear hers that are pink and too big."

"Baloney," Cap said, "they're not lost, they're still at Turtle Hole. Oh, it's beautiful there, Lenny, wasn't it beautiful? I thought this morning when they got us up they'd found out everything, but it was only because you didn't wash the dishes right." And Cap jumped up to dance Lenny around in a circle, half shaking, holding her. Buddy skipped the stream to slip himself between them and tangle their legs; when they fell down with him their bodies were heavy and warm and smelled so different from Mam, they smelled like warm candy with a bitter tinge, like something he could eat. He thought about the rolls this morning, rising in Mam's camp ovens, the way the bread got so big it grew up from the pans and spilled over swollen, and he felt so dizzy he held on to Lenny's waist, clasping his hands across her stomach even when she tried to pry him off. He felt the tension of her muscles and the cleft of her buttocks against his face and he was silent while she laughed. He pressed hard against her and squeezed his eyes shut until the girls tickled him, digging their fingers into his ribs till it hurt and he squealed and let go.

Then they were stacking the piles of plates and gathering things like he wasn't there, and he yelled out how Frank and him were going to trap a rabbit, Frank and him were making a rabbit trap out of Mrs. Thompson-Warner's lectern crate, Frank and him were going to get a rabbit for a secret pet, Frank and him were going to keep the rabbit at Frank's tent in a cage so Dad couldn't eat it. Buddy saw the girls didn't believe him about the rabbit but Frank's name got them looking, they looked at each other and wouldn't talk anymore, only stacked the plates and cups in a basket to take back to the campsite while Buddy stepped into the stream, splashing, and sang out, "Frank, Frank, Frank . . ."

Lenny smiled at him. Then her serious voice said, "That's enough now. Be quiet."

And he was quiet. The clearing was quiet and they were walking back up through the woods toward tents he could just see through the leaves. Those tents sagged from their rope sides and smelled like rope and hay and dust. Buddy liked them. They were better than any house because you could tie up the walls. He liked how you walked in the front but you could fall off the back, the way the floor stopped six feet in midair. When the Seniors were at breakfast he sometimes circled back up to their tents and found Lenny's cot. He stayed in her tent, lay on the cool wood floor and looked at the hill dropping off below till the start of the woods and, far down, the tops of the trees. He couldn't see the rest of camp and camp wasn't there, only this place that could be a tree house or a ship in the air, and he put his face on Lenny's pillow and his hands on her green army blanket and once he looked in her footlocker. He found a white T-shirt wadded up at the bottom, a shirt like a boy or anyone would wear. Seemed like she didn't want it anymore; Buddy folded it into a square and put it in the front of his own shirt to take home. In her stationery box there were stamps and pictures, little gray ones from the picture machine at the drugstore in Gaither. He saw that Lenny had been younger even than him, a little kid, and her hair had been white then, like his was, and the woman who didn't smile must be her mother. The blond man in the pictures had strong arms like Dad's but he didn't have tattoos like Dad, no heart with a sword, no *Lucky Devil.* The paper in the box was pale pink and too thin to be much good, and down underneath there was a ring with just a smear of hard glue where the jewel should be. It came to him: Lenny would want a jewel, not a rabbit.

Now he took the crumpled spinach leaves from his pocket and threw them into the air. He moved his feet in the cool of the stream and pretended to look for jewels, combing the smallest pebbles with his toes, stirring up clouds in the clear water. He heard Lenny and Cap walking, running, moving down the trail from Highest to the quad. He wanted to be with them, following rules, but the day stretched before him, limitless like all the days. At the dining hall Mam would be serving up breakfast. There, the long tables of girls made a noise like acres of cackling birds. In the kitchen their roar came and went, admitted and closed off by the swinging kitchen doors that opened and shut as Mam and two other women from her church carried forth heaps of food in big round bowls. Buddy wanted to be there but Mam said he was underfoot during meals, *get on out of here, I'll land on you like white on rice.*

So Buddy went anywhere and everywhere he wasn't allowed to go. Mealtimes, while the dining hall rumbled like it might burst, Buddy could make his rounds of the cabins where the Junior girls slept, look in the unlocked trunks, inspect the counselors' rooms that were always straight back of the foyer. Those were tiny little rooms where two grownup girls lived and kept their dirty underwear in plastic bags, underwear that was shimmery and small, girls' things, not like Mam's. Early in the mornings, he made his excursions to the empty infirmary, to deserted Highest. Later he went to the swinging bridge to watch the men lay pipe. The camp floated in a dream, the heat seemed less hot, a breeze was discernible, the flag could be heard to gently waver if Buddy stood just at the foot of the tall pole. No birds wheeled in the sky.

There was only Frank, reading comics and listening to his transistor radio. Frank's tent was in a clearing by the woods, not so far from Turtle Hole. Buddy could only visit if he brought Frank presents — candy bars, jawbreakers, a Pepsi filched from the kitchen, or a cold beer of Dad's, if Dad was drinking enough not to notice one missing.

Sometimes Buddy took a beer and tried to drink it himself, or he sat on the swinging bridge that moved above the river and dripped the cold liquid down his legs while the workmen dug dirt and dragged pipes. He called them scary men and pretended they were the Russians; he could watch them from the bridge and think he was a spy. Every day he looked at them and heard their far-off voices laugh and mutter and curse. They wore uniforms the color of dried mud and smoked cigarettes that hung from their lips when they talked. They looked like Russians to Buddy, but he'd never seen them up close. Afternoons he sometimes sneaked into heritage class and heard Mrs. Thompson-Warner talk about Russians to the Junior girls, about the fiery furnace Russians had built in the basement of their embassy in Washington. The furnace could burn bone to ash and people had gone into the embassy and never come out. Buddy didn't know what an embassy was but he thought the scary men could build a furnace that burned people up, they were like the devil, they could make a fire that hot. And the words he heard them saying through warm, still mornings and sweltering afternoons were *hell* and *damn* and *sweet jesus christ* and *goddamn you fucking fool.* The words swam along under the rattle of the river.

The river was gentle now but Buddy knew how wild it was in spring, how snow up the mountain melted and swelled the river to a torrent, how broken trees rode the crests of the brown water and caught in the bridge, tore the bridge loose nearly every year. Mrs. Thompson-Warner said how Russians didn't believe in God, but even the scary men would shut up in the spring when the river was raging, they wouldn't be digging here so close the banks. Next spring the river would be thunder and kill their voices and suck the heavy pipes into itself. If they were still here, the river would get them, but meanwhile Buddy spent his time on the bridge, carving one small cross in each plank with his sharp stone. Crosses kept the scary men below him, and lately he had known to carve the cross in the morning, not wait too long in the day. He thought he might as well go now and he felt in his pocket for the pointy rock he always carried. The rock was good and sharp but not too big, so it never worried a hole in his pants. He could turn it end to end in his pocket and he turned it now as he walked alone on the trail.

Lenny and Cap were far below him, their voices distant and fading. If he cut off through the trees and dropped straight down, he could still beat them to the quad, he could sneak in at the back door of the kitchen and grab some bacon before the girls even sat down at their table. He could be eating and running the far boundary of the camp, along the river to the swinging bridge and beyond to Turtle Hole. Cap had said Lenny's shoes were at Turtle Hole, but girls never walked that far, they never swam at Turtle Hole, they swam in the river across the meadow from Great Hall. Their swimming place was marked off with yellow ropes and they swam in teams, back and forth, and the youngest ones wore life jackets so they wouldn't get their faces in the water. They all wore tight rubber caps and kept their hair dry and some of them paddled like dogs. Buddy had never seen Lenny swim but he thought she must curl her long body and pulse forward, fast and liquid like a snake on a surface streak.

Buddy swam fast and silent too; he liked to swim naked at Turtle Hole and dry in the sun, sitting crouched on the diving rock. Often he went swimming after doing his time at the swinging bridge. The cool water of Turtle Hole drove scary men out of his head. He'd swim to the center where the water was deepest and kick his legs, excited he'd made an escape; he'd imagine the crosses he'd carved, stretched out across the entire bridge like the tiny tracks of some creature the devil would always fear. Today he could carve the cross a little later. He wanted to go to Mam and see her serve up breakfast. Maybe she'd sit him down with a big plate of food and he'd stay quiet, invisible, and watch. Mam had told him how the Holy Spirit was invisible; that was true, but Buddy knew he could hear the Spirit and smell it and see its tracks in the woods. Now when he was bounding down the mountain, taking the steep grades so fast he didn't have to think where to put his feet, how to grab branches and direct his slide, he thought he heard the Holy Spirit whistling past his face. The Spirit breathed on his face and in his ears, filled him up, smelled of pine and dirt and wind, made him full and perfect and he could not make a mistake, he flew and the earth fell away beneath him.

## ALMA: STARS AND BREAD

At breakfast everyone was encouraged to eat some of everything; snacks were not offered between meals. A great roar of gluttonous eating and talking crested in the dining hall, a building smaller than Great Hall though large enough to accommodate the many rows of girls on white benches at long white tables. How many tables? Later they might all try to remember, but it seemed a vast confusion of tables and platters, with the swinging doors to the kitchen propped open and fat Hilda Carmody, the head cook who lived in the shanties farther up the river, scraping fried potatoes from a great black skillet into a voluminous bowl. Little Buddy hung at her skirts and she shook him off like a floppy dog, and as he hit the floor one of the doors was abruptly shoved to from within. The platters were in place on the tables and everyone sang grace. Grace existed in the dining hall like the eye of a storm. Those in the storm's eye heard, even in a moment of stillness, the echo and rattle of the circling wind; they were meant to sing only when the food was in front of them, mixing its smells and steam in the brief cool of the morning. Their joined voices climbed a breathy stairsteps and startled them all with the round, windy sound of their prayer. *God is good and God is great,* they asserted in a questioning tone, then answered themselves with grave words, a request for what was owed, a benediction. *By His hand must all be fed, give us Lord our daily bread. Amen. Amen. Amen.* And this last utterance of solemn assent was drawn out to five musical tones. They might have been angels. Many of them closed their eyes. They touched their own clasped hands with moving lips, feeling the breath and shape of words that tasted of familiar flesh. Bread was in evidence, endless mounds of warm homemade rolls served in dented metal pans. Alma thought of the rolls as the fruit of a living being — they were so warm and dense. Of course Mrs. Carmody made the dough in the afternoons, stirring with a great wooden ladle in the crockware vat they'd all seen in the kitchen, but Alma wanted the bread to have been grown by the body of a woman, laid like eggs from her private parts, or dropped from her fingertips like immediately edible fruit. Browned and buttered, the rolls tore like innocent, bloodless flesh. Alma ate them; Delia liked to crush one in her hands, worry and roll and squeeze it, turn it into dough again as though the whole enterprise had been a mistake. Alma obliterated hers with red jam, the same jam they'd eaten at school hot lunches all winter; it came in big plastic jugs and Alma had seen those jugs in the camp pantry.

Alma was a little scared of Hilda Carmody. When Hilda lifted her big arms over her head to grab some implement, she breathed heavily and the flesh of her arms hung down like wattles. Her hands were dimpled and she worked relentlessly. Each day she kneaded dough by hand, lost to the elbows in the big vat. She gazed down at what she lifted with an expression of placid concentration and never saw the girls watching her, looking in the kitchen windows on their way to or from activities. The way Hilda moved, working rhythmically at something unseen, rocking her great body, reminded Alma of that man at the drive-in movie, the one who'd stood behind the cement block refreshment bar and kept his hands in his privates, pulling and tugging. Alma had thought he was urinating, the way he kept his head lowered and stood with his feet apart, and she'd stepped back in the shadows to look, away from the kids in line for Cokes. The ground was littered with the dirtied, red-and-white-swirled rectangles of crushed popcorn boxes, with cigarette butts and crumpled playbills. The man never looked at Alma, never looked up, but turned to face her so she could see what he held in his hands. There was a slapping sound, fast and violent. He was hurting himself and something came out of him; he bled milk like a broken plant. She could hear her own heart beating and she stepped away into the light, dirtied by her own curiosity, dirty because he was dirty and she'd watched, dirty because she'd left him standing there. A groan escaped him as she turned away. His eyes had not caught her but the sound he'd made found its mark. She could never be sure she was remembering exactly what she'd seen, but her memory of the sound never altered. That strangled, satisfied *Oh*, like something maimed and alive. Alma heard it in her sleep. When she saw Mrs. Carmody through the kitchen window, glimmered by the dust on the old screen, Alma thought the big woman knew the sound too, and felt it in her hands. Hilda Carmody slapped the dough side to side, staring into the crock as into a well or pool, finally lifting the crock itself to her breasts with both arms. She'd carry it to the black iron stove and cover it with cloths as though it were a being requiring warmth.

The warmth of the food made Alma sleepy again. She squinted through curling steam above the platters to see Mrs. Thompson-Warner seating herself at the other end of the table. Today it was their turn to have Mrs. T. as breakfast guest. When she sat with one of the three tables of older girls it was called a mealtime lecture, since the Senior girls of Highest were too busy in the wild to have heritage classes, but when she sat with the Juniors they were meant to converse. Alma always tried to sit near her, which meant Delia was forced into the same vicinity out of loyalty. Delia regarded Mrs. T. now with sullen skepticism, then, dutifully resigned, stood up and shifted places as Alma led her closer to Mrs. T.

Alma knew a secret. Yesterday, after archery, she'd helped collect equipment and overheard the counselors talking in their cynical whispers.

"You know the story about her, don't you?" someone said. "Her rich husband was a suicide. Shot himself early one morning in some public place."

"Right, so she wouldn't have to find him. Sick."

What public place? Alma couldn't ask. And what did it mean, sick? He wanted someone else to find him? A bridge was a public place, though no one ever went to Mud River Bridge, or walked along it, or did anything but drive over it. The bridge was not beautiful. It rattled. Some people in Gaither said Nickel Campbell had driven off the bridge on purpose, but he'd never seemed sick at all. The man Alma had seen at the drive-in was probably sick. And Mrs. T.'s husband must have been. Sick. In a public place. He'd wanted to be discovered, like a secret. He must have known secrets, his own secrets or secrets about Communists. Alma sat down now beside Mrs. T., her forearm nearly touching the ample, satisfied wrists of Mrs. T. She watched Mrs. T.'s every gesture and expression and linked each one to an entry on a list of details she kept in her head concerning Mrs. T.: the dead husband, pamphlets about Communism passed around in heritage class, the sick husband, the wedding ring with the big diamond and the other rings Mrs. T. kept in her room, the gun, the public place, the books about Lenin and Stalin on display in Great Hall, the silver hairpins Mrs. T. wore. Somehow the details linked up, the lists corresponded, like those pages of lists in grade school workbooks, those tests where kids drew lines running corner to corner between "wood" and "mahogany," "fruit" and "cherry," "morality" and "rules." The penciled lines would get mixed up and erased and drawn again in web-like combinations.

Alma tried to make conversation. "Mrs. Thompson-Warner, do you live near Gaither?"

"Gaither, dear?"

"Our town, where we're from. It's near Bellington, and Winfield."

"No, I live in Pittsburgh, in the Shady Side section. You know it? I am a widow. My late husband worked with Bethlehem Steel, advising them of European developments in the industry." Mrs. Thompson-Warner ate with one hand on her lap — the left hand, with the diamond — and ate only with her right hand, shoulders squared, tilting her head to gaze directly at a speaking girl, a slouching girl, girls who ate too quickly, girls who didn't eat.

Delia, reprimanded just yesterday, kept one hand out of sight. She held her fork by the recommended method and pinched Alma's knee under the table with the method that was always most effective: impale and grasp. Alma ignored her. "Did you call your husband Thompson?" Delia asked Mrs. T.

"What?" Mrs. T. opened her roll with her fingers. Never, she'd instructed the girls, cut a fresh roll with a knife, it ruins the dough. "No, his name was Berwick Thompson-Warner. He was British, you see. He'd lived through the Blitz in London."

Delia was silent and Alma threw her a stern cautionary glance. Alma would pay her back later if she didn't stop; maybe she'd refuse to walk with her at hiking. "The Blitz was during the war," Alma said, "in England."

"Yes, certainly." Mrs. T. nodded approvingly. "The Germans bombed the British day and night for weeks. It was a terrible siege. Mr. Thompson-Warner remembered it well and appreciated freedom for what it is — a great gift."

Delia, separating her scrambled eggs from bits of syrupy pancake, trained her hazel eyes on Mrs. T. "What happened to him?"

"Pardon me?" Mrs. T. leaned slightly forward.

Alma felt herself redden. How did Delia know things, without knowing?

Delia was expressionless. "What happened to your husband?"

Mrs. T.'s fork, poised in midair and tuned to some fine frequency, appeared to vibrate. "We ask personal questions, Delia, only of those with whom we are on intimate terms. Even then, we speak personally only in private."

Alma heard her own voice murmur, "Delia's mother is a widow too."

"I see." Mrs. T. nodded and her fork came to rest on her plate. "She has my sympathies. I hope it's not recent?"

"No, it isn't." Delia picked up the job jar and peered through the glass at the numbered plastic chips inside.

It wasn't time to pick jobs. Alma was afraid Delia would begin shaking the jar like a maraca, or even hurl it the length of the white table like a bowling ball. The white chips would fly out and snow down on them all, cover them with numbers so no one would know if they were a two or a six, a scraper of plates or a stacker. *A storm would be wonderful,* her mother had said, *it might as well storm.* They'd sat in the car outside the funeral home while Audrey tried to stop crying so they could walk inside. Far away, Mrs. T. was saying, in her voice that let in all these pictures, "Alma, I look forward to your speech. You're doing the supper speech for your cabin tonight, aren't you?"

"Yes ma'am."

"I hope she gets to go last," Delia said, "because the one that speaks last always wins the most applause for best."

"I'm afraid your observations are correct," Mrs. T. said. "Still, perhaps tonight will be an exception."

"I doubt it," Delia added. "It's so loud with all of us doing our jobs and carrying dishes back and forth, nobody can really hear, anyway."

Alma sighed and began to load her plate with food. She didn't want to think about the speech, and she wished the end of the day would never come. She reached for the syrup pitcher.

Every breakfast was the same, an endless bounty of soft, warm food heaped in piles, in aspect not unlike Hilda Carmody herself. The scrambled eggs were hot and yellow and moist, mounded up like whipped potatoes at a Thanksgiving, and there were plates of pancakes, their speckled surfaces stacked ten and twelve deep, and saucers of sticky, browned sausages, their links unbroken as though whole boxes had been fried at once. The syrup was cold and thick and Alma poured it on her plate with abandon, not caring if the sweetness permeated every color and shape. Then she didn't have to distinguish one thing from another, note the limits of this or that, allow for discrepancies experienced many times, look out for new ones. She knew her table manners were atrocious; her mother had said so. *Don't mix your food, honey, and don't sit there staring at your nose. Make people aware of you, converse . . . impolite to say nothing and pretend you're alone at the table.* But sometimes Alma liked to pretend she was alone. She looked at her food, not really seeing it, and heard all that was said. The food was a warm soup, and the Senior girls trooped in amidst the cacophony of another breakfast.

"Alma," Delia said in low tones, nearly in reverence, "there's Lenny and Cap. They're late."

They were later than all the other Senior girls; Alma wondered why. Seated across the hall, she watched her sister as a stranger might, a stranger in possession of stories and facts. Facts were facts, but Alma didn't know what the stories meant. Even so, they accumulated in her mind, bolstering one another, and most of them were images, pictures with no words, or words that didn't match. Not long ago she'd gone down in the basement at home to get Wes's tape measure out of his toolbox for Audrey. In with the hammers and screwdrivers, the small plastic boxes of nails and washers, Alma found a wallet-sized plastic portfolio. It was creased and dirty, nearly empty of snapshots, but when she pulled one free from its cloudy envelope, Alma recognized Wes and Lenny. They were a different version of themselves, Lenny a child with white, flyaway hair and an open grin, Wes holding her with both arms, laughing, the two of them staring into the camera. It was a machine picture, taken in a photo booth like the one at Hart's Drug in Gaither. Maybe it was the very same machine where Alma and Delia sometimes spent a dollar on Saturdays. There were two more photos of identical size, one of Audrey, staring soberly into the dark screen before her, and another of the three of them. They were all laughing, crowded into the picture. *I don't know,* Audrey had said when Alma asked, *probably from some wallet that wore out. Lenny should have these — Where were you? You weren't born yet, or maybe you were on the way, just barely. See that look in my eye? There you are.*

"Where were they?" Delia said, her face so close Alma smelled the peppermint tinge of her breath. "They must have gotten in trouble."

"Yeah, probably so." Alma watched Lenny across the dining hall, knowing her sister would never tell her what the trouble was. Just now Lenny kept her eyes on her food and didn't look over at the younger girls. Lenny looked different at camp, Alma thought, less cared for, the way her hair was never really combed, just pulled back tangled in an elastic, and her lips, maybe chapped from the sun, were redder. She looked more rugged, or brave. And she didn't even need to be more brave. Lenny never told secrets or talked about troubles. She didn't talk to their father because Wes himself never talked. She didn't talk to Audrey because, well, just because she didn't. And she didn't talk to Alma. She and Wes were both like stars Alma saw in the sky from the earth of home, with Audrey. Alma could look at the stars or wish for them, but she couldn't tell them her own secrets, surrounded as she was with Audrey's voice and talk, Audrey's stories of how things were.

"Want to try to talk to them after breakfast?" Delia pretended to keep her interest low.

"No. I'm not going to ask them a thing. Anyway, there won't be time. Activities is hobby hours, and they always rush us over there."

Alma sighed. The noise of the dining hall seemed to swell and crest around the seated bodies of the Senior girls. Far away, they broke bread. Alma and Delia shifted closer to one another, leaning into the current.

He sleeps alone in the shack. He has left the truck with the other men at the river and walked back to lie down on his narrow pallet. Sleeping is like falling. Sinking into his own body.

The girl who was a fish circles deep within the bowl of Turtle Hole. Parson feels her undulating movement in his body as a sliver of silver in his chest, and the silver moves like a bright minnow into his belly, cool in the heat of his sleep but hurting like a burn. He knows he should wake up. But he holds still, careful, trapped in his own dream. She travels within his sleeping length, seeming to whip and move in his darkness that is vast and deep as the dark of Turtle Hole. She is shining in that water, shining inside him, long and thin. Her darkness lengthens, skating through water like a snake. The glow of her yellow hair pressed flat to her head has become the shine of her dark flesh. She is a snake with human eyes and the wide gaze of the angel of death, and in the dark water of Turtle Hole she sees the children floating in their bubbles of air. They are sleeping, all of them, curled into themselves, and she opens her gaping slash of a mouth and swallows them whole before the evil can touch them. The water is crowded with shadows that moan for light and air; Parson hears their reedy, warbled voices and feels their wavering approach. But the snake moves through them, limitless and closed, shooting for the surface in a long black streak that shines and contracts, a rapid S, and when the head of the snake breaks water, Parson sits up in his sleep. She has found him.

Before he opens his eyes, still dreaming, he knows the door of the shack is ajar; he feels air on his face. Early morning. Waking in the fever of his dream, Parson watches himself get up from the pallet to pull on his khaki pants. It is then he sees the snake, lying motionless along the edge of the floor, just in the shadow of the slanted wall. Come from Turtle Hole, Parson knows, along the narrow path through the trees. He imagines the silky, comfortable slide of the snake through dense shade, through trailing vines barely disturbed by its passage. The snake is a long straight form except for the half oval it curves around the shoes — Lenny's shoes. The shoes sit abandoned, their shape so approximate and human that Parson has imagined Lenny standing in them in the dark. Not Lenny herself, but a shade of Lenny, a shadow whose patient form exudes a rustling whisper. The snake has heard and drawn close.

Parson approaches slowly, grasps its jewel-like head, and pulls it along the rough floor of the shack, a big snake — blacksnakes, people call them, a rope of flesh redolent with the feel and smell of the reptile. Lukewarm silk, Preacher used to say, dead and alive, and he never touched the snakes his parishioners brought to services. Parson did. Some folks up the hollows were snake handlers and used copperheads for their cleansing poison, but Preacher's people only kept garden snakes, river swimmers, pest eaters. Snakes hunted vermin; their sliding, secretive forms could tempt evil and draw it out. In prison Parson had stopped talking. Before, as Preacher's shouting boy, he'd thundered over the jostling heads of the faithful: snakes are the living memory of evil, respect and fear them. As Lucifer himself was an angel fallen from grace, so these shades of the Devil are fallen from the mantle of evil, thrown alive from the whirling vacuum of hell, humbled, crawling on their bellies toward the scent of redemption. Perfect power, perfect shame, Parson preached, extending his arms for the snakes to climb as that room in Preacher's Calvary house shook with ecstatic bodies.

The room of the shack holds still. The snake is no messenger; it is a probe of God. Parson holds it waist high before its tail end clears the ground. He raises it higher to see the quick tongue slit the air. The snake contracts, lowering, looping its lower coils to stand like a one-footed creature on Parson's thigh. He still holds the compact head, a solid bullet, but feels the snake rise of its own accord until its long straightened length has reached his height. And he feels her there, the girl who was a fish, long and cool in the head and length of the snake. Parson peers into her bright eye as though into binoculars, wanting to know, to see, but the eye is a flat glass of power and rejects his gaze. He sees only the reflection of his own searching eye. Startled, he loosens his grip, and the snake moves through the curve of his hand. Takes him over, begins to coil along his arm, travels upward to his shoulder and around his neck. He makes a basket of his arms for the snake to fill and it does, coiling rope on rope to an inverted bowl of flesh, and when Parson steps to the broken front windows he knows he will see an angel at the water, and it is the girl, Lenny.

The silence through which she proceeded was full of scattered bird-song, echoing its hidden search and answer in the trees above and around her. The grass looked lit up, the river fresh, transparent, too clear to be real. Last night the dark water had seemed a solid, disturbed surface roiled from below. Now the river only murmured, a somnolent, rushing murmur that faded and pulsed as she followed the rocky path off through trees to Turtle Hole.

Here in dense shade the ground was spongy with moss, the rocks overgrown with fern and lichen; Lenny no longer heard her own footsteps, only felt the odd slipping of Cap's pink sneakers, too wide and long for Lenny's feet. Only Cap would come to camp with three pairs of shoes, one of them pink — and the laces were round, like cord. Shoes from New York City maybe, or some other city Lenny had never seen, and she had pulled the laces tight to make the shoes stay on, but nothing made them work. They were useless shoes. Cap couldn't wear them at all in the dust and dirt and mud of Highest camp, and Lenny couldn't wear them either. She had to find her own shoes, and she trespassed here while the others were en route to Highest with supplies. No one would miss her in the few minutes it would take to get the shoes; she could circle back up and emerge into camp from her own tent. But she didn't want to be in camp; she wanted to be here, invisible, alone in the woods like a ghost. Girls and women: with all their noise, tramping, cooking, eating, Lenny thought they were mere shadows in the dampish, rough-hewn buildings, in the tents that smelled of dirt. And the men had seemed, from the beginning, shadows — the workmen seldom seen, Frank doing his peripheral chores, Buddy, the little man, the elf, appearing and disappearing. The camp was meant to be empty as the trail was empty now. Empty, and so full of sound and light and dense, liquid shade that Lenny entered it and nearly forgot herself, forgot what she was looking for, wanted to lie down and be lost. What had happened last night was nothing to this place: the three of them only sounds, movement in the water, barely discernible in the dark. She held her breath, stepped into the open.

Turtle Hole spread out in front of her, still and deep. Last night the circular water had seemed illumined, lighter than night and clouded with mist. Today the surface was blue, a flat mirror to the open sky. She circled the water, watching it, felt herself track round it like the hand of a clock. The shoes should be just there, somewhere in the rushes where she and Cap had stood to watch Frank on the rock. Lenny moved into tall grass, feeling its moist scent stick to her legs, feeling the delicate slide of Cap's cool hands on her ankles, taking off the shoes. She thought of Buddy's reedy voice, talking his mixed-up song this morning when he'd found them at the stream. Frank, Frank, Frank, rabbits his dad might eat, rabbits for secret pets. Rabbits would always remind Lenny of secrets.

Last winter she'd stayed with Cap nearly every Friday night. Cap's parents were always off somewhere in the big house, the maid working in the kitchen. Left alone like adults, the girls shut the door to Cap's room. They took long baths in her bathroom, coiled together like eels in the wide tub. Then they'd wrap up naked in the old rabbit coats Cap's mother stored in the closet. The skins were torn, the silk linings soiled; Cap would turn the coats inside out and the girls pulled them on like bathrobes. At first the fur was so cool and shivery it made the hairs on Lenny's arms stand up, but it warmed and was so soft she had to rub herself against it. Cap would smoke a cigarette and then they'd tell each other stories, and the stories were supposed to be true. They called their stories the rabbit game, because they had to wear the coats when they talked, and they had to be naked, to make it harder to lie. When it was Lenny's turn, she never lied, but she framed real things with lies so she could tell the truth. She might tell how she'd seen a man biting and kissing her mother, a man who'd come to the house selling dictionaries. In fact the man had been Mr. Campbell, Delia's father, the same one who'd driven off the bridge last spring. He'd brought Delia over to stay the night with Alma. Wes wasn't home and the girls had all been watching TV. Lenny had looked into the kitchen from the sofa and noticed the clock, the second hand moving around, and realized there was no talking. She'd moved into the hallway and seen her mother with Delia's father, pressed against the kitchen counter, their eyes closed, oblivious. Lenny didn't even consider telling her father. It seemed women's business, mundane and mildly horrifying, like menstruation. She thought about telling Alma; unofficially, Alma was in charge of Audrey. But Lenny told Cap instead. In code. He was biting her? Cap had asked. You mean her neck was bleeding? No, he was like, sucking on her neck, like a vampire. The girls had dissolved in laughter. Or Lenny might tell how she'd learned to like beer, how her dad drank at night, outside on the porch, and once she'd sat with him and drank two cans before he'd stopped her, the beer so sharp and cold and bitter, and that night she'd had a dream about a man standing in her room, watching her sleep, then slowly pulling her twisted nightgown down to cover her belly, her thighs. You're lying, Cap had said with authority, you lose! Maybe Cap knew the dream was real, that it was Wes who'd touched Lenny in that gentle, deliberate way, then turned and left the room. But the rabbit game was a way to make things that really happened seem as though they never had, make things that were magical, dangerous, waiting, fade into shadows. Lenny and Cap could hold the shadows, tangle up in shades of lies, Cap grabbing Lenny, lying on her, sucking at her shoulder to make a warm, soft bruise, both of them laughing until it became an experiment just to play with the dreamy, tingly feeling, stay sleepy, silent, a little drunk.

Part of the rabbit game was silence, and touching each other was a lie they were allowed to tell inside the game. When Cap was judged to be lying, Lenny often sent her downstairs to steal another bottle of sherry or wine, or more cigarettes; Lenny's customary penalty was to have to lie on her stomach under the heavy, silky fur while Cap took off her own coat and crawled under Lenny's from behind. She started with her fingertips on the soles of Lenny's feet, inching her hands upward. Then she slid her whole body under — her long arms, her boyish broad shoulders, her breasts, face, laughter. It was like she crawled under Lenny's skin, licking, tickling, pinching with her teeth, pushing her fingers into Lenny's mouth to try to make her speak and lose this version of the game. Lenny almost never lost. But late at night, somewhere in their dark sleep, Lenny always lost. She was the one who woke to hear Cap's funny cooing moans, saw her trap her hands between her thighs in a neat pyramid as though she were praying to wake up and couldn't. Her eyes moved rapidly behind their shell-smooth lids. Once, tears coursed down her expressionless face. Watching her, Lenny ached. She tensed until her muscles stung, knowing she could shake Cap, try to rouse her. But Cap never fully woke, only reached blindly for whatever she could touch. She would get too close. She might straddle Lenny's thigh and press against her in a rhythmic, rolling motion. Lenny would pull back and push her away, hoping Cap wouldn't wake up enough to get scared and flail wildly around in the bed. Or she let Cap do it, not helping her, only watching how she tensed and pushed, moving toward one moment again and again until she was in the moment, falling through it. She opened her mouth and panted, delicate short pants. Lenny looked away then, into the meaningless space of the room, and cried, she was so desolate. She cried silently, like Cap, but she was awake and alone.

Finally Cap's mother found an empty sherry bottle and cigarette butts under the bed, and Lenny wasn't allowed to stay overnight anymore. Even after Cap's mother left town and went back to Connecticut, the girls continued to follow her edict. Sometimes in the spring they'd still joked about the game. Cap would say she was hungry, starved, but now she was allergic to rabbits. They'd never played the rabbit game at camp, as though it were all part of the old world of stories and lies. This was the new world. The new world opened, one secret opening against another.

Today when Buddy found them at the stream and talked about secret pets, about rabbit traps and Frank, it was as though he knew about the old game. He was strange, he knew things, he really could move like a rabbit or a raccoon. He was like an imp the grownups ignored. Maybe he'd followed them, seen them with Frank — he might have been out late at night, alone in the dark. Or he might have been in his house nearby with Hilda, the big cook, Hilda cooking all night like she cooked all day, their little house an oven in the warm night, and Buddy dreaming about Turtle Hole, seeing whatever touched the water, knowing everything. The old games were over and Frank was part of the new world, the world that opened. It was like all the sick wanting Lenny had pushed under in herself had burst out of her in the warm dark of Turtle Hole, and it wasn't bad or good or anything she could think about. She wanted it again but she was afraid, afraid without Cap and the water and the dark. And where were the shoes?

If she didn't find them she'd have to call her mother, and Audrey would drive out with new shoes and lecture her, and want to see the tent, and eat in the dining hall. Lenny thought of home with a kind of panic. Nothing from home belonged here, home would take it all away. She thought of her father at the dinner table, his mouth, his teeth on his food, his hard, sinewy arms, the way he would sit outside after supper, spring, summer, fall, Gaither darkening around him, lightning bugs lighting the field he watched, while Alma and Audrey banded together in the house and Lenny was forced to choose. She remembered the other life and she felt soppy and indistinct, warm, banked, saved up. She heard herself moan with frustration and she peered into the depths of the rushes, sweeping them aside with extended arms. She began to walk systematically back and forth across a small area. It was from here she'd first seen Frank on the rock, she was sure of it. She stopped and turned.

Then, somehow, a break in the forest cover caught her eye. It was a sort of path, or a place where the green of the cover was mashed into what might be a path, as though dogs had run there, or kids, breaking things down a little. Just up a rise, nearly hidden in leaves, something shone, caught the sun. The light cut and turned like a tiny knife. Lenny felt herself startle, as though someone saw her, watched her. She walked toward the light, seeing it turn and glint, and when she got to the cover of the woods she bent and saw the shack itself, the glass of its broken windows shining in jagged shapes. Tar paper hung from the sills in strips. The little building was a lopsided rectangle. One end of it seemed to have sunk into the earth, and the other had buckled up and tilted, as if the shack itself had seized up, or tried to stretch itself around a curve like a house in an animated cartoon. Buddy could live here; it was just the place for a woods elf. Lenny had heard he lived in a shack with his mother, but this one was much too small for Hilda. Poised in its twisted shape, it seemed a house for rabbits or mice, a child or a lost wraith. Lenny never considered going inside but she wanted to see, to look without touching, as though to touch would taint her, bewitch her, cast a spell she'd feel for years. She walked soundlessly closer. There might be animals inside. From here she could see the ground was dug out a bit along the front side of the shack; there was a long, narrow hole under the floor. Like a crawl space, and Lenny could see bits of dirty burlap merged with earth as the space descended into dark. She could barely see inside the shack — there was a melamine plate on the floor, and beside it an old bucket. Cicadas were trilling in the trees. Maybe they had sounded all along, but now Lenny heard their noisy, urgent rattles rise to a crescendo.

She looked back at Turtle Hole and saw a man walking around the water, round and round it — one of the workmen, she supposed. He was wearing khaki pants and no shirt. Lenny thought he couldn't see her but she crouched, watching. She saw that he held something dark in his clasped arms and strode purposefully along, not looking at it, like an Indian chief walking a private ceremony. He came abreast of the path to the shack and suddenly flung his arms out; the dark thing he'd held against himself snapped out, rope-like, toward the water. Then he let it hang in one hand and turned toward the woods, his arms outstretched. Lenny saw that he held a snake. He walked toward her, into the cover of the trees. She lost sight of him but felt him moving toward her, along the path.

## 🈀 ALMA: PHANTOM RADIO

McAdams marched them to hobby hours at Great Hall. She even called out double time as the line of girls broke from the trees into the quad. Double time meant they raised their knees high and more or less danced across the open green, heads bobbing. Double time was a gait unlike any other, unlike running, certainly. Alma watched from the rear as her compatriots hit the clearing and swung into rapid action. The line of girls resembled a giant centipede in electroshock, but no one giggled anymore. Delia didn't and Alma definitely didn't. Double time was a grim odyssey, almost as grim as required swim in Mud River. Staying in step while galloping in a controlled jerk and bounce required concentration. There was no room for laughter, as double time engendered its own weird momentum. By the time they reached the overhanging porch of Great Hall, Alma felt jangled and listened for a ringing in her ears. She'd assumed everyone marched, since McAdams was so fond of it, but Lenny had set her straight.

Alma usually tried to talk to Lenny after breakfast, before the Seniors picked up supplies and hiked back up to Highest. The older girls had to carry jugs of Kool-Aid, boxes of hot dogs, bags of potatoes, graham crackers, water bottles.

"Do you have to march all the way up, toting that stuff?" Alma had asked, trying to make her tone disinterested.

Lenny laughed. "They march you because you're too old to hold hands, like the Primaries. It's just to keep you in line and rush you along."

Cap gave Alma a look and a sigh. "Crowd control," she said, "purely for Junior crowds."

Now Alma smiled, imagining how B wing must look from above, glimpsed from one of the lookouts along Highest trail. She thought of the Seniors as rugged angels, able to view the whereabouts of the younger girls at any moment. Alma knew she would spy on everyone if she were a Senior, on the girls and the counselors, on Frank, on Mrs. Thompson-Warner. But Seniors had no interest in lower camp. They were up there in the woods like soldiers, cooking, chopping trees for lean-tos. They never set foot in Great Hall except for opening and closing assemblies.

Great Hall was beautiful. Standing in the massive doorway, Alma could already feel herself enter a wash of cooler air, night air collected through dark hours in the vast, eaved space, sheltered from morning sun. The air was chill and smelled of stream water and pine, the knotty pine of the walls and ceiling, of the enormous beams that angled high above the girls' heads, a series of inverted V's. Looking up, Alma thought of church, a deserted church; no matter how many girls converged in the space below, their bodies, their noise, seemed temporary. From each towering apex of the ceiling beams hung powerful lights, their green glass shades shaped like Chinese coolie's hats. The hall was so cavernous that the lights stayed on all day. Before McAdams switched them on there was a wonderful dim ocher in the big room. The stone fireplace at the far end was a shadowy monument six feet across, flaring to the ceiling itself. Mrs. Thompson-Warner had positioned the state and national flags to either side, and hung the banner of Girl Guides from a pole. The three brass poles stood mute below the picture of Jesus. It was the same picture Alma remembered from church school, but this version was so large that it seemed entirely another likeness. Jesus was nearly in profile, his face bathed in golden light. Behind him wavered a fluid darkness, as though he stood in the foreground of an oily water. His visage was lengthened and gaunt, his eyes soft, uplifted, mournful. He was clothed like an angel, like a Roman, in the requisite white gown. Where had the face come from? Someone had invented it. Now it was shown to children at camps and schools, printed on keepsake cards for funerals.

Alma knew who had built Great Hall. Wes used to drive big machines before he began to sell them to the mines; he knew about buildings and he'd told Alma that all of Camp Shelter was WPA work.

"What is WPA?" she'd asked him.

"Means it was built during the Depression. Jobs for people who wanted to work, feed their families. Stonemasons, carpenters, road builders." He fixed her with a quizzical smile. "You're going into seventh grade. Haven't you studied about the Depression?"

"No, not yet."

"Nineteen thirties, when I was a young kid. Everything went bad. I remember standing along the road when I was seven or eight, and a flatbed truck would come by and pick up my dad and my older brothers, take them off to dig ditches. Dollar a day."

"Was that in Gaither?"

"No, we lived in Bellington then." Wes shook his head, considering. "People worked with their bodies more, had a pride about it."

"Did your dad work to build Camp Shelter?"

"I don't think so, but men like him did. Those halls will last into the next century, if they don't burn down. Those stone chimneys, all by hand."

Alma was enthralled that he knew of the camp, admired it. It was almost as though he knew of her life. "Have you been there, Dad? Did you go to camp there?"

"No, they didn't send kids off to camp then. Kids weren't kids. I mean, we worked. But yeah, I been there."

When Alma looked at the giant fireplace, she wished there were a fire burning in it. The iron grate was the size of a baby's cradle. Alma had never seen it full of logs and flames, but the stones and mortar behind the big portrait of Jesus were discolored, as though some heat had passed blindingly over the surface.

Now she walked away from the fireplace toward the rear table, the one nearest the windows. Delia had already reached it and staked out seats. It was the table most removed from supervision; Alma would do Delia's picture as well as her own, and they could eavesdrop on McAdams and Pearlie. Resolutely on break during hobby hour, the counselors sat nearby and talked openly, as if the younger girls had been struck deaf. Even their trivial remarks were of great interest. Pearlie sat sipping a soda she'd bought from the machine in the hallway. Alma was already leaning over to inspect bowls of materials set out for the day's collage — sunflower seeds, lengths of brown twine, cotton, pastel paper straws, a quantity of the smooth pebbles people bought for goldfish bowls. Alma actually liked hobby hour, though she pretended to be bored. Delia sat gazing aimlessly into the hall.

Nickel Campbell had died four months ago. Alma thought it miraculous that Delia was still Delia after her father disappeared so suddenly, buried in a box that Alma herself had touched. Alma was usually afraid to ask questions, afraid to remind Delia, afraid Delia would see through to what Alma knew. Every time she thought of Nickel Campbell, Alma heard the pitch of her mother's voice rising and falling, droning on like a phantom radio no one could turn off. *Nickel Campbell comes from a good family up in the north of the state. Nickel was his mother's surname, and where they got their money . . . The family were mighty unhappy when he married Mina, and moved down to Gaither to start over with no help. Of course, now he admits they were right about Mina, if nothing else. Sometimes we talk about how it could have been if he'd met me before I tied up with Wes.* Lights in Great Hall flicked on as McAdams and Pearlie stood long enough to call out instructions. Under their directions, Audrey's voice raced on in Alma's head, as though time were limited. Her hand was on Alma's wrist, arm, shoulder, like a restless bird trying to light. *You remember that barbecue we all had summer before last, your dad's birthday? We invited the Campbells and Lenny asked the Briarley girl? Well, I guess that was the start of it. He walked down through the yard to stand at the fence and watch a Piper Cub land at the airstrip across the field, and I realized he'd wakened up, like me, and found himself in the wrong life. And you don't even know what I'm talking about, do you, sweetie?*

"Alma! Hurry up. Sit here." Delia indicated the chair to her right and shifted her own seat to make room.

Dejected, Alma sat. More than anything, she wanted not to be her mother's sweetie, but miserably, she knew she was. The metal folding chairs of Great Hall were sharply cold, as though they'd been refrigerated. Later, during archery or hiking in the heat of the day, Alma would want nothing more than to come back here and lie down across four of their hard, cold seats. *Not many women can talk to their daughters like I talk to you. Thank god I have you. I can't talk to any of my friends. Why, I'd sooner print everything in the newspaper. Oh, I know he's not my husband, but he wishes it were different, the things he says. No one ever talked to me like he does.*

"I'm going to set up my picture," Delia hissed, "to make them think I'm interested. Then you can change it around. Do yours now, OK?"

Alma dumped a fortress of white pebbles into the center of the manila sheet. What did it mean, the wrong life? Nickel Campbell had died because he drove off the bridge. Alma knew the facts, but it seemed to her that Audrey was guilty. Well, Audrey had always been guilty (seemed like always) but the guilt was secret. Now the secret was bigger, deeper. And a secret had to be paid for. Delia was angry, angry at everyone and everything but Alma. Alma wanted to feel the anger rain down on her, wanted a series of screams that opened out until the earth shook, howls that would shatter glass and stone, cries that were empty like the wind is empty, a voiceless keening that would let Alma go, let her betray her mother.

Below him the empty quad sits still like a square green jewel as above it he tilts and leans, nearly falling closer, he moves so fast. His steps on rocky slants and layers of leaves are so sure that even as he stumbles he rights himself and slides into balance. He doesn't even think about his body, he hears a heartbeat and the air he moves through, and the other snatches of sound, birdsong, skitter of dislodged pebbles, simply fold into what he enters. He breaks the cover of the woods, finds level ground, feels the lack of resistance as a push from behind and runs flat out, as though some winged predator glides above him, poised to strike. Across open space the dining hall sits like a stone shape meant to echo Great Hall, and he must run past the steps and the columned porch to the back, where Mam is cooking, she must be, breakfast is nearly over. The girls are inside. He feels at this distance a surge of buzz and clamor, more vibration than sound.

Once inside the screen door he leans against the pantry wall, gulping a fragrance of hot butter and bacon, batter and air. He tastes and swallows, seeing the whole reach of the big kitchen in an uproar. They're serving second platters and Mam thunders near him, sees him, bends down to peer into his face as she opens the heavy oven door to retrieve another deep pan of crisping meat. They are both panting, her smooth skin moist; it's as though she runs this fulsome oval while he runs the lines of the camp; he is cutting through, slitting space open with the slender blade of his movement, and she is filling a sphere that grows more dense and full with each revolution of her big body. The smells and the food and the rising bread all seem to evolve from the heat she generates in each repetitive pass and circle.

She jerks her head toward the little table where he usually eats and raises her brows at him, meaning she can't take time now he's so late but sit down and stay out of the way, and she's gone back out to the dining room as he moves toward her. He glimpses through the swinging door the long benches filled with girls, the double row of long white tables all laid with place settings and tray after tray of food. He sees Lenny and Cap cross the front of the room just as the kitchen door swings back toward him, and he is maneuvering around to look again, watch the two girls sit down, see Lenny put food in her mouth like all the rest, when his errant arm catches the protruding corner of a big rectangular platter of scrambled eggs. He is too close to the sideboard and the platter hits the floor, sliding a few inches on its steaming contents. A groan goes up from one of the other women and Buddy moves as she turns to grab him, then she changes her mind and hustles away to find wet cloths and towels. Buddy opens the door to Mrs. Thompson-Warner's little room and scuttles inside, shutting the door so silently he knows he is safe; they'll think he's run off across the quad. No one is allowed here; no one will find him.

First he sits motionless, waiting. There's Mam's heavy tread back and forth to the counter, the blam of big cans set down hard, water running in the deep sinks. He's never seen inside the old redhead's room before. It smells of sugar and it's dark, nearly dark, or seems dim after the bright kitchen and the noise. Her filmy curtains are drawn shut, with the bright shape of the window behind them. In the filtered light from that one square he sees the neatly made cot and wants to touch it, touch the white spread that is covered with little yarn bumps like popcorn and drapes nearly to the floor. The bed is edged all round with a fringe of these little balls that tremble on their strings and jump when he kicks them. Sometimes when small things move or jerk he does want to kick them, hurt them, not animals but insects and the small toads he picks up in the grass after a rain. *Frogs for their watchdogs:* he tries to remember Mam's singsong rhyme, the one she used to say. But Buddy can't think straight, like Dad has squeezed his head. He watches the fringe on the bedspread ripple; the little balls dangle, spin lazily in some repetitive current, like a long line of tiny animate creatures. Buddy feels a wash of air and realizes the electric fan on her bureau is turning its small round face from side to side, the blades encased in a circle of metal cage. *Ain't no cage can hold me, you mays well forget trying to settle my hash.* Dad said that. Hash was little cubes of potato with corned beef from a can, Mam fried it with pepper and the meat was so salty Buddy could pucker his mouth, just thinking. He feels his hunger as a vague burning and there's a sound past the door. He crawls under the bed to disappear and all around the hem of the bedspread those little yarn nubbins jump, like a shiver runs along them in time to the sweep of the fan. *I told you I'm not stayin around here on no dirt road end of nowhere.* Where was Dad going and when would he go? Maybe soon, in the car. He'd said so. Then it would be all right. *Take you with me, get her goat, wouldn't it.* And Buddy feels his stomach seize up like he's so empty he might get sick, and then Mrs. T. will know someone has been in here when she left the door unlocked. He presses himself flat down on the floor, feels in his pockets the small, sharp rock he carries and the hard bulk of the leather bag of marbles. Always before, Dad has given him bubble gum or a jawbreaker, like what they sell in penny machines at the liquor store. *You and Mam.* He does things to her too, behind the blanket that hangs down. Mam knows everything but she doesn't know about Dad, or she does. Buddy knows she's afraid. She makes noises at night, and the old bed moves. She doesn't have to answer questions like Buddy does, but Dad talks to her in the same voice. Like he's got hold of them both. Like if they move he digs in deeper. *Arch up there. You be in trouble you rile me. You like trouble, have some.* Buddy stayed still in the dark. Dad forgot about Buddy unless he got mad at the end. *Don't hush at me, I'll make some noise he can hear.*

Mrs. Thompson-Warner's room is quiet. Buddy hears water in the wall pipes. Washing up. He has to stay here now till breakfast is over, and sneak out through the dining hall after Mrs. T. gets to yakking at those girls, the younger girls that take her class about Russians. Mam has to clear off so those girls can set up the room. Mrs. T. might turn out the lights and run a film, and Buddy could get himself out the other door of her room. Two doors and neither goes to the outside; her room is just a corner between the kitchen and the vast dining room. Big old closet they punched a window in, Mam said, and nailed up plyboard around a toilet that used to be for the kitchen workers. Mrs. T. had to have her own bath; the other women could use the bigger restrooms in Great Hall. Stop work and walk all the way over there, like they had all the time in the world. But the plyboard would be ripped down when Girl Guides camp was over and Mam and him might take it home and nail it up in a tree, floor for a treehouse, Mam said. After while Mam would forget about the spilled eggs. Under Mrs. T.'s bed, the smooth floor is cool against Buddy's cheek. Not even dusty. He flattens his face against the boards and breathes; little white feathers from some pillow skitter along just out of reach. White wisps. He puts out his hand to catch one; the filaments are downy, lighter than air. Lenny's hair is not that white, but the white starry shapes of feather against the dark floor are like her when she is walking, the way she looks bright against things. He follows with his eyes the border of the shadowed space and over against the wall he sees a shape. Crawls carefully, soundless, until he touches a round silky box pushed back between the bed frame and the wall. Buddy zips it open. Some money folded up inside, and hairpins, a brooch with a ghost face, and two, three rings. He feels them, tries them on. One has a sparkle piece like glass and the gold band is cut with swirly shapes, a ring for a queen, that's what, a ring for Lenny. That old redheaded woman has a lot of rings; she could think she lost this one. Buddy sees Lenny's eyes, the sweep of her lashes, the plane of her face as she holds the ring close to study it. If he gave it to her she'd ask him where he got it. No, he would put it in her footlocker, in that little cardboard box where she keeps stamps and pictures amongst pink sheets of paper. She wouldn't even find the ring, most likely, until she left camp; he could put it into one of the envelopes and lick it shut. Hidden.

Suddenly the door to the kitchen opens. Mam coming for him, she's found him out. Buddy holds his breath and sees, in the crack of space allowed him, Mrs. T.'s shiny black shoes, or the toes of her shoes, pointed toes, and her silk-stockinged feet. Buddy stares. Inches from his nose, the shoes are still; they're like slippers with heels. Mrs. T.'s fleshy hand reaches down to fool with the ankle strap. Then an exasperated sound from above, and the shoes turn round so Buddy sees the heels. The bed gives with a creak as she sits down hard, and the sagging box spring droops just low enough to pin Buddy fast. He nearly cries out, watching her fingers tug at the tiny buckle. He must breathe in with a desperate little wheeze but she grunts as she heaves herself up, doesn't hear; he closes his eyes, sweating. Something elastic snaps far off, is tugged, rolled down. He hears her sit, then her stream of urine clatters into the bowl of the toilet Buddy hasn't seen behind a makeshift curtain. He imagines a long acrid water falling down a hole, falling and falling, but there's no bottom; the clatter keeps rattling down, then levels out in silence as the paper turns on its wooden roller. He makes his mind blank. Then she's up, the snap and pulling, a discreet huff, the toilet flushes. Her shoes cross the floor toward the kitchen in eight hard steps. Slam. The turn of the key in the lock. From outside.

Buddy pulls himself to the edge of his shelter, peeks out. Pulls himself forward on his elbows and looks at the ring where there's enough light to really see. The stone looks clear as rain, but he can't see into it or through it. Cut in minuscule angles but not sharp. He puts his lips there, tasting. Lenny's hand. *Do what a girl does.* But Lenny wouldn't do that. Dad could never make her. Buddy sees her hand, still and open, like a flower. Pale in the air, a ghost of itself. In her fingers, a music he can't hear. He puts the ring in his pocket, thinks again, pulls the pouch of marbles free and loosens the drawstring. Drops the ring in with the other glass.

Now he stands up. At the window, the opaque curtains move. Buddy steps closer. He could climb out the window, but he sees Frank in the back, stringing a length of rope to the side of the building from a utility pole. Clothesline for Mrs. T. Buddy will have to sneak out through the big dining room when she has the lights off. If he gets well into the room before she sees him, she'll think he's snuck into her class again from the kitchen, or from outside. He has the ring. He waits at the exact center of the little space for some time to pass. The fan whirs its quiet noise from the bureau. On the bedside table, the second hand of a wind-up clock moves round. Beside it sits a pitcher of water. Buddy sighs and the brimming water stirs.

It never occurred to her to run, to move, to get away. She stood listening. She wasn't hearing him with her ears; it was like she heard him in her head, his footsteps separate from the forest sounds, and she stood in her own space, understanding it was possible to know what she could not actually sense with her body. As though she'd always heard sounds that lay hidden under other sounds, and never quite known what they were. She had no questions. Now she was conscious of the shack behind her on its rise of ground, broken down, overgrown and hidden, exuding a specific warmth. The hum in the earth moved up through her feet. Beyond the trees Turtle Hole shimmered in the sun, oval as an egg.

She looked at the trees, which were absolutely still, and felt him, closer. He breathed near her. She remembered suddenly: the white bars of her crib, feeling her father come home. Feeling him move through the air along the road to the house, like a spirit. A wailing in her chest, winding out like an unwieldy banner that licks the air, tasting for him. She senses her mother as cloudy, fading off like smoke on a floor. There's just Wes in his undershirt, younger, thinner. Lenny wanted to study the apparition but it vanished, went back inside her, or fled into the trees. No, something else was in the trees. The clearing motionless, densely shaded. Where the trees broke by the path she discerned a particular light, a cast of sun or gold. Lenny kept her gaze trained on the color to be certain it was there, and listened: the interior sound of his footsteps, his breath, the weight of his body. She was conscious of the heat she stood within, the turn of the humid morning as it grew denser. The sun climbed and the day was thick and still. Yet she saw the leaves move, begin to move as though a breeze riffled them. Then she felt air on her face, distinctly cool air that played across her skin. Her forehead tingled with perspiration, with the glaze of her sweat. The air was not breeze or wind; the air seemed to fall across the little clearing in a column, a long shadow, a cold space like a slice. Then he appeared, holding the coiled snake in his arms.

Lenny stood motionless. He was a shape in the trees, wearing the same type of khaki pants her father had worn as a laborer years ago. Soft with washings, faun-colored. She felt a tug of memory, an image that pulled at her consciousness like a fish on a line. But it was gone, eclipsed in the face that loomed into her vision, very close: his dark, curly hair, a swarth of close beard, and the sculpted look of his mouth, perfect and red. He was grown, a man, but younger than her father, darker. She wasn't afraid. Instinctively, she reached up to touch him, to see if he was real; the whiskers on his face were long enough to feel soft, not bristly like her father's weekend beards. If he was real, this near her, then everything was real: the colors and the coolness in the air, the way he had come close to her without seeming to move.

"Why is the air cold?" Lenny said. She felt she was speaking into a tunnel. Her voice sounded far away and thin. She wondered if she'd thought the words, not really said them.

He shook his head impatiently, as though considering the air were a waste of time. His eyes were dark and full. He lifted his chin to indicate what he held in his arms. Lenny glanced down but the snake was gone and she saw dark vines in his arms, vines looped one over another, with dark reddish leaves the color of wine, and closed among them were long blossoms with curved petals, still and opalescent, nearly black.

Lenny touched the flowers and they stirred, cool beneath her hand, rolling and smooth. The flowers seemed to flatten, move and coalesce in a darkly patterned blur. Lenny saw the trick, the spell he cast: how the vine became the snake and the snake became the vine, shining, moving over him. His crossed arms were sinewy and firm, sun-dark, close to her, and she felt the cool glide of the snake just at the level of her chest. Again, a picture of Wes, or a sense of him, flashed into her. Throwing her toys over the top bar of the crib into his arms, soft toys, fuzzy bears, a white lamb that wore a hat. Lying flat on the mattress. The blur of the white bars, the toys raining down on top of her and the mattress bouncing. Then the pictures blurred like film run too fast, and Lenny stepped back. Immediately, the man with the snake stepped closer, one step, no more, a mirror image of her own movement. He filled her vision and she focused on his mouth, his parted lips, the line and shape of his upper lip like a tipped bow, the roseate color deep, lines in his flesh deep, the flesh thick, cushiony. He seemed about to speak but he only breathed, his mouth pursed, open. She saw his teeth, the pink tip of his tongue. All around, the light seemed by turns shaded and bright, as though clouds blew quickly across the sun. Or a light was lifting and settling in her head; she heard a window shade in her room at home, pulled fast by the wind, blown forward, pulled fast, and the other curtains were drawn. It was all confused; her father was there. She saw herself in a crib, falling asleep. After something. Sleeping with his finger in her mouth, the smallest finger of his right hand. The pulsing of her tongue against him, sucking. She pushed out hard with both arms, pushed away, heard the sharp exhalation of her own breath. Again, the man with the snake moved with her, leaning far back with the force she'd exerted, then moving back toward her. Two of them, moving. She understood he was not going to hurt her, that he was, in fact, waiting for her, waiting for her to see. He only stood near, not touching her. She put her hands on his chest and felt the thud of his heart, a pounding inside him that seemed to ripple through her and into the ground. She was certain she saw a glow move across the planes and curves of his shoulders, his throat, up into his face. She couldn't look into his eyes; she saw his wide brow, his dark, tousled hair. The glow seemed to move outward and emanate, a violet blue, completely transparent, like a rainbow, or the light that shows motes of dust moving in bright air. She could see a whiter glow around her own hands, her forearms against him, like a buzz over her skin, an after-image.

He was telling her something without speaking. She suddenly heard him, in the interior way she'd heard him walking toward her, in the way she must have heard other things, a long time ago. Ways she'd forgotten. She leaned subtly closer and found herself seeing into his eyes. Instantly, the sounds and images came clear; a deluge of rain, and glass between them, like a long, curved window. She seemed to look down at him through glass, a glass box, or he was in a box, enclosed. The air felt fluid, as though the water from her dream this morning were all around her, the water of the stream she'd lain within, floating. But he was real; she felt him moving onto his knees and looked down at the top of his head, at his upturned face. He had knelt in front of her and her hands were on his shoulders. The vine was around his neck, the dark vine that was alive, and the dark flowers were turning and moving. They were slender, closed blossoms, turning up their barely open lips, glisten-ing. He extended his arms and Lenny saw how the flowers were the dappled black of the snake's hide, the darkest gleaming, shining, moving over him; she felt the snake on her own wrist, how it moved, a heavy shiver, undulating and smooth. The weight of it moved along her arm to her throat; she felt the flick of its tongue, the small, blunt probe of its head. It moved along her skin, across the cleft of her collarbone, long and blind and silken. She could smell burnt sugar, the buttery, darkened sweet of the burnt sugar cakes Audrey would make Wes on his birthday when the girls were little. Caramel icing she stirred with a spatula in a tin saucepan. He drank that dark, bitter beer with the sweet black cake; she saw her mother's lips on the mouth of the bottle. A burnished liquid fell through space. She felt the white heat of someone's touch, a finger-tip tracing each of her ribs; she saw the room, her parents' bedroom with the high windows along two walls and the lilac branches waving outside. She couldn't see who else was in the picture. A white form lay its head on her chest, and the light cracked open and shut; everything grew bright, and the long flowers in the flat leaves of the moving vine were white. He was giving them to her, lifting them with his arms, and she knelt down in the bright white that was left, in what was there when the colors had bled away, before the picture went blank.

## ❈ ALMA: HERITAGE CLASS

Heritage class and the supper speeches were the only difference between Girl Guides camp and other camps. Heritage class was in the morning after hobby hours, while the grass was still drying and the heat hadn't grown too intense to forbid indoor gatherings. Supper speeches were meant to reflect what the girls had learned in heritage class, but to Alma the class was like storytelling, and the stories were meant to be scary. She sat in the dining hall now, trying to finish her supper speech on the blue onionskin stationery her mother had given her for camp. *I'm the first B-wing girl from our cabin to make a supper speech about freedom. I think freedom is like a long road or a trail that winds to where we can't see, but living in America means we go there together.* That was true, but a heritage wasn't just about freedom. Mrs. Thompson-Warner said it was their Christian duty to be informed citizens because Communists were godless. *Each county of our state has sent at least one girl to Camp Shelter. We come from cities and towns and farms, and we pledge allegiance to Girl Guides, our state, and our nation.* Alma read her own lines and wondered if the Russians believed in magic, then; anyone who hadn't heard of God seemed to believe in magic, in spirits of the forest or the air. She wrote: *The forest is all around us and we're like a country inside it.* The woods were full of sounds and silence, but her speech had to be about protecting Democracy. Mrs. Thompson-Warner told them numerous stories and facts about Communism; Alma jotted down details that seemed related. Russia was a very large country partly because it had taken over smaller countries and made them fly the Russian flag. People were arrested just for criticizing the government and taken off to prison. Everyone knew these things, but not everyone knew the Communists were trying to take over America.

Heritage class was held in the dining hall. Each morning, the Juniors bumped their shins moving twelve white benches away from the tables and arranging them in even rows at the side of the big room, just in front of Mrs. T.'s lectern. She had a record player and a projector set up there on a rickety table, and a screen on a stand that pulled up from its metal tube.

"Alma." Delia was nudging her in a confusion of milling girls. "Put your speech down and help me move the bench."

Struggling, trying to match her steps to Delia's at the other end of their long burden, Alma heard a rasping sound as Mrs. T. struggled to raise the portable screen taller than her own height. Today she had a broomstick with a hook in the end that she used to push the screen as high as it would go. Now the pictures would look bigger.

"Wonderful," Delia said, "another film strip. Where did she get the broomstick? It's perfect for her."

"Will you sit with me?" Alma set her end of the bench down in line with the others and waited to be refused.

"In the first row? No way." Delia always sat in the back and tried to read comic books after the lights went out. She'd brought *Millie the Model, Richie Rich,* and her *Classics Illustrated* version of *Lorna Doone;* she read in the light from the kitchen, the comics concealed in her materials folder. She even had tracing paper strategically placed over the pictures of Lorna she wanted to copy. Alma sat up front and was buffeted, swayed, enveloped by the words of Mrs. Thompson-Warner, who spoke after showing a film strip or presenting a program.

Alma wanted company, wanted Delia to join her in the camp of the alarmed, but Delia declined. "You don't listen," Alma hissed at her now, "because I do listen."

"You're dumb to listen," Delia said. "She makes it all up."

"She can't have made up the film strips."

"Someone made them up for her."

"What about James Worth? Did she make him up?"

Delia shrugged. James Worth was a man who said he'd been a prisoner in a Russian slave-labor camp, and he'd written a book with a man in chains on the cover. Somehow Mrs. Thompson-Warner had gotten him to come all the way from Pennsylvania to talk to the girls in heritage class. "Maybe she didn't make him up," Delia admitted, "but she must have made up his hairstyle. He was wearing at least a bottle and a half of Vitalis. His hair looked wet. And he was sweaty. He looked like he'd just been swimming."

"That doesn't mean he was never in Russia." Alma frowned, remembering his squinty eyes. She supposed he squinted because his cell had been dark, and the snow in Siberia was endless and white. He'd worn a suit and tie in the heat of Camp Shelter, and kept his fingers laced together in front of him while he talked, as though he still wore handcuffs. Or maybe they just used rope in Siberia. Alma was certain he was genuine; there was a terrible heaviness about him, in the hunch of his shoulders, in the way he turned his head to look to the side, so slowly. She remembered a line from her speech: *If people aren't free, they can't think.* James

Worth was like someone who'd been asleep a long time. He spoke normally, but with such deliberation and weight, as though he'd once forgotten how to talk. Mrs. T. said he'd done a great deal for his country. What did she mean? *We know what President Kennedy told us the day he became the leader of the Free World.* Alma had written that in her speech, but when she thought the words now, she only saw James Worth, how careful he was, like someone who'd had to learn again to move, to smile.

"Something happened to him — we don't know what." Delia sighed. "Look, I'll see you later. I'm not going to sit up here." She walked to the back as Mrs. T. turned on the record player.

Alma took her seat, rustling the thin sheets of her notes. A reedy soprano voice floated through the hall as girls sat down on the benches. *Show me the prison, show me the jail . . .* It was the voice of an angel, resigned to sorrow. The lights went out and grainy black-and-white picture stills filled the screen: a woman with a guitar on an outdoor stage in front of a crowd, her long, wan, romantic face and straight dark hair. Immediately, Alma wanted to be one of that crowd. *Unfortunately,* read the words across the bottom of the screen, *many of our most popular youth entertainers are Communist-inspired. Many of them have publicly attended Communist meetings.* It was a kind of war, Alma thought, the cold war Mrs. T. talked about, all done with spies. Alma closed her eyes for a moment and saw her mother's mouth, closer than a kiss, saying silently *secret, secret,* and *spy.* But she had never said *spy*; it was a word Alma thought, remembering the big doors of Souders Department Store in Winfield, and watching Nickel Campbell step out of her mother's car after one of their Saturday meetings. Alma saw them pull up in the car again and again, like pictures on a reel. "You shouldn't be in the car together," she'd told Audrey, "lots of women from Gaither shop at Souders. I see them all the time." It wasn't true, but after that Audrey always drove up at exactly twelve noon, alone. Alma would watch for the car, numb like a spy must be numb, seeing familiar things look strange.

Now she sneaked a look at Mrs. Thompson-Warner, who stood watching the film from her usual position beside the record player. Mrs. T. wore old-ladies' jersey dresses, slick to the touch, patterned in small prints, buttoned down the front with a fabric belt around the waist. Mrs. T. was big and the flowered dresses were vast, like fields. Her voice was large too, deep and shrill at once, and her shoes had ankle straps. Even in the heat she wore silk stockings, and her seams were always straight. The whispered swish of her heavy thighs touching as she walked was a sound not unlike the repetitive soughing of wind in some hidden leafy place. Mrs. T. really was like a forest, with her faint patchouli smell and her clothes that were printed with the images of tiny leaves and curlicued creepers. Her skin was so pale she looked chartreuse and her long red hair escaped strand by strand from the tight French twist that bound it. Her hairpins, Alma knew, were sterling silver; she used exactly six, and all had been wedding gifts.

Alma had last week fetched a lantern to the room of Mrs. Thompson-Warner; to Alma it was unthinkable that Mrs. T. actually slept at the camp, but she did, in a small room behind the kitchen of the dining hall. There, according to the counselors, she was accorded the special privileges of coffee, hot rolls, and jam before breakfast ("served on a tray, don't you know"), and an electric fan. The room had a door that led into the kitchen, and another that led into the dining hall; maybe it had been a cook's bedroom. The one window had no screen, but it had sheer curtains Mrs. T. had brought with her. She'd also brought her own mirror, a large round one in a gilt frame. She'd stood before it, pinning her hair, when Alma was admitted with the lantern. One of the pins dropped and Alma picked it up, observing at close range Mrs. T.'s silk-sheathed toes. Thanking Alma, Mrs. T. confided that she couldn't manage without her pins, made for her by a Bond Street silversmith and given her by her husband's family at the time of her marriage. She spoke of her marriage as an inalienable, long-past ceremonial event, like a coronation. She seemed to pretend her husband had gone down at sea or perished in a courageous struggle. Now Mrs. T. lifted the needle of the old record player and began the song again. *Show me the hobo who sleeps out in the rain* . . . Mrs. T. stood contemplating the film, pleased and stern, a tense smile playing about her lips. Watching her, Alma thought people could be convinced of anything as long as they didn't know the truth, or didn't remember it. She wondered if Mrs. T. remembered the truth about things that had happened to her, if she had secrets she'd made herself forget. Nickel Campbell was gone and no one but Alma and her mother knew the secret about him. Audrey would stay at home now, wouldn't she, and not leave like she'd said she might; Wes would stay, though he might leave for a week, two weeks, as always, and not say where he went. Ten years would pass. Lenny would grow up and go away. Alma, in her turn, would go away. She tried to imagine being grown up: all she knew would be layered over, made less sharp, made softer, older, buried. She gripped the bench and held on.

The singer's voice ebbed and flowed, punctuated only by a muffled banging of pots and pans in the kitchen. Mrs. Carmody would be cleaning up breakfast or starting lunch; the swinging doors to her domain trembled as usual. On the far side of the same wall was the door to Mrs. T.'s room. Alma gazed absently beyond the screen and saw Mrs. T.'s door open slightly; she thought she glimpsed Buddy's round, pixie face before it disappeared, but she wasn't sure. She was nearly asleep and might have dreamed him; she was never sure what Buddy was, the way he hung on the edges of things, skinny and wispy, there and not there. The clear tremolo of the song continued to float behind the grainy, subtitled stills. *There but for fortune.* What was fortune? Sleeping, Alma looked for Mrs. T. but couldn't find her. Even in dreams, she couldn't think of Mrs. T. as a being involved in real life, walking along streets — not like she imagined, in stark detail as her eyelids fluttered, the sounds from her parents' bedroom, or her father's rough touch as he shoved Audrey away from the refrigerator when she planted herself between him and his beer. He would tell them to call an AA meeting, Audrey and Alma, two girls, teetotalers. At this time of morning, Audrey would be hanging out the wash in the yard, in the corner where the clothesline was strung. Alma heard the hymn-like, sorrowful song and behind it sheets were flapping, snapping, filling with air and billowing. Alma dreamed there was wind at home when there was not even air to breathe in Camp Shelter. Audrey was half hidden as the sheets twisted, dropped, flew again, her naked arms upraised, her hands urgently working. Alma heard the wind as though surrounded, like her mother. She saw Audrey's hands pinning the double-hemmed sheets with wooden pins as the flapping cloth tugged hard and tried to sail away, waft like flags over the green of the spring earth. The ground was spongy with water and the dream smelled of water, and when the lights went on Alma was shocked to recognize the electric smell of the projector. The fan had failed again, the projector was in pre-burn, the bulb had gone out.

"We seem to have technical difficulties," Mrs. T. was announcing at the front of the room. She fanned the projector with her wide, pale hands before she remembered to turn off the switch. The hum of the machine died away.

"Is it going to catch fire?" Alma heard herself ask the question in a faraway, disinterested voice.

"No, of course not." Mrs. T. looked at them brightly and clapped her hands together once. "Now then, girls, what do we mean when we say 'Communist-inspired'? We mean that certain entertainers, though they may not be members of the Communist Party, have attended Communist meetings or publicly expressed support for Communist points of view."

"What's a Communist point of view?" someone asked.

Mrs. T. nodded, pleased. "A Communist point of view is the opinion of a person who believes Communism to be the best form of government, and who wishes to see all governments become Communist. Or a Communist point of view may be held by an uninformed person who has been duped by a Communist individual into believing that that individual is different from Communists in China or Russia."

Alma shifted on her seat. Far back along the shadowed rear wall, she thought she saw the doorknob to Mrs. T.'s room turning first one way, then the other, as though someone were trying to get out. Unaccountably, her heart leapt. The door quivered and was pushed ajar just slightly. One bright eye appeared in the opening, so near the floor that Alma thought the creature about to crawl forth would be an animal, scuttling on all fours. The eye was like a little jewel, a subtle glitter, and Buddy's small face emerged behind it. He held so still that no one saw him at first. Alma held still as well, looking past Mrs. T. as Buddy edged into the dining hall thirty feet behind her and silently closed the door. Glancing at no one, he began to move rapidly along the floor in a cat-like crouch, huddling near the wall, his body parallel with the dark baseboards. He wagged his fuzzy, yellow, close-cropped head in time to his own quick movements and was utterly silent. A few girls had seen him and began to titter.

"Certainly," Mrs. T. said, "it *is* laughable. It's ridiculous. And ridiculous that some Americans find it fashionable to admire Fidel Castro, who promised to liberate the people of Cuba and instead enslaved them, just a few miles from our own national borders!" She paused for emphasis and regarded her audience as they responded in a chorus of ragged giggles. She lowered her voice and said flatly, "I assure you, it's no joke."

Helpless, the girls laughed. Alma lowered her head and bit her lip, trying to stop. It came to her that Buddy was both an animal and an enchanted creature, nearly always alone, appearing and disappearing around the camp like a small ghost the wind blew through and lifted up at will. She wished she were like Buddy, so strange no one could own her, and she laughed harder, her eyes tearing, her stomach sore.

Mrs. Thompson-Warner looked over her shoulder to her left and caught sight of Buddy as he reached the corner and began moving straight along the wall to the double doors of the dining hall. She crossed the floor in several heavy strides and hauled him up by his arm. "Little *boy*," she said, "do not *ever* interrupt my class again. Go into the kitchen and stay with your mother and *obey* her from this moment onward!"

Buddy seemed to dangle in her grasp, still in motion, straining for the doors with his eyes. He kept his fists clinched and then tilted his head to look at Mrs. T. He gazed at her for some seconds, staring, his mouth pressed into a tight smile. The girls quieted and Mrs. Thompson-Warner released him. He seemed to hop in place, then he skittered across the floor and was hidden by one of the swinging doors to the kitchen, which moved ever so slightly in response to his entrance. Alma looked after him longingly. She thought she could still smell his dusty, woodsy smell. He didn't care about the Russians, even if he was a sort of spy, always trailing someone, looking around with his whole peculiar, watchful face — not just his eyes but his raised brows too, and his little pursed mouth, and his short-cropped hair that stood on end.

Mrs. T. folded her arms and looked at the girls. "As I was saying, Cuba is no joke. You may remember just last fall, when Castro and the Russians were ready to attack us with missiles launched from Cuban bases." She paused as the children grew more silent. "How many of you had air-raid drills at school, in case the Russians attacked?"

Alma glanced back at Delia and raised her hand. The sixth grade had been herded into the girls' bathroom and told to crouch along the cement-block walls with their arms over their heads. Delia wouldn't raise her hand, but Alma heard her call out in a loud voice, "We had drills, and at recess the boys pretended to be Russians and knocked the girls over."

"The boys are Americans and they had better *be* Americans, even in games, because I assure you, the Russians are not pretending." Mrs. T. held one finger up and jabbed at the air to emphasize each word. "Certain Americans have *vanished without a trace!*"

Alma's face burned. She remembered how Nickel Campbell had looked in his casket at the funeral home when her mother had sent her in to pay respects and sign the book "Mrs. Swenson and Alma." They'd gone early in the morning one day before school, when none of the family were there, and Audrey had stayed in the car and cried and said she couldn't look at him and Alma would have to sign.

"Vanished!" said Mrs. T. "For instance, there is an open runway at Dulles International Airport in Washington, D.C., where Russian planes take off and land with no official clearance. No one knows who comes and goes on those planes."

Alma heard Delia's accusatory voice from the back of the room. "Why don't we read about that in the newspapers, then?"

"Not everything is printed in the newspapers or reported on the news," said Mrs. T. "Some disturbing facts remain secrets."

Alma knew it was true.

Nickel Campbell had not looked real anymore; his body had been in the river for hours — maybe that was why. Someone had put a long stone doll with paints on its face into the casket. The doll was not like a man asleep, it was an empty doll with no man inside. The doll wore a gold watch on its wrist and the watch was ticking. The voice of the watch was like a whisper that knew all Alma knew, and the whisper wouldn't stop. Now Alma heard footsteps and she raised her eyes to see Mrs. T. standing near her, casting her hushed voice over Alma's head.

"It's a fact," said Mrs. T. quietly. "I've told you before and it's true: the furnace of the Russian embassy burns at temperatures hot enough to *cremate human bones.*"

The girls sat rapt. In the wake of their stillness came a sudden onslaught of noise as the catch on the film screen gave way and the screen rolled down into its metal tube with a rasping mechanical shriek. A few girls yelled short, nervous screams. The screen, reduced on its metal stand to the stature of a lowercase *t*, seemed to tremble before it fell with a final resounding crash. Heritage class was over.

## 𝕏 PARSON: MEANT TO DO

Walk, keep walking. Back toward camp, find the others.

Lenny falls asleep inside him; he walks along the river trail and she is still falling asleep, leaning forward to get as close into his neck as her face can push; and when he's walking he's not afraid of letting her fall away, he feels her mouth, sentient, asleep, on that pulse point in his throat, as though she won't ever leave him, and there are sounds in the woods that echo the rushing warble of the river, as though it all draws up around him, a tunnel of sound meant for passage, his passage, what he's meant to do. Dreaming and walking, he feels the weight of the coiled snake in his arms as the perfect form of her head, as though he carries her sleeping face, contents of a basket, carefully, not to wake her. *Know what it's like to kill someone, kill them with your hands? I killed her and I'd kill her again.* Carmody had laughed, squeezing the sponge over the bucket in the bathroom; those days they cleaned latrines in D block, he'd talk on and on and Parson mostly kept still. The sponge moving over the gray tile was a dull yellow, and the medicinal smell of the

139

bright green disinfectant was on Carmody's hands and chest while he talked; Carmody knew about Proudytown, knew Parson had done time there too. He jeered and teased when he heard about the "resident rooms," the "counselors," the "library" whose dull windows were barred with ornate iron. *Yeah, an when I was there in the forties they called it a home. Prison for kids, some fuckin home. And kids do get fucked, right? Thing I could never figure out, how do they decide which ones?* Carmody, leaning closer to wink, bat his eyes, blink like Parson's own shuttered memory, making blocks of pictures that floated in slants of moted sunlight. *Baby flesh, so tasty. So many of those guys, they can't resist. Who can blame them, eh?* The urinals were a long-necked row of cracked porcelain forms, laced with shadow, supplicant, open-mouthed. Carmody swore, wielding his long-handled brush in and out the bucket of bitter potion, *cleaning up piss, all my life I been cleaning up piss.* Shoving the bucket along on its squeaking wheels: *I get outa here, I'm gonna piss on the world.* The wheels squeaked and Carmody said about his mother, how she smelled like piss, drunk in bed and he hated her, he was a little kid in diapers, then a big kid who couldn't wake up and pissed his own bed, both of them smelling like piss, how that made him know he was really her kid, worthless, and from the time he was eleven or twelve he could knock her around, he could throw the bottles by her bed out the window or against the wall. A bottle could shatter and spray the couch, the rug, till the place smelled fermented, pissed and whiskied, her bed a sot's padded nest, which is what she was, a sot, a whore and then a sot, and when she was a drunk and not a whore he said he hated her worse. *Men knocked her up and knocked her down and none of them could hit her hard enough. Finally I took over.* Then he'd smack the toilets one after the other with his wooden brush, walking up and down till the long row rang out like a dull xylophone. Which ones. The tiled room seemed to spin along in a death orbit or free fall Carmody directed. Pictures tugged at Parson: limited frames, like glances through the slats of a broad venetian blind. *Parson ain't no name. What was your real name, Bobjimbill? Uh, Mike? You know, the name your mother handed over when she dropped you on the trail. Sure as hell dropped you, your head is so bent. Don't know, do you, don't even fucking know.*

It was like Parson had floated a long time in the shadow where Carmody lived. Parson was a curled form that slept and grew, hurtling through a dark space in which Carmody hit his mother till she was nearly dead, and Carmody, sent to Proudytown, got fucked, fist-fucked, fucked with brooms, still his mother's child. Carmody, a sixteen-year-old private, lied to get to Korea, posed with a gun he didn't have to steal. Then Carmody in a cage, his first real cell, the cold mountains east of Manchuria, where *certain phrases* got him rice and bread crusts. These were pictures, memory transplant; they were Carmody's. Other pictures, more fragmented, far less detailed. Whose were they? Flashes that were only the angles of objects. Big objects rushing and falling, sharp or cold, muffled in a world of giants. Like Parson had lived in that world, asleep and curled up tight, and the orphanage in Huntington was what he saw when he finally opened his eyes. *Orphan kid. Just as well. Why know? Wish I was like you, big strong zombie blank.* But it wasn't blank, it was the wall beside Parson's bed, printed with a cracked thirties wallpaper of fish with legs and top hats, fish with parasols. The paper was blotched, water-spotted, and the faded patches were the pools into which the fish disappeared. Four years old, Parson would get out of his bed in the dark and walk straight along the back wall, one forefinger tracing the paper to where it disappeared altogether in the far corner. The matron would find him there, standing in the corner where the fish had vanished, and lead him back to bed. There was something warm beyond the wall, a place the fish went, and the enveloping sagged mattress of his own bed was a sliver of that place in his dreams. *You got a few tricks though, zombie, do the heat trick. No kidding, I'll wait, just do it.* Carmody standing in the prison bathroom and Parson could close his eyes, see the pattern of that paper with the fish, and the objects and fragments of the other echoes all fell into the pools of white fade he remembered on the orphanage walls. He'd stand an arm's length away and extend his hand, hold still. He could feel Carmody as a murky, cold smoke, see inside that face, peering out, a devil-child, evil and wet, whimpering, with eyes that bled. Parson would have to pull back into the fire of the spirit. He'd feel the heat in his chest first, like a weight he balanced by focusing, until the liquid heart of it overflowed and fused down his spine in a circular ripple. The same heat coursed down his arm, into his hand, and Carmody's devil-child drew back, opened its black mouth and turned away. The points of its teeth glittered in a bright sweep. Then there was darkness, purely, the starry drift of the Devil's light fading, lonely and beautiful. The surge of heat seemed to burst in Parson, easing, an emergence through pressure and weight. *Like a fuckin furnace out of your hand. You crazy loon.* Parson would open his eyes to see Carmody staring, very near, his face screwed up in a tearful grimace. Sobbing, the sobs wrenched out of him. Cursing, always cursing, fallen down in what the Devil kept at bay. *Sonofabitch. Too bad you can't get some sparks going, get yourself on TV.* There were no sparks. But there were colors Carmody couldn't see, colors darting off around the dark shell encasing his empty form. The Devil, beaten back, beaten in, small and disappeared, left a black, sucking space in the shape of Carmody, in the sound and smell of Carmody. The space yawned, emitting a neutral hum. Carmody's voice talked through it. *I ever tell anyone about your crazy shit they don't believe me you fuckin asshole you don't prove nothin with all your bible crap you fuckin maniac.* Carmody weeping, shaken with effort and rage. *Spirit my ass you're just a fuckin nut like everyone else.* Carmody's long fingers tinged brown with nicotine. Tales of what he'd do to get cigarettes in the joint, like his body was nothing, he was nothing but the need to breathe, smoke, keep walking, drink whatever rot-gut he could find. *Then how do you do these fuckin tricks you sorry loon.* Carmody, eating the prison slop, sucking up to whoever for cigarettes and whiskey, getting his workload reduced, scrambling like a rabbit jerked through holes. Parson knew him, saw him: Carmody was a pit the Devil had filled, a pit to drown whatever touched him. When he pushed at Parson, jabbed at him, sharp elbows, knees, his long thin frame pushed close, mouthing offers and taunts, Parson had to flatten him, walk over him. And still Carmody got what he wanted, the touch and the push, the damage piling up. His tears would burn and sting on Parson's hands. Carmody cried like something squeezed.

Not like her.

Keep walking.

In the river weeds, cicada vibrato. The water a long form hold-ing still. Here, cut through woods. Safer now, walking in the shelter of the trees. At the work site near the bridge, men are digging. How the dirt flies up. Warm loamy smell of something old, folded in for eons. Foreman standing over the mounded earth, the rest of them gathered in a knot for cigarettes. Leaning on their shovels and pickaxes. Not like prison, where the men empty out and time all around them swells up, ripens fit to burst. Time here is different, a level plain. See things coming from a long way off. The men on the camp crew brag like kids, laugh with their eyes closed. Full of plans.

The snake moves in the bowl of his arms. Careful not to spill it.

*Sorry fuckin loon ain't you full of yourself.*

She's full. Densely near him. Like he keeps walking in the shaded heat, moving through a pulse of aura she has lent in her touch. Holding on to him, her eyes swimming up. Some cousin to the one he watched in Carolina those nights, swimming the darkened main corridor of the cellblock. That one a figment, a wisp he couldn't feel; sometimes she was only light, dark neon turning like an eel. But Lenny grabs on to him. He walks and feels her hands. Her eyes fill, washed clean in her open, knowing face. Her tears must taste of salt but his face against her comes away glowing. She smells of milk, sweet and strong, but she is not so pure. She carries some damage around, holds it out from herself. Damage as dead as the moon. Parson tastes her now and walks; just here the earth is dense with golden needles, second-growth pine and balsam grown close together, so he moves between slender forms. Air smells of pine, no sound but his footsteps. She lies on the grass, back near the shack: he feels her lie there still. Old weight of the snake in his arms. Moving away from her body, the ground her body graces. He sees his own work boots, step after quiet step, but he feels himself floating, following the course of his body. The boots muddy, scarred, same boots from a world ago, boots issued him in Carolina. They called it work detail, short-timers and trusted convicts saving state money. Cutting brush. How the scythes sounded along the roads, men fanned out, swinging long knives from their shoulders. Like a line of clocks. Time cut up in airy whistles. The tall grass flying, the wet, cut smell.

Camp smells like that, only sweeter and bigger. So many children, and Carmody's big wife cooking food whose odor wafts even to the far ends of the trails. Here in the woods, leafy bower, Parson can still smell the fried lunch meat, smoking American cheese, toasted bread. The quad so open he stays in the shade, and the boy, Frank, angles toward him, calling out.

"Hey there," Frank says, "you guys on a break?" He walks closer, nearly as tall as Parson, a stringy kid still filling out.

"Yeah," Parson says, "lunch break." He lets the snake wind out, drop its length down.

Frank whistles in admiration. "What you got there?"

Parson doesn't answer yet. Just at the rise of the trail, he sees the little girls, their shapes moving toward him like shadows. Carmody's kid follows them, drifting behind and between them like he's hiding till the last second. Like he knows there are black streaks in the air around his head, like he's ashamed to breathe out what Carmody has poisoned.

"What you got there?" Frank says again.

And the little girls draw near.


## ✖ ALMA: INTO THE TREES

"Alma, come with me to get mail." Delia moved the benches back in place. "Sweeping is the worst job in the jar. You have to wait till nearly everyone else is done, and then pick up all the food people have walked on."

"You go ahead. I never get much mail anyway." Alma dragged the wide push broom back to the kitchen. She shoved open Mrs. Carmody's swinging door and propped the broom in its place. The cooks were loading scraped plates into the big dishwashers and one of the machines was already running, whistling its shussing, watery noise.

"That's not true," Delia called after her. "Anyway, there's no line. Look."

Alma walked back over to look out the big front window onto the porch. Everyone was allowed to check mail drop after lunch. Mail drop was really just a series of alphabetical plyboard slots mounted on an old door. The door itself was attached to the stone wall of the dining hall porch with metal hooks; across the top, someone had scrawled "Instant Post Office," but Mrs. T. had painted that over with the neatly lettered legend "Shelter Missives." Alma wasn't sure what "missives" meant, and if she didn't know, the other Juniors and Primaries wouldn't either. Possibly it was some play on "Miss," some British way of saying the messages were for girls. The mail slots were arranged by cabin or campsite, then alphabetized by last name, except for Mrs. Thompson-Warner's and Frank's. Alma supposed they had their own slots because they had no campsite. It was funny, Frank and the directress, side by side as labeled slots. Mrs. T.'s read "Mrs. C. W. Thompson-Warner" in little typewritten letters, and Frank's was just scrawled on in pencil, with his first name. Frank's handwriting, Alma assumed. Sometimes she saw the image of his penciled name when she closed her eyes, as though the letters weren't really a name at all but a drawing or a gray and white painting that shimmered in and out of focus. The image was so restful that she'd begun to use it to fall asleep. If she was awake and walking around, the image wasn't strong enough to counter her other thoughts, but in the dark, the careless letters enlarged and relaxed and crowded out the other pictures. But now it was daylight, just after burnished noon, and the nearly empty dining hall still seemed crowded with the fading vibrations of girls' jostling, high-pitched voices.

"Hey," Delia addressed her impatiently, "you're finished, aren't you? Let's check the mail before we run out of time."

"Go ahead, am I stopping you?" Alma pretended to be peevish, but she smiled. "Remember the note we wrote Frank, and how we were too chicken to put it in his box?"

"Don't remind me." Delia rolled her eyes, as though the memory were long ago and utterly sophomoric. In fact, so many girls had written Frank notes that Mrs. Thompson-Warner had outlawed notes and announced that only stamped mail would be put into the mail slots for pickup. She said the girls were really much too busy to find time to write notes to each other, or to anyone else, and if they found a moment they might write to their parents, many of whom had scrimped and sacrificed to send their fortunate daughters to Camp Shelter.

"Fortunate daughters," Alma stage-whispered now. "Find a moment."

"Come on," Delia whispered back, "no one's around now to see if you got anything. And anyway, so what?"

Alma shrugged. Usually she refused to join the lines of girls formed across the broad porch every day; she often received no letters, and she allowed herself to check only if she happened to get out of lunch chores late. Then there was no waiting and no one but Delia to know. Who would write her? Certainly not Wes. Alma had never seen him write on anything but his business papers. She hoped for another box of chocolates and gum from Audrey, but didn't look forward to her letters. They weren't normal letters like Delia got from Aunt Bird or Mina. Audrey sometimes sent blank pages with pieces of grass or pressed flowers folded in them, or a poem she'd copied from somewhere. Her last "missive" had been some pages torn out of *National Geographic*, an article about Italy with pictures of mountains and a walled town. No message at all, no scrawled comment in the margins. Alma had stared at the images, intrigued, until she remembered one of Audrey's comments from last winter. *He speaks Italian beautifully, Alma. He says it's a language for shouting or whispering. He wants to go back there so badly, but Mina says it's an insane way to spend money and too far to travel with the kids. Can you imagine? How we'd love it, you and I.* Siena. It was the town where Nickel Campbell had lived in a villa before he was married, before he knew Mina. Where had Audrey gotten those pages? She must have gone to the library and found them. Is that how she spent her time, with no one home and the weather so hot? Quietly ripping pages out of library magazines? She'd included a stamped, addressed envelope so Alma could send the pages back, and Alma had, immediately, folding them up and sealing them in the minute she realized why her mother had sent them.

Now she let Delia link arms with her and propel them through the heavy screen door onto the broad porch of the hall. Even in shade afforded by the deep eaves, the heat of the day enveloped them. Alma sighed, peering across the quad while Delia checked through the C box. The grass seemed a yellower green by noon, dried out, and the dirt track bordering the woods appeared to waver. She let her gaze rein in and quickly peruse the wall of mail slots: there was Frank's name, the familiar picture of his hasty scrawl, and in the slot below was a single pink onionskin envelope. Lenny's stationery. Like Alma's, except Alma's was blue. Without even considering, Alma angled her body slightly and leaned against the mail slots. Watching Delia, she deftly slipped the thin envelope into her back pocket.

"I checked yours for you. See? You got two things." Delia looked up, distracted and triumphant, holding out the envelopes. "One of them is just from Aunt Bird. I can't even read her boring letters. But who sent you this?"

"I like Bird's letters. At least she tells us how Johnny is." Alma took the white legal-size envelope Bird always used for her notes about the weather and the shop. The other letter was stamped and addressed too, but again, Alma recognized Lenny's stationery, and her heart lurched gently. Lenny had sent her a note, and Frank too.

Delia held out the pale pink envelope. "Who's this from?"

"It's from Lenny."

"Lenny? Lenny wrote to you?"

"With a stamp and all, so they wouldn't confiscate it." Alma took the envelope and slipped her finger into the fold. It was barely glued down.

Delia stepped back. "What does she say? If it's secret, don't tell me."

Alma unfolded one thin sheet and read the words. The message was two printed lines, but it wasn't Lenny's writing. Alma stared.

"Well?"

"Here. Read it yourself. I guess it's to both of us."

They were alone on the big porch. Delia looked at the words, then read in a quizzical whisper: "'You and Delia sneak away from campfire tonight and meet us at Turtle Hole. Don't let anyone see you.'" She turned the paper over, then over again. "Lenny didn't sign it."

"It's not Lenny's handwriting, just Lenny's paper," Alma said. "It must be from Cap."

"Oh. Well, they probably share everything. More than us, even. I mean, they're older." Delia handed the letter back, looking non-committal. "I guess it's important. They've never written us before. We could get away pretty easy. No one would miss us till after, in the cabin. Campfire goes on so long."

"Two hours, anyway."

It was true. The counselors couldn't notice exactly who was there; it was dark beyond the flames of the big fire, they were busy leading songs and chants, and all the girls were mixed together, crouching loud and faceless in their tangled circle.

"We could just go to the latrines, separately, and not come back." Delia looked interested. "Maybe we're going to drink beer or liquor and go swimming. I heard Cap drinks. Isn't that why your mom made Lenny stop sleeping over at the Briarleys'?"

"Where did you hear that?" Alma frowned, annoyed. In fact, it was the Briarleys who'd requested that Lenny not sleep over anymore, after they'd found an empty bottle in Cap's room, as though Lenny were the bad influence. "Gaither is awful," Alma said. "Everyone knows everything, except they get it all twisted."

Delia dropped her eyes and looked away, studying the quad.

Quickly, Alma took the other letter from her pocket and ripped them both once, twice, three times, crumpling the pieces. "I better tear this up. Maybe we'll sneak away, maybe not." She threw the paper into the big trash can by the door and stepped off the porch onto the broad steps. Delia was just ahead of her. They moved into the light, and the sun assaulted them full force.

It was the hottest time of day. The dining hall seemed to have shut its doors forever, and straggles of girls drifted toward the wooded paths to regroup for hiking after lunch. Already, most of them were swallowed by the big-leaved trees; Alma and Delia were last. They dragged their feet, growing later and later as the heat ate minutes away, absorbing time. Noon, and the sun was too bright to see, all alone in the blue sky like a fire.

"Walk faster, will you?" Alma stiffened one arm and put a hand flat against Delia's back. She could feel, in the exact shape of her palm, the weighty heat of a body. That's how it was: slow, the blouse damp to the touch, and a heartbeat measuring each step.

"We're already late," Delia said. "They're lining up by now and filling canteens. Pearlie is saying how we're the very last ones again. We'll say I got sick and you stayed with me. It'll work. I'm going to *be* sick in a minute." Delia stopped then and half turned, shading her eyes. "Look, where the path goes into the trees. Who's there?"

They saw two shapes, black against the sun where the ground rose. The little hill looked black as well, a curve before the trees began. There were two men, motionless, staring at the ground. One of them knelt.

"It's Frank," Delia whispered, her lips so close Alma felt the shape of the words against her ear. "It has to be."

Both girls drifted forward; the heat seemed to push them from behind. Alma felt her face nearly glow with some fire, but the tips of her fingers were cool, as though she'd touched some frozen, smoking cube. Dry ice, like in science class, ages ago. Yes, it was Frank; suddenly they were standing right beside him. He wore white cutoffs and a T-shirt with the sleeves rolled up. His hands were empty and Alma was inches from him. Her eyes followed his long legs to his tennis shoes, unlaced so the worn tongues flopped out. He seemed to have been dusted with phosphorescent color. His legs were downy with golden hair; his arms, dark beige, glistened with the same yellow sheen. He looked hard as stone, he was so lean, yet she saw the vulnerable swell of his biceps and thought there was something tender about him. A fierce bravery overcame her and she reached out and touched him, the gesture completed before she could stop herself. Her fingers grazed his upper arm, moved, testing, and stopped.

Beside her, Delia gasped. She moved as though to protect Alma, pull her back, but she was staring at the ground. The man kneeling there was a stranger, maybe one of the river workmen, shirtless, in sagging brown khaki pants. The ridged soles of his heavy boots were caked with dried bleached mud.

"It's a blacksnake," Frank said. "Can't hurt you."

Alma dropped her hand. He'd thought she was afraid! The distant, limitless trill of a locust rose and fell, a wilderness siren echoing a hidden shade in all this glaring daylight. Dimly, she wondered if she could faint now and not be here, her face was so hot and her hands so cold, and she peered into the depths of the ground at their feet. The ground moved and she saw the snake. The workman, his arms smeared with light swaths of dry yellow dirt, held the flat head of the snake in his fist. He held it carefully, like a weapon he respected, and something about him was like the snake. His black hair was wet and long, plastered to his head in ringlets, and he had a new beard. His face looked pared down, the broad cheekbones flaring under dark, almond-shaped eyes. His ears looked too small, they were so perfect, tight to his head, and he smelled. The odor of his sweat was pungent, faintly sweet, like the spoiled, smeared flowers of some unknown vegetable. Like snakes might smell, Alma thought. Beyond his big arm the black coil of the snake lengthened and swung, sidling along the ground as if the human grasp impeding it were of no consequence.

"Who are you?" Alma asked. But she was staring at the snake, the movement itself, the black, shifting coil that looked so mindful and graceful.

"He works down by the river," said Buddy.

His funny, piping voice rasped, almost as though he wasn't used to talking. He was suddenly there among them, had caught up and pushed among their elbows and got next to them. The top of his fair, bristly head against Alma's arm tickled like a brush.

The man nodded. "That's right, I lay pipe by the river." His voice was low and smooth, a singsong of even tone. His unshaven face was sun-dark, dark with close, tufted beard. In that shadow his mouth looked well defined, his lips pink, like they were lined with the kind of lipstick pencil Alma had seen Mina Campbell use. She'd lean into the mirror by the front door and draw a line around her lips; when she filled in the space, Delia called it *painting up*. Now the stranger pursed his lips and sat up taller, on his knees, and gestured with the head of the snake, turning his fist as though to give the creature full view of Buddy's face. "I know you, boy," he said softly. "You know me?"

Buddy seemed not to hear. "I might not have got a rabbit yet but now I can get me a snake," he said, as though to himself.

The man stood, holding the snake tightly away. The length of the creature swung like animated rope, unfurled, and hung straight.

Frank spoke. "That's the biggest blacksnake I ever saw. Where'd you find it?"

Alma heard his voice with her head and with her chest, as though she vibrated when he talked. She eased closer in the tight knot of them all. Just by releasing her held breath she was bigger, took up more room. She brushed his body with hers, from her shoulder down her naked arm to her hip and thigh. She thought her clothes were just a shadow on her and she was breathing Frank's breath.

"It found me," said the man with the snake. "Come from the river." He looked at Alma, as if it were she who'd asked.

Delia was talking at Buddy, fast and nervous. Alma hadn't heard her until now. "Some snakes can swallow rabbits whole," she was saying, "and the rabbits are alive but they can't breathe in the snake —"

"Not around here, snakes don't swallow any rabbits," Buddy said.

"They do in Africa. I saw a movie at school. Didn't we, Alma?" She pulled at Alma's wrist, tugging hard. "Say so, will you?"

The workman began backing away from them, beckoning them farther into the shade of the trees. "Come here with me now," he said, "look at this." He dragged the snake along, its black length sliding through grass.

"No, we're supposed to be at the bridge for hiking." Delia looked up at Frank, emboldened. "Frank, you too."

He shrugged. "Go on ahead. I'll be there."

Now they were silent in their little knot, the circle broken. The workman moved back near them, around them, his gaze fixed on the snake. The long shape slid through grass with a sound like rope on silk, whispering. The whisper drew them on. Frank moved first, following the workman into the shade. "We'd better get someone," said Delia, but even as she spoke, she was drifting toward the towering oaks. Looking up, Alma thought the big leaves were the size of elephant's ears, flopping and heavy, concealing some intricacy. She felt Buddy pressed up against her, moving tight to her side.

The stranger waited, looking at them. He gestured impatiently. "Hush and come over here," he said. "Watch here." And he held the snake high as they moved in close, secret again in shade, where the air had even a different smell than sunlight. He held the snake higher. They saw then the outline of the eggs within the black hide and the rhythmic, internal working of the snake. It hung limp and straight in the grip of capture; its tail end eased an oblong cylinder onto the grass.

Alma crouched down to see. The egg was perfect. It looked smooth, opalescent. She half expected to hear a sound from inside, a hum or a blurred murmur.

"Don't touch it," came Delia's voice.

Alma let her hand draw near. The shadow of the workman fell over her. In that instant Alma felt him to be different from them, a different being, as though he were an animal or a ghost who only looked like a man. He bent, hovering close, reaching past her face with both arms. The snake he still held was like a long muscle, its flat head hidden in his fist, its tongue flicking out through his fingers. Alma was enveloped in the dense air his body made.

"There," he grunted. Gently, he grasped the egg with two fingers and let it roll back into his hand. He straightened, held it out to Buddy flat-palmed, like sugar to a horse. "You touch it, boy," he said.

Alma had moved a little away, was trying to move; she was never actually sure what happened. Buddy must have touched the egg but it seemed to break apart before he could. There was a barely audible sound and the egg seemed to fly apart with the force of a tiny explosion. Delia screamed and ran and Alma was running too, deeper into the trees, hearing Delia's short, shrill, directive screams. Alma followed, stumbling, wiping frantically at her face with her hands until she realized the wetness was tears.

# ⬕ BUDDY CARMODY: DUST OF THE ROAD

His feet on the dust of the road made smoky pops. The dust was soft, warm, blond; Buddy dragged his heel and made a long dent for the scary man to walk through. He wiggled his toes to make scratchy marks like chicken tracks. He'd wanted to circle up to Lenny's tent, hide the ring in with her special things, things no one else touched. But he couldn't go when someone followed him, watched him. The scary man could follow him easy and Buddy guessed it was a game. He'd come slowly after when Buddy left Camp Shelter to go on home. He kept walking but far behind; Buddy only saw him as the road turned, through the trees, still holding the snake like pendulous treasure. Buddy had seen him all along: he was one of the river workmen but he didn't curse with the others. He drove the pickup for Mrs. T.; he stood outside the kitchen and took the trash away. He was a scary man but he was a stranger, strange among them, not laughing with them, taking time to peer up at the swinging bridge when Buddy sat there, when Buddy carved his crosses one to a board and dangled his legs over the water. Now Buddy felt for the pouch of marbles and pulled the ring free. He held it up to the light and put his finger in and out the circled gold, touched the sharp little stone. He wondered about sitting by the mailbox at home, waiting for the scary man to walk up and giving the ring as trade, but no, he should keep it for Lenny. Maybe the stranger would give the snake, just leave it, what did a man want with a blacksnake? Those girls had run away so fast, maybe the stranger was taking the snake a far ways from the camp, and he'd leave it with Buddy for no trade, nothing. Buddy could keep it in the empty rain barrel, bring it spiders. Bring it the big grasshoppers he found in Mam's tomatoes, bring it the praying mantis bugs he trapped under the broad furry leaves of the squash plants. A mantis looked grown wrong, the way it picked along so slow and stiff, all drawn up to pray.

Buddy knew he'd sinned, stealing. When that old redheaded directress sent him back into the kitchen, Mam was at the big sinks running the water, her broad back turned. He'd scuttled into the pantry and outside, quick, careful not to let the screen slam, that door a flat knife tall as a wall. Walking now, he touched the ring inside his pocket, pressed the stone hard to hurt himself. Stamped

153

his feet to make smoke. Fly up, dust! A snake had hide that was dead and alive and a mouth straight across like a slash. Some snake might swallow a ring and keep it hid from Dad. Dad would take a ring and sell it, that's what, now he had that old car of someone's. Someone who, Mam would say, some rip is who. But Mam would take the ring too, take it back to that old redhead and tan Buddy's backside, make him tell at church what he'd done.

He stopped, turned, looked back along the road. The stranger came on like he walked with steady music, holding the snake before him like a torch that lit a path. But the sun was bright and the day glared with heat. Like frying in a pan, Dad said, no river mudhole can cool a man. In Florida there's white sand beaches, ocean like diamonds, you could squint and see the water flash all the way to where the sky lit up. Then Mam banged plates on the table: so go there, don't need you here drunk all day, mean as a viper from hell and just as useless. He'd give her a shove: hell ain't no hotter than this trash house of yours, I get me some cash and I'm gone. No sense waiting, she'd say, go right on. She wasn't afraid to talk back in the daytime, but she was careful, like she was careful with fire when she burned trash in the steel drum by the stream. Piling up dirt, moving things that might take a spark. She talked at Dad and kept the table between them, didn't turn her back. They yelled, pushing their faces close each other's eyes, and Buddy tried to pay little mind until later, when he was by himself in the woods, on the road. Then their voices floated near him, flaring up out of nowhere. Dad's laugh was like a jay's scold, a robber bird's fat screech: *I'll take that kid with me and teach him what a man likes to do.* Now the words played over and over in the bright daylight. The words were in the bushes and up in the trees, holding still. A man liked to do. Buddy sat flat down in the road and waited for the man with the snake.

Dad might still be drunk from this morning. Or he could rouse up from a drunk sleep if he heard Buddy and be out his head. You could never tell what might set him going. He'd rip off his own shirt and thump it with pillows. Or he'd get to throwing things at the light bulb that hung from the kitchen ceiling on a cord, pelt it with rocks or coins from his pocket. Mam didn't keep a bulb in it anymore but he still got riled and swung the cord all around, yelling words that weren't American. Mam said he learned those in the army in Korea, and he didn't talk foreign unless he was drunk. Then he got afraid. Afraid of what? He'd been in prison in Korea, Mam said, long time ago, but not for doing anything wrong. Just for being a soldier. So you got in jail for being a soldier. No, no, he was captured by his enemy, in a war back then. And the jail was like a cage. He don't like being closed in, so what does he do but throw over a job in the mines and go rob him a gas station, get himself in prison. You mean down in Carolina? Yes, but you know there's no need to talk about it to people. He gets scared locked up. Least he wasn't drinking then. That's what saved him, Mom said.

But Dad wasn't saved. Not like they said about saved at church.

A snake would keep him off Buddy. For sure he'd be afraid of a snake. Dad would take a rabbit and skin it for fun, but he wouldn't touch a snake. And he couldn't shoot it because Mam had taken all the ammunition and hid the boxes in the camp kitchen. She'd washed Buddy's hair under the spigot, saying there's no shells around here now, not even pellets for your BB gun, till I see about Dad, what he's going to do. Buddy heard her talking, her big hands circling his scalp. Her soapy knuckles on Buddy's head rubbed and kneaded behind her voice, getting rid of all the dirt. Dad's been down some hard roads, she said. Got himself into the service out of Proudy-town, barely sixteen. Proudytown, what a name for a work farm. Nothin proud about it. Just kids with no folks who've got into trouble. What kind of trouble? Never mind. I stand here between you and trouble, you know that, Buddy. And her voice would get full. He knew without looking that she was biting her lip in one straight line.

Dad wouldn't get over. Dad was moving one way. And he had hold of Buddy, like Buddy's wrist he held on to, Buddy's arm, carried the print of Dad's strong hand. Dad was moving and drifting and maybe he scared himself. The snake would remind him, it was so long and black and quiet when it moved. Dad might forget to put Buddy in the car then. He'd go away alone, drive off, forget about Mam and Buddy. Buddy sat still on the road and put both hands in the yellow dust. Go down dust, flat like a powder river. A snake could move without moving, crawl out of its own skin, climb and swim. But Dad would get drunk in that car, forget to steer, forget Buddy somewhere in the dark. Here it was bright in the sun. Buddy slammed his hands hard to see some smoke fly up, rise like a fat ghost and spend itself. He would be a ghost if Dad took him away; he wouldn't know how to get home, how to get to school in Gaither and find his bus back to the road and the woods. He wouldn't know to say the right words if someone asked him. If he was far away and Dad had got him confused. He practiced now and said out loud: Gaither, Camp Shelter Road, Mam, Buddy Carmody, and his bus was Number Two. But if he was scared to talk, things got loud in his ears. Like the loud sounds in the trees. They were sounds Mam made at night when Dad was fighting on top of her, grunting and swearing, trying to climb in. Buddy shut his eyes tight and panted like he did then in the dark, shutting out their sounds; he panted and felt for the ring in his pocket, the ring and the bag of marbles and his pointy rock. The marbles he emptied out across the road. They turned their bright ripples over and over and the colors shooting through them rolled into the ditch; Buddy kicked the bag away from himself. Today he'd taken the ring instead of carving a cross on the bridge — it was no use now, because the stranger with the snake was not at the river anymore with the other workmen. He was here, just out of sight. But who was a devil? Who was a ghost? The stranger walked and nothing scared him. The crosses might have kept him away but the ring had drawn him close. He knew Buddy had the ring, that's what. He might be the Lord's own angel, come for vengeance, like Mam said angels did. But it wasn't the ring he wanted, because he could come and take it. He wanted to follow Buddy.

Buddy wanted the stranger to follow closer.

He got up and kept walking. He looked back and saw the stranger come up. The sounds in the trees were louder now, long-drawn breathing, sighing, not Mam's sounds but sounds that sat behind heat and light. Buddy had heard them before, roaring like water or wind through the trees' heavy limbs. The trees held still in the heat but what was about to happen roared behind the stillness. He looked back and the stranger was there, just at the rise of the road, coming on slowly and letting Buddy see. He nodded at Buddy to go on, like he knew where they were going. The snake was curled up small in the crook of his one arm.

Now the house was in sight, nestled in brush to one side of the curve. The red car was still there, parked askew. The high board front of the porch was a storage for hoes and rakes and junk, and Dad would be sitting up above, looking over the road, waiting for something. Or asleep on the porch, waiting. Drinking on the porch, if there was something to drink. But Buddy couldn't see him. He stepped to the side, behind the brambly chokeweed, and looked back to see the stranger was waiting too. Waiting for Buddy to go on. The light was different back there, like the trees were a cooler, lighter green, and the dust of the road looked gold and thick as fur, like someone could lie down in it, cover up. The stranger stood carefully, in the open, peering into a hotter light. Buddy was close enough to see his eyes move side to side, taking in the picture; he looked like a man in an army comic, tawny and dusty, his bare chest the color of the dust. He put his finger to his lips, nodded at Buddy, pointed forward with the same finger.

Buddy looked and saw Dad, standing in the road, come back from behind the car. He looked to be blind drunk, leaning up against the driver's door. He was trying to get in the door and then he fell down and was feeling above the tire. Buddy heard the hot roar of the trees above them all and he walked into the sound. He could feel the stranger behind him, standing and watching. So the stranger knew who Dad was, knew enough to wait. And he knew more: he stood right out in the open, like he knew Dad didn't see past his nose if he was drunk. If the stranger was an angel he would bind Dad up: *tongues of heavenly flame* like they talked about in services; angels in the pictures couldn't burn, their feet were on fire but they walked in a gold light and didn't feel any hurt. If he would make Dad leave in the car. The car could be the flame.

Dad started talking when he saw Buddy. He was sitting in the road by the tire and at first he didn't seem to know who Buddy was. The sound the trees made stopped; the warning was over and Buddy was standing in the center of the picture. Buddy watched Dad: the gray eyes, hooded in his gaunt face, looked flat and pounded. Then his wandering gaze snagged on Buddy, passed over Buddy, came back. Suddenly his pupils seemed to go small and dark and he held still. Like a cat gets still.

"Gimme the key," he said. "Empty your pockets."

"I got no key." Buddy moved back a step, looked over his shoulder. The stranger was gone. Not there.

"Turn your face back here. You got the key. You took it off me earlier when you had me up there on the porch."

"You mean the key to the car?"

"Key to the car, key to the car," Dad mimicked in a high sneer. He was up on his haunches now. "You damn girl. I'll get that key and take you for a ride."

"I never saw no key."

"You want yourself a good long ride. You gonna get one."

Buddy moved to run, started to yell, but his breath went out of him when Dad sprung, tackling Buddy's feet and bringing him down so hard he felt himself bounce. Dad's hands came up and got him by the pants and upended him. He pulled Buddy into the air by the cloth of his shorts and shook him in a fury. "You got the damn key," he screamed, his voice breaking. He rammed his hands into Buddy's pants and for a terrifying instant there was a fire that came on bright and hot, everything frozen in the heat, but then his hands were out again, ripping at Buddy's pockets. Dad was crouching over him on all fours and he had the pointed rock and he had the ring. He flung the rock down and turned the ring side to side, rubbing at it, smelling and tasting it. "What's this? Jesus. Where'd you get this?"

Buddy was trying to breathe and Dad had him by the back of the neck, his long fingers squeezing, nearly meeting in front where there was a small space to get air. Dad had pulled him up to sit forward, and Dad's shape was black, and behind Dad's black head a bright sun moved back and forth like a ball. Sparkles came off the ball. "Camp," Buddy whispered. "In her room."

"What room?" He was scrambling his hand around, feeling Buddy's pockets for more.

"Mrs. Thompson —" Buddy started to say.

"She got more? Answer me. She got more?"

"Just a couple more, in a box."

Dad's hand was pinching shut on Buddy's throat and the spot where the air came through got ragged and tiny. Everything got darker. There was a sort of tunnel Buddy could still see into and Dad's face was in the tunnel. A hand came from behind Dad. The

158

hand had Dad by the hair and jerked him up so the tunnel split apart and Buddy fell backwards into the dust of the road.

The trees that arched over the house were just an outline of themselves, silvery, then green, and the stranger was holding Dad by the hair, lifting Dad half off his haunches like a dog with his front paws floppy. Dad had the ring in one hand still and his eyes were rolled up, trying to see what had him. The stranger had a low voice, a growl Buddy could hear inside, like the stranger talked and Buddy thought the words. "Don't hurt the boy," the stranger said. "You hurt the boy again, no matter what is supposed to happen, I'll kill you."

Dad held the ring up, held it higher.

But the stranger just gave him a shake, pulled him up a few more inches. "I'll break your fuckin neck. I could do it now." The voice was quiet and low, a whispered monotone.

Dad went still.

"I know what you do," the voice said. "I see it all."

And he dropped Dad.

For an instant Dad stayed crouched, motionless. He was looking at Buddy but he didn't see Buddy. It was like he was looking into the picture he'd made Buddy see, when he choked Buddy and all the colors bled away. He listened, frozen, then he scrambled for the handle of the car door and got the door open a space and slid into the car. He sat hunched down, looking out the open window, like he'd hid himself.

The stranger nodded at Buddy to get up, get up off the ground, and Buddy did. He stood still and watched. He'd never seen Dad scared of anything real, anything he wasn't just seeing in his head.

Dad looked hard out the window, peering down the road. He kept darting his eyes at the stranger, like it wouldn't do to look directly at him. "I know you ain't really here, you devil." He still held the ring in one hand, and now he put it in his shirt pocket. "I seen you before here, in the dark." He was feeling frantically along the dash, over the seat, for the key. He was trying to drive away, that was what.

Buddy stepped hopefully toward the car. He saw the key in the ignition, with a thin little chain swinging from it. The little chain swung because Dad was gripping the steering wheel in both long hands, jerking on it like he could get the car to go by banging himself against it. "Dad," Buddy said, "the key. Right there."

"You ain't here," Dad said, "you ain't talking." He was looking at the stranger and he felt for the key. He turned the key and floored the gas, and the car rocked and lurched. The brake was on but Dad kept pumping the gas, his face in a clinched smile. "You can't find me, devil. You ain't even alive."

"Let off the brake," Buddy said. Then he wondered if Dad was right, if the stranger was real. But other people had seen him, Mrs. T., and the other men by the river, they worked beside him. And the girls had seen him earlier, and Frank had talked to him, and he had the snake, and eggs had come out of the snake onto the grass. He had the snake now, still coiled up in his one arm. Tight circled up, like it slept. Buddy wanted to go back and look, find more eggs. Touch the cool leaves. But now he felt a real arm, hard and warm, circle his chest and pull him sharply back. The car shot forward, squealing, veered to the opposite side of the road, and disappeared over the bank, down the slope of the shallow ravine. Immediately, there was a thud and a squawk of scraped metal.

The car had left a burning smell. But there was no smoke and the road was quiet, like nothing had happened. Buddy saw streaks in the air, long subtle falls of light, like the air was rearranging itself where Dad had been. The stranger stepped back away from Buddy and went to the edge of the road and looked down. He motioned for Buddy to stay. The snake he let go, the snake he held by its small head, and the length of it uncoiled and hung down, heavy, like a black rope. The stranger walked down the bank holding it until Buddy couldn't see him anymore. Buddy heard him walking a few steps in the long tangle of bushes and briars, then he heard nothing.

The engine was still running; Carmody had managed to roll down
a sharp descent of scrub and hit the only two pines big enough to
stop the car. Just here was a sort of clearing, bigger trees shading the
ground so dense, nothing of much size had grown up. If Carmody
weren't such a drunk fool he might have kept going a ways, steered
around trees and driven himself through the woods a half mile, right
into Mud River. Carmody should have done that, with the Devil
bright inside him, gleaming off his hands and burning. But he sat
slumped over the steering wheel, passed out. Parson reached in and
turned off the ignition. The throbbing car fell silent. But there were
sounds in the woods, the crackle and slide of evil slunk from its
host. How evil moved like sun through trees, in patches, dappled
and patterned. Parson heard an airy giggling behind him, here and
gone, like patchy reception of a child's laughter. Like Carmody's kid
might laugh, wasn't laughing, standing back at the road and listening. The kid should stay there; Parson glanced up but he thought
the boy wouldn't come down. Too scared. The giggling continued,
tinkling like bells; Parson tilted his head and heard the sound move
off to the left. He felt the snake shift in his grasp and he stepped
closer to the car. There. The bullet head probed along the metal rim
of the open window; the snake began to glide forward. Parson slapped
Carmody, once, twice, but he didn't stir. He must have knocked
himself good against the wheel, but there were no marks on him,
no cuts, and the windshield of the car was intact, not even a crack
in the glass. Wake up, you evil fool. Then the laughter came again.
A kid's laugh still, but high-pitched, strung out. It was a joke,
Carmody asleep like a baby, like any drunk who had run his car
down a hollow.

"Hey, mister," came a voice. "Mister?"

The words floated down, unanswered.

Parson shoved Carmody's inert body out of its slouch. Now
Carmody lay back in the seat, one arm against the door. Parson
watched as the snake slid along the edge of the open car window
and began to climb Carmody's shoulder. It swung itself in a drooped
coil onto Carmody's slack leg. The head moved in its slow S, testing,
along the back of the seat.

"Mister," the voice said again, "you down there?"

"I'm here," Parson yelled up.

"Can I come down there now?"

Parson looked up along the bank, nearly blinded by a slant of light. "What's your name, boy?"

A pause. "My name's Buddy."

"Buddy, you stay where you are. And be still, real still."

Parson had to listen. There, the laughter, and a sound like a rush of wings. He felt in his pocket for his knife. Blade of a knife, no handle. Just a razored edge, blunted round with a strip of corrugated cardboard he'd fastened tight with a rubber band. The blade was sharp, sharp enough to gut fish: he'd thinned it both sides with a lump of whetstone. The blade had been part of a rusted army knife he'd found at the dump, the one piece untouched by rust, and he'd freed it from its smashed red carapace, hard, with a rock. He could do Carmody now, here, and the kid would be all right. It would all be all right, and Parson could leave.

But Carmody only slept, his mouth hanging open. The snake had looped itself around his neck twice; now it probed the air with its darting tongue. Parson unwrapped the blade and drew it delicately across the flesh of his thumb. Blood sprang up. Quickly, he marked a cross on Carmody's forehead, and another on the inside of the windshield.

It wasn't enough. Carmody was empty. Nothing to kill in him now, just a sleeper, drunk and stupid. But he would wake up. The Devil would feel his feeble scrambling and rush back inside him, fast and silent as a blast from a ray gun. That hot light would curl up in Carmody's guts, peer out through the holes in his head. No, there had to be more, a sign Carmody would recognize and fear. A sign to prove Parson had seen him and touched him, pulled him off the boy. Parson held the blade up, angled toward the sun. He could direct a slice of reflective light across the leaves, across Carmody's sallow face.

Slice of light. He would have to slice the snake. Parson leaned forward. The laughter came again, so quiet, like a whisper inside his own head. Do it, then. Carmody would wake up and feel a weight on his chest, have to pull it off. Know Parson was here, waiting for a time the Devil was home, swollen up big and bright in Carmody's lanky frame, in Carmody's pale eyes. Carmody would come to and fling the snake off himself, shaking and cursing. The snake heavy and bloody on his shirt, no drunken dream. Parson reached out with the blade. He wanted the snake to move, slide away fast. But the snake was still.

A cascade of pebbles. The kid was coming down the bank.

Do it quickly then. And when he pulled his hand away the woods were quiet, and he heard the boy close behind him.

"You killed that snake," Buddy said. "Why'd you have to do that?"

Parson made his voice quiet and smooth. "'Whoso breaketh a hedge, a serpent shall bite him.' Ever heard that, boy? You know your Bible?"

"I know some." His big eyes looked open too wide, like he'd seen a lot and still thought he could climb over it. He looked up at the trail the car had made rolling down from the road. There weren't any hedges, just crushed blackberry and chokeweed. "Is Dad snake-bit?" he asked.

"He's passed out," Parson said. "He'll come to in a while."

"You mean he ain't dead?"

"He's full of poison."

"Blacksnakes ain't poison. Anyone knows that."

Parson smiled. "Wasn't this snake that bit him. He's been poisoned a long, long time."

The boy seemed to consider this.

"I think you know it," Parson said.

The boy only glanced across Parson's face, looked away. "I was going to fix up that snake some shade in the rain barrel," he said, "with branches in there, and a lot of grass and leaves —"

"You ever played a harmonica?" Parson asked.

"Yeah, I got one. Mam gave me one."

"Ever play it?"

"I play it some."

"You know how you hold it and blow the music through it. How you blow, that's how the music sounds. Harmonica is something to use, that's what it's for." Parson wiped the blade off carefully on his pants, held it down in front of the boy, and saw his own face reflected on the surface.

The boy moved closer to look. Not so scared as he seemed. Parson watched him lean in so his head nearly touched Carmody's laden chest.

"The Lord uses what he needs to make a mark," Parson said, "leave a sign."

The snake's head was level with the boy's face and he peered at the lens of its cold, still eye. In its black depths lurked a diamond of glitter. The diamond seemed to move, as though a shine of eyelid flicked across sideways, fast as an instant. The boy stepped back, but reached to touch the flat plane between the ridges of the eyes. Parson knew the feel of the snake's head was hard and smooth, like the dome of a pearl.

"Get away now, boy," he said. "You get on back to the camp. Stay with your mother."

The kid fixed Parson with his blue gaze. "Can you get me that ring Dad took off me?" His voice was a fast whisper. "I got to have that ring back. It's in his shirt pocket."

Parson touched the back of the boy's head. Smooth, the hair shaved so short it felt like peach fuzz. "You don't want any ring. You don't need any ring." He nodded up the bank, then bent down and said, quietly, "Get on back up the way you came, and get to the camp."

The kid looked at the ground, then turned and scrambled up through the brush. He was lost in leaves even before the sound of him stopped.

Parson began walking toward the river. He didn't look back. The car sat like a bent toy in the quiet, but everything else would move forward now. They would all line up, like a sum to be figured, or a design on a flag. Like the girls raised the flag in the morning and took it down at night, and walked around the quad on white gravel paths that cut straight across like bright slashes. Flagpole in the center. How the heavy flag hung down in the heat, limp and useless. Parson had seen it there, a bright rag for children to salute. Jails have flags, and prisons, courthouses, orphanages. Yes, even that far back, there was a flag.

Parson walked, wrapping the blade again in its cardboard sheath, crossing the rubber band around it three times. At the dump there was no flag, no tall pole with a banner. There was a place nobody claimed, a squat of spoiled land in a clearing that looked to have been seared off. It was an open space in the trees that pulled at Parson and spooked him. The clearing was octagonal and dark. Tree stumps stood up in burnt configuration, silent amongst the shapes of discarded furniture, torn motorcycles, piles of tires. The stumps were jagged and splintered, weathered a few years yet blackened where ash had washed away. Tumbled with them was a spread of damaged goods, and Parson took from that damaged bounty this thing and that thing. He drew sustenance, like a creature at a water hole. Like that exposed creature, he took and he listened, alert, ready to bolt. The sky looked big above the clearing, and the road emptied into it like there was nowhere else to go. He'd found the blade by the coils of a broken box spring: piece of a knife the size of his palm, just right for his hand. He'd bent to retrieve the metal shard and there was a silence as he knelt down, a kind of sanctuary.

Now he put the knife back into the pocket of his baggy pants. The pants were loose; he didn't need to eat much, only the coffee they gave him at the site and the evening meal he took at the roadhouse the men had shown him, where traffic hummed on the two-lane road, not far from the dirt road to the camp. The place smelled of hamburger fried with onions and the food was the same as food he'd eaten everywhere: eggs flattened to a yellow sheen, grits with pooled butter. He'd always thought to see Carmody walk in there; Carmody never had. Other people came and went past the booths, and the electric fans made a humming that was nearly sleepy. Parson wanted to go to the roadhouse, sit thoughtless and still in the familiar sounds and smells, but he would go back to Turtle Hole and wait.

None of the other workmen knew about the shack. The boy wouldn't tell anyone about Carmody, about anything Carmody did. The girls wouldn't want to explain to anyone about the snake, and Frank had laughed it off. Carmody would come to and blunder toward Parson in his own time, in his red panic and his rage. Parson would go to the shack but he knew Lenny wouldn't be there. She got farther and farther away from him. She moved higher and higher.

# ✖ LENNY:
## THE VOICE THAT DOESN'T TALK

She lay across his big chest, holding on to the narrow straps of his white undershirt; his eyes were closed and she disappeared because he couldn't see her. His body moved them to and fro like a boat and their laughter seemed far away, secret and careful, sounds through a gauzy wall. She kept her eyes closed, and behind her lids his white undershirt came loose and rippled in space, all alone like a shaken flag. The shirt grew smaller and disappeared in a black pool as she rolled to one side and the other of his long form, and the room cracked open. He was gone and she saw herself lying still, a white shape on the black ground; she saw the whole of the forest as a massive shadow darkly green around her, and the oval of Turtle Hole was the black pool she knew could tilt and move through trees. She knows someone else was here with her, someone who seemed a dream but was not; now he is lost to her as well and moves away from her, leaving her. She remembers his broad, naked back, the moist feel of his skin, his arms full of vines. Nothing to hold but his shoulders, his hands; he walks away and she hears his footsteps as though she were in his head. But the pictures he seems to have left in her are older and rush through her, darting and flashing: the two windows of her parents' bedroom, rectangles blocking the sun, and light falling in long bars from under the blinds. Her father and mother asleep on either side of her. Light plays across the foot of the bed; sparkles swim in the lit air as though swirled by a wind no one can feel. But when Wes ran under the clothesline he was the wind and she held on in the glaring sun, legs clasped tight around his neck, holding her arms high to touch the dangling sleeves of shirts and blouses. They ran into the field and there was no fence yet and the house looked bald and small with no bushes around it, Audrey laughing, calling them back, and Lenny tries to open her eyes. *Open, shut them, open, shut them. Give a little clap!* Her mother played that game, covering her face with her hands. Sleeves of the shirts hung upside down and Audrey let Lenny hold the pins she kept in a special apron, a heavy apron with big pockets that sagged, and the pins with hinges could snap your fingers. *Open, shut them, once again. Put them in your lap.* In the big bed she keeps

166

her eyes closed but afterward she can reach the string on the window blind by its little ring and pull it all the way down. The blind reaches to the floor and Lenny sits hidden between the blind and the wall, a narrow white space like the inside of an envelope. Cross-legged on the floor of the room, her chin level with the windowsill, she can see her mother far down in the yard, near the field. Audrey hangs clothes on the line, appearing and disappearing between the shapes. Lenny hears the shower go on in the bathroom and she calls to her mother in a voice that doesn't talk, but her mother never hears. Far away, Audrey pins up the damp, heavy sheets, white sheets that are vast and square. The sheets are white and the bed is white and the walls and the ceiling are white. Rumpled pillows along the tall headboard. Lenny's knees drawn up as the bed darkens, enfolding and layered. Low sound, a growl or murmur that stays near her face yet moves, rolling, against the side of her hip, the one part of her broad enough. Muffled and careful. Then a white cloud of canopy over the bed: Cap's room in Gaither. Lenny awake, and Cap's white chiffon curtains tied back with ribbons. Sounds Cap made in her sleep. Lenny hears Cap's little moans and feels a thrill of fear. Don't look. Go to the window, safe in the white envelope. The sound like a song until it's over and stops and leaves an emptiness. Like when her mother danced with her and the music on the hi-fi ended. Phonograph needle knocking against silence and Audrey whirling around in her full skirt, swinging Lenny faster. Dizzy, the sideways ceiling, white and high. She wakes up at night and hears the raccoons shriek near the field, near the garbage cans Wes has chained together to keep them from being toppled. She sees him bending over in sunlight, pulling chain through the handles of the metal lids; she can't see his face, only the khaki side of his leg, his long clothed thigh. His big hands with their squared, clean nails, moving her up beside him in the white bed. Milky Way bars from the freezer. The frothy chocolate in her mouth got warm and she heard the shower go on and she stood by the window and her mind was white. *Open. Shut them.* How her mother stood against the sky, straddled tall as a bridge between the flapping clothes when Lenny helped with laundry and looked up, peering through her fingers. *Right up to your chin.* His one hand holding her, a warm tight seat, and the white cotton of his shirt on her face. She moves, gliding on the hide of a long animal, and someone still kneels with his face on her belly, helps her stand amongst black flowers.

She opens her eyes and the colors are washed out, fading in slowly: she sees the shack on the rise behind her, and the path through the trees to Turtle Hole. Above her the sky is an amazing blue. She stands up inside it, puts her hands over her ears to stop the sound she hears, the sound that fades: a white cloth twisting in black space is sucked inward, swallowed and gone.

Lenny begins to walk toward camp. She sees her feet negotiate brushy ground and rocks; she takes the fastest route, through thick trees, up over the ridge that will bring her out at the periphery of the quad, lowest point of the path to Highest. She moves quickly, grasping and climbing, her arms around her face when she moves under the drooping limbs of long-needled pines. She doesn't look at the pictures in her head. If she looks, the images will disappear again. She lets them shuffle, like cards, waiting for the one at the bottom of the pile. She looks for Alma and can't find her. Alma was always there, but Alma's gone.

The house empty. No one home. Or someone on a white bed, in the bright, white, middle of the day. Home sick from school, reading picture books, tick-tack-toe on a board with a magic lift-the-flap. No, that was later, not alone, Audrey in the kitchen making soup, smell of tomatoes simmering. Alma in her own room when they both had chickenpox, and Lenny gets her parents' bed because her fever is higher: the big bed feels cooler and she pleads to sleep there. Alma, playing paper dolls, not sleeping at all, yelling for Kool-Aid, how things seal off for a while behind the pair of them, the two girls. They smell warmly of illness, the oil of the bumpy rash that splatters them back and front, between their fingers and legs, inside their ears and mouths. *You're covered, covered,* Audrey marvels, but in the last days of the quarantine they build tunnels in the sheets with pillows, hide under the skirt of the bed in dust and forgotten shoes, listen to her calling, calling them. Dolls and plastic horses, appaloosas, palominos, Percherons, Alma sets them up on towers of books behind the couch. *You girls get this cleaned up,* Audrey says, *don't ignore me just because you've survived.* Summers they don't clean up anything, ever, they're in the field being horses they call Fury and Patches, horses that walk on their hind legs like men and drum their forefeet in the hairy milkweed. Alma throws her shirt down in the weeds but Lenny stays covered in the approaching dusk: Wes is outside while their mother washes the supper dishes. Lenny stands deep in the overgrown field; she sees him through hollow stalks, brush or feed corn in tall rows, sitting at the picnic table and smoking, watching them. *Run!* she tells Alma, *run away,* and she drives Alma farther into the field, not letting her stop till they've run clear to the creek, and the lightning bugs flash on and off like constellations.

Later, he was never at home till nearly dark. Audrey will slap them but he never touches them; supposedly he's afraid of his temper, *all up to me,* she complains, *like everything,* and he no longer works with his hands, he's a salesman and their mother irons his shirts, spraying the wrinkles with water from a squeeze bottle. In a dream Lenny has, he holds out his hands for inspection, to show he hasn't taken anything; the hands show open palms against a white field that gets so bright the hands are blotted out.

He doesn't wear khakis anymore, he doesn't drive a truck or work a night shift, he doesn't come home any longer in the middle of the day.

Lenny keeps walking, stops and bends down to tie the lace of her shoe. Cap's sneakers are too big and she pulls the laces tighter, she hasn't found her shoes, she will have to wear these, get used to them. It doesn't matter. She wants to see Alma, talk to her about any stupid thing. Stand beside her and look down along the straight part in her brown hair, her high brow with its cat scratch of a frown. *My beauty and my beast,* Audrey would joke, her joke being that Alma was the beauty, curled up with her books and her serious glower, always seeming to watch her feet when she walked, and Lenny the beast in her long body and mane of hair. After all, pretty is as pretty does. *What did I ever do to you? Why don't you talk to me?* The phrases are Audrey's, plaintive and insistent, as though she's repeated them for years. Lenny feels herself respond with an old silence, but she hears, in the trapped quiet, another answer which seems to have been there all along: *You can't hear me. You could never hear me.* Startled, she looks around her at sumac and rhododendron, the waxy green leaves that flop and arc. With almost no awareness of effort, she has gained the steepest part of the trail to Highest. Below her the greenish river meanders. It will be dusk soon. How bright the water looks here at night, shimmering and black, and the shadows seem broad and safe. But at home the dark in her room is a mash of shapes, fuzzy and diffuse. Cars turn the curve on the road that runs beside the house and cast their headlights across her wall, shadow play, pale yellow like a searchlight, falling across the empty wall and disappearing, disappearing. Don't look, go to the window instead. She wants to talk to Alma about anything, even Delia, or Delia's baby brother or Delia's crazy aunt in the beauty parlor. Or funerals, but only when Delia's not around, and their mother can't hear. Alma still has to think about all of it, like she borrows it from Delia, like it was *her* father who drove off the bridge. Lenny stands still on the trail and closes her eyes, sees Wes drive across bridges, silver structures with crisscrossed steel beams like Mud River Bridge but bigger, higher, wider, and he drives so smooth and fast, the familiar Chevrolet doesn't even touch pavement. Her point of view shifts and turns magically, gliding closer: she sees Wes talking, his lips moving, and she wants to make out what he's saying so intently, all alone in the car.

When she hears real voices, a confused talking and laughing far below her, she holds to a branch and leans over the ravine to look. The Juniors are crossing Mud River on the swinging bridge. Frank stands in water hip deep, holding the bridge steady as the girls step onto it. Lenny sees the top of his head, and a view of the bridge halfway across. She looks for Alma and Delia, but the girls are anonymous in their similar uniforms.

The girls all wear green but men doing construction wear khaki, men on crews. The man she saw at the shack must be one of the workmen, but his clothes were a disguise. The way her father was in disguise in his dark slacks and open-necked shirts, his sportcoats he wore to Henry Briarley's office and other offices, driving in his car, working away from home.

She sits down. Everything is solid. The picture in her mind is just the shape of that window in her parents' room; the image comes clear. She sees her mother again so many years ago, down by the clothesline, calls out for her, keeps calling through the glass. And when Audrey finally turns, Lenny sees her form in the loose dress, how she leans back to balance her bulk and carries the empty clothes basket to the side, her round and swollen front so big there is no room.

## ❧ ALMA: DRAGON SPOONS

The swinging bridge was old. There were a few blond boards where men had repaired winter damage; Alma tried to imagine Mud River in winter storms. The wind blew at night and snow thrummed against the walls at home, drifted on sudden wind. When snow fell from the eaves it landed with the *thunk* of some long body falling and lying still. That cold seemed to have happened in another world: the river was low and lazy now, like something in a bowl, colored the beige of coffee with milk. By day it looked to be the temperature of old bath water, mute, barely moving, but it was full of snakes and turtles and gluey mud. How could there be rapids in the spring, ice melting and the banks ripped by a rage of water so high it tore the bridge? All that and no one here to see it — the camp empty, the cabins shut tight like closets and the tent sites just rows of wood platforms layered with leaves, snow, rain. They'd all been some-where else then. Frank was from Bellington, a town whose Main Street was only slightly longer than Gaither's. The private college there was Methodist, not Presbyterian, and the football team played in the Triple-A division, and the high school was new. The county was bigger and had money, her dad said, if anyone in this state did. Wes had grown up in Bellington; there were two or three big coal companies, and a couple of factories. But Shelter County was mostly mountains and forest preserve. Wes said all the state cared about were those trees, like people were only camping out and didn't need jobs anyway. When Audrey complained about Henry Briarley, Wes retorted that Gaither would shut down if it weren't for Consol Coal, and Bellington did seem richer and busier: cars always bumper-to-bumper down Main Street on Saturdays, and a Strawberry Festival in the summer, when bands came from all over the state to march in the parade. There were three drive-in restaurants on the two-lane route that led into town. Frank was old enough to have a learner's permit; Alma supposed he went on dates, school dances with the Bellington kids, but her mind's eye faltered at imagining his hands on someone, ceiling decorations above his head in dim light while music played on an intercom. He must have taken driver ed. last year, all boys did. Probably he'd lounged in the dark watching movies of wrecks while Alma sat beside Delia in Gaither, twenty miles away. Math class, texts with printed sums, notebooks, homework pages with ragged edges torn free of the binder. The clock ticked as they recited answers, one by one, and everything had been different then — Nickel Campbell worked for Henry Briarley and went to Winfield on business every Saturday, and Alma and Delia went to Girl Guides after school at the Baptist church on Wednesdays. They'd taken home pamphlets from Camp Shelter and their fathers had written out deposit checks.

"Alma." Delia's whisper came from behind, as though to remind Alma that past was past. "Think Frank will remember us?"

"What, that we're the ones who ran away from a snake? No, we look like everyone else. He won't notice us."

Alma watched him on the opposite bank. He was pulling on his waders so he could walk into Mud River and hold the bridge, mostly so the timid girls wouldn't be too scared to cross. The bridge was a concoction of wood boards knotted together with rope and tied to steel cables, two on the bottom to support the bridge and two that ran above as handholds. The counselors had strung rope sides along the cables in a continuous pattern of X's. There was the illusion of safety, but no one really knew if the rope would support the fall of some particularly clumsy Girl Guide. The sets of cables wobbled and swung, not necessarily in tandem.

"Everyone's late because Frank's late," Delia whispered.

"But we were late too, and no one noticed, thanks to him. Right?"

Alma watched Frank wading into the water to hold the bottom cables. Supposedly he kept the bridge from swinging so wildly, his weight a ballast as the girls walked cautiously across.

But the long line of girls jostled and hung back. At least two Junior groups were milling together, trying to cross the bridge and then take separate trails to Highest. Despite the counselors' urgings, the scene was one of lackadaisical confusion. A few girls bawled like cattle, which prompted snickers and jeers from the rest. They were a sort of herd, Alma thought, waiting in single file. They had to walk across five at a time, in carefully spaced intervals.

The line was moving. They began to advance on the woods like a platoon avoiding land mines. Alma and Delia exchanged glances. Acutely embarrassed, Alma began walking, her eyes on the planks beneath her feet. She could feel Delia's footfalls behind her, exactly in step. Midway the river was too deep for Frank to stand; he stood thigh deep on the other side. Alma kept walking until he was directly visible through the rope sides of the bridge; she saw him foreshortened, hanging as though crucified, his form abbreviated by the muddy water. The river was not so slow and somnolent as it seemed: the water eddied around him, lapping at his legs, licking at what disturbed it. Distracted, Alma glanced at his face and found he was looking up at her. His eyes met hers and he winked. Immediately, she looked away. She felt her face burning and hoped Delia wouldn't look at him, knew she wouldn't; Delia hated the river and the bridge and only braved the crossing because she liked hiking. Often the girls were allowed to spread out and meet at a preassigned landmark, and Alma and Delia would find themselves nearly alone in the quiet of the trails. Alma reached the other side and stepped onto land. What had he meant? Winking to flirt was sleazy but she realized, humiliated, that she wasn't even a girl in his eyes. He'd winked as though he were the grownup and she the kid, the stupid kid, the nervous kid afraid of a snake egg. But if he were so grown up, why hadn't he run after Delia, and held on to her and gotten her to stop screaming. McAdams would have. He wasn't a counselor, more like a junior custodian. Maybe he wasn't allowed to talk to the girls; still, no one would have known. He wasn't grown up and he didn't know anything about them, and he didn't care. Suddenly Alma hated him for being so ordinary. She couldn't believe Delia was afraid of a snake egg, or even of snakes. Really, she was afraid of something else getting broken, and Alma was afraid as well.

Alma glanced back and saw Delia step off the bridge. She was completely calm now but nearly stumbled with fatigue, as though the day's work were done. It was hard work, screaming. Alma had never done it, but when she'd caught up to Delia in the woods and held on to her, the screams felt like blasts coming out of her, a ripping apart Delia had to aim toward the outside. Once Audrey had made sounds and not been able to stop, but her sounds were more like howls than screams, and they'd never ended, really. It was like those sounds had just gotten soft and small and seeped inside her. Delia's screams had finished, like a siren. She took deep breaths, like she'd finished an exercise, and the girls had even begun to laugh.

"Alma," Delia said now, and nodded off to the left of the trail.

Alma followed her. They climbed steeply sideways awhile, staying over the river, and came to a rocky enclave. The rocks made a kind of leaning outpost on the high bank. If the girls knelt down they could see most of the bridge and scan downriver nearly to the bend. The big boulders curved away from one another like spoons and formed a kind of hard nest.

"We'll stay here," Delia said. "It's like a fort." Then it seemed to occur to her to be polite, and she added, "You don't mind, do you?"

"You don't want to keep going? The Seniors are up there. We could find out what's supposed to happen at Turtle Hole."

Delia shrugged. "Tonight we'll go there and find out." She smiled sleepily, slid down on her haunches, and leaned back on the rocks. "We don't have to walk any further. I'm your excuse. They all know I need my rest."

Alma sat close beside her. The rocks were mossy near the ground, and cool; Alma felt for pebbles and chips and found a small rock nearly as round as a ball. She balanced the rock on her palm and looked at Delia. "Table tennis?"

Delia yawned, and followed Alma's gaze. The crowd of Juniors had nearly finished crossing the bridge, and Frank was almost directly below. "I think you could," said Delia.

Alma stood. "Aim," she said.

"Fire," finished Delia.

Alma did. There was an instantaneous lag time, and Frank spun a little to the left, craning his neck to look up. The rock seemed to have grazed his shoulder.

"Is he annoyed?"

"Confused," Alma said, "and it must have smarted." She let herself slide down close to Delia.

"Let's hope so." Delia closed her eyes.

Safely wedged in the rocks, they waited as the troop of girls passed, climbing the trail a little below them. Soon the trees obscured all the patches of colors, and voices trailed back like echoes. Then the woods were silent. Alma could see the river below, and pipe stacked down along the opposite bank, and the workmen moving about in their khaki clothes.

"Do you see him?" asked Delia.

"No, I don't think he's there. Weren't there five of them?" Alma sat without moving, as though witnessing a ceremony, her eyes trained on the repetitive movements of the workmen. They dug with large picks and shovels, throwing the dirt off onto a growing pile of soil. Soon they began to move one of the big pipes into place, girding it with chain and tugging, two men to each end.

"Now there are only four," Delia said. She must have opened her eyes and looked.

"I do remember that movie you were talking about," Alma said, "the one we saw in school." She spoke in a near whisper. It seemed to her that Delia was shivering. Their bodies were pressed together by the formation of the rocks.

"The one in the auditorium," Delia answered.

A few times a year, the school saw a movie in assembly, the whole student body present in folding chairs arranged in rows. Topics of the films were sometimes inexplicable. A movie about deserts, for instance, or about World War I. Occasionally an old print of *Treasure Island*, or *Tom Sawyer*.

"It was about rain forests, jungle animals." Alma didn't look at Delia but talked softly, wanting to hypnotize her into seeing the exact image Alma couldn't forget. "There was a snake that flew, or glided, from one tree to another. It made its body flat and whipped itself in coils to catch the air. Do you remember? It flew like a dragon — or the native people called them dragons."

"I don't know." Delia sighed.

"People made up stories, and they carved pipes and bowls and spoons, all with dragon's heads."

"I remember the jungle trees, all mossy and grown over with creepers, like they couldn't breathe," Delia said. "Those movies. I only remember that one because it was the day I came back to school."

Alma rested her arms on her knees and cradled her head, looking down at earth through the tunnel of her own body. Yes, that was the first day after the week of the funeral. Beside Delia at assembly, Alma had kept her eyes on the screen, willed herself into the forms of the animals. The snake was most deathly and most alive, throwing itself into air and cracking like a whip. It was dangerous and free, like Audrey had been that day in the yard. After school, in March. Audrey had stood by the fence down behind the house and looked out at the field. She was weeping, sobbing, not with her head bent, hands covering her eyes, as she wept when she was "in a mood," but out loud, her face a contorted mask. She'd answered the phone and spoken to the secretary of the Women's Club, who'd asked her to bake a pie for the Campbells: Nickel's car had been pulled out of Mud River and the ladies would all be taking meals to the family.

"Delia," Alma asked softly, "did your mother cry a lot when your dad died?"

"I was at school when she found out, I don't know. Later she did, or her eyes were just red all the time. Aunt Bird came and picked me up from school and threw all the beer and liquor out of the house. Mom always had some around and Dad let her, but Aunt Bird threw it out. Mom didn't come home for a couple of hours, and Bird didn't tell us anything until she got there."

Alma listened to Delia's whispery voice. A hint of breeze stirred Camp Shelter and the trees made hush-hush sounds up high in their leafy canopies. The whole story seemed a dream from here, just a dreamy world with rippled images, the way the sky looked upside down through a rain puddle. "The week after the funeral, my mother didn't cry at all," said Delia. "We watched *Morning Movie* and then *Midday Matinee*, eating toast on the couch. Sometimes she fell asleep."

Alma, curved into cool, hard rock, could still hear the sounds Audrey had made, a kind of yelling, *Oh, Ohhh, Oh,* circular and endless, emptied into the tall grasses that ran all the way to the creek. Blue beads, remembered Alma, she'd been looking for her blue beads in Lenny's tumbled bureau and had gone to find Audrey, demand she make Lenny tell where she'd hid them. But Alma heard the weeping as soon as she stepped onto the concrete porch. She'd closed the door of the house to keep the sound outside, and walked toward the field. She thought at first that some animal was bellowing in the grass, dying maybe, torn up by dogs, and she'd walked out to see. But it was her mother making the sound. Even with Alma standing beside her, she couldn't stop. She'd gasped, *Leave me alone,* her voice an odd, strangled bark; Alma had gone back to the house and told no one. Lenny hadn't heard anything. A few minutes later she'd given Alma the missing beads, but Alma threw them into a drawer and hadn't worn them in all the months since.

"Aunt Bird was so funny, " Delia went on in her dreamy voice. "She put the liquor in the trash but she put it in our neighbor's barrels, not ours. On purpose."

"She thought if your mom really wanted it, she would get it out of your trash. That's what alcoholics do."

"Aunt Bird is a lunatic." Delia dropped her head onto her chest.

"Maybe it will rain tonight," Alma said. "It hasn't rained the whole time we've been at camp."

"Tonight is your supper speech." Delia pulled Alma's arm close around her. "What will you say?" she asked. "I'm glad it's you and not me."

"I should talk about that movie," Alma whispered. "The dragons and the jungle."

"No, " murmured Delia, "Communists."

Alma was silent.

On the far bank the river workmen pulled and tugged, setting pipe in the leveled ditches they'd dug. Some of them moved in and out of the shallow water near the bank, wearing waders like Frank's, and no shirts. They were wiry men with sinewy arms. Alma wondered if men made, ever, the sounds her mother had made. No. The women made the sounds while the snakes flew, and the men held the snakes while eggs appeared in the grass, delicate, glowing with sounds that broke free and caused everything to fly apart. Alma fit her body closer and felt herself flying deeper into cool rock, sleeping beside the sleeping Delia.

## ❧ BUDDY CARMODY: SAY AND SAY

He crouched near the top of the steep bank. Through patches of leafy branch he saw the stranger turn and walk toward the river. The stranger's brown back and the beige of his pants were visible through the trees in broken pieces. There were sounds in the woods again, quiet sounds Buddy knew and heard now, and birdsong close by, far off. Nothing stopped because a car sat in the woods. If it sat here all fall and winter, the snow would cover it and melt, cover it and melt. The sound of the woods, the wind and sun and snow and dew, took in whatever secret, paid no mind. Buddy heard the stranger walking on layered leaves and needles until his steps across the ground were a faint scuffle that disappeared.

The pointed rock was gone; Buddy would never find where Dad had flung it. He crouched close to the vertical earth and measured with his eyes the long swooped scrape where the car had slid. He ran his hand along an upended furrow of ground, then inched his body over to sit in the tire-width track Dad had dug up. The earth was soft and black under its cover of weeds and roots; Buddy began to slide, soundless, down the incline to where he could see the silver bumper of the red car. The car was tilted into the pines and sat catty-corner so the bumper looked to be a silly lopsided grin. Like those cars and trucks with faces in the Golden Books Mam used to buy him at the grocery store. She'd get him one every time from the notions rack, since they'd always just cashed their assistance check; Buddy would let her read the books out until finally he wouldn't listen anymore and she found one in the stream, all the pages floating off and the talking cars and trucks erased. Then she taught him checkers and card games till he could shuffle the deck so fast it blurred. He didn't like those snaggle-faced fire trucks and buses with eyes. A car was not supposed to sing and wink; a car should be a machine and fly by on the two-lane, either side of those double lines, sounding a low hum before it even came in sight from around the trees. Bellington was up the road and Gaither was down the road and the cars ran from one to the other, never stopping or turning, and this car could have taken Dad away, got him far off so easy. Buddy could have told Mam how Dad had got drunk and gone off in the car; he could have said how Dad was never coming back and not been lying, and how there wasn't going to be any prison they would have to visit either.

But maybe Dad had gone off. The red car sat still. The stranger had said how Dad was passed out but it didn't feel like Dad was here: the woods were big, empty and full at once, like they had been before Dad came. Buddy inched closer; he thought he could be a shadow when he moved, nothing could hear him, smell him, feel him circle: in his dreams he could walk the swinging bridge, dance across it, and the bridge never moved or swung, only held still. Like a feather moved above each cross Buddy had carved in the wood. Now he stepped down the spongy, leaf-strewn earth of the steep bank, pretending to fly. There, he was beside the car, and he looked in to see what the stranger had made. It was like a picture: Dad was still and the snake was still and the front of Dad's shirt was dark like he'd sweated through it. The snake was vanished; it was only hung loose around Dad's neck like a piece of round tube, and the dull color of the tube hung down along Dad's leg to his knee. The snake wasn't real anymore; it was just a thing, empty like dead things were empty. If Dad could be empty, like a shell, Buddy thought there would still be a space of air around him, a space where things hummed and tried to get away.

Quietly, both hands, Buddy pushed down the thin metal handle of the door latch. The latch gave and the car door swung open. Buddy stepped closer, see if Dad was breathing. Dad lay back like a sleeper; he never slept so quiet. Always, passed out or drowsing, on the porch, in the bed, at the kitchen table, he twitched and moved, like he was awake and raging somewhere. Now he just lay still. In his shirt pocket, Buddy saw the round form of the ring. He exhaled a whisper of breath and the breath itself seemed to draw his hand near. He let his hand hover upwards, closer, closer, then down. He fixed his eyes on the little circle beneath the fabric of the shirt and saw the cloth move as his fingers touched inside Dad's pocket. He felt the sharp gold prongs of the setting with his forefinger. There. He let his eyes close, just for an instant. In that moment, he began to step back and away, and he heard Dad's eyes open. A click, like a sound inside a lock.

Dad's hand shot across to grip Buddy's wrist. His long fingers closed like a vise and no one moved, as though the hand grasped and pinched of its own accord. They tottered on a line or an edge, then Dad's voice said, in a questioning rasp, "You. Who you been."

Out his head, Buddy thought. "The car wrecked," he said.

Dad pulled himself upright, nearly lifting Buddy off his feet and through the open door of the car. "Get me out," he said, and pitched forward. He fell sideways onto the ground like a sack of stones and the stones smelled sour. Buddy fought to get out from beneath him and thought the stones were full of rot and pulp, breaking inside the bags of Dad's clothes. Dad's shirt was ripe and wet and his pants were stained and the juice would leak out on Buddy and the juice would burn. Buddy kicked to get free and felt himself pummeling air as Dad rolled him over and threw him in the car. The door slammed closed and Buddy was in the driver's seat, his face pressed to the open window. Just level with the blunt rim of the rolled-down window glass, he saw Dad's eyes peer in. Dad's eyes moved side to side in their lit slits and his forehead was smeared with red in the crease between his brows.

The long form of the snake had fallen away. It must be in the grass at his feet. Dad's hands appeared over the edge of the open window. He was panting, holding on and looking. He disappeared then, and Buddy heard him circling the car on all fours, slapping the metal chassis with his open palms, staying low like something in the car might see him. Buddy felt him jumping onto the rear bumper again and again as the car bounced, and there was a tearing, ripping scrape as the front of the car nosed downward through the woody flesh of the pines. When Dad opened the other door and pitched himself through it, the car finished its three- or four-foot drop back onto four wheels. Dad sat very still, whistling through his teeth. Then he crouched down low, his long legs folded into the floor of the passenger side, and turned himself to kneel across the front seat, his arms bent at the elbows. His eyes darted to one side and the other, and he pulled a rope from under the seat.

Buddy lunged for the open window on his side, but Dad got him by one shoulder and pulled him nearly flat. The rope whipped around his arm in a flurry and Dad tied the other end to his own wrist. "You gonna drive," Dad said, and pushed him back upright behind the wheel.

"Ain't no road," Buddy whispered.

Dad was crouched down below Buddy, half on his haunches, and he moved to turn the key in the ignition. He shifted himself around to face forward, half on the seat, and straddled one leg over to reach the gas with his foot. Buddy felt the car throb, then Dad put it in reverse and they lurched backward, the tires spinning for purchase in the soft earth. "Turn the wheel!" Dad shouted, and Buddy did, and they rammed backward again, and backward and forward till the car had tilted away from the trees and was easing slowly down the grade. "Now steer around them trees," Dad said, and he stayed low, like something in the woods might see him.

The ground leveled out and the car bumped over soft ground and big roots. The grade of the earth pitched gently downward and Buddy felt Dad lift off the gas so the car idled forward slowly, humming. The trees were white pine whose scraggly lower branches started twenty feet up and flared to feathery plumes. Buddy could see off in every direction through their staggered, singular forms, off to where the trees grew smaller, closer together, and the layered floor of needles stayed brown. Buddy knew these woods were the oldest; here were the tallest trees, the towering conifers whose piny, top-heavy shade kept the forest floor free of brush. Nothing grew in such dense shade but dappled mushrooms and jewely ferns and the scaly fungus that ran like reptilian stripes on the north sides of the big tree trunks. Light cut through in bright bars from a long way up, and the shady air itself seemed nearly golden. Needles inches deep muffled all sound and the car seemed to ride on pillowy swells. They rose and fell in subtle waves like the ground breathed into them and out, and above them the dense, green-hung branches subtly moved. Dad hunched down lower in the seat. He sighed and the noise was like a whimper.

"Ain't nobody out here," Buddy said.

Silence came up around his words.

"I know what's out here," Dad whispered.

They were passing through a slant of heightened sunlight and the air seemed moted with dazzled particles. Long brown needles dropped at intervals, twirling down along the top of the car in soft, minute tappings.

Buddy listened. All the sounds came to him like secrets, with little directions inside. He kept trying to hear; he felt quiet, like he was waiting. He knew Dad might have forgot about the rings. He might have forgot about everything.

"Where we going?" Buddy asked softly.

"We going to a place you know," Dad said. "Place you been to. We're gonna hole up awhile, till it gets good and dark and they're buildin their goddamn fire and you can skedaddle your ass in to get more of what you got this morning." He laughed a harsh, single squawk. "Chip off the ole block, except I ain't your ole block, am I." He peered into the forest, his eyes just clearing the dash.

The stranger had made the car safe. It was like Buddy steered in slow motion, easing over bumps and shapes, and the metal wheel hummed a soothing vibration through the little grooves where Buddy's fingers fit. There was a red smear on the inside of the windshield and Buddy fixed his gaze just below it, where the big trees seemed to mark a path of widest passage. Steering around one or the other wooden column, he glimpsed alligatored bark, ridged and mossy. Buddy wanted to stay here in the car, in the woods, where Dad wouldn't move much or look at him. He could hear Dad in the stillness.

"Uh-huh," Dad said to himself, "get to the river, outa them trees."

Buddy gripped the ridged black steering wheel. It was hard to talk, like his mouth was full of cotton air, and his heart hammered, muffled, a long ways off, in his ears. "You going to hurt me?" he asked softly.

"Hurt you?" Dad spit through his teeth and a glistened spray of saliva moved out through the open window. The spray seemed to move in one feathery arc, so slowly. "I ain't never hurt you," he said. He turned to look at Buddy and his face was lit in the gold light. Buddy saw the blond hairs of his brows and the glimmer of his red lashes and the deep-cut lines around his mouth. "What you know about hurt," he breathed.

Buddy was careful not to move, only whispered, "You getting set to leave with them rings, right?"

"I get me a stake. Damn right."

"And you won't be coming back here neither, I bet."

Dad's eyes looked wet. He leaned in closer, his head level with Buddy's shoulder, saying each word in a sharp hiss. "No, I ain't coming back. You going to have her all to yourself again." The gray of his irises looked faceted and shattered, like lit-up glass, and his pupils were tiny black spots. The spots seemed to pull at Buddy, suck him in.

"I'll help you get those rings," Buddy said. "You don't have to tie me up or nothing. I'll help you leave."

"Bet you will."

"You better off by yourself," Buddy said. "Then can't nobody keep up with you."

"That a fact." Dad laughed a long, syrupy growl in his throat and pulled his shoulders in tight, staying low. His eyes left Buddy's face and shifted side to side, raking the concave frame of the windshield. Beyond the glass the giant far-flung trees were giving way to smaller pines as the car made its way into brighter light. Suddenly Dad reached over and turned off the ignition. The car shook and they lurched to a stop.

Buddy breathed. The car sat like a beached boat in the green. They waited in the burnished sun of late afternoon, all the green color bright and still after the shade of the pines. Buddy heard the chatter of creatures and squirrels and, not far off, the hushing roll of the river.

Dad motioned him to keep still. He opened the glove box and took out a big flashlight and a pint bottle in a paper bag. "I got me a headache," he murmured, "hell of a headache." He took the bottle out of the bag and drank a long swallow, then jammed it into the rear pocket of his pants. The flashlight he went to put in his shirt pocket, but first he took out the ring. He held it up to Buddy, then put it on the second finger of his right hand. It fit just below the first knuckle, and the stone seemed to blink like a little star.

Suddenly the door was open and Dad was pushing him out, clambering after him with his long limbs unfolded. "We're down-river of the camp," he said quietly. "Ain't nobody gonna see us, and you're gonna keep your mouth shut." They walked fifty feet through trees and came out at the riverbank. Here the water was not so wide as up above. They walked down the bank a ways to where a big stand of oaks had fallen over into the river, their tangled roots flung up in a wall of earth. "We gonna cross here," Dad said. "Walk across these trees and swim the rest."

The oaks spread in a flung gash across the water, though their uppermost branches fell short of the opposite bank. "I can't climb over them trees tied up to you this way," Buddy said.

"You ain't gotta climb nothing," Dad said. "You get on my back. I'll do the climbing. That way I know you'll hang on."

Buddy stepped away but the rope tugged and Dad grabbed him by the arm and pulled him up over his back. Dad was walking on the tree and Buddy had to grasp him round the waist with his knees and hold on with his arms. Like being tied to the lurch of a bandied horse high in the air, the whole river to fall into. He shut his eyes to keep from struggling, not to upend them both. Buddy could swim the river, he'd done it before when the water was calm, but he wondered if Dad could even swim. He might go crazy if they hit the water, pull Buddy down like a flailing log, and the river would close like a flood around them. Dad tilted and lurched, leaving it to Buddy to hold on, and Buddy listened for the river, its hush and swoop, the warble of its deep spaces eddied around the bridge of trees. Once he opened his eyes and saw them surrounded by a throng of whale-gray branches, the uppermost spires half naked of leaves, and he thought he felt the beginning of a gargantuan give and roll, a little groan as the trees shifted, but he held on and Dad kept climbing, grabbing and lurching.

Then he stopped, and they were at the farthest point of the big trunk's spread. Buddy moved as if to slide down, plant his own feet on the broad curve of the bark. "Stay where you are," Dad called out. He nearly had to yell over the sound of the river, and he threw the flashlight the rest of the way over the water to the bank in one strong heave. Then, before Buddy could talk or move, Dad jumped. Buddy opened his mouth wide but no sound came, and they were dropping through the air. The river must have come up fast but Buddy saw it approach for a long moment, like a wet wall with all the colors swimming in its greeny slosh, and there was a loud bang, like a crash, as they went under.

But there was light around them, light in the heavy soup, like they'd dragged down splashes of daylight, and the darker, bluer deep of the water pulled at them, surging and cold. Buddy felt himself stretch free, as though the water had taken hold; he spread his limbs in a watery glide, floating off on the tether of rope. The rope tugged. Dimly, beneath him, he felt the surge of Dad's motion, colors and glints in the dark wet moving past him, and the lifted strands of Dad's light hair wavered up like a long weed. Buddy grasped its wafting length with both hands and Dad pulled him through the dark glitter like a fish. The river grew thicker and heavier, cut with swoops of light, and the water had begun to rumble in Buddy's ears like a fast-approaching train, squeezing him, when they surfaced in a sharp crack. Buddy gagged and choked. Dad tossed his head and the water flew off him in strings. He gained his footing and hauled Buddy along by the rope, and they were walking out of the river.

Dad didn't wait for him to get his breath, only heaved him over a high shoulder and carried him like a sack of feed up the soft bank. Buddy heard himself gasping, breathing long drafts of air, and he could make out an upside-down version of the woods above Turtle Hole. Finally he saw a glimpse of the oval water far to his right, and Dad had walked through the trees to stand behind the diving rock, the big boulder that overhung the water. He slung Buddy down to stand against the rock.

They were at the entrance to the cave, an elliptical hole not quite obvious behind brush and grass.

"I ain't going in there," Buddy said.

Dad leaned close, pushing Buddy to a near crouch, and pointed into the dark. "You tell me you ain't been in here?" he asked softly. "You ain't been in this cave?"

"I only been in a little ways. I don't like going in." Buddy set his foot against the wall of rock and tried to brace himself.

"You say you don't know I had my stash in here?" Dad pretended to be surprised. "You didn't come here and find my stash while I was gone? Why, who took it, then?"

"I don't know. Anybody coulda —"

He grabbed Buddy up sideways and aimed him head first through the opening. He had to bend down over Buddy's face to clear the shallow entrance. "She sure as hell didn't," Dad said. "Never woulda told her what I had. Wasn't more'n three hundred bucks, but enough to get me outa here."

Buddy felt the moist dark yawn up around them like it was alive. Mouth of a wet animal, shaggy and cold. And the throat of the animal was deep in, blacker than any dark. Farther on there sounded the rattle of a stream.

"Don't need that stash anyways, do I now. Wish I could see her fuckin face when I told her you stole from that rich cow, all on your own, like." Dad giggled, drew his breath in sharp. Buddy heard him unscrew the metal cap of the pint, and he reared back full height and drank.

The cave must open up. The cave must get big. It wasn't always so small and tight. Buddy felt a wash of air pass by them, fast, like something big and billowy and cool had rolled over them.

"Ah," Dad said, like he hadn't felt it. He screwed the cap back on and Buddy heard the bottle slosh as Dad put it back in his pants pocket. "Guess all that goddamn prayin you two did, didn't do a lick. Did it, girls."

"I took it for a reason," Buddy said, soft.

"Did you now? Well, ain't we all got our reasons." And he dropped Buddy.

The floor of the cave was damp rock, and there was no dirt here. *Whomph.* The fat air flew past above Buddy, then he sat up quick, looking all around. There were streaks of deeper purple in the black when he moved his head, streaks from the corners of his eyes. Buddy sat on his haunches. Dad jerked the rope so he pulled Buddy's one arm up straight, like Buddy was putting up his hand at school.

"I see you," Dad said. And the flashlight went on bright in Buddy's face. Dad's voice was behind it, like the circle of light was talking. "I know what you think. You think I been drinking and you

186

can get away if you wait your chance. You ain't so dumb. You ain't dumb at all." He jerked the rope. "You just a fuckin girl, is your problem."

Buddy blinked into the light, and listened for the air Dad couldn't feel.

"Say it, girl."

"Girl," Buddy said.

"Say it all."

"Goddamn girl," Buddy whispered. He heard skittles of delicate sound beyond the light and he listened hard. Airy rustles. Live things. Bats, must be. But they weren't the same as what he'd felt before, the rolling of air no one could hear. Felt it, not heard it. Like it took up all the room for an instant, rolling through the cave on a pulse, and Buddy heard it in his guts, inside himself, but Dad didn't seem to hear it at all.

"That's right, you a girl." Dad shone the light on his own face. His face hung in the black, talking. "Now you listen, girl. You might get away from me, but even you did have the light, and you don't, you couldn't get yourself outa here. I could leave you here right now, you tell me you ain't goin back in that bitch's room to get whatever else she's got." He waited. Purple dots ranged across his face. "You gonna tell me that?"

"No."

"No. You ain't. And after I get my ass outa here, you gonna keep your mouth shut."

"Mouth shut," Buddy whispered.

"You don't, I'll be back to talk to you about it. Open your mouth."

Buddy opened his mouth and the light trained down, a white flash. Fast, Dad's fingers were inside, clamped hard over Buddy's lower teeth, and his thumb held Buddy's chin. He jerked Buddy's head up and down. "You gonna do what I say? Say yes."

Buddy only breathed, his head vibrating.

"Got yourself a fat pink tongue there. Like yer Mam's tongue. Why my, my, my. Lookee there." Dad flashed the light back on his own face and waggled his long tongue in and out. "Know what a tongue's for?"

He shook Buddy's head side to side.

"Nah, you don't know. Maybe I show you, show you some things while we waiting."

Buddy shrank back but Dad pulled him to his feet. The beam of light was jumping and bouncing; they were walking on a sort of shelf, back toward the entrance a little way. The walls of the cave seemed shiny. Buddy stumbled, and the fan of yellow showed a rumpled sleeping bag shoved into a pile on the rock floor. Dad shone the light on a metal lunch bucket beside it. The metal looked dull and corroded, and when Dad opened the metal buckles Buddy saw crumpled bread bags inside. Dad pulled them out and trained the light across the words. Wonder Bread: Buddy knew what the letters said, he didn't have to read to know. Yellow and red and dark blue polka dots, and the letters.

"Had the bills inside them bags, one inside another, keep em dry. But when I got back and got in here, there wasn't nothing." The light flashed off. He spat, and Buddy heard the screw cap of the bottle turn, and Dad drank a good tug. Then he was on his knees beside Buddy. "Can you believe 'at? A man's hard-earned savings. Being a criminal yourself, you can appreciate."

"I ain't no criminal," Buddy whispered.

Dad lunged against him and Dad's breath was on his face and the smell of whiskey was strong, like a smoke, and Dad's hands were on him, turning his head. "No? Well, now what are you, then?" He shone the light up along the wall of the cave, and the wall curved up and bulged. "Maybe you a brain surgeon. Or a scientist. Lookee at this, mister scientist."

There were crosshatches on the wall, like a bird with forked feet had burned its sharp prints into the rock. The marks tracked upward, like overlaid arrows that pointed; the light bounced from one column to another, and there was color in the deep scratches, some lighter color that made the marks seem to float. It was writing, Buddy thought, some kind of writing, but it didn't have to make words. It was what writing should be. So old it looked to be grown in, older than letters or numbers.

"I ain't never lit it all up, but I figure this whole wall must be covered," Dad said. "What's it say, there, brain surgeon?" He plunked the big light into Buddy's hands and grabbed Buddy under both arms, lifted him straight up, like he could read the wall if he were a little higher.

Buddy's feet dangled, and he felt Dad's arms start to tremble. He held the light on the marks. They tracked clear up and he couldn't see where they ended.

"Well?" Dad said, and a wheezing moan was in his voice. "You better say what them marks are meaning. You better say and say —" He began to shake Buddy, and the light jumped big and small across the writing.

"It says," Buddy began, and squeezed his eyes tight shut, "stay here, and when the bats fly out from inside, you'll know it's dark. It says —" He opened his eyes, and when he looked at the wall again the marks seemed to glimmer, firing on and off across the rock. "Sleep here," Buddy said, "sleep here and lie still, and don't ever tell nobody."

One more shake. "Tell nobody what?" came Dad's voice in the dark.

"That you been here," Buddy finished.

Silence. And he did feel tired, so tired. Buddy felt his head nod once, and twice, and he let his arms fall, holding the heavy flash-light, and the beam of light traced downward. Dad lowered him to his feet onto the rumple of the sleeping bag. Buddy's legs wouldn't hold him and he crouched down, shivering.

"Well now," Dad said softly, "I don't plan to tell nobody nothing." He took the flashlight from Buddy and turned it off, and splayed one big palm across the top of Buddy's head, pressing.

"I got to tell you," Buddy said, and tried again. "There was someone there, when the car wrecked."

"What you saying?" Dad was swaying Buddy to and fro slowly, holding on so Buddy rocked from his heels to his toes and back again.

"A man followed me when I walked from the camp. And he knew you. You told him you seen him before, in the dark, when he wasn't real. But he was real. I seen him behind you."

Dad took his hand away. The flashlight went on, licked across the floor of the cave, and lingered on the lunch bucket near Buddy's feet. Dad's hand fumbled inside and brought out a pack of matches. The light went off again and the black was deeper, more purple.

There was a crackle, and the match flared out like a flower, the bright glow curling orange, black-edged. Buddy saw Dad's eye squint through the flame, and Dad's thumb was beside his eye, the mooned nail streaked with yellow. "A man," Dad said, and his voice was in the black. "And what was the look a this man?"

Buddy's eyelids fluttered. The orange light was pulling in and folding. "He was tall as you, and big like you, and he didn't wear no shirt."

"Maybe it was me you seen," Dad said. "Maybe you seen me twice."

The little flame dipped and guttered out. "He had black hair," Buddy whispered, "not yellow hair like yours, and he said —"

"He said what?"

"I'm too cold," Buddy said. "I'm mighty cold in here." He had begun to hiccup and there were tears on his face. He hunkered down on his knees and pulled the sleeping bag up around his shoulders, and the quilted material was colder still, full of the breath of the cave and the old smell of the marks on the walls. Buddy let himself fall over and crawl deeper, until he was under the damp fabric, pulling it closer and tighter, and he could taste the dust on his lips. He felt the pull of the rope but he unclenched his hand and thought he could pull free, falling away, deeper. He didn't have to be here anymore, he was gone, he fell far away in a density that churned, darkest green and lovely. A furred wing grazed his face as he fell and the layered trees gave way; the shadows of their limbs and their rooty hearts came up around him.

PARSON: HIS LEGION

He has some paper sacks he found among newspapers and magazines Mrs. T. sent to the dump; he will pack what he needs to take.
When he shakes open the paper bag it sits on the floor of the shack
in an empty rectangle. He takes off his work boots and settles them
in the bottom. He puts his Bible into one of the big boots, and his
socks that were prison issue, and he folds his khaki prison trousers
on top. The trousers are stenciled inside, but he can still wear them.
No one will see in his clothes; no one will see inside him. The
prison shirt he has long ago thrown into the crawl space under the
shack, but he folds the khaki shirt given him by the pipe-crew
foreman and puts the twenty dollars left from his pay in the front
pocket. He puts the shirt in the bag.

His cloudy legion watches him, all of them, floating up along
the incline of the peaked roof. They float in front of and behind that
wormy beam, and the forms of their lustrous shadows waver with
the waver and slant of the boards.

Harkness wears his blue postal uniform and today he keeps his
eyes closed. His breath furls near him, blue and cloudy, dense with
the smell of whiskey, but he has no need of breath and the cloud
only drifts near his mouth like a memory. In his arms he cradles the
old iron grate from the fireplace, empty and blackened, cold now;
his whole body curls toward the square iron shape as he rocks,
disturbing the gray ash that still clings to the bars. The ash is a
backward snow, spiraling among the faces, collecting on Preacher's
hat brim, that black hat Preacher wore traveling. Preacher's face in
the hat talks on and on, even if no sound comes out. This time he
looks as he did when Parson first saw him at Proudytown, yes, that
first day, preaching to a crowd of boys in a quiet voice that drove
through stories and Scripture, offered twelve-year-olds a captain in
Jesus, a hideout, a shield and a weapon; he stalked back and forth
across the room then, but here he drifts gently, nearly disappearing
at times, the hem of his black topcoat frayed and flaring out behind
him. Preacher gave Parson books of Bible stories, then a large-print
Bible meant for the half blind. That Bible was Parson's text, his
dictionary; he learned to use a dictionary to read the endless pages.
It was a Bible thick as a footstool; much later, Parson had to leave

it in Preacher's ramshackle house, stacked among Preacher's books in the front room. He'd never been back after Preacher got shot. Months in a county jail while his court-appointed lawyer tried to argue Parson was crazy; the voices talked outside and around him. Preacher spoke whole pages of Scripture in Parson's head, page after page of bold print from that first mammoth Bible. Verses with Christ's red words glowed up bright and lost.

But someone has retrieved Parson's Bible. The girl who was a fish swims the slant of the shack roof; the thick dark book fills her extended arms, glows like a beacon that pulls and pushes. She moves in a neon fluid that blurs behind her shoulders; years in the rain have washed away all but color and motion, a dark radiance like the refracted neon in oily puddles. Other forms shimmer in her long wake, turning in silent meditation.

The stringy kitchen matron from Proudytown, jerking her head in time as she chops chicken parts on a board.

And the woman from the orphanage, way before that, the one who sat knitting in the corner while the little boys fell asleep at night. Summer evenings they could still hear car horns and the cries of other children in the busy street. Seemed like there were a lot of beds in Juvenile Boys but maybe there were really only four or five. Still, she seemed far away in her chair because Parson was farthest from her in his bed by the wall. She read from a volume called *Children's Bedtime Bible Stories*, about how Jesus knocks three times: *the first knock is the knock on Father's door by the little boy or girl who has been naughty and is sorry for it.* When she read to them she kept her head lowered, her eyes downcast, and the light moved across her face and throat like a bath from the moon. *Now, the second knock is the knock of Jesus on the door of our hearts. To every boy and girl, He comes at some time and says, "Behold, I stand at the door, and knock: if any man hear My voice, and open the door, I will come in to him and will sup with him, and he with Me."* She would clear her throat and lift her head, and something glimmered across her face. *Think of Jesus inviting himself to supper! Yet that is just what He loves to do. And sometimes He comes unexpectedly; you never know when He may call. So it's really best to leave the door ajar and tell him to come any time He likes.* Parson remembered her buttoned white collar and her long white sleeves against her dark dress; he thought parts of her body were good and seemed to shine. *The third knock is the knock that comes too late . . .* The others fell asleep before she stopped reading; Parson saw how the shadowed light moved across her until he couldn't see her face anymore, only the front of her chest, dark, rising with her breath. *I hope you never have to knock like that . . . Knock now. It is dangerous to put it off. Be sure to give that first knock now.* Later, when the others were asleep, Parson heard the pipes behind the wall and tried to count the ghostly thumping: she was wrong about three knocks, the knocking went on all night. Like someone was lost, up and down between the walls and floors, but never gave up looking. She didn't hear. She sat with her head bent over her knitting, the needles clicking in dim light from the hallway, and she peered at the measured commotion in her hands as though something unfolded there. Parson thought she composed the pictures in his head, what he saw and heard when he couldn't keep his eyes open anymore. There were hallways thin and dark as those wandered by the lonely Christ in the walls, and shouted phrases in a musical language Parson didn't understand. There was a tub of water in the center of a floor, and steam poured in from a kettle, and in the tub a body whose breasts were long; the broad-backed body turned and was smooth like a column. Parson was under a table and the aluminum leg of the table was a silver post; he couldn't move far from the post, and when he pulled to get away the table shook. There were more pictures and sounds but the knocking in the orphanage walls drew him close and let the pictures fade. He slept in the shelter of a luminous body whose robes enveloped all pictures and all sounds.

But that was a dream. Parson has never seen Christ, only felt in himself powers he couldn't own or direct without permission. He thinks something entered him long ago and pulled him back from darkness, but the memory of that darkness lives inside him like a stain he can bleach with light. Even before he lived with Harkness, desperate creatures appeared to him, creatures that feared light. He knew the creatures were bad and thought he was one of them. But the fire burned Harkness's farm to singed rubble and the creatures were driven back. They feared what fought them, and Parson began to dream of flames. At Proudytown he set fire to the chicken coop, but the moldy straw was old and wouldn't catch. Then, from the first time he heard Preacher speak, Proudytown became a sanctuary: Parson knew he could name the creatures and oppose them. Preacher told the boy his visions were knowledge, warned him not to speak of what he saw except to the elect, in services, and Preacher began to negotiate with the officials to let Parson leave, live in the home of a Christian man and study the Scripture he'd learned to quote so extensively. Parson began to lead prayer meetings. He did speak well, though he'd come to the institution a nearly silent ten-year-old.

So at sixteen he was released into Preacher Summers's foster care, with the stipulation that he finish high school the next year. And he did, class of '53, in a brick building near the same river in Calvary that ran by Preacher's weathered porch. His classmates were those whose Scots and Welsh forebears had left hardscrabble mines and famine to settle the hollows and mountains; they were ruddy and fair, cared for football, called him Dago or Wop. The boys were passionate warriors who might have borne Parson's different look and silent ways if he'd joined their cause. He was big and the coach asked him to watch practice, the pounding and grunting in pads and helmets. At Proudytown the boys had worked hard, raising food in the gardens, caring for animals raised as food, cleaning the halls and the floors, and washing the worn sheets and towels before feeding them, wet, into the mangle that stood like a grotesque engine in the center of the basement laundry. But they hadn't played on teams, dressed in uniforms: they fought each other to maim and defend, not to score touchdowns. Parson watched the team line up to lunge at sandbags impaled on wooden frames; behind their shouting and grunting he heard some whispered chorus he couldn't make out, a breathy music that rose above their heads, rich and various with female voices. Parson heard that gravid hymn ebb and swell while the boys in helmets shouted a punctuation by turns: *Kill! Kill!* and the hard bags quivered under their lurching shoulders. The boys turned round in frantic, identical scampers, growling, oblivious of the clouds of mist swirling about their feet. They hit the bags, hit, hit, and the air furled whiter, pearlized, until the dusty field was banked in cloud; Parson turned and left.

He'd kept his mouth shut at Proudytown, and in Calvary, but

194

he was never confused by what he saw or heard. Even as a child he had known what was real, and what was more than real. His visions were opaque, as though made of different, unbound matter; they spoke in symbolic objects and charged the air with an electric moisture, a rainy smell. The Devil and his wraiths smelled of vague rot, of flesh reduced in some far place. They reeked of dread. Only the mist had confused Parson, when he was young, first seeing it in his room at Proudytown. Just arrived, he'd thought the place was on fire, like his last rooms in Harkness's house. He'd thought the slow white furls were smoke, but there was no acrid odor of fire, no choking sensation. He came to understand the mist was like a promise, like the laden smoke from Harkness's burning roof. Parson remembered the slant of those warm shingles, and running back into the barn to open stalls. The white goats had circled once, like dancers, before they streamed out in a line.

After Preacher died and Parson waited in jail for the trials to finish, his visions deserted him. He was blinded in those months, only heard Preacher's voice, heard Scripture trapped in his head. But in Carolina everything came back, stronger than before. He was Preacher's emissary: seven years in the silence of the barred tomb, in the realm of the man beasts. He hurt one of them and the others left him alone: the men were like the rock of the walls, pulsing with the rage of the ages. Parson waited, did as he was told, and in the second year Carmody came, rife with the knowledge of evil. He could not see or hear as Parson did, but he seemed to sense any presence, any power. *You got that look on your face, you loon, you fuckin nut case. So do it, bend the bars, deliver us sinners, God man.* Carmody knew, and his taunts and whispered jeers drew the visions forth, stronger and more lustrous. *But why should you, you ain't even here, you ain't here like us, you God loon. Leave when you want to, won't you, walk out when you're fuckin ready.* Carmody knew that Parson saw through him, into his head, his thoughts. During the months they shared a cell, he thought Parson sent him the pictures in his nightmares. He would wake up at night, raging or contrite. *Damn you how do you know, you stop her talking, you make her put me down, make her, you loon.* Carmody wept and begged like a pilgrim but he was wholly damaged, what was in him plummeted and sucked, a presentation of the Demon, a work long tended, and during the time they shared a cell Parson waked and slept in clouds of glory. He could move his mind as never before, unbound, free to oppose the Demon.

Carmody's voice says things in the shack at night, things Carmody might say if he were saved.

*Deliver me,* he says, and, *Let me lie down.*

*Let me sleep in the Rock of God,* he says, *the Lamb is lame.*

Mist envelopes the words, whatever they are, as though Carmody, saved, becomes a prize beyond value, a treasure loved above all.

There is no mist in the shack now. Parson's legion moves above him, comes together in the quiet. He thinks of the snake, its animated form, and he hears Carmody weeping. He knows the sound is inside his head; he hears it because it's the truth, not because it's real. The stone buildings in the camp, the boards and rope strung for a bridge over Mud River, are real, like the road and the sky. Within this frame the dark forms wander in their sphere — singular, hungry, and fervent.

Parson stands still in the center of his wooden room. The shack is a cave in the woods, a sacred place. He raises his arms and feels a renting of veiled air across his flesh, as though he touches these lit forms, saved, all of them, their limbs and faces mixing, pulsing. Torn back from harm, from the rot of the Devil's smell and need. There is a fast chattering beyond the walls of the shack, a frantic, guttural patter; Parson feels its vibration through the floorboards. He breathes slowly, steadily, feels himself move through his hands, lifted, drawn up. He sees an extended pattern of colors and shapes, and the pattern tilts like a broad view glimpsed from above, the land, the country, pine forest and stands of chestnut, wild-grown fields and stripes of rippling water. Onslaughts of light and dark, rising and falling through a rush of days and nights. He climbs the swept air of Shelter County and sees below him a ribbon of pavement, the gleam of a silver bridge. Closer, and he hears the shudder of the weight-bearing beams and pylons. Hidden, blinded, panting, and wet, he is under the bridge in the shelter of its weedy arch. It is dawn in another, colder season and he hears the water sluice and stream, an engine grinding of gears, the carcass of an automobile drawn up by its snout through muddy water. There is a massive chain and a hook, movement and shouting on the bank. Parson lets himself sink into Mud River, for he recognizes this place, and he swims, instinctively, away from the voices, deeper into the maw of the brown river. But when he feels earth beneath his feet and walks out of water, he finds himself on the oval shore of Turtle Hole. An electric tension gleams along the lines of his body and he knows he has slipped through, gone off. Near him on the ground sits the carefully folded sack of his possessions; he has brought it here and yet been elsewhere.

Twilight has fallen; Turtle Hole reflects the early risen moon. Parson touches the surface of the water and the image shies away from his flattened palm, quivering.

He can see the shack through the trees. Only because he knows how to look, he knows the shack is there.

He stands and begins to walk the rim of the shore. Turtle Hole plummets to its center, rounded and dense, an egg of water nested deep in its rocky cropping. Parson circles, moving and listening. He must stay here now: meant to do. He hears Carmody cry out and locates the sound in his own chest. The great boulder that overhangs the water looks nearly blue in the fading light and the ground is littered with worn stones. They are old stones, stones that have surfaced, and Parson touches them. Slowly, deliberately, he begins to stack the rocks, balance them in conical shapes. He will build seven shapes from stones, for in Revelation there are seven churches, seven stars, and seven lamps of gold. Seven years he waited in prison before coming to this place. Far up in the hills he hears the sound of some cacophony, a drifted blaring of mixed noises, and he looks up from the work of the stones to see Harkness's six white goats across the water. They stand quite still, the evening pale and thickened around them, small clouds of breath at their muzzles, and then they turn and clatter off through the snow.

She emerged from the wooded trail having walked it fast, leaning forward into the narrow ascent. She carried no burdens and so used her hands, pushing off the trunks of the second-growth saplings that bordered the path. The common area of the clearing was nearly empty. All the girls seemed to be in their tents, as though activities were suspended, and the few who were milling around took no notice of Lenny. Perhaps she was invisible. But she could hear herself panting now, breathless; her pulse pounded in her temples. She'd flung herself the rest of the way up the mountain, racing the green-shaded trail to get here, be back inside, but camp looked different, removed, as though glimpsed from outside the group. She thought of retreating onto the trail, backward from this place. But she stood still and the pull of the trail fell off behind her.

Highest trail was steepest in the last hundred yards, before it emptied into their rocky, ever ascendant campsite, twelve tents clustered on their platform floors in a staggered semicircle. There were three rough-hewn picnic tables, the same weathered type supplied to roadside parks by the state, and a broad fire pit centered exactly in the middle of the clearing like a bull's-eye. The pit was scooped out slightly and circled with rocks. Successive troops of campers had built up the stone ring, balancing more rocks until the ring itself rose perhaps two feet off the ground. At night Girl Guides and their counselors sat by the fire on their low stones, singing rounds or hymns, cooking meat on sticks or marshmallows that caught fire and blackened, tracing strings of light in the dark as the girls waved their sugar torches. Lenny liked the sticky globs black and crisp, with the sweet white insides hot enough to burn her tongue. She'd suck the sweet white goo from its black shell in flickering light while they all sang "Onward, Christian Soldiers," probably the most maligned and ridiculed forced march in their repertoire, but they'd learned a soprano harmony on the high notes everyone liked: *with the cross of Jesus* drawn out and trilled at length, falling off to the ponderous tromping of *going on before.* They sang out in the dark and it seemed they clung to the side of the mountain in their settlement, with their fires and chores and tents, while the oblivious peak soared on above them. The trail ended with Highest camp and any progress farther up was slow and picked out, hands and knees, more like climbing than hiking.

The top of the mountain was not so far, Lenny thought, they were all nearly living there. The big rocks on top looked pushed up, squeezed from below by some brute force, just as the diving rock at Turtle Hole looked to have been dropped there from an immense height. But the tall boulder must have emerged slowly, a dense, upright egg, and the flat water at its edge was that same oval shape. Turtle Hole held still in Lenny's mind as she skirted the clearing of Highest and turned to the left along the row of tents whose rear walls faced the drop of the hill. She reached the last one over and stood in the entrance. Only one of the rear flaps was raised and the interior was darker than usual. Cap stood in the center of the space, simply waiting.

"Where have you been?" she said. "If the counselors had been here to know you weren't back, you'd be in trouble."

"Guess so," Lenny said.

The tent seemed so familiar. Not welcoming, exactly, but plain, singular in purpose. Cots, trunks for tables. Sticks and rocks they'd saved, arranged just so. Dirty clothes in a pile. Lenny felt as though she'd been gone for days, that she should have stayed here in the woods with Cap, with the sounds of the crows at sunrise and the stirrings of the group filtering through like the start-up of a tiny village. So many people, and so much room, like the woods and the vault of sky went on forever. Home in Gaither seemed so small, the four of them cramped together so tight the others felt it when anyone moved. Staying up high was easier. Lenny walked to the back of the tent and looked down on the field weeds and the border of the woods, and the trees and the woods, descending plateaus of colors. "Cap," she said, "how can we leave here?"

"We're not leaving," Cap said. "We've only been here ten days."

"Right," Lenny said.

"Are you OK?" Cap stepped closer and stood toe to toe, surveying Lenny's feet. "You find your shoes? Your shoes were your mission."

Lenny let her head drop forward and pressed her brow to Cap's. Sometimes they played at staring each other down until they both saw spots, but now Lenny closed her eyes. "Does it look like I found my shoes?"

"Well, no. But you can have those. The length is OK. You'll just tie them up tight."

"So where are the counselors? No wonder it's so quiet." She moved past Cap to lie down. The squeak of her cot always sounded midway between a whine and a sigh, and if she turned or bounced she imagined the springs cried out in some limited, anxious language. "My cot is talking again," Lenny said.

"Don't pay any attention." Cap sat on the edge of the metal frame. "What's wrong with you, Lenny? You're all sweaty. Close your eyes and I'll tell you a bedtime story."

"Really? A real story? Or another one of your plans?" It wasn't even a question, Lenny thought, because Cap didn't tell stories. Not like Audrey. Audrey was full of stories to be fended off. The stories surrounded her, next to her skin, as though she were wrapped in yards and yards of stories, like bandages. Lenny thought of her mother, standing in the kitchen in Gaither, wrapped like a mummy in her complaints. Only her eyes peering out. Audrey couldn't seem to plan at all. Cap was always planning and her plans were about the world. How to do this or that. How to navigate.

"I can hypnotize you," Cap said now. And she began moving her fingertips lightly across Lenny's forehead, harder up to her hairline, down again, across. "Your eyes are growing heavy and you're listening carefully. This is the plan. Tonight we'll skip the mob scene at campfire and have an adventure."

"Not sure I want to," Lenny said.

"Yes," Cap whispered in her Natasha accent, "you vant to, you can't resist."

"Ve must resist," Lenny whispered back, "resist ze mysterious water, ze call of ze wild . . ." She was laughing but she felt so tired, as though closing her eyes brought back what had happened near the shack at Turtle Hole. Everything had changed; she couldn't say how, she couldn't catch hold. "I'm going to see Alma tonight," Lenny said slowly. "Later, after singing and campfire." She thought she might go to sleep, and sleeping would be perfect. She could talk to Alma in her sleep, find out what she wanted to say. She could see Alma and watch Alma. She tried to focus on Alma's face but the image slipped and Cap's face intervened, so naturally, the features of one melding into the other and back again, both of them watchful, listening or waiting, both of them still.

"We will see Alma," Cap said, "I'm sure of it."

"How do you know?" Lenny felt Cap's fingers flicker and change direction. She opened her eyes.

Cap shrugged. "We'll see them. But first we'll go swimming."

Lenny sat up and hugged her knees. "Let me guess where."

"That's right. And who knows. Anything could happen." Cap smiled her slow, secret-pact smile. "You know," she added then, "it doesn't work with you. You're one of those people who can't be hypnotized."

Lenny stared at her. There was no way to tell her about Turtle Hole. The man with the snake and the flowering vine. A sense of him washed over her. Hypnotize. That's what he'd done, like a magician, but with no tricks or stories. What was he? Lenny thought she'd fallen through him, long spaces full of pictures. He was big, bigger than his body. In confirmation classes, years ago, she and Cap had studied little books with color pictures, with choral readings of Scripture, and there was a color plate of an angel holding a rod that became a flowering branch. Rod to branch to serpent. Serpent to rod to branch. It was only a picture. Someone's powerful hand, skin that glowed. An angel, mesmerized. But no one could have made up the pictures Lenny had seen: the window in her parents' room, the shape of the window, the view of the yard. Again she saw the yard behind the house, the way it was then: she held it still and looked. No fence at the field, and the clothes were on the line, not summer but spring, a little season, short and cold, and her mother wasn't there. Where was she, why didn't she come, and where was Alma, always there, always underfoot. Alma, who knew too much and stayed awake at night with Audrey's stories, and if those weren't enough there were other stories, whole books of them to read with a flashlight, Alma dragged out of bed on school mornings, Audrey going on about books hidden in the pillows, about shadows under Alma's eyes.

"Hello?" Cap said. "You're not hypnotized. Don't pretend."

"What do you think about Alma?"

Cap let her expression loosen and paused to consider. "There's

Alma. And there's Delia. I don't know. They're like two brown mice. Delia is the mouse with curls, and Alma has no curls at all. Right?"

"That's not what I mean. There's Delia's father."

Cap shrugged. "I barely knew him. I mean, I saw him around. There was that party your mother had last summer, that birthday."

"My dad's birthday," said Lenny, impatient.

"Yeah. Your mom seemed to know him. Delia's father, I mean. Did she know him?"

Lenny blinked. Of course Audrey knew him. Or they might have kissed on impulse, that time in the kitchen. Lenny couldn't imagine anyone kissing her mother, taking that kind of chance.

"They were standing down by the fence, like this." Cap folded her arms in a defensive wait-and-see. "Looking across the field, at the airstrip or something."

"So what?" Lenny said, irritated. "It doesn't matter. I'm talking about the accident."

"Oh," Cap said. Her green eyes shifted and clouded. "The river and the bridge."

Outside they heard shouting, and the hand-held bell began to ring.

"Well?" Lenny said.

"Well," Cap repeated. "Alma and Delia are two brown mice, and suddenly Delia has this big, big story, like some big cheese full of holes the two of them crawl around in."

"And what do you think about us?" Lenny said softly.

"Us?" Cap glanced toward the opening of the tent. "We don't like cheese. We're spies, not mice."

The others had begun to gather around the rough picnic tables to divvy up chores. The sun had set and they had lit lanterns, but the light was still a dark, informed gold. The tent flaps drooped. Through them the camp seemed a picture whose burnished, faraway movements the girls glimpsed through shadowy bunting.

"Lenny," Cap said, "I want you to come to school with me."

"What do you mean?"

"My dad will pay for it."

"Your mom would never —"

"She won't know until it's too late. My dad will pay for you, to spite her. And because I want him to. My grandparents pay for my schooling, it's in the custody agreement. He's getting off easy."

"I don't know," Lenny said.

"Your mom would let you, if it's paid for. She'd love it."

"Why should the school take me?"

Cap moved to sit in front of her, fill up her vision. "Your grades are good. You were in accelerated math too, remember? And you'll have your own scholarship."

"The sidekick scholarship," Lenny said.

"So what? No one would know unless you told them. Anyway, what does it matter how we get things." She grabbed Lenny's hand. "Do you really want to stay in Gaither, after camp, forever?"

Lenny made a move to pull away.

"I have to go," Cap said. "My mom tied it all up. Even my dad says I have to, or he'd be in trouble with the court. He would never agree to let me live with her, but he says I have to go to school, as long as it's no closer to her than to him. So she's got it all fixed."

Lenny heard tears in Cap's voice and looked past her, through the drooped opening of the tent. "I don't know," she said again.

Cap let go and moved away. She kicked the metal frame of her cot once and the bed skittered across the board floor with a jangle of springs. Then she folded her arms and took a deep breath. "It's just a plan," she said softly. Then she said, "We're not alone here, you know."

"What?"

"Here in Highest, Lenny. We're not just here on our own. The troop deputies are in charge."

"Who are the troop deputies?"

"They're those two girls from Winfield, the big city creatures. Just appointed." Cap arched her brows, Natasha-like, and stood to indicate the darkening campground beyond with a sweeping gesture. "I believe I can bend them to my will."

"Oh, Natasha," Lenny said, "you nasty Russian. You Communist."

"Boris, don't try to flatter me. Just rise" — she made a minister's mock "all rise" with both hands — "and follow me."

"Take up your pallets and walk," Lenny murmured, standing.

"We're not washing dishes in a cold stream tonight. Know how that happens?" Cap bent down to pick up a shopping bag full of snacks. Lenny saw she'd gone through both their trunks and taken out all the bags of chips and popcorn and cookies, and there seemed to be a whole new contingent of dark salamis and butter crackers.

"So that's what I smelled." Suddenly Lenny was so hungry she nearly gasped. She thought she might burst into tears. "God," she said, "give me some. I'm starving."

"My grandparents," Cap said. "A whole box from some mail-order cocktail party. Cornichons and olives and pâté in tubs, and four, uh, tubes of meat." She turned and headed for the tables, shouting she'd brought dinner.

Lenny stepped out of the tent behind her. There was a circle of light around the tables, the part lit by lanterns, and there was the darker light, the light of the clearing pitched with tents. There was the light that seemed to hover above the dark of the trees, the trees that stood sentinel, ragged and big, at the border of their country, and there were the trees and the woods beyond, so dark they seemed to disappear, as though nothing really existed but this island.

Confusion of voices. "We're in charge here," said a voice off to the right. "We're making spaghetti," said someone else.

"Right," Cap said, "with that dehydrated tomato powder."

"Forget it," Lenny said loudly.

Cap snapped off a salute. "Please, my captain, permission requested to feed the masses. Why make food? Food is here."

"And you've all got more in your trunks," Lenny said, "attracting mice. Bears, even. Who knows?"

"Bats," Cap said.

"Exactly," Lenny said. "And there's more where this came from. You'll all get stuff this weekend in the mail. And if you don't —"

"I'll give you some of mine," Cap finished.

"Now go get your contribution," Lenny ordered. "Dinner is served. And put away the mess kits. All you need is your paws."

"Stop it!" someone said. "That's not what —"

"Overruled!" Cap shouted, and the others took it up as a slogan, yelling and laughing.

Lenny picked up the bell and began to ring it as girls moved back and forth between the tents. A table was soon covered with cellophane bags of popcorn and chips and crackers, piles of fruit and packages of Twinkies and cupcakes, tins of homemade cookies and bags of Oreos. Someone got a knife and slit open all the packaging, and Cap cut the meat into hunks. They all began to mill around, eating and singing, but not the usual camp songs. Someone began a raucous chorus of *in the jungle, the mighty jungle, Girl Guides never sleep*, but the words soon gave way to high-pitched, melodic howls. Someone else imitated an ambulance siren and then several sirens emerged, keeping time to the banging of the unused mess kits. The girls from Winfield gave up all pretense of uninvolvement and began to bark, imitating aroused guard dogs. Anyone who wasn't doing a specific sound in time simply yelled or screamed, and Lenny stood on top of a table to conduct the various parts. They found that short, sharp screams were effective as a kind of base line, and Lenny designated a group of screamers to keep the beat. They were amazingly shrill and they kept it going maybe fifteen minutes, everyone else cooperatively eating and banging pans and barking and singing siren sounds, when a group of adults streamed into camp from Highest trail. Camp was a celebratory cluster of girls, raucous and fierce, and suddenly the adults were there, the four Highest counselors and three others from lower sites, all carrying lanterns and flashlights and backpacks full of first-aid supplies. They'd obviously run all the way up Highest trail and stood panting, playing the beams of their lights over the group of girls, who abruptly fell silent. There was a stupefied instant in which no one spoke.

Lenny jumped to the ground from the end of the table, grabbed a handful of potato chips, and began to eat.

"Hello," Cap said to the counselors. "Care to join us?"

"Do you know how you all sounded from down below?"

"We didn't know *what* was going on up here —"

"Is this the way you handle responsibility, by shrieking —"

"It sounded like you were being attacked."

"By what?" Lenny asked.

"Gee," Cap said quickly, "we're really sorry. It was just, well, a spontaneous thing. Didn't realize you'd hear us all the way down at the quad."

Their own counselors stepped forward. "We did hear you," one of them said. "Now you can hear us. I want all this snack food thrown away, sealed up in garbage bags and brought down the trail to the Dumpster behind the dining hall. Any food you receive from home will be held at Great Hall until further notice. As soon as you finish cleaning up, you will go down to the quad and lay the campfire. We'll discuss this further tomorrow morning. Everyone is *required* to participate in that discussion."

There was some groaning and sighing, but in fact they'd all eaten voraciously, stuffing their mouths, and couldn't have consumed the rest; the meat was gone and the ground crunched with trampled crackers and apple cores. They held open gigantic green garbage bags and swept the refuse in with brooms. It was full dark as they negotiated the trail, dragging lumpy bags fastened in knots. Lenny and Cap, in the rear of the jostling line, were careful not to carry anything. They dropped back and slipped away, following the silver line of the stream to the river and Turtle Hole.

## ✖ ALMA: WISE WORLD

There were wieners and sauerkraut and mashed potatoes swimming in butter, and baskets of warm rolls heaped in piles. The beets made a wine-red soup around themselves in their deep bowl; Alma thought they were like bulbous Christmas ornaments with tails, swollen with juice and smell. The girls' plates were full and Delia proceeded to spear her wiener with her fork and eat it vertically, bite by bite.

"Dear," Mrs. Thompson-Warner said, "put your food back on your plate. You are not at the races. And even if you were, knockwurst is not finger food. You have a knife — please pick it up and use it appropriately."

Mrs. T. demonstrated by slicing her wiener neatly down the middle, then carving it across into remarkably matched, narrow slices. The girls began to titter in reference to various jokes about wieners, but their covert laughter was swallowed up in the noise of supper in the dining hall. Alma sighed into her hand, aware that everyone was on seconds and very soon they would begin to clear for dessert. She knew it wasn't actually their turn to have Mrs. T. at their table for dinner. Her presence indicated interest in Alma's supper speech, and a form of moral support difficult to ignore. The other girls suspected as much and responded by passing the onion relish, an item no one would touch, back and forth under Alma's nose repeatedly. Finally Mrs. T. secured the relish and sprinkled her mound of beets with a ladylike portion.

"This relish is a specialty of Mrs. Carmody's," Mrs. T. said reprovingly, "and it's delicious. It's made with Vidalia onions, locally grown — those are sweet onions, not at all bitter. You really must try it. I myself don't normally eat onions" — she wiped her mouth with her paper napkin — "but tonight I make an exception. You know, girls, you may not realize just what an excellent cook our Mrs. Carmody is. To cook for so many, so richly, with such variety —"

"It isn't just her cooking, though, is it?" Delia took another bite of her upheld wiener, but her wrist began to wilt and lower in the glare of Mrs. Thompson-Warner's direct gaze. "I mean, she has two other women helping her."

"Yes, of course, but she is responsible for organizing and planning every detail. In addition, she must supervise and direct the help. No small task. And much of what we are fortunate to receive is made by Mrs. Carmody herself — the relish, for instance, and the wonderful breads. Her breads are the equal of any served in the best restaurants of London or Paris, I assure you." Mrs. T. nodded emphatically.

Delia leaned close to Alma and whispered hurriedly, "Listen to her. She's here for the food!"

"What was that, dear?" asked Mrs. T. "In private, we speak to each other. At table, we speak to the group. Would you like to repeat your remark to all of us?"

"No," Delia said.

Alma sighed audibly.

"Pardon me?" Mrs. T. sat up straighter and raised her penciled brows.

"No, ma'am," Delia said, "I would not like to repeat my remark for the group."

"Then you'd best not make further remarks. Silence is always preferable to rude behavior." Mrs. T. took a sip of water. "As I was saying, one day some of you girls will find yourselves supervising others" — she looked specifically at Alma — "whether in business or academia, or in family life. You will then appreciate your experience here in a new and larger way." She looked pointedly at everyone in turn. "You know, when things are done efficiently and well, we often benefit rather unthinkingly. For instance, we've come to expect Mrs. Carmody's delicious, bountiful meals. Of course, there is plenty of fresh, inexpensive produce available from the local farmers, and they're eager to sell to the camp in bulk, but not every cook would know how to take such productive advantage of her resources." The other tables were clearing, and Mrs. T. reached for the job jar. She screwed off the lid and passed it without a break in rhythm. "When things are badly done, we notice immediately. If our food were bad or tasteless, we would wish for better food, though few of us would have the expertise or talent to provide it. Even if we've never experienced an environment that is well organized and productive, we wish for that environment."

That was right, Alma thought. And all the girls were listening, despite their resistance. Alma felt for the folded pages of her supper speech in her pocket, though she kept her eyes on Mrs. T. It occurred to her that Delia disliked Mrs. T. more than anyone else did. As though Mrs. T. told them things Delia didn't want Alma to hear or believe. It was true Mrs. T. was odd, with all her particularities and her secrets about Communism. But no grownup had ever said before that there were secrets everywhere, dangerous secrets someone should do something about. Alma knew it was true. And Delia knew it too, surely.

"We wish for a world attentive to our needs, a world perhaps wiser than we are," said Mrs. T. She paused and the table was still, unmoving, as the rest of the dining hall populace ebbed and swirled around it. The girls sat suspended, each holding a numbered tile from the jar. "That is why our system of government is so important to each and every one of us," Mrs. T. finished, and the spell was broken.

A and B wings ate together, twelve girls lined up on each long white bench. Finally they all began to shift and stand, scraping plates and stacking them. Alma glanced at her tile and saw she was a clearer. It was her job to help take dirty plates to the kitchen and bring back dessert; she began the first of several trips with her arms full of heavy china. The plates were plain and white, sectioned into portions like the plastic plates used in school hot-lunch programs; each had a faded green rim, barely a shadow, as though the plates were older than the dining hall itself. They were solid and dense, like flat stones; Alma felt she carried them from one turbulent universe to another. The clatter of the dining hall gave way to the noise of the kitchen dishwashers, their slosh and hum, and the passings back and forth of the cooks. At every entrance, Alma searched with her eyes for Hilda Carmody, as though to locate the source of gravity and power in this cosmology, but Mrs. Carmody seemed to stay in the rear of the big room, her arms hidden in a deep sink as she sprayed the massive cooking pots. The water from her flat-nozzled hose was so hot it steamed, and she seemed to supervise numerous pourings and tumblings and watery machinations from within a cloud.

Alma put another stack of plates on the metal sideboard and wondered, idly, where Buddy might be; he was usually scuttling around or crouching under this very sideboard so that the girls had to dodge stepping on him. It was always their peril, not his; he seemed to move so fast and so quickly, Alma couldn't imagine what could ever actually touch him, lay hands on him — he seemed an evasive streak capable of outmaneuvering even a force as powerful as Hilda Carmody. How could someone so big be the mother of a kid like Buddy? Alma could imagine him emerging as vapor from the top of Hilda's head, as swirled smoke from the center of Hilda's chest. Herself and Lenny she saw as logical extensions of their parents: Lenny for Wes, claimed and left to herself, as though he'd drawn a magic circle around her and then stepped away. Alma for Audrey, claimed and reclaimed and fed and pulled. And Delia, well, Delia was her father's, left behind. Alma stared across the big kitchen at Hilda Carmody's broad back, and the look of Nickel Campbell's face came through to her, so strongly, as if from some other place. She realized she'd forgotten the look of him, the expression in his eyes. Not the way he'd looked at her, or at Audrey — that she'd ever seen. It was the way he'd looked at Delia, with such waiting and accepting quiet, like he knew all about her and asked without speaking. Asked what? All those days after school at Delia's house, and the Sunday afternoons, all of them Sundays following Saturday trips to Winfield, Alma would look at Nickel Campbell and he would be looking at Delia. His look was something too old for the world, an idea from one of his books. Like *Ivanhoe*, one of the novels from the set he'd given Alma. *I beseech thee.*

Alma grasped one of the big pans of faintly warm apple crisp with both hands and backed through the swinging door. That's what it was. Wes lived with Audrey and went away, leaving and returning, and Lenny was away, at home, and Nickel Campbell had gone away, farther and deeper than anyone. People went away from Audrey. But maybe people were always moving, on their way somewhere, and Audrey tried to stand in front of them. Maybe it was all older and bigger than Nickel Campbell. The way he looked. Had he always looked at Delia that way? Alma couldn't remember, but she thought she hadn't been awake to know. It was like she'd woken up in her mother's car on the way to Winfield, driving to or from Nickel Campbell. And she'd wakened reading his face, his look that bathed Delia like atmosphere, his look that asked Delia to forgive him, years in advance.

Walking, Alma saw Mrs. T. at the head of their table, standing and gesturing. She looked to be a sort of island, imperious and pink in her flowing dress, smiling expectantly. She took the warm pan from Alma and leaned close, as though to impart some confidence.

"Dear," she whispered, "whipped cream?"

"No, thank you," Alma said.

"Ask Hilda for it," said Mrs. T., nodding pointedly back at the kitchen doors.

"Oh." Alma turned to retrace her steps. She realized dessert was in full swing all around her and the whipped cream was late. She heard spoons tapping on glasses and the first of the supper speeches begin as she pushed her way back through the swinging doors.

Hilda Carmody's realm had grown quieter. The dishwashers rested mid-cycle and a group of counselors stood in the middle of the room. They stopped speaking as Alma entered, but she saw them hurriedly packing backpacks from a big first-aid box sitting on the sideboard. Alma recognized Lenny's counselors, and McAdams was among them as well. Hilda Carmody suddenly loomed close and gave Alma a big stainless steel bowl of white puffed cream. The bowl was so cold that Alma flinched when it pressed against her, and then she heard something. The windows were open — of course, the windows were always open — and the rear of the dining hall was downmountain from Highest camp, directly below it, and sounds seemed to fall straight down, like water pulsed from a rapids. There were screams. Shrill screams, edging a continuous howl. But the refracted sounds seemed to circle, approach from all angles. The sounds bounced around and faded and came on stronger, like sonar and interference, like something tracked through weather.

The counselors turned abruptly, nearly running, moving through the back door of the kitchen; they turned on their powerful flashlights though it was barely dusk. Alma saw the weak beams of light cross and lengthen through the kitchen window, then there was no one, but the sounds kept on. The other two cooks had gone outside to listen, but Hilda Carmody stood by the sideboard, touching its metal rim with both hands.

She didn't look at Alma, but she seemed to want someone to hear what she said. She spoke toward the open window, as though the words moved through the old screens into the blush of the evening. "He always helps Frank stack wood for the bonfire," she said. "He thinks the sun rises and sets on that Frank."

Alma realized she'd never heard Hilda Carmody's voice. Its timbre was purely soprano, melodic and slow, the words drawled quietly. Alma leaned closer, wanting to hear more. There was something miraculous about Hilda's voice, and surprising. As though she cradled that voice and kept it carefully apart, a last remnant of what she had been before anything happened to her.

"You better get on in there with that cream," Hilda said. She spoke in the same calm tones, so slowly that the words seemed important.

Alma had backed up to the swinging doors into the dining room, but Hilda was still talking. "Don't you worry," she said, like a lullaby. "It's just those girls, into some foolishness or other. Girls will do some fool things . . ."

The door closed and cut off the sound, and Alma turned to walk the main aisle between the rows of tables. But the atmosphere had changed, as though what was in the kitchen had entered stealthily as smoke. The speeches had stopped. The big windows all around the walls of the room were cranked fully open, and everyone was listening. Most of the girls had stopped eating. Someone, one of the little Primaries, began to cry. Two or three others began to whimper, and Mrs. Thompson-Warner stood up. She banged a serving spoon on the table in front of her, then clapped her hands.

"Girls!" she said. "We will postpone tonight's speeches and go directly and quietly to campfire. Please leave your tables as they are and line up as usual. Girls! Proceed quietly —"

Everyone stood and began a rush for the doors. Mrs. T. was clapping her hands and shouting. Alma and Delia fell in beside each other and Delia linked their arms to make sure they weren't jostled apart. Alma looked for somewhere to put the whipped cream.

"This is going to be easy," Delia said.

"What is?" asked Alma.

"Turtle Hole," Delia said. "Let's go."

She reached into the bowl of cream with one hand and filled her palm with froth. Then she blew it away.

## ❊ BUDDY CARMODY: CARRY US

You know how you blow music through it, the stranger was saying, and he held the knife in his hand tight against Dad's neck. Buddy and the stranger were standing by the car again, like before Dad woke up. The woods were quiet and the trees watched. The stranger brought his hand away slowly. He held the knife down for Buddy to see, and the head of the snake lay aslant on the blade, wide as the silver metal. The snake's head was so close Buddy's face that he could see inside the mouth. The snake had fangs now, like a copperhead. Something was lodged inside. Buddy put his hand close the blade and the slit of the mouth drew back, exposing the delicate fangs to their roots. A round white pearl emerged, like a tiny egg, and dropped into Buddy's palm. The stranger pulled away. He took the head of the snake in his fingers and pocketed the blade. Then he held up one finger, as though for silence, opened Dad's mouth, and fixed the head of the snake between Dad's teeth. The head stuck out from Dad's lips like the whole snake wound its way down his throat, and the stranger was pulling Buddy away, tugging him by his wrist, and as Buddy woke up under the folds of the sleeping bag he knew from the moist, mossy smell and the dark that he was still in the cave.

It was Dad pulling at him, and his wrist was still tied to Dad's. Dad was moaning like he did, asleep, calling out in small words, and Buddy struggled to pull back, sink again into his own dream. He pulled his knees in tight with his free arm, tucked his head, rolled his forehead hard against his knees. He wanted to call out for Mam but he stayed still and he could hear her say, in a deep whisper like a secret, words from the singsong rhyme she used to tell him: *white owl's feather*. He saw the feather standing up in the dark like a slender torch. Suddenly, behind and around it, all of space reverberated. *Whomph*: the big air flew through the cave and moved the earth, filling all of space with a pulse that might light up like the sun if it were bright. But the air was blind in the darkness and searched without eyes, *whomph*, again, rolling through, knowing Buddy, what he was. In his dream the rolling air was Mam, standing by the diving rock and bending down to peer in through the slanted opening that looked too small to be the door of a hole that tunneled through a mountain. She was too big to get in, so she put her hands on either side of the rock wall and threw her mind inside to fill it all until she found Buddy. Her mind so big she didn't even need to say his name, he didn't have a name, he was like the marks on the high wall and the ceiling of the cave, older than names. Buddy knew she wouldn't be looking for him now at the camp — he always helped Frank carry wood for the bonfire and lay the kindling. But Turtle Hole wasn't camp anymore. And somehow she'd found Buddy in the narrow, dark crack Dad had made in their days and nights, the crack Dad filled if she left the house too early in the morning, too late at night, so it wasn't safe for Buddy to sleep late, not safe to say he wouldn't go to church of an evening. Not safe to sleep at all because all of night was cracked and turned around behind the blanket she'd nailed to the ceiling, the blanket that hid their bed, hid the voices and dark shapes. Dad had her and she had to do things. And Buddy had to. But she would never let Dad make Buddy stay in the cave; if she knew, she would come, and it was Mam pouring through in the flash of a second, shaking rock in the black dark with her searching eye. Buddy saw her eye, big and wise as the world, peer in at the opening of the cave, the colors darting and moving, and the iris of her beautiful eye was hard with facets like a jewel, and her gaze lit a path through the dark. Buddy could stand up and walk in the light, dragging Dad along behind him. Dad was still tied to him but Dad would never wake up. Wasn't so hard, walking. Buddy only had to pull Dad along to get out, and then Mam would know what to do.

But the light that lit a path guttered like a flame and went out. Buddy felt himself curled flat on the rock floor and Dad was behind him. Dad was talking in the dark. He was saying those foreign words and then he stopped and Buddy felt him twist around, tugging the rope at Buddy's wrist and talking on.

"Off'n me," he said, "get off." He made a low whine, like a dog might, pulling at a trap.

Buddy waited.

"Get outa me," he said, and jerked, and when he moved Buddy heard the pint bottle skitter away across the rock floor. It slid like something empty.

Buddy heard Dad move, sit up maybe.

"Ah," Dad said.

It was so quiet Buddy heard a rushing trickle of water, far off, deeper in. The water sounded, a whisper and a clatter.

Dad heard it too and he leaned forward, pulling Buddy with him. "Who's there?" he rasped, "who's in here?"

Buddy sat up from under the sleeping bag and found he could see Dad's shape in the dark. Just barely, in the black. Like he'd learned how to look in his sleep. He knew Dad couldn't see nothing at all. Dad turned his head side to side, fast, like he was blind and had a panic in his ears.

"It's just the water," Buddy said. "There's a stream back there."

Dad jerked the rope and pulled Buddy in tight. "Where you been? Where did you go?"

"It was dark," Buddy said. "I fell asleep."

But the cave wasn't so dark as before, when everything was black, sucked in deeper and deeper. Buddy couldn't tell why. He thought he knew which direction was front, toward the opening, but there was no light at all that way or the other, like they were stuck mid-throat in some big animal. A thing so big it couldn't feel them or be bothered to swallow them.

"Asleep." Dad nodded. He flailed his arm out sudden and fast and nearly knocked himself over. "That's right, I went asleep."

He kept on rubbing at his face, like he was spooked by spiders, like he was wiping at spider webs. Buddy could see his arms moving. There were tracings in the dark where Dad moved, some outline that barely shone. Buddy watched Dad, looking hard, then he felt something and wanted to turn, look behind him. But he nearly couldn't. He had to breathe deep in his stomach and try hard, slow, turning, and he faced the wall of the cave and saw how the writing in the rock glowed up. He couldn't see the light if he looked straight at it, but when he moved his eyes across the sweep of high stone he saw shapes glimmer, and a gold dust swim the air. Buddy thought about magnets: he had him a magnet that was shaped like a horseshoe, painted in red stripes, and nails stuck to it, and tacks, and the powder that came from the writing in the rock shifted in the air like it was pulled. It didn't fall or sift like dust. It was more like a smoke that moved, drawn together, and Buddy could see it around Dad's face. It clung to Dad's arms and shoulders. The cave had lit him up.

Dad stared out blind. He lurched to the side and rubbed his face with his sleeves.

Afraid of the rope now, Buddy thought, scared of the feel of it. Aloud, he said, "It's that there rope. Got to untie that rope on your arm. It's dragging over you, ain't it?"

Dad fumbled with one hand at his wrist. "Gimme that flashlight," he said, and his hand was on Buddy, feeling him, pushing him aside.

The dark was chocolate around Dad's shape. Buddy could make out the little box of the flashlight beside Dad's leg and he grabbed for it, pushed it into Dad's hand, but Dad dropped it so Buddy picked it up and turned it on. The slant of light was bright yellow and Dad brought his arm to his mouth and pulled at the rope with his teeth, his fingers, till the loops came undone and the rope was off him.

Dad was lit up in the circle of the flashlight and he pulled at his face with both hands.

"All that rope," Buddy said, "the rope's all got them things in it." And he thrust his wrist into Dad's face and Dad worked at the rope and pulled it loose, and threw it far from them like it was alive.

"Gimme that light," Dad said. "Don't think you're goin anywhere. You can't see nothing."

And the yellow beam flared around wildly, Dad taking hold of it and fumbling like he was burnt. Buddy could only see the light, how the black against it was dead again, so black they could fall into it, and Dad did fall, standing up, but he got to his feet and stood behind the light. He aimed it at Buddy and Buddy stared straight in. He knew not to turn away or shield his eyes.

He could hear Mam talking, behind the light. *There's a spirit goes along with us,* she said. *Sometimes it goes along and sometimes it picks us up and carries us.*

The light was so bright it seemed to flare red at the edges, vibrating. "You still got that ring?" Buddy said it loud, into the center of the fiery circle. "We got to go and get them other rings."

An arm came out of the light and picked Buddy up. He was gathered up at his neck, the collar of his shirt bunched into a knot that held him. He felt himself lifted high and pulled into a heat that flared at his face, tasting him.

"Course I got the ring," Dad said. "You want to wear the ring, little girl?"

His words steamed, like an animal's insides steam when it's gutted and the entrails lay out sudden in the air, smoking.

"You want the ring," Dad said, "you got to do some favors."

"I don't need no ring," Buddy said. He kept his eyes wide open in the light.

But Dad held him high with one arm and kept the light on him, and began to turn, slowly, till Buddy couldn't tell anymore where the walls were, where the sound of the water came from, which direction was the way out. And Dad's rasped whisper was everywhere — not a whisper even, but a breathing that said words and got into Buddy's head till it took up all the room and he couldn't hear anything else.

They were turning, smooth, like a planet and a moon. It felt to Buddy like they were falling sideways, falling and falling.

"You need it," Dad said. "You want to do them favors. You got me on the porch those times, and you had me behind the house, that time you run and got me on my knees. You didn't want to do it, you think I woulda known to make you?" He shook Buddy hard, one time. "You think I woulda known?"

Everything was light. Dad's head and the cave were light, and the arm that held Buddy pulled him closer to the white eye of the light. The eye was all heat and fire, burning, and Dad's voice said, "You didn't want to do it? You a girl, ain't you?" The fire wavered, and then it roared, "Answer me!"

"No!" Buddy screamed. "You did it! You wanted to! I'm no girl, I'm a boy, I always been a boy!"

And the light burst apart, falling back in fiery shards. An onslaught of rushing air exploded from behind the flared core. The bats seemed to flow through by the hundreds within that black pulse, scattered and streaming, rippling from high up, far back. In the air of their wings Buddy heard them all around, an infinite rapid crackling like snapped flags, pulsing forward like a grid in buoyant motion. The grid spliced around and beyond him and closed past him in a surge, pouring through.

What held him bobbed and weaved and fell down, and Buddy was talking in the dark. "They ain't going to hit you," he said. "They can feel where you are."

The light had dropped and flared round, a vertical, empty beam drawn upwards, and Buddy saw the bats pass through its edges like a tremor. They poured forth, separate and connected, a flickering smoke. Their sharp little faces seemed to dip and glint in the high rattle of their passage. They were like fist-sized foxes, with their pointed ears and lifted lips, tasting the air over Turtle Hole, all of Camp Shelter their dense, moon-fed food. Dispersed, glimpsed far up over trees, they contracted like skeletal birds and fluttered, blurred and ashen. But here they were animals. Looking and surging for the hole at the front of the cave.

"It's dark now," Buddy said. "We got to go out."

He dove for the light but Dad grabbed it first. Dad crouched down and held it tight between his knees, all folded over it like a long-limbed bug lit up from beneath.

"No," Dad said, "we ain't going anywhere."

The light only shone through from underneath him, in lines.

"We got to go now," Buddy said. "They all at the bonfire. I can get them rings now."

"No," Dad said, "I think we stay here now." He hunched farther down, rasping each word. "You gonna do me a favor and then we going to stay here. We ain't going to go out."

"You afraid of them bats?" Buddy said. "Bats ain't going to hurt you. It's this dark you got to get out of."

"Ain't dark," Dad said. "I got the light. You ain't got it."

"I can get them rings," Buddy said, "for your stake. You don't need no car, you got a stake that can get you a far ways. All the way to Florida, to that white sand —"

Dad kept his hands on his face and he was talking and murmuring words. "You lie, you lie," he seemed to say.

"I ain't lying," Buddy said, "I can get them —"

Dad talked on and Buddy realized he was saying his foreign words. Dad was all turned around. He'd believe a lie and he'd turn off the light. Buddy thought he might be able to see again if the light was out.

"Turn the light off, then," Buddy said. "Them bats will fly toward that light. You keep that light on, them bats will head for you. They looking for the light, get outside to the water, all them skeeters over the water —"

The light went off.

Buddy thought about the elliptical hole of the cave entrance, the lopsided hole in the rocks. He saw it, the way it looked from the outside, with sunlight playing across the stone and scrub pine grown up around it. Out there the air was so big it went clear up to the sky, and Turtle Hole lay still and blue in a dark so soft it was only shadows. The look of it was like a picture in the utter blackness of the cave, a black fierce and close as the dense hide of an animal. Buddy could still hear bats pass above them, swooping disconnected now in isolated, drooping glides. All in one direction. He turned and walked two steps, three more. He wanted to put his hands out in front of him and feel his way, but he made his hands stay down and looked with his eyes. The wall with the glimmering writing should be to his right. He swept his gaze across again and again but he saw nothing. Fly up, dust, sift down like gold — but it was like Dad's flat palms were clapped tight against his eyes. The gold had clung to Dad, the shadow lifting in a pool around his form, pulling at him. The cave wanted to keep Dad, Buddy thought. Dad was supposed to stay in the cave. He could only get out if he went away from Dad.

"Boy," Dad called out. "You get back here."

Buddy heard the bats flying around him, silent far up, and closer, rattling gently just above his head. Couldn't hear their eerie, ringing sounds but he could feel the shapes of their calls and screams expanding in curves and bells all through the dark. If only he could find the entrance before the cave emptied, Dad would be too scared to turn the light on, Dad wouldn't find him. He looked back to see if Dad had moved and he could see a hunched body behind him, a shadowy hump, yes, dimly glowing. Smoky with the gold dust.

"You!" Dad yelled. "Where you going." He stayed put and craned his head like a turtle might, coming up from water.

Buddy turned his eyes back sharply and thought he saw some-thing move in front of him. Something small, no bigger than a cat. He stood still to look and the form vanished. He tried moving forward, balanced, so still, on the balls of his feet, and the form coalesced again, this time far to his left. There was a sparkle, like a tingle in the dark, or a shudder, and Buddy saw a face in the creature, a textured face drawn down in folds. The mouth moved like a cat's mouth, in a long, luxuriant yawn, and one of the stumpy arms held up a shape, opaque and golden. It held the shape up like a lamp, but it wasn't a lamp, only a gold glow. The creature stood on two legs and turned away to walk, and Buddy followed a faint outline in the dark, trying to get closer. He thought it wore clothes, and its head was an odd shape. It came perhaps to Buddy's knees, were he to get close enough to stand near, and it moved with a trundling motion, like a two-year-old or a midget, but it could surge forward. Or seem to disappear and reappear to the side, or farther ahead. Buddy realized the cave turned to the left, and he wondered if the creature was leading him out or deeper in. He stopped walking and the creature paused and turned. The face, twenty feet beyond Buddy, was an old man's face, yet strangely animal. It wore a hat, conical, like a soft clown's hat, and a bulky jerkin. Suddenly Buddy remembered: *green jacket, red cap.* Mam's rhyme. *Fear of little men.* But Buddy wasn't afraid. The creature shimmered and beckoned him, jangling a silent urgency, and Buddy started forward again. The rock beneath his feet slanted upwards and he could feel space narrowing, as though they moved through a tunnel and the tunnel grew smaller as they progressed. They seemed to be moving quickly, without effort, and there was a shine to the rock sides of the world. Buddy blinked his eyes. Dad could never follow him here. It was so easy to walk now. Ahead was a circular formation, a wreath as big as a door, and the rock was dark gold, lustrous; the stones felt warm when Buddy came up on them and touched them. The creature was gone or escaped, Buddy thought, for he peered through the circular rocks and saw the slanted hole to the outside of the cave. He stared, trying to make sense. There was a blue space beyond the hole, and that was evening, and evening had so much blue that it was not dark at all. Buddy understood: he was looking at the hole from the wrong angle. He had come another way, from the side. Dad had walked straight in, but the cave was full of ways to move, and Buddy went forward and climbed through, raking his arms to clamber down and through the shelf-like hole.

He got outside and everything smelled of plants and dirt in the dizzy blue, and the blue rolled over darker in the air that led to the sky. The ground Buddy stood on was springy with moss, so soft he staggered and sat. He sat down and pressed both hands flat; he looked, to watch himself, and he saw Dad's broad hard shoe beside his hand.

Dad's shoe, like a wall no one could get over.

"Well, what the hell," said Dad's voice. "Beginning to think you wasn't coming out."

"I shined the light all around," Dad's voice said.

"You hadn't heard me yelling, why, you'd been in that cave till you laid down and quit," his voice said.

"Reckon you got me to thank," said Dad's voice. He reached with both long arms and lifted Buddy to his feet. "Get to walkin. We got a job to do."

Buddy felt Dad's hand on his neck, pushing him along the narrow trail behind the diving rock. Buddy knew there was no job. None of it mattered; Dad wouldn't leave. Dad would never leave, and if he did leave, he would always come back. Buddy stumbled. The truth stretched round him vast and circular as a dead world. Dad steered him past the side of the boulder, onto the sandy, pounded ground that circled Turtle Hole. The water spread out still and satiny, flat like a blue egg. Buddy heard sounds, and then he saw the girls. One of them stood still in the water. She turned, and he saw Lenny's face. Startled, backing away.

But Dad was in the water too.

## ❧ PARSON: THE CLOCK AND THE GATE

The goats have fled into the trees and stand waiting at the border of the woods, their soft muzzles visible through the leaves. They hold still like threatened deer. If Parson tries to approach, their images waver, begin to fade. So he stands quietly. From here the seven markers of stones near the diving rock are directly opposite. Parson sees them across the darkening water and feels he is far away, too far from the stones, and he begins to sweat. Steps barefoot into an edge of water and out again, back upground to a border of neutral space halfway between the water and the woods. To calm himself he thinks about the stones, how they felt in his hands. He looks back into the trees and the goats nod their long heads, peering sideways. He knows the stones were big enough, each a little larger than his hand, heavy and flat-bottomed, balanced. Even from here they look placed, deliberate. A low boundary, an entrance, a remnant of a gate.

He squats, then kneels, breathing. He sees light begin to move, first where the trees begin, then along the shore and among the stones. The light is strong and weak, melding, separating. Tracers of movement. Among the stones. Then he sees the girls' bodies across the expanse of water, moving. The older girls, Lenny and the other one. And two younger ones. Glimmering. A convocation. He hears them laughing, calling one to another, but the words are blurred.

He sees Lenny walk into the water, wade in to her waist.

The others separate, calling to one another. Among the stones. Lenny is swimming farther out.

Behind them the diving rock turns. Shifts in space. Parson sees it turn like a moving wall, glow in the dusk that is layered, furred with shadow.

He sees the boy walk round from behind the turning rock. And Carmody, close enough to grab him, not needing to, attached to him like a dark hole, shining and empty.

As though she feels someone approach, Lenny hesitates in the water. She turns, executes a smooth circular glide, begins swimming back to shore. Parson hears a gong struck, a hollow, resounding break. And Carmody leaves go the boy, walks through stones, is in the water. He swims like a powerful horse; Parson knows how Carmody swims.

*Do it, you fuckin loon. You want to do it.*

The water is blue beads, like a long cord Parson swallows. A cord he pulls into himself. He feels every stroke, swimming just beneath the surface as though to break the skin of the water would slow his progress. *Lethal, ain't you, loon. You can pray over me.* And it is like prayer, this clocked glide in heavy space timed to his heart's thud. But he surfaces and sees Carmody reach her, begin to drag her back to shallow water. He erupts in fire like a hunger.

They walk hand in hand where the trail is wide enough. Alma feels Delia's shoulder near her own and they lace fingers or grip each other hard as the path rises and falls, swells and drops, winds around rocks, and the rocks themselves are more than the hard slabs they seem by day, more than a kind of dead furniture thrown up suddenly in the woods. In dusk the lichen dappling their pumiced surfaces light up in scaly lines. The leafy canopies of the trees droop down, as though darkness creeps through them in lengthening shadows. Far off, the campfire flares orange and jagged and Camp Shelter is singing: *Rocka my soul in the bosom of Abraham.* The song spins out in rounds and Alma hears the sound as echoes trapped somehow behind her.

"It doesn't sound like 'rocking my soul,'" Alma says. "It sounds like 'rock of my soul,' like, you know, a soul is a rock inside a bosom."

"A man's bosom." Delia shrugs. "And who's Abraham? If you know, don't tell me."

"I don't remember," Alma says. "One of the Bible fathers, I don't know. But I know we don't have a flashlight."

"So what? We won't be out all night. Anyway, I could walk this trail blindfolded. Couldn't you?" Delia lets go of Alma and moves ahead, singing under her breath, *"Oh, rock of my soul."*

There was that old story about the Pied Piper, Alma thinks, where all the children in the town disappear into a rock by the sea. All except the lame boy. His soul is too pure, or not pure enough, and he can't keep up. Can't be taken in, like treasure, which was always hidden in rocks. Like the treasure in one of Nickel Campbell's books, *Arabian Nights,* buried in a cave inside a rock, and the rock had a door. Then there was the rock Jesus lay within until the third day, and the door of the rock was rolled away. And Lenny had made a game once where the girls collected a treasure of rocks and sank them in the stream, far down in the field behind the house. The rocks fell through beige water, slowly and deeply, and mud furled up like smoke around them when they hit bottom. But Nickel Campbell had floated, floated away, out of his car into river water, and Alma imagines her mother's soul, stuck like a shard of rock in the center of his chest. Wet that day, in the muddy river, buried now. Audrey's soul really would be hard and dense, buried or hidden like a nugget or a seed, like a jewel with her voice held tight inside. Or the voice had found a way into Alma's head, with all its words intact. *I don't know why I was brave enough to be so foolish, phoning him at work that first time. Maybe I was just desperate, not willing to go along nursing some little hope. I told him it was Audrey Swenson, please not to say anything, that I knew he went to Winfield to do banking for Consol every Satur-day, I wanted to meet him there, this week, at noon at the bus station, I wanted to talk to him, more than anything in the world, please if he would just not ask questions and agree . . .* What question would he have asked? Sometimes, driving to Winfield, Audrey and Alma had played Twenty Questions; Alma paid close attention to every clue, and she was better than her distracted mother at guessing answers. Animal, vegetable, mineral. Bigger than a bread box.

"I bet we're going skinny-dipping," Delia says. She turns to face Alma, a band of sunburn across her nose and cheeks. She blinks and her eyelids look pale. "Cap will have cigarettes, of course," she says. "Alma, do you ever smoke with them?"

"I don't like smoking," Alma says. "I cough. And it smells awful."

"It doesn't. And Cap wears that French perfume. If you stand near her you can smell it, and it mixes up with any other smell. She told me she wears it for camouflage."

They've come to the clearing, where they leave the swinging bridge and the river behind, and move off into the woods toward Turtle Hole, but Alma bends down to tie her shoe and Delia stops on the path beside her.

Alma frowns. "When did Cap tell you that?"

"One day after breakfast," Delia says, nonchalant. "We were talking. What's her perfume called? She wouldn't tell me, like it's a secret."

"I know."

"Well?" Delia asks.

"Let's play Twenty Questions," Alma says.

"No, it's boring."

"Twenty questions about Cap. The name of Cap's perfume."

She peers up at Delia, then reaches out to pull down Delia's socks. "Your socks fell down."

Delia crouches to pull them up, moves to shove Alma off balance. "So tell me your speech. Let's hear it."

"What, now?"

"You wrote it, didn't you? You know it by heart, I know you do. You were only going to read it off paper to keep from looking at them all." Delia's eyes widen and she leans forward, cocks her head sideways and fits her face to Alma's. The scab at the side of her mouth is a hard little shape. This close, her lashes brush Alma's eyelids.

"I don't have to give it now, not ever, and I'm glad." Alma closes her eyes. She does know all the lines of her speech, but their sequence seems to have jarred loose; the order is gone. *President Kennedy said not to ask what our country can do for us.* The phrase floats clear in Alma's head, detached from any other, and she smells Delia's skin, Delia's hair. She thinks how like themselves they both still seem, and how different they've become in this place. They smell different now, more like earth, less like their mothers' houses.

"You think she'll forget about it?" Delia laughs, moves away. "Mrs. T.? Not likely."

"She might," Alma says. "The schedule would get messed up if everyone from tonight had to talk tomorrow night —"

Delia makes an impatient noise in her throat, grabs Alma's hand. "But tell it to me. Tell me now, the lines you remember. About the secret furnace in the basement of the Russian embassy. How hot it burns. You were going to say that, weren't you? It's Mrs. T.'s favorite story."

"I don't have to, Delia. It doesn't matter anymore."

"It does matter. Tell me!"

Alma sighs, and she hears how still the woods are. She will have to say something, tell Delia. "All right, listen," she says, and she leans close to Delia, whispering each word distinctly. "Blue on blue. Heartache on heartache." She wonders if Delia will hit her, slap her.

But Delia moves closer as well, and whispers, "I'm . . . Mr. Blue. When you say. You're sorry."

Alma smiles into her flecked eyes. "Blue on blue. Now that we are through."

"She wore blue," Delia says softly, "velvet, and in my heart I —"

Beside them the river moves like twisting fluid dropped into a trench. There's a sound close to the bank, jump of a frog or a fish, a sluice of escape and a plop.

"Look," Delia says.

And the fish jumps again, flashing like a comma, falling back in muscular surrender.

A soul could be like that too, Alma thinks, that silver color, or a kind of smoke. The way lines from songs curled and drifted, peculiar, real and airborne, if you took them away from the music people moved to, the music that begged and pushed. Words could push too. But Audrey's words only waited in Alma's head. It was Alma who seemed to push them, remember them, try to hold them up. She wanted to move them. A soul could fly: hadn't Wes let his go, drifted upwards and blown about like hair? Her mother's voice stated facts to make a gravity he escaped. *I never knew your dad drank until after I married him. The man is a secret still, but he's an alcoholic as surely as Mina Campbell is. That family has been through hell, I know all about it from hearing Nickel talk and hearing women gab. Years ago now. Your friend Delia was only three or four. Mina's still OK but they all walk on eggs.*

Last Easter, Mina had said how Good Friday was the holiest day for Christians, and the Resurrection the most joyous event; Christmas was pagan really, the trees and the lights. Alma had stayed overnight at Delia's that weekend, and they'd skipped church Easter Sunday but dressed in good clothes and gone to the cemetery with flowers. They'd have a picnic and an egg hunt instead, Mina said, just the five of them, and the gossips in church could talk about someone else today. Nickel Campbell had died a few weeks before, and Mina drove Bird's station wagon up the winding cemetery road, steering with one gloved hand and smoking a cigarette. Alma and Delia were sitting in the back with John-John between them, and Alma could see the shape of Mina's face reflected in the rear-view mirror. The short black veil of her pillbox hat moved with her breath when she exhaled little puffs of smoke and her dark pink lips showed when she talked. Bird said to put out that cigarette, Mina would smudge her gloves or catch herself on fire, one or the other. Bird was like Audrey that way, Alma thought, always telling people what was going to happen, or comparing one story to another.

*You've not been through what Delia's seen. Even so young, kids remember. I never let your dad drink at home. He'd just go out and drink and be gone; he wouldn't ever say what happened. I think it's because he didn't remember. It's all secrets from him as well. And I never knew why he went off. It never seemed to have anything to do with me. If he's not drinking now, fine. He's gone so much I wouldn't know. It's all him, his whole life is him. I'm just a bystander.*

Delia and Mina and John-John are never gone. They don't even have a car anymore; they drive Bird's car.

"Hey," Delia says. She leans toward Alma, into Alma's face. "Let's go. You're taking so long, we'll miss them."

"I wonder how John-John is," Alma says. "Don't you always think about him at night? Where does he think we are, I wonder."

Delia stands and turns, leaving the path to move off through the trees. "He thinks we're at camp. Anyway, that's what they told him."

"He's too little to remember, or know what camp means." Alma has to move faster, skipping to keep up.

"Bird will explain it to him," Delia says, and laughs, because they both know Bird isn't capable of explaining anything. Bird mixes everything up and changes it around.

Delia moves on through the trees and Alma lets herself fall just behind; she can see Delia's white blouse through leaves. Delia is singing again, and they've left the drifty sound of the campfire singing behind; there's only Delia's sometimes lines and phrases, floating back disconnected. *Oh, rocka my soul,* she sings, and *white silver bells, upon a windy hill . . . that will happen only . . . when the faeries sing,* all camp songs she says she hates and can't stop thinking.

Like she can't stop complaining about Bird. Alma peers ahead and sees Delia turn smoothly in stride, wheeling around to look up into the trees, as though relieved of any care. Like a soul could fly up in this place. Resurrection, Alma thinks, means back to life, and she keeps moving, barely fast enough. Easter was a long time ago now. That was the weekend Delia got so angry at Bird. Alma had stayed with the Campbells, Lenny had stayed with Cap, and Wes was gone too, so Audrey had gone away as well. She said it didn't matter where she went, as long as she got away from all the lilies and the florists' trucks that were ever present on the streets of Gaither, even along the country roads, as though each house had to have one of those three-headed monstrosities with its pot swathed in bright green foil. Mina seemed to like lilies; the Campbells had three or four in their living room, ribboned and foiled and tagged with somber little cards. Nickel Campbell's grave still looked new, and Mina had left one of the lilies beside the big headstone. The stone had a crest carved over his name, discreetly, Mina said. Very discreet, Bird remarked, you had to read it with a magnifying glass, and anyway, a lot of good it did these kids for his folks to spend all that money on a gravestone. If they wanted to help, why didn't they pay off Mina's mortgage?

Delia began screaming at Bird to shut up, what did she know about it, shut up and leave them alone. Delia was carrying all the eggs they'd colored the night before, three dozen nestled in egg boxes, and she opened one of the boxes and started lobbing eggs at Bird. Bird actually crouched down behind the gravestone because the eggs were as hard as little rocks, and Delia kept throwing them, dodging Mina until Mina finally caught up to her and grabbed her. Delia had thrown mostly her own eggs, screaming at Bird all the while; there were still plenty to hide for John-John. The night before, she'd marked each one carefully with an initial in wax crayon, so there'd be no confusion and they'd each have twelve eggs when the hunt was over. Alma and Delia had both done six for Johnny, hunched over the kitchen table with paints and stencils.

The kitchen of the Campbells' house seems years away. Alma looks back along the trail, with the sound of the river falling away, and thinks the trees seem flattened shapes, like someone has stenciled them black against the deep blue dusk, and the blue keeps darkening, purple as a bruise. "Johnny won't know where we are," she says aloud, because she knows Delia's too far ahead to hear. "He'll think we're never coming back, like your dad didn't. Delia? Delia, where's your dad. Where is he?"

Wherever he was, that's where Audrey was. She only pretended to be at home still. She let Alma stay with Delia anytime, but she never quite cooperated, and she avoided ever speaking to Mina on the phone. All the arrangements were made by the girls themselves, and Audrey would forget to send the dress or the toothbrush, or the homework Alma needed to do, until at last Alma packed her own overnight bag, and by then she had her own toothbrush at the Campbells' anyway. At Easter, Audrey had still made a pretense of organization, but she'd forgotten to send Alma's good clothes, so Mina ironed one of Delia's dresses for Alma. And while she ironed the girls dyed eggs, and Delia complained. Why did she have to go to the beauty shop every day after school, why did Bird have to go everywhere with them, why couldn't they get a car of their own, like the one they used to have, instead of using Bird's old station wagon, with Bird in it, and Mina said back to her, Why why why. She said why and it was like Audrey was behind the ironing board too, and the Campbells' kitchen was moving the way the room of the car had moved on the trips to Winfield. *It seems terrible that I tell you so much, but is it always terrible to tell a child the truth? When I married at twenty I believed all the fairy tales, and they didn't get me very far. I knew Lenny would hold herself apart, like Wes always has, they were born that way, like animals with protective coloring. You're so like me and I don't ever want you to fade away and then have such trouble coming back from the dead, have to deceive and turn yourself inside out.* Back from the dead. No one could come back, but Audrey thought she had. Well then, that was a resurrection, like Easter, like Jesus, and it should be forever. It shouldn't be over because of the river, because Nickel Campbell died in his car. Alma remembered painting over the mistakes on Delia's eggs, while Delia got madder and madder at Mina. You don't need to be mad at Bird, Mina kept telling Delia, nothing is Bird's fault. But Mina never looked up from the ironing and no one ever said whose fault it was, and Delia never asked. John-John sat in his highchair in his pajamas and banged his spoons and opened and shut his hands over his ears; he thought the change in the way things sounded was funny. Alma wished she could cover her ears that way, or that she was too little to be bothered about anything, like Johnny, and then she imagined herself a baby and Lenny a little girl, both of them in the car with Audrey on the way to Nickel Campbell, with all the windows rolled down and the wind so loud it seemed like a hurricane. *He didn't hesitate, just answered like he'd been waiting for my call, Yes, I'll see you then. He said nothing for a moment, I said nothing, but maybe I sighed, some sound I couldn't stifle, and he said, so calmly, It's all right. Alma, you don't know what feeling is, comfort, gratitude, until you've reached a certain point, and then you'll tear out your soul for it.*

"Delia, Delia," Alma calls out suddenly, her voice rising nearly to a scream. "Delia, wait for me!" And she hears Delia stop ahead, reverse direction, come running back. Alma presses both hands to her mouth to keep from calling out again; she wants to bury her face in John-John's feathery hair that smells of baby powder, she loves Johnny more than Delia does, she knows it, why is it true, and she thinks about the new part of the graveyard where no one was buried yet, the part they ran to while Mina cleaned eggshells off the gravestone and talked to Bird about Delia, how the soft ground was all long grassy sweeps, cleared and gently rolling, drifted with loose grass the mower had left, and how John-John kept pulling up handfuls to throw at the girls, and they hid what was left of the eggs for him to find in the short grass, and Alma helped him peel them. She helped him and the colors cracked apart but the membrane underneath fit tight as a glove, and it was hard to get it off without running water. *Being with him was the worst wrong I ever did but it felt the most like belief; I still believe things he said. I don't have any shame in my mind about that time, just a still white calm, like there's snow over all the pictures and the words.* "Delia!" Alma screams, and she sees Delia running toward her, her white blouse, her white socks and shoes glowing up in the near dark.

"What is it," she says, "what's wrong?" And she pulls Alma's hands down from her face and grasps them hard, searching Alma's eyes. "You're scared, aren't you. But it's only bats. And they're flying way high up over the water. Come and see. Like a flock of birds. And Lenny is there. By the diving rock. We're all going to go swimming."

And they are both running then, through the woods, and the dappled beech trees before Turtle Hole are stalwart and massive, bending this way and that, dense with boughs. The oaks and overhanging willows are heavy and green, as though their miles of roots have drunk the deep heart of the water and forced it through their limbs. Just here on the shore the land is bare, the soil moist, pounded flat like an earthen beach. Cap stands gazing toward them, smiling, and nods her recognition. Alma looks for Lenny and finds her, standing in water to her knees, her clothes wet, her hair streaming. She raises both arms in greeting and presentation, as though to give Alma this place, this water and the colors mixing above it. The girls have made piles of stones, Alma sees, waist-high towers that stand in a staggered line, stacks of single stones that are still and blank, like markers, like a place for a ceremony. Alma moves among them, delighted, careful not to touch.

## ❧ LENNY: BEAUTIFUL SEA

Delia and Alma came running out of the trees, suddenly apparent in the same white shirt and dark shorts, like troops, excited and released, escaped perhaps, and Lenny gestured they should come closer, as though some mystery or secret would make itself known in the shallow water. She raised her arms high and felt the delicious pull of her muscles, reached higher until it hurt, and the younger girls had arrived.

"Good, you got my note," Cap said softly, pleased. "We're all here now. We're just waiting for someone."

Lenny looked into Alma's face, saw her expression lighten and darken almost in the same instant. She thought about picking Alma up, how it had felt, struggling to carry Alma back and forth to that red wagon they'd played with in the field, the one that always got stuck in the tall grass. Audrey would have to come from the house in her apron and pull the wagon for them, telling Lenny to put Alma down, she'd drop Alma and hurt her, Alma was too big to be carried now, she could walk on her own, put her in the wagon and pull her and stay up in the yard, what if she got separated from you in these weeds, she could wander off and you'd never find her.

"No," Alma said now. "We're the only ones."

"What do you mean?" Cap asked.

Lenny watched Alma pause and consider, but she was thinking about the field, how high it had seemed when they were small. The towering blades of the rushes and the fat milkweed had moved in one piece, like water, like the sea must move. Audrey should have known about the field; how any movement in the grassy depths made a wavery trail and left a flattened swath anyone could see from the yard, from the porch, from the air, even. It wasn't possible to get lost; someone could always tell where you were.

Alma's gaze met Lenny's. "I just know," she said then. "I have a feeling." She looked up, searching the sky for the jagged movements of the bats.

"They're like birds flying," Delia said, "all coming up from behind the rock."

Far above, bats continued to flare into the sky, nearly silent, dispersing high in the air. Moving, they flickered and seemed to contract, shaken like creatures compelled to rise by some power in the sky itself. A few stragglers veered low over Turtle Hole, out over the trees.

"So who else do we need?" Lenny found herself smiling. She walked out of the water and began to step carefully among the stones, between the low totems, her arms dramatically outstretched, and she saw the others begin to follow her, laughing.

Delia stepped along on tiptoe, drawing herself up haughtily and holding her folded arms before her to represent a burdensome décolletage she didn't possess. "Indeed," she drawled, raising her brows in unmistakable reference, "we can now appreciate our experience here in a new and larger way." She snuck a glance at Alma.

But Alma only nodded, extending a chivalrous hand. "Mrs. T., what a pleasure to encounter you in this unexpected place."

Cap moved near them in an exaggerated glide. "We'll discuss this further tomorrow morning," she said, pirouetting, "and *everyone* is required to participate in that discussion."

"What was that, dear?" inquired Delia, lifting her chin and sniffing.

"Would you care to repeat your remark," Alma said slowly, in her normal voice, "to all of us?"

Delia advanced on Cap in a threatening mince and raised her voice in a morally superior rendition of hysteria, enunciating with precision, "*Never* cut a fresh roll with a knife, girls, it *ruins* the dough!"

Cap held her ground, batting her lashes and staring down into Delia's narrowed eyes. "Is *this* the way you handle responsibility, by *shrieking?*"

Delia smiled and stepped to the side, swaying, provocative. "If our food is bad or tasteless, we wish for better food." She pursed her lips and grasped Cap's hand, holding it up for inspection.

Alma slipped between them and intoned reproachfully, "Dear, you are not at the races. Put your food" — she trapped Cap's palm in both of hers — "back on your plate. You have a knife. Please pick it up."

"My knife! My knife!" Delia flung herself at Cap and grabbed her around the waist in mock frenzy.

Alma pretended to comfort her, firmly, reasonably. "In private, we speak to each other," she reminded them all. "At table, we speak to the group."

"What," said Delia, "are we at table?" She indicated the series of silent piled stones with outspread arms, and the water beyond seemed to move subtly, as though it were breathing.

Trick of the light, Lenny thought, and she began to sing, softly and deliberately, "By the sea, by the sea, by the beautiful sea . . ."

"You and me . . ." answered Alma.

And they all began to turn and move in easy, seeming ignorance of one another, like members of a tribe. Lenny turned toward the water, closing her eyes, sensing Alma's movements between the stones. Alma seemed to move within her; Lenny didn't have to know about her, or look at her. It was as though she didn't have to think about this one thing; she could live separately from Alma without ever leaving her, the way people left people. People did leave, like Wes had left, whether he was off somewhere or sitting in the kitchen with them. He would sometimes shake his head and complain in irritation, half mockingly, *Too many women*, as if sheer numbers explained his difference from them. Too many *men*, Alma would retort under her breath, glowering, as though even one were too many. Her hair was brown, like Delia's but without curls, average, Cap would say, but her brows and lashes were darker, as though she hadn't yet grown into her face and something more dramatic might evolve. *Don't frown,* Audrey was always telling her, and Alma would try to recompose her expression, smooth the minor scowl of concentration she fixed on nearly any object of her attention. But she wasn't frowning now. Turning, lifting her arms, Lenny framed a round window with her hands and saw her sister glide away from her within it, expressionless, spellbound, perhaps. They were all moving in measured, circular steps, relaxed and drowsy, and above them the bats were as silent, flaring up again into the dark violet sky, and this time they seemed to rise more slowly. It was all very slow, wasn't it, then, and Lenny thought she heard echoes, her thoughts were so clear. She heard herself tell Alma, as an excuse for bossing her, *I'm supposed to take care of you,* and Alma would snap back, *No,* I'll *take care of* you. How she could ignore Alma for what seemed months, all the time depending on her to exist and be exactly as she was.

Lenny let herself circle the curious arrangement of stones; turning, she saw the water, then the blur of the woods with the girls moving past. As though they all only flowed through, flowed past. She thought dimly of the summer Alma was born, when Alma was just "the baby," a creature Audrey rolled outside in the buggy. Lenny's first memories of Alma are indistinct shadows and textures, yet she remembers the buggy, a huge contraption that rocked on its springs like a boat, whose spoked wheels were as big as a bicycle's. She tried to think if she'd seen the buggy recently, some piece of it, entangled with other castoff relics in the basement. The hood had folded down like an accordion in the hot evenings, when the family ate supper outside on the picnic table. Audrey would cover the boat with sheer mosquito netting before she wheeled it over to the side of the yard and knelt down in the garden to weed. Lenny and Wes were supposed to stay occupied, *give me half an hour of quiet, I've had the two of them all day, and the house like a bake oven.* Her father Lenny remembers, so intensely, as though it were just the two of them and Audrey were lost to them both, huge with her pregnancy and then numb, gaunt, giggling with fatigue, or crying while the baby cried, or yelling about some mess Lenny had made. She drank pitchers of sun tea in the long afternoons to keep her milk up while Lenny sat on the steps of the front porch in a daze, worn out, refusing to nap, watching the two-lane down in the curve for a sign of Daddy's car. He would arrive and the day seemed to begin again, even though supper was cooking, and the long, dead August heat began to lift the moment he picked Lenny up and flung the screen door open for them, striding through the house to the icebox for a cold beer, two cold beers; Lenny carried one and Wes drank the first down fast. Supper made a splattering sound in the frying pan and Lenny saw it cooking from atop his shoulders, but they were always outside by the time he finished drinking his beer, crumpled the two cans and smashed them under his work boot. Those big boots. He took his shower and never wore them later, after supper, making fun of what Audrey called the garden, a few rows of toma- toes and beans, farmer Audrey. Lenny laughed at whatever he said and tried hard to play catch, she had a little fake-leather mitt, but she was only three and finally just chased balls into the field, what Wes called the ocean, and the hills across the stream were France, starred with dogwood in the spring that flung their frothy bursts out like popcorn. But now the trees were leaved and green and Daddy ran after Lenny into the field, all the dense twilight pushing him from behind; his girl had never seen the ocean, no, it was nothing like the stream beyond the field, where they caught tadpoles in the yellow bucket and Wes was persuaded to carry the mud-colored, darting creatures all the way back to the house for Lenny to watch in the bathtub. But what was France, and why was the field an ocean? Because the wind blew and the field swung, like soup, along its rim, the way the bath water sloshed, and that was waves on a beach, and then the tadpoles were back in their pail and Wes cleaned the tub with the big sponge. Lenny was in the water and his hand was the troopship, long and broad, bigger, bigger, steaming toward her with an engine sound, a wake like a tail along the surface, all of it up and down with the waves, and an ocean swallowed ships, lots of them. Like the submarines, hard cigar shapes that sunk and spied before the troops could land. That was a beach called Omaha, like Nebraska, and that was France, and the field was like the sea because it hid things, but it moved in the pull of the wind, not the moon. *The men hid in the dark and landed in waves on the beach,* Lenny knew that line, all its words, and the picture she'd thought to go with it, countless little men sitting motionless on burgeoning water like people in a theater.

"Lenny, Lenny, oh, Lenore," Cap whispered now, gliding suddenly close, rustling her voice at Lenny's ear, draping an arm across her shoulders. Then she pulled away as though inviting Lenny to follow.

But Lenny didn't; she turned toward the water instead.

Once she'd asked Cap if her father told stories. About what? About the war, or anything. No, and who cares. But Wes had told stories, talking to Lenny, stories Alma was too young to remember, stories he hadn't said anymore by the time Lenny was eight or nine, when he was gone, when he was home. He must have told her stories, stories she might have confused. He seemed to have told her things, given her things he'd thought she was too young to remember. She saw his dark forearms, furred with golden hair, his sleeves rolled up, the watchband on his wrist turning and darkening. She caught her breath and felt the rolling shift of the ground beneath the picture. That was in the field, when they were hiding in the grass. Or Lenny hid and he came to find her, lying down so the weeds closed over them.

There really was an ocean or a field that kept whatever happened, and nothing moved from where it first touched ground in the fluid grass.

Lenny stood still and looked up, searching the sky for the jagged movements of the bats.

"There were so many," Delia said, her voice soft with wonderment or disbelief. "They're all gone."

The others stopped in place as well. But the bats had vanished, they'd disappeared. Lenny watched Cap and Alma and Delia, their faces upturned in sifting dusk like so many flowers, and she turned away, deciding not to talk. Then no one talked, they were all in the water and they were laughing quietly, secretive, and the water was warm in long spaces, bath water tinged olive. Or Lenny was in the water alone and they were on the bank, the shore; they would remember it both ways, Lenny in the water, already swimming farther out, or the four of them splashing and shoving, but quietly, so they can hear the water, hear the water take them, pull them in, or they only walk in to their ankles and fall back, moving among the stones, because it's Lenny the water really wants, Lenny who swims deeper in, and they've discovered a stage set, a pastoral, Audrey would say, the stacked rocks spaced just so where the water meets the bank, stones stacked high enough to touch with their hands as they move, dipping and turning, the water stretched before them as they trace this path and that among the stones. They move, catch what remains of the light reflected in a glimmer along their arms, holding nearly still to see that effect in the water at their feet, in water to their knees, the water watching them, certainly a presence, heavy with time and forgetting, the long, rippling water Lenny swims through, turning to look at them, showing only her white shoulders and her opalescent face, her wet hair flat to her head and floating out around her, swirled like fabric when she turns.

The girls on shore, tall from her vantage point, move among the rocks like performers, wet to their thighs, laughing, posing for one another, and Lenny swims farther out. The water was colder, deeper in, she moved through stripes of cold, kicking hard, she wanted to move to the center of Turtle Hole and look back, stay afloat where the water was deepest and plummeted down, she wanted to look back to shore and see the girls dancing, pretending to dance, pretending to forget about her, knowing she was watching. She called out to them, she called but they didn't hear, not really, and she started to swim back, as though what she had to say was important, as though she wanted them to hear. Maybe she felt some movement in the water, felt the approach of some entity she nearly recognized, maybe she wanted to draw that power closer to shore, closer to the other girls, whose danger approached from behind. She began swimming back but she couldn't have seen Buddy yet, or Carmody, steering Buddy forward like some vestigial appendage he might at any moment detach from himself and hurl away. She had stopped and turned, treading water, to locate the sound behind her, the sound of Parson's limbs cutting the surface. She must have seen Parson first, swimming hard toward her. She saw him, close enough, his face, his eyes, saw he didn't look at her but past her, toward the shore, his focused gaze completely honed on some other object. Something bad, something wrong. Lenny moved quickly then, instinctually, toward Alma, toward the shore and the stones; then she saw Buddy. She saw his eyes, saw his mouth begin to open in some warning, some plea, and a force behind him, almost a blur, long and powerful and dark, came for her with its arms outstretched.

## ❧ BUDDY CARMODY: FAR FROM ANY OTHER

Lenny's eyes were wide open; wet, she looked smaller, her hair tight to her head. She seemed to crouch in the water, her shoulders white and ghostly in her wet white shirt, and Buddy wanted her to disappear, didn't she know to disappear, but her eyes came at Buddy, searching inside him as Mam's fierce eyes had searched the cave. He felt her search for a way through the dark crack Dad broke in the water, the crack that reached across to find her and hold her. She didn't back away or stop moving toward shore; she moved to the side as though to edge past what filled the water and the world above the water. As though the circle of clearing around Turtle Hole and the water that went so deep were one world, far from any other. She was in the water and Dad moved past Buddy like a lunging wall. He stepped into the water and Turtle Hole did crack apart; Buddy saw it crack jagged and black across its whole surface. The light cracked too, on and off, and lightning flashed so far up in the sky there was no thunder. For a moment Turtle Hole was lit up, silver, and in that silver instant Dad was in front of Buddy's face: he saw nothing but Dad's long back and Dad's shoulders, high and rounded, and the strip of Dad's belt, and he reached up and clung on. The silver lit a dusk that was not day and flashed off; Buddy felt himself dragged into water past his knees. Dad swung round and grabbed Buddy up with one powerful hand and held him dangling just above the surface. The water broke when Buddy moved, tried to stand, he

238

felt his legs jerk as though he ran in place, trying to make the water hold him, lift him up.

"No!" he said. "No!" He kept shouting it, grabbing at Dad, grabbing at the arm that held him.

Dad howled a sound without words. Lenny had come toward them, not away, or they had reached Lenny and found her, and Dad had Lenny by the neck.

"You got to come with me!" Buddy heard himself screaming. He twisted his body, kicking at Dad with his feet. "They're at the campfire now, you got to come with me —"

There was a roaring above the water, blowing along the top of the water and billowing up. Dad made a sound in his throat, an answer, and he threw Buddy at Lenny, like Buddy was a stone to crack her open, a rock to crash a way inside. Buddy felt Lenny stagger, trying to stay on her feet. Dad had pulled her round in the water by her hair and turned them both so they saw the tilted shore, the forms of the other girls frozen, all of it silent, like a scream too high-pitched to hear.

Then it broke open and Lenny grasped Buddy with both arms; she was pulling and tugging his body away, and he heard her yell, in a clinched, bitterly defeated scream, "Give him to me!" She had turned a little away, trying to stand straight enough to throw Buddy out from her, farther into the shallow water they all seemed to struggle toward. Buddy was turned round too, slipping deeper in, his head nearly submerged, and he looked up to see Lenny, her eyes closed and her face contorted, and Dad's face above her, behind her. Buddy felt some shift in their locked embrace and Dad half lifted Lenny, pulling both her arms behind her so she had to let Buddy go. Beyond Dad and Lenny appeared another face, dimly recognized, the dark eyes starkly fixed: he arched from behind and above them as though descended, but water sprayed round him like an aureole. He rose out of Turtle Hole and hung suspended above them: Buddy saw him for a long moment, a slow whirling when all else seemed to move in a spiral circling from him, fierce and clear. Then there was another crack and Dad pushed Buddy under.

He was under water and there were sounds, globular and far away: something fell on Dad and Dad pressed down on Buddy, fallen and scrambling. Buddy was under Dad and he couldn't move. He opened his eyes and saw Lenny's legs moving above him, slowly, in a bicycling motion, bubbles all around her like a glow that was all he could see of the air. There was a kind of music as he moved deeper into the water, deeply beyond Lenny and Dad, and he saw that it was the stranger who had pushed Dad down. The two men grappled, sinking, heavy and dumb, and Buddy felt the whole world drop with a thud, with the same rippling pulse he remembered from the cave. He was trapped in the dark water and he saw the dappled bottom of Turtle Hole, all spotted with light circles and soft with dust that stirred. He let himself drift down as the others struggled above him. Something turned in the depths, curved and pale as a shell, and he looked deeply after that object, trying to follow it with his eyes. Suddenly, as though emerged from what fell away, a white owl flew straight up at his face, wings flared in the water, talons outspread. The hooked bill opened, and the white ruff around the staring eyes became the lined, miniature features of the creature in the cave. Wavering, unmistakable, rolling with the motion of the underwater world. The little man's odd, drawn-down face looked at Buddy hard, reprovingly, and the short little hand made a lifting motion. Instantly, Buddy felt himself forcefully buoyed up as Dad and the stranger plunged into the water past him, beneath him, locked and rolling. Then Buddy was breathing, long, ragged gasps, and the water was too deep and Lenny had him by his shirt, pulling him behind her, and he felt her stumbling, knew she was walking, pulling him out, but the men had come after them; Buddy felt them just near, a tumult falling haphazardly closer.

Buddy was coughing, standing on his feet, trying to walk, and he heard Lenny yelling at him, at the other girls who were milling toward them. He couldn't really hear, his ears were so stopped with water, but he felt the muffled explosions of her words pushing him along.

They were on the shore, on the rocky dirt that bordered Turtle Hole, and the earth itself seemed to move and slide, and the stranger had hold of Dad, had dragged him out of the water and fallen beneath him, and Dad had got a rock from one of the stacked piles fixed along the water.

Buddy heard Lenny then. "Alma," she was screaming, "Alma!"

And Dad hit the stranger with the rock along the side of his head, and the rock made a sound when it hit.

The stranger got up, holding on to Dad, and he fell back down. Buddy heard Lenny screaming, "Run! Run!"

Dad was yelling too, and he was laughing when he yelled. "Run," he said, like she did, and he had her by both arms and moved her forward with his knee. "You gonna run! All a you run!" And he pushed Lenny down with his knee and she was on the ground.

There was a roaring in Buddy's head and he had the rock in his hand and he darted forward. Dad was kneeling on Lenny's back and Buddy hit him with the rock. He hit him on the top of his head, and Dad lurched just a little, and put out one hand to steady himself.

Lenny had twisted under him, trying to hold him off with her arms. "Cap," she cried.

And Cap was beside Buddy, and she brought a rock down on Dad's head. She held it with two hands, and she hit him twice, and he fell sideways, grabbing at her, and the rock dropped, and the other girls screamed and came forward with rocks, and Buddy was pushed back. There was just the sound of the rocks hitting Dad's head — dull, separate sounds, like steps they were all walking, deeper in. The girls came together, hiding the ground in a wall of ragged sounds, their arms moving scared and rapid, and Buddy thought they should keep hitting Dad, just there, on his head. Dad's head hurt him; there was something so bad in Dad's head. He would get all of them. None of them would get away from Dad now if Dad got up; none of them would ever get away. Dad was like a stone that wouldn't bleed, but the inside of Dad's head could fall in, hunch down small and smashed the way Dad really was.

Then Buddy heard a silence that was empty, seeping around and between them all. The girls staggered, their backs to him, reaching for each other. Buddy thought they would fall down, fall on their knees: they were scared to be where Dad was, scared of where Buddy had been. Buddy saw through their clasped hands, their bodies that touched and drew apart. He saw Lenny crawling out from underneath Dad, trying to stand up.

A voice said, "Buddy."

But he couldn't look away.

They were screaming, she heard them dimly, Alma distinct from the rest, her guttural repetition of Lenny's name ripping out meaningless, keeping time. He was on her back with one arm under her, pulling her hips off the ground like he was going to rip her open from behind. She hit the ground hard under him, her breath sucked into a hard, bright point of pain at the base of her spine. Maybe she closed her eyes, or the ground grew a luminous black, and she saw Buddy across the stream from her in the woods. The woods were lit up and Buddy was a little animal crouching on his haunches, trying to make them laugh, disappearing across a divide; in her mind she took hold of him and pulled him to her over the bright line of the water. From somewhere above them all she saw Buddy dart forward, the only one to move, hurling the rock with all the force of his body, jumping into the blow. What gripped Lenny faltered and she twisted under it, struggling to see, to breathe, and the girls' faces appeared above her, contorted and weeping. They weren't looking at her but at what held her; it all ground down, slow and silent. The blur of their moving arms seemed to continue a long time, as though they were pounding a stake into the ground, deeper and deeper, and Lenny felt the impact of each blow as she was hammered into the earth beneath his dark, dense weight. They seemed to be hitting her in a part of herself she couldn't feel, desperately, forcing her down and down. She fell away from them and saw the evening sky beyond them, aswirl and starless, alive in its convex field, and she knew she would never leave this place. They kept hitting him, too terrified to stop, to touch him or pull him off her; she tried to crawl toward them to tell them, *stop, stop, you're too late.*

But they had reached for her. She stood up shakily in their embrace, into a still instant.

Everything stopped.

Lenny could hear the air. Clouds of mist turned in their slow descent, drifting and dissipated. She felt the others near her, a bitter warmth above his sprawled form. They stood, looking down. A silence rippled out from him and the silence seemed to coalesce, heavy and calm, holding them all in place. So near, and so far from her, Lenny heard the hushed voices of the others.

"He's not moving," Delia said.

"He might get up," said Alma.

"He won't get up," Cap whispered. "He was crazy, like an animal."

"We should never have come here," Delia said. She began to sob, but quietly, as though any sound might waken him.

"Shhh," Lenny said. "He would have hurt Buddy." She dropped her own voice to a whisper. "He wanted to kill Buddy."

"Don't we have to tell someone?" Delia put her hand in Cap's, tried to pull at her, but Cap didn't answer. She didn't raise her eyes from the shape on the ground.

"It's over now," Lenny said slowly, evenly. "But if we tell someone, it'll never be over. We'll have to tell it and tell it. We'll never be able to stop telling it. Nothing else will matter anymore, ever."

Cap turned her head to look at Lenny. Her eyes were wide, startled, so close Lenny saw the facets of her green irises. "Then what?" She mouthed the words silently, over the heads of the younger girls. The wind tossed a coppery strand of her hair across her lips, and Lenny looked away. Dense woods circled the open clearing of Turtle Hole. The giant beeches and willows arched their limbs, nearly bestial. Their branches stirred and moved, hulking, protective. Lenny strained to hear the sound of the leaves, as if there were words in their lissome rattle.

"It should stay here," Lenny whispered. "It should all stay here."

"Look at him," Cap murmured.

The shape on the broad dirt shore hadn't moved. His legs were twisted and his upturned hands were empty, the fingers curled. Lenny looked at him and her body stung in the moist air, limb by limb, as though it were painful to come alive again. She imagined lying still. He would have stood over her like this, or reached for the others. Which one? She pulled them all closer. The world would not be as it was. She saw that there was no world but this one now, full blown and dense with shifting air; they were born into it, mourning. He lay at their feet, unmoving: now he looked like a man. Above them the far-flung sky arched away and dusk gathered, blurred and soft, rolling like a wheel that only rolls and darkens as it rolls.

He moves to stand and knows he can't, not yet, but his vision clears and the colors separate into forms. He sees the boy first, a shape light and then dark, a profile finely etched against a cataclysm of sparks. He calls the boy's name once, twice. There is a hush and that quiet holds still. He sees the boy for what he is: a piece of light with dark scars on his wrists, at his throat. Someone is sobbing calmly, but it's a sound like water pouring from vessel to vessel, a sound like an undercurrent. Parson thinks it's a sound he has heard and brought here with him, an old sound that goes on a long time. The boy moves toward Parson and the sound fades; the light gives way, becomes Buddy's face, Buddy's hands on him. He gets to his knees. The boy wants to hold on to him, takes his arm as though to show him, lead him closer, but the girls stand with their backs to him. Parson can't see what's in front of them.

He stands and the knot of their bodies loosens. They say nothing, they only wait, and Parson edges them all a little aside, moves into the circle. Carmody has turned nearly face down on the bank of Turtle Hole at their feet; there is an absence, a blank around his body, and the absence is empty: everything has gone away. Parson bends down, kneels, reaches beneath the body to unbutton Carmody's shirt and pull it off. He wraps the shirt around Carmody's head and face, and ties the empty sleeves to keep the shirt in place. But there is not much blood. It's as though whatever was in Carmody's head has withdrawn, pulled back, moved on; now he is only what's left. He has a weight, dense and quiet; he sleeps in a layered dream, a dream so deep he has sunk far from whatever he knew, far from all of them. Now it would be wrong to hurt him, and impossible. He is delivered; it is already done.

Parson looks up to see the girls standing motionless, a still configuration. Lenny with her arms around the younger ones, each wedged near like a shadow, and the other girl then, standing just before them, one arm flung out in front of them all. She holds a rock in her other hand, as though Carmody might stand and lurch toward them, as though it might all begin again. Parson hears them, hears someone, gasping.

He stands up and nearly loses his balance; he does lurch toward them but Lenny moves closer and places one hand flat against his chest. They are all moving, tilting, standing near him. There's a smell coming off them, a smell of tears and sweat, new and smashed, sweet. Like clover reduced in someone's hands, worried until it's moist. A panic smell, but they're standing in their own silence.

Parson looks at Lenny and tells her, "Stand with the little boy."

Quickly, while they're moving, Parson stands between them and Carmody's body. He puts a foot against the nearest stack of piled rocks and shoves hard; the rocks topple scattered on the ground and Parson picks up the largest, the stable, flat rock from the bottom of the pile, and lifts it high with both hands. He brings it down on the back of the hooded head but the body never twitches. Still, they can't know. Parson has taken it on.

He whirls round in a smooth progression and topples each pile of rocks. One hard, balanced blow, a well-placed kick, and the rocks fall in a pummeled, nearly circular grid no one will know how to read. No one will come here looking, not for years and years. They'll look for Parson somewhere else, and they'll find him, and it won't matter then.

The boy steps forward, his pale, peaked face round as a moon, as blank and wan. "You got blood on you," he tells Parson.

Parson only looks at him, and Buddy comes closer, gestures for Parson to bend down, puts one hand on Parson's shoulder. "You got blood here, where he hit you," Buddy says, and Parson feels Buddy's hand on his temple, a touch as light as some wafted petal, a pale and waxen touch. Buddy brings his palm down then and opens his hand to show Parson the red stain, and he moves into Parson's arms, fits himself closely. He folds himself in and sighs raggedly. Parson stands, holding him, and they walk into the water just far enough for Parson to crouch down, immersed to his chest. He cradles Buddy in the water easily, with one arm, and he tilts Buddy's head back, only slightly, as though he will rock him, to comfort him.

"You can wash it off," Buddy says. "You can get it clean."

Parson nods and puts a finger to his lips, widens his eyes in a signal for the boy to be quiet. He palms a sluice of water into his hand and touches Buddy's head, first with his wrist, then with the heel of his hand, fingers opening, a slow, practiced caress.

Buddy looks, interested, into Parson's eyes. As though he's watching a man shoe a horse, Parson thinks, or load a gun, or make a pie. Cupped water from Parson's hand courses down his face, but he doesn't blink. His wet lashes are fixed in starry points.

Holding the boy in his arms, Parson lets himself sink into the water. The boy only nestles closer, light, lighter than air, Parson thinks, like some bird just resting, an intricate, airy works, densely packed, nearly weightless. Parson lets them turn in the water, thinks of stopping here, but he stands and begins carrying the boy back to shore. Buddy touches his face.

"Mister," he says, "let me see." He slides his fingers over the throb at Parson's temple.

Parson feels the ache as a separate pain for the first time, as though the pain responds to the delicate pull of the boy's fingers. "He clipped me one," Parson murmurs. Hears, doesn't see, the hip-high swak of water against them. Holding the boy, Parson lets him float, moves him forward in the water like a cradled ship.

"Not too bad," Buddy says, still peering at him through near dark. "No one's going to be asking you."

"Don't matter," Parson says. "I'll get away, lie low." He looks at Buddy, wanting an answer. "No one knows me here. You're the only one could even say where I came from."

They hear an owl call across the water, the sound a question and exclamation, hung in the air to fade.

"You know me?" Parson asks softly. "Do you know me, boy?"

Buddy looks up at him, smiles. "I saw that owl in the water," he says.

"They fish off the surface sometimes," Parson says, "frogs and peepers."

"I saw him deep down," Buddy answers. "Flew up at me from them lights on the bottom." Then he goes quiet, lapse of a heart-beat, and says, nearly too fast to make out, "Dad wanted me to steal them rings the old lady has in her room, so he could take him a stake away with him. He was fixin to go. He was going to take me too, then he was going to let me stay if I got the rings."

"He did go," Parson says. "He has gone and he won't come back, and you don't have to be afraid."

The boy finds his own feet and stands, walks out of Parson's loose embrace as they come up on shore. Parson feels his movement and lets him go, and the two of them move close to the girls until they stand, all of them, at Carmody's feet. Carmody's wet khaki pants are smeared with red mud, and his boots turn in awkwardly. The soles are pitted, dug in long scratches, as though something has clawed at them.

One of the little girls is still crying, sobbing.

"Delia," Lenny begins, stops, takes a breath.

Parson looks at her, at all of them. They raise their eyes to him, even Delia, each gaze cutting space like the spoke of a wheel. "You can finish it," he tells them quietly. "The body has got to be put somewhere."

The one called Delia shakes her face free of her tousled, curly hair. She looks into Parson's face and her wet eyes look blasted awake, alert. "The water, then," she says.

"No," Parson says.

"I know where," Buddy says. He is looking along the ground, walking a few steps away, and he stoops and picks up a box-like flashlight. He cups his palm over the plastic front and turns it on, and his hand shows suddenly red, the light pouring round his feet like something spilled. He switches it off. "Got to have a light," he says quietly. "But I know where."

"We can't carry him far," Lenny says.

"It's not far," Buddy says, and he tells Parson, "You best leave, before someone's looking for us."

Parson stands and listens. It has begun to rain gently, as though the shadow of a watery hand draws closer. He hears rain on leaves, a sound like a sigh all around the water, and far off he hears singing in faulty patches. The others are still at the campfire but they'll stop now, in the rain.

He looks at Lenny, doesn't speak, but she says, soft and deliberate, "You should go."

Parson takes a step back, away from them, watches Lenny take Carmody's hand, no, his wrist. The younger ones position themselves at his feet.

"Cap," Lenny says, "help us."

The other girl seems to rouse. She drops the rock she's holding, looks at Lenny. Their exchanged glance seems to pull her in, closer, until she too reaches for one of Carmody's wrists.

"Do it fast," Parson says. He knows they've got to do it now, together, and he remembers the bag of his clothes, his boots. He grabs the sack where it sits, near the rock. A curtain of rain begins to fall quietly across Turtle Hole and Parson is turning, walking. He thinks it will rain all night; he'll put on his clothes when he gets into the trees near the road. Soon it will rain hard and no one will wonder that he's soaked to the skin; men driving between towns on a wet weekend night will stop for him. In fact, they will: as a green Ford Fairlane shudders its way over Mud River Bridge near Gaither, he'll shut his eyes in the dark, whispering to himself in the back seat where no one hears him over the blare of the radio. And he will still see the girls, dragging the body around the diving rock, the body a spent slab they don't try to lift.

## ✖ BUDDY CARMODY: DARK PARABLE

The rocky path to the diving rock is a broken road, a road that never was, and the grassy, weed-choked border of the path, the dense, leafy woods beyond, are suddenly full of sound. The rain is just beginning, a fine spray, a drift of cloud. Insects chorus in the clarified air, in the safety of the dark. Hundreds of crickets, Buddy thinks, more, maybe thousands, what are thousands, and he sees numbers in his mind, a one with endless zeros, points beyond points, and the crickets and beetles are small as zeros, darting hidden, hard as jewels, deep down near the white roots of the onion grass. He feels himself move among them, tall as a mountain. The girls follow him, tight together, and a bright elation stabs through him; the world has turned round and made real a scenario too surprising to have dreamed or hoped. They're like a team in the dark, a team in a group in a line, *trooping all together,* and for a moment he forgets what the girls hold in their hands, why they're struggling to keep up, their breathing a ragged, balanced cadence urging him on, pressing against him, their staggered footfalls moving him. And the dragging sound between them moves him too: the heavy thing they pull along the ground, the wound that hangs down, and Buddy's head goes black inside. At the edge of his darkness a bright thread jumps like a nerve, moving off into a separate space Buddy can't think about with what he knows. If he were really a mountain, the girls would be part of the dark, all four of them on the path with their cargo, unseen from way up high. Nothing lit from far away but the stranger who has left them and moved off, his trail a line of light through trees toward the road. He has to be moving, careful, in the cover of the trees, Buddy thinks, or stopped like a still point, standing on the road shirtless with his wet trousers clung to his legs. Or he could wait in the woods until real night comes, wait to leave, and far off on a road the car or truck that will pick him up is already moving toward him. Sound of an engine. The stranger will walk through trees to the road, and Buddy knows he'll come out two curves and a straight piece from the dirt turnoff that leads to Camp Shelter. Leads past the church with blue windows and farther on to Buddy's house. The car that picks up the stranger could head back past Shelter Road, past the wide berm where Buddy and Mam stand when they wait for the bus, on toward Bellington and across the whole country of America. That's where the road goes if you never stop, Mam says, clear to the Pacific Ocean, and Buddy thinks about the stranger plunging into the sea, not a man anymore but a long tail of light, like the comets he's seen in pictures at school. Or the stranger could head the other way, over Mud River Bridge into Gaither and quickly through it, like a thought going away from them, vanishing. There's an ocean on that side too, Mam says so, not so far either, a big cold ocean, and Buddy sees the stranger taking away everything that's happened, taking it all away into water so big and deep nothing ever comes out again. Buddy fixes the stranger in his mind, the way he looked, arched high out of the water of Turtle Hole and bearing down on Dad, suspended, come from nowhere: Buddy holds him still and looks at him. He did look winged, bronzed and dark, his big shoulders and the whole of his body curved, flared inward, an attack bird, a sprung predator poised to drop, and Buddy remembers a pounding, his heartbeat in his ears when he was pushed under the water, nowhere to go but deeper, the thrashing above him a flailing mix of limbs and white streaks. How big the water was, how cold as he went deeper, with the dappled gold color like circles inside circles, spangling the bottom that sank farther away as Buddy drifted toward it.

"I hear something," a voice says behind him, and the procession slows, hesitates.

Behind, in front of them, the sound reverberates in the rain, fragile, a breathy calling that hangs in the air.

"Alma, it's just doves, or owls," Lenny says quietly, "owls in the trees."

"In the trees," Buddy hears himself say, like an echo.

"Don't stop walking," Lenny whispers back. "It will be too hard to keep going."

"Where is he taking us?" Alma asks her.

Buddy doesn't turn to look but he says, still moving, "This way, around the rock. I know a hiding place."

And he hears them fall in again, resume their march. He thinks about them marching and lifts his own knees higher, walking, not running, a troop is a team that walks: *airy mountain*, and the ground does rise here, toward the back of the diving rock, the door of the cave, the slant of shelf-like hole that opens, and Buddy feels a rush of fear, a tremor along his spine so chill he can't be drowsy, but he stifles a yawn that makes him shake. A little sound escapes him.

Lenny reaches out, puts a hand on his shoulder. "Shhh," she says, "quick now."

"Lenny," Cap says, "did he hurt you?"

Buddy knows her, the girl Lenny stays with in her tent. Cap. A name like a hat.

Lenny whispers, "Don't talk about it now."

"We can't ever talk about it," Cap says.

"We can talk," Lenny says, "but only to each other. It's only ours to talk about. We're the only ones who were there. We're the only ones who know what happened."

One of the girls is crying, on and on.

"We'll talk later," Lenny says, "not now."

"Delia," someone says, "shhh, shhh."

"Never mind, Alma," Lenny says.

"Delia, some of us could have run away," Alma says quietly. "But we couldn't leave Lenny. We couldn't leave Lenny, Delia."

"I know," Delia sobs, softly.

"Let Delia be," Lenny says. "She's all right."

Buddy turns to look. Lenny and Cap are barely able to drag Dad over the ground. The younger girls seem far away, holding his ankles up, as though they only keep him from taking root in his heavy parts, melding into ground like a fallen tree gone powdery and rotten. But Dad is not rotten; he's someone asleep, with no face. His hooded head hangs down and his white chest is like a face. His bare back scrapes along the dirt. Buddy doesn't look, he doesn't look at Dad's long legs or think about Dad's belt. The belt with the buckle will stay in the cave, the buckle like a treasure that won't change, metal like a coin: Buddy knows about coins, how they last and never rot. Like animals rot on the loamy ground of the forest, like Dad will rot, all of him gone away to powder. Not big anymore, not fast, in front of Buddy and behind him and all over him. Buddy takes a skip, jumps in place, like he could help them lift, but he can't touch, no: Dad is too heavy for him. Buddy has the light though, he has the light, not Dad, and he'll turn it on when they get to the cave. Now he shows them how to go, here, around the back of the rock that anchors sheer above them. They can still see to follow, this dark is not really dark at all. Buddy knows about the real dark, the black inside the cave. Now he sees the back of the rock, the little rise of dirt leading to the hole. The scrub pine around the hole moves, pale, showing its underside; there's a wind picking up, a soft rainy wind to blow leaves and needles backwards. The pine tosses itself gently against the rock. Buddy grasps the damp, springy tendrils with his hands, pulls himself close, and kneels at the hole.

She's there beside him.

"It's a cave," Buddy tells her, "a big cave deep in."

She watches as he turns the flashlight on, shines it quickly inside. "You go in first," she says, "and hold the light on us."

Buddy can smell the cave breathing its cool air into the rain, like a smoke no one can see. He crouches and crawls in; he doesn't look to the right or left, only turns back around and plays the light across Lenny, across the space where she'll appear. He sees her hands, her arms, reach through, and her hair hides her face. She pulls herself in tighter than she needs to, crawling through like the opening is smaller than it really is. When Dad came through he only crouched down double, but Dad could move like an animal, bending and sliding and folding himself. Buddy yawns again, shivering, then Lenny is beside him on all fours, and she touches his arm to signal he should shift the beam of light. He hears her panting, and she reaches through the hole to motion Cap inside.

Buddy sees her hands on Cap's hands. He moves to make more room and Cap is inside. Both of them lean back through the opening into the bluer night. Buddy can taste the night in his mouth like a wish, a night so big, so warm and wet and full of air, falling away forever like the sky falls with its stars.

"Give us the hands," Lenny says, "here."

Buddy sees Dad's hands reach in, the fingers splayed, and he stumbles backwards. Dad would crawl in out of the rain, he'd do it like that, long, on his belly, out of nowhere — like his foot, his leather boot, had appeared beside Buddy's hand when Buddy got out of the cave. But Lenny and Cap take hold of Dad's wrists, and they have to pull so hard, like Dad doesn't want to be here anymore, he wouldn't go out, he won't come in, they have to pull so hard their hands slip and they grasp his fingers, holding on.

Buddy shines the light. Dad's hands look like anyone else's now. They don't look like Dad's hands anymore.

"You have to push," Buddy hears Cap say through the hole. "Inside there's a slant downward, but you have to push to get him in. Hold his legs and push."

And Dad's covered head is inside, wobbling, and his white shoulders. And his blank white chest. Then the rest of him slides down the incline of the rock, slides so fast he reaches darkness, and the faces of the other girls appear, lit and golden, in the rectangular frame of the hole.

"Come on," Lenny says, "hurry." And she reaches out to them. Alma slides inside and walks the slant of rock to stand near them.

"I don't want to," comes Delia's voice. "I can't."

Lenny stands at the slanted hole of the entrance. Buddy thinks she's talking to the whole world outside the opening. "You were brave, Delia," she says softly. "You kept him from hurting me."

"I was scared," Delia sobs angrily.

"I was scared too," Alma says. "But we stayed together —"

"We weren't wrong, Delia," Cap tells her. "There was no one to help us."

"Wait," Lenny says. "Delia, do you want to go back to camp and get someone? If you do, tell us now. We'll come with you. All of us."

There's a pause. No, Buddy wants to tell them. No, don't bring anyone, don't tell.

"Delia," Lenny calls quietly. "We can't make it so that it never happened. But we can make it stop here, and stay here. We can, Delia."

"I don't want anyone to make me talk about it," Alma says, almost absently. "I want to think about it ourselves, just us."

Delia's face peers through the rock slash of the opening. One long beam of light trained on the stone ceiling casts a glowy nimbus around her. Buddy knows she sees through to find them in the dark soup beneath her, all of them shadows. She shouts into the cave, where the sound disappears. "What if one of us tells," she cries, her voice breaking.

"Delia —" Cap begins.

"No, wait," Lenny says, "she's right. Any one of us might tell . . ." She is quiet a moment, then starts again, seeming to find words as she talks. "Tell someone, sometime . . . Tomorrow, or next year, or in twenty years."

"A hundred years," Alma breathes, as though it's a fairy tale.

"And what then?" Cap says.

"Then maybe we'll all talk about it." Lenny stands quite still.

"We'll have to," Cap says.

Alma steps closer, floats her clear voice up to Delia. "Or one of us might tell someone," she says, "who'll never tell."

Everyone stops speaking. Buddy waits in the silence, hearing the water rattle deep in, deeper than any of them knows. He thinks the cave could go so deep it holds all of Turtle Hole, holds the bowl of the water in vast rocks and deep spreads of space that crawl down and down beneath Camp Shelter.

"Delia," Lenny says softly, "what do you want to do?"

"I want to come in," says Delia's voice.

Buddy shines the light on the opening. And Lenny reaches up to help Delia through, guiding her legs, nearly lifting her inside. Buddy plays the light around the dome of the entrance, follows the curve of the rock just over their heads. He lets the glow fall to hold their faces, their white collars and shoulders. Gravely, they look into nothing, relieved, afraid, completely still. Buddy hears them breathing, and he can't swallow, or think what it is he has to do.

"We should have some twine, some string," Cap says, "to find our way out again."

"Buddy," Lenny says, "you've been in here? You know the way?"

"I know," Buddy answers.

"We'll stay directly behind you," Lenny says. "We won't go any further than we have to. When we come out, we'll walk with a hand on one another's shoulders, in a line, so no one gets lost." Lenny blinks once. In the yellow bell of light Buddy sees the quiver of two long blond hairs that are caught in her eyelashes. "Buddy," she says, "give me the flashlight."

"I can turn it off," he says, "to show you how black it gets."

"No!" Lenny says, and her hand is at his wrist. She has the light and keeps hold of him, pulling him nearer. "Stand just in front of me. Face forward. There, don't move. Listen," she says to everyone, "we have to go further in, just a little further. Buddy comes in here, other people must."

Buddy shifts in place. He hears them shuffling, wordless, taking up their burden. Lenny nudges him, gives him back the light, keeps one hand on him. He begins to walk, straight back, the way Dad walked. He knows the path runs along the broad wall of the cave, the wall with the writing, but he keeps his eyes on the filmy light at his feet. He doesn't want the cave to come alive, he wants to take them in and out. Behind him, he hears someone crying again, but they all keep walking, steady and still. He stops a moment to play the light along the rock floor. Off to the side, he sees the rumpled shape of the sleeping bag and moves the light back to center quickly. Now they all hear the stream in the dark, a tinkling like music, and they are moving closer to the water, back farther than Buddy has been before. They seem to be walking gradually downward, as though the cave dips low to hold its rattle, to hold whatever runs through it.

"Alma," Lenny says quietly, "you OK?"

"Lenny, it's far enough," she answers. "Delia can't stop crying. She needs —"

"Delia," Lenny says, "soon we'll go out. We will. Soon."

"Go to the water," Delia says.

Buddy stops. The stream sounds close. He feels the rock, damper and colder on his bare feet. He moves forward one step, two, and catches the edge of a shining line with his light. Closer, and he sees the narrow run, a rocky sluice smaller than it sounds, and as he squats to see it better he slips on the slick stone and sits down hard, dislodging a run of pebbles that seem to skitter down a long slant and fall off an edge to the left. They all wait, motionless, hearing the pebbles fall. The little rocks seem to drop and plunge and drop again, rattling a long way down.

"We're at the stream," Delia says. She has stopped sobbing.

"Buddy," Lenny says. She reaches down and hauls him gently to his feet, pulling him back. "Give me the light for a minute."

The light plays on the stream, though it's not a stream really, just a bright, narrow ditch. They could almost jump across, but the other side is wreathed in darkness. The girls kneel in a tight knot and move forward carefully, on their knees, to the edge. Lenny sweeps her cone of light over the still black water, then holds her other hand just beneath the surface. Buddy finds himself behind them all, in darkness, but he can see the lit water, her wavering hand. In the pool of light something stirs across her palm, disappears, moves across again.

"It's a minnow," Cap says, "a little fish, all white."

"A blind fish, must be," Alma says. "Fish in caves are blind." She puts her hand in the water too, lightly touches her fingertips to Lenny's. The sieve of their fingers draws tighter in the circle of light, but the fish has disappeared.

"We have to put him in the water," Delia says. "The water will hold him."

There's a silence.

"But maybe this water feeds Turtle Hole," Alma says. "Or maybe it feeds into the river. And the river floods. There are rapids. In the spring, the water gets high."

"It does, doesn't it, Buddy," Lenny says. "So high sometimes it breaks the swinging bridge."

"Don't break it," Buddy says. "Never has washed it away. Just takes some of the boards."

Lenny trains the light all round them, picks up a rock, and throws it sideways. Again they hear the long slide, the drop and tumble of an object falling end over end.

"The edge is close," Cap says. "Back behind us, that way. You can hear it."

"Buddy," Lenny says, "you stay exactly where you are. Delia, you stay right beside Buddy. Then Alma, and Cap. We'll move in a line, slowly, so we won't lose each other. I'm going to be in front. I have to find the edge."

"You'll have to crawl," Alma says, "and feel with your hands. Take the light, and feel way out in front of you. I'll hold on to your ankles."

Lenny lights the girls' faces. The three of them well up out of blackness like a reflection on the surface of a pool. "All right. Cap, you hold on to Alma."

"Delia will hold on to me," says Alma.

"Right. Now, everyone but Buddy. Slowly. It's slippery here." Lenny waits for them to get into position, then she moves the light and turns away from them. Buddy sees the yellow cone play over nothing, and he reaches out in the dark to touch Delia. She has knelt beside him, and he feels the top of her head, the soft curls of her hair. He leaves his hand there.

"I'm moving now," Lenny says. "I'm going slow. Everyone will have to move with me. We'll see how far it is."

Buddy hears them, like a string of wary animals in the dark. He closes his eyes so he won't try to see. Even Delia stirs, begins to move.

"Buddy," he hears her say, "you have to kneel down. Hold to my leg, here."

He squats down and feels her take his hand, move it to her

ankle. He keeps his face turned toward the stream, toward the sound of the water and its lonely singing, and he can feel the chain of their bodies pulling away from him.

Suddenly he remembers the ring, round and gold, jammed halfway onto Dad's finger. Dad still has the ring. Buddy will have to get it, find Dad's hand in the dark. Now, before the girls come back. He doesn't want them to know about the ring.

"I feel the edge," comes Lenny's voice. "It's here."

Buddy keeps his eyes closed and reaches behind him. He touches Dad's side, his leather belt, his long arm. He feels for Dad's hand. Dad's fingers are curled up, fragile and curved, like he's let go. He doesn't want the ring anymore; he doesn't want anything. The ring is half off Dad's index finger and Buddy turns it gently and pulls it away. He puts the ring in his pocket, his heart pounding: what will he do with it now? He longs for someone's voice, someone to tell him.

Lenny is talking from the dark. "I'm backing up now. Everyone, move back slowly."

Buddy opens his eyes and sees the conical light inch back with her. The light appears dimmer, farther away, and the girls seem to reel it in until they are all at his feet as he stands up. Below him the cone of light reaches out, looking, until it finds the body behind them, a half-naked log with its head wrapped up. Buddy sees the cuffs of the khaki shirt now, hanging from the knot the stranger made when he tied the sleeves tight together. Across the blank of the covered face, dark patches have surfaced like a message or a claim.

"Bleeding," Cap says into her hands.

"No," Lenny says, "wet. It's wet in here. Even the air is wet. Buddy, you hold the flashlight."

She puts the plastic box solidly into his hands, and he aims it toward her, trying to see her, but he only finds her back, her shoulders and Cap's, as they bend over Dad and grab Dad's two flung-out hands. His naked hands. And they pull. They pull until Dad lies in front of the line of girls, and they put his arms straight along his sides.

"It's not far," Lenny says. "And the floor drops down before it stops."

"It stops?" Delia sounds sleepy.

"Like a cliff, " Lenny says.

"And below the cliff there's a long space," Alma says softly, "closed off in the rocks."

"Like a grave," Delia says.

And they are moving the body, turning it before them. Like Dad is a heavy rug, rolled up around some secret. Buddy keeps the light playing over them as they move off. The girls' dark shorts, their hips, don't register in his vision; he just sees the pale, interrupted field of their four white shirts moving in a staggered line.

"Buddy," Lenny calls to him, "don't move. Just hold the light. We'll see by the light to come back to you."

He can hear the girls moving; he strains to hear, but some whispery intervention crowds closer, near him, spirals of hushed murmuring that run over and over each other, fast talk he can't understand, now urgent, now drifting.

He hears Lenny, calling to him. She is saying his name. "Buddy. Buddy? We're at the edge."

He tries to make himself answer, say a word. But he can only think the word he wants to say.

"Buddy?" Lenny is still calling him. "Buddy, was he your father?"

*Except I ain't your old block, am I.*

Buddy tries to push those words through his brain to his mouth. And he pushes so hard that when he makes a sound he thinks his voice will be a scream. But his voice sounds calm and quiet and the words arrive unbidden. "No," he says, "I had to call him Dad. But he wasn't no part of me."

Silence. Then Lenny says, from over there, "Now, let go."

"No," Delia says, "we should say something. Some kind of prayer."

"For who?" Alma asks.

Lenny's voice. "Then go ahead, Delia, pray."

"A prayer is like asking," Delia says, "because we didn't call the police."

"We didn't call anyone, Delia," Cap says. "No one could change it or make it not happen."

"The police found my father." Delia sounds dreamy, as dreamy as Buddy feels.

"They were supposed to," Lenny says. "He knew they would. All of you wanted them to." Then she calls to Buddy, "Buddy, do you want anyone to find him?"

"No," Buddy says.

"Does your mother want them to find him?"

"No," he says.

He hears them say more but the whispers crowd in between, fast and hushed, and he understands those hurried words are the girls' voices: he's hearing everything they're going to think and not tell, even to each other, years of phrases turned round and round, left here in the dark.

He hears Delia's voice. "What's down there? Is it water?"

"It could be water," Lenny says.

And Buddy knows it is. *Like unto a net* is what they say in services, and they say it every time in the church with blue windows, and in Mam's big Bible at home there's a slick picture in satin colors. Angels flying down to walk on water with the net. Their billowing gowns and open hands. Lightning on one side of heaven and sunrise on the other, and the water leaping up; there were dragons in the water but the angels weren't afraid. That was the kingdom of heaven and the dragnet in their hands, and the good and the evil all taken up.

"Now," Lenny says.

And when they push Dad over, Buddy has crouched down with the light between his feet; he claps his hands over his ears hard but he still hears the waves leaping and crashing around them all. He feels himself float away, dragged and tossed, and there's a pounding like a roll of drums, and air so sweet he opens his mouth to drink, and the voices he finally hears descend through water, parting the white sheets.

The tumble of rocks charting a depth plays on in Lenny's head, distinct and delicate, a far-off clatter that sounds and falls, sounds and falls. But her burden has no sharp edges, lies before them heavy and inert, rolls unevenly. Lenny thinks about rolling down hills, holding her arms above her head and clasping her hands to make her body longer, tighter, and still she bumped over the ground, clumsy and lopsided, until she closed her eyes and concentrated not on speed but on how her body met the spongy grass, turning slowly, more slowly, a slow-motion rotation in the dark that let the ground fill any recess in her body, make her smooth. Sunlight bright red against her closed lids, and when she rolled into the shade that color changed and the grass felt cool. The floor of the cave is cool and damp, no earth anywhere that she can feel, and she remembers the flare of the sun with an intense thirst, as though she could drink it. The dark is so black they could be crawling in space, moored to this rock surface in vast, turning space, and when they let the body go Lenny thinks it might float away from them, released over a chasm it will never find. But it leaves their hands and begins to slide like a bag of earth. The drag of the slide stops abruptly and stops her breath; she reaches forward into nothing, too late. Falling, the body makes no sound at all. Soft, like fruit or meat, empty of the wild force that defined it, empty of anything at all. Abandoned, Lenny thinks, dragged all this way and let go. For the first time, she thinks about his hands on her in the water, how there was a roar all around her, nothing but rage or hunger in him, as though he were an animal with his teeth in his food, and when she wrested Buddy from him the boy was like an object he dropped in order to tear her apart. Death grip: now she knows what it means. And she veers away in her mind as though the feel of him skates fast and vicious inside her, a shadow to sidestep, a remnant.

"Don't turn," she says aloud, quietly. "Back up, straight back. Everyone, move back slowly. Buddy has the light. Stay together and move back to the light."

Lenny hears Delia whispering, making words under her breath, and wonders about the words of the prayer. She can't believe in any prayer made of words: she understands now that she doesn't believe in words at all. None of it translates. Like the taste of the beer her father gave her, sharp and bitter and golden like a potion. And running deep into the field with Alma, urgent and fast, driving her with a long weed they pretend is a coachman's whip, both of them so young the waving grasses rush at their faces. Alma's body flickers through tall stalks and both of them fly, fly away, and their father watches from the yard, not calling them back. And Camp Shelter the first night, throbbing with sound in the dark, the shrills and trells of unknown, miraculous creatures pressed against the canvas of the tent in moonlight; Lenny and Cap sitting on their bunks, looking at each other, listening. Those were prayers, and crying was, and groaning. Standing in Cap's mother's closet, looking together at the clothes she'd left behind: that was praying. Delia was wrong; a prayer didn't have to ask. A prayer could be brave enough not to ask at all. When they were all at Turtle Hole, separate and together among the rocks in the dusk, that was a prayer, and that prayer held them together at the water when he came. It was why no one ran away, even when Lenny told them to. It was why they all hit him after Cap couldn't stop him moving: because it was done, come upon them, and they took it on together, closed themselves in. Whatever happened would happen to all of them. And Buddy, Buddy had been praying all his life. Walking and running and living in his house.

"Buddy?" Lenny calls out. She twists back again, close now. Buddy's light spills across the rock floor and they've nearly reached him, so much faster than their tortuous movement forward.

"The light!" Delia gasps, almost to herself.

Delia doesn't know she prays without talking, Lenny thinks, doesn't understand her father is a prayer that twists, a prayer Delia carries around in her hazel eyes, her curly hair the same brown, like dark honey. A picture slams into Lenny clear as a snapshot: Nickel Campbell with Audrey, Audrey backed against the kitchen sink, holding him, his mouth in her neck. Then the picture moves, they move inside it, forward and backward in their tiny history like film on a reel. Slow it down and look. They were moving, weren't they, like dancing in place, no, more like floating on what eddied and slowed and moved them both, and Lenny thinks about Mud River, Nickel Campbell's car blunt as a metal beetle, spraying water when it hit and disappearing when the river closed over. Audrey backed against the kitchen sink. Lenny hears the roaring, far away from her, like some dim apprehension. There should be water in the cave, more water than the rattle of the stream, there should be water at the bottom of the drop, she'd promised Delia, she'd told Delia there could be water to float the body down and down, safe, where it could never come out, float underground through some watery vein into Mud River, into Turtle Hole. The cave would never let loose, give things up like the river did. How they dragged Delia's father out with steel tools, and pulled the car up, and floated the news through town. Accident or not, they should have let him be. The river took hold and there was no struggling or turning back. Like when Carmody had hold of her, her arms pulled tight and his knee in her back. Everything Carmody was had flashed for an instant in that look on Buddy's face, the look he'd given Lenny when he recognized her in the water, and the dark blur beside him surged toward her. He'd cried out to her in some frequency she can still feel. She imagined Buddy in Carmody's grip, shaken like a rag. Yet it was Buddy who'd suddenly hit him. Buddy's bare feet rushing forward as she lay with her face pressed in the dirt, the dull impact of the stone, and Carmody's loosened grip, like a hesitation in the mechanism of a machine.

They've reached Buddy.

"Buddy's here," Alma says. "He's lying on the ground." She picks up the flashlight that lies beside him, shines it over all of them as though to be sure they are all here. Then she runs the bright stripe over Buddy. He seems to be sleeping, curled on his side with his hands tucked in, like a baby.

Lenny bends over him, cradles his face in her hands. "Buddy. Buddy. Wake up."

"What's wrong with him?" Cap's hands are on him too.

"I don't know. Let's get him outside. Alma, you walk in front with the light. I'll carry Buddy and try to keep one hand on your shoulder, and Delia, you come behind me."

"I'll stay behind Delia," Cap says. In the short cone of light, she lifts Buddy onto Lenny's back, slides him up over Lenny's shoulder. Lenny feels his weight, his head hanging at her breast. She pulls his limp body a little more forward and clutches his wrists with one hand.

"How do we know which way to go?" Delia asks.

"We go straight back from the stream," Cap says. "Buddy hadn't moved. The stream" — she reaches out to direct the light in Alma's hand — "is there. Alma, walk that way, we'll follow."

Lenny balances carefully, her feet slightly splayed to support Buddy. She doesn't want to lean on Alma, throw her off. She gets in position behind her sister and waits to feel Delia's hand. When it finds her, tentative, reaching up, Lenny says, "Hold me at my waist, the belt loops. Easier for you." She grasps Delia's hand for a moment, guiding it, then touches Alma in a signal to move forward.

If she could only close her eyes, Lenny thinks, carry Buddy and just walk. But she can't help peering into the black, a dark deep as oil, pierced by the beam of the light. The black takes on its own shimmer, like an absence of colors that sucks and turns. Fear licks up in her, a tongue at her wrist, in her chest: without Buddy to lead them, they'll never get out. Stay here, tracing paths back and forth to the stream until the batteries give out and the light disappears. Lenny tries to see; her own thoughts seem to roil and turn like black scarves in the black around her, floating and vanishing like the white fish that moved across her hand. There, the stranger, the workman who was some magician, some angel, walks through trees into air itself, rising, rising away from them, contracting in mist over the water, pulling in to curl like a fetus and float, mindless, away from them. Behind them, the monster she felt on top of her at Turtle Hole peers after them in the dark, tasting their departure and waiting, hungry, so hungry and empty, a monster still wet from Carmody's body, wet the way newborn babies are wet, slathered with fluid and suddenly alone, the monster that threw Carmody away and passed into the summer dusk, seeking a darkness like this. Or she was wrong: the body she'd thought was empty had pulled Buddy after it, wouldn't let him go after all. She stumbles, pitching forward.

Alma stops in front of her. "Lenny?"

"Yes, keep going."

On her back, Buddy doesn't move or twitch; his head bobs against her with the motion of her walking. But she feels his warmth, his borne-down weight. He's only sleeping, she thinks, so he won't remember this part. Tears well in her eyes and she gazes rapidly to the left and right, never turning her head, amazed to see a glowing crosshatch of markings arc above them. The marks seem to float, they aren't stationary, then they disappear. She looks again, tries hard to focus, takes a deep breath. *They've done a terrible thing.* The line floats into her head like a story about someone else. She knows what it means but she can't feel it. She knows something terrible happened, came to get them. She feels it in front of her, breathing on her. Like the air of another world, this world, the world that shifts and moves beneath what she knew. What had they seen, each of them, what did they know? A world inside them all, dark and velvet and ripped. Suddenly come upon and taken in. Like he took them in and showed them: what was in him roared like a cyclone, a hurricane; it was the sound that ate Carmody and turned him loose and Buddy had turned it all: Buddy with the rock in his hand, no plan, no thought, what he knew broken through in him at the only possible moment. Strangely, he'd saved them, and they had saved him, made sure Carmody never got up, never, to come and get him, find them, find Buddy. *They did something terrible.* And when he'd fallen and lay there, still, with his feet turned in and his long arms loose, the roaring dropped him like he'd dropped Buddy. What it raged inside was only a thing, a possession. Where had it gone? Lenny imagines a black wind tearing through the night sky over Turtle Hole, ripping at trees and bridges, ripping along the two-lane to Gaither, imagines Audrey alone in the house, opening the door. And the roaring is Lenny's own voice, poured through like a message, a long, rattling, unmistakable sound, perfectly rendered.

"Lenny," comes Cap's voice from behind, "I can carry him for a while, let me —"

But Lenny finds herself on her knees, her face hot, and it's hard to breathe, somehow she's tripped over nothing, and the beam of the flashlight tours wildly around to find her. "Alma! Don't turn around, don't move!" She hears her own ragged sob behind the words, and Alma's panicked denial, "I'm not! I'm moving the light, only the light!" and Cap, reaching forward over Delia, "I'll carry him now," and in all the sounds it takes a moment to feel Buddy's hands clutching at her neck, her throat, then he moves his head, burrows in like an interrupted sleeper, and Lenny holds still just to feel it, relief breaking over her.

"Shhh," Alma's saying, "wait. Be quiet a minute."

And they all hold still.

"I hear something," comes Alma's whisper.

And there is a sound, far off, like applause.

"Rain," Delia breathes.

"We're close," Lenny says, and she pulls Buddy higher onto her shoulders, shifting him with both hands, gets her legs solidly beneath her and stands. They move forward again; Lenny can feel Alma veering off a little to the right but the sound leads them, closer, and they smell it, warm and wet, and they're almost at the slanted entrance before they see it.

Even through the thudding downpour, the color of the dark is a pale charcoal in its rock frame, and the color floats; Lenny has to focus to see its exact dimensions, the line of rock around it. She realizes their light was nearly useless; they would never have seen the opening against the dark, never found it after dusk without the sound of the rain to lead them. The others are yelling, screaming with pleasure, and Cap is pushing Alma up, through the shelf of space to the outside. Then they are lifting Buddy away, pushing him through to Alma, and Lenny finds she can stand upright, touch the rock face, reach through to feel the rain pounding into her hands. But they push Delia through next before Cap nudges Lenny, helps her up the incline, and when she slides into the world she is instantly drenched, and she opens her mouth to drink, reaching at the same moment back inside for Cap's hands, Cap's arms, and they are rolling over in the loud rain, crouching around Buddy, squinting in the force of the downpour, and they bend over him, water running off their arms, and he opens his eyes and looks, in the refuge of their faces, their shoulders, their breathless shouts.

They all listen. And then Alma can feel it, smell it, move toward it without the light, the very air pulls her as though the rain could breathe them in, and when she reaches the opening she has to feel for the shape, reach up to grasp the rock before she sees it, and the rain pours off her hands, splattering. It's as though they all fall out at once, up into the world, washed in the downpour, and their noise wakes Buddy up, their noise and the drenching rain, and the girls actually join hands around him, whooping and revolving until Lenny pulls him upright and begins to move down the path around the rock, back toward Turtle Hole. They are sliding and falling, not talking, Alma has hold of Delia and the broad wall of the diving rock beside them streams with rain. Water gullies and flows down the path, fills Alma's shoes; she sees the prints of Lenny's bare feet fill like puddles and disintegrate as they all flash past. Turtle Hole is dappled, pounded with rain, brimming like a bowl, but Lenny leads them away, back up into the woods along a trail that is only mashed weeds through overhung trees, and the trailers and vines drag on Alma's arms like wet hair. The night is truly dark but awash in shadows even through the rain; there's no moonlight, no lightning, no thunder, only the sky split open, falling down driven and polished. Alma watches the slippery ground; they're nearly on the shack before she raises her eyes. A torn screen door hangs off one hinge, slanted like the walls. Alma steps up, inside, onto a board floor that gives under her weight.

They move, all of them, carefully, and for a moment they simply stand together, motionless, listening. Rain pours through the pitched roof here and there, drums on the board floor, spreads in a wet oval on the mattress tick, one like theirs, Alma thinks, but older, ripped into the cotton batting, shoved onto a kind of shelf a little off the floor. Someone has arranged things in front of it, like a display, just so. Alma moves to flash on the light, go closer, but Lenny touches her shoulder.

"Stay here," Lenny says. "All of us, stay here."

"Don't we have to go back?" Delia asks. Her hair has sprung into wet, shoulder-length curls; she bunches them in one hand and squeezes water onto the floor.

"They would all have sat by the fire until the rain began to really pour," Cap says. "Then they'd run everywhere, scatter under the porches."

"Sitting around in the cabins," Lenny agrees, "with the troops all mixed up. I don't know if they'll even miss us. If they do, we'll say we got caught in the storm and waited under trees, in the woods."

"We did wait in the woods," Alma says. "We were under the trees."

"In a shack," Buddy says in a small voice.

"He stayed here," Lenny says. "These are his things."

"In here," Buddy says, "and no one knew about him."

"What things?" Delia says. "Look at them. Shine the light."

"Wait." Lenny takes the flashlight from Alma and turns it on. She shines the beam along the walls, along the line of the tilted floor. It all looks empty in the dim light, swept with a broom maybe, but there is no broom, and the inside has a hay smell, like clean dust, even in the rain. In the splintering pour of the storm there is such a silence, like a church or a cell, a cloister, empty, and rain courses down the broken glass of the block-paned windows. Some of the jagged glass juts up like tongues, other panes are shattered intact, jeweled in their frames in webbed configurations. A metal kitchen chair with the vinyl seat laid open stands near the door. There's a bucket with no handle, and a bowl. The beam of light comes round to the pallet, the long shelf filled with the mattress, and Lenny walks closer, Alma so near their arms touch in the small space.

Objects. Trash, Alma thinks at first, or not trash: things from the woods. Each is placed deliberately, as though the interlude of space around each one is perfect and the spaces are not to be touched. Lenny shines the light and they bend close to look. There's a piece of honeycomb, long abandoned, its miniature grid intact. There are leaves, one brown-laced leaf placed atop another, stacked neatly like irregular, desiccated papers. Bones. Vertebrae like knuckles, and a jawbone studded with little teeth. A snakeskin, placed lengthwise, under the rest. And the metal blade of a broken pocket knife. Beside it, a piece of cardboard folded round like a sheath.

"That's his knife," Buddy says. "I seen him use it."

No one answers him, but Lenny lowers the light.

"Dad had hold of me," Buddy says, "and he come and got Dad off me, but Dad run the car over the bank. And he cut a snake with that knife — trying to scare Dad, I reckon." His voice rises at the end of each phrase, as though he's reciting a series of questions. "Mam and me," he says softly, "we was waiting for Dad to leave his own self. He kept saying he was going to leave, but then he said he was going to take me, not tell her. Make me go with him."

None of them moves. Outside, rain seems to wash the world away. A piece of Turtle Hole is visible through the broken windows. The sky is light gray and mist drifts through it like smoke behind the rain.

"He was wanting me to take all the stuff from that old lady's room. I had got me one ring — I got it for a reason, but Dad took it and kept it. I took it off his finger in the cave. I took it when you was all gone from me, looking for the edge." Buddy reaches into his pocket and shows them the ring, flat on his palm.

"You keep it tonight and you put it back tomorrow," Lenny tells him. "At breakfast you put it back, before she misses it. She won't be looking for it tonight, with all the confusion and the storm."

Buddy puts the ring back in his pocket, speaking slowly, as though to himself. "I'll tell Mam he's gone, he's left. She knows he was aiming to leave, and she won't be looking for him to come back."

Lenny swings the beam of light off the floor, up to the rafters in a bell that expands and fades, a circular tour, back to the pallet. They see the knife, small as a nail file, and farther on, just at the head of the bed, a pair of white shoes. Canvas sneakers.

Alma walks over and picks up the shoes. She walks back, three steps, holding them in her arms. She turns them one way and another in the yellow wash of the flashlight, as though to be sure. They sit on her flat palms like objects on a tray. The frayed strings hang down. Inside one, the fabric decal of Mickey Mouse, worn nearly smooth.

The rain still pours, a pounding, murmurous constant. They all sit down, knees almost touching, and Lenny sets the flashlight on its end in the center of the circle. The light shines up, a low lamp. She takes her shoes from Alma, and puts them on.

EARLY NOVEMBER, 1963

## ❧ BUDDY CARMODY: HIS KINGDOM

He climbs to the top of the rock nearly every day; even if he can't see the whole camp, he knows he stands over it, and he spreads his arms out and stands straight up and turns himself, slow, like he holds all below him in a bubble or a globe. School days, they get home before five and while Mam makes supper she lets him stay out; he has him a secondhand bike she got from someone at the church and he rides it down the road and straight through a stand of level pine till he can see the swinging bridge. Then he runs; he knows the light is going and it's not much longer she'll let him out like this near dusk, the wind blown around wild, a sudden rush in the trees while leaves fly up, like the wind blows him into the needle of the bridge and rocks him in its swing. He loves how the bridge looks to be a different color now because the sun has got a darker shade, like a fireball in a brown box, glowing through to turn the brown box red and tinge Mud River. The river is louder, faster, floated with leaves that rush away, like it knows the ice will crawl across it, choke it off narrow and more narrow till the water only runs hidden and slow, a deep channel no one sees. Buddy sees the little crosses he carved once on the bridge, a code at his feet as he runs across the moving planks; the crosses look like chicken scratches or a one-legged track that disappears, and he likes the unmarked part of the bridge, the part he'll never have to write on. He runs faster then and takes the flat part of the trail by the river at top speed. These shoes aren't like the leather ones Mam used to get him, or the boots she'll make him wear later in the cold; he can run now fast as the painter cats never seen around here anymore, faster than anyone at school, even the oldest boys. The long dirt track on the riverbank where the crew lay pipe is covered over now. Men brought in a bulldozer on a flatbed truck, edged it down a ramp and roared it through the woods from the road; how the big machine crashed through brush and throbbed, the August heat rising up from its yellow sides in lines. And the hills of dirt the workmen had dug up and piled like a ridge along the ditch began to disappear. The lengths of pipe were deep and still and linked and the dirt began to cover them, little trees and green bushes pulled in and crushed, the limbs cracking and the dozer jerking back and forth, roaring. There's still a long mound where the trenches once lay open; Buddy has run up and down it, stomping and tramping, talking to the hard dumb pipe that is buried. He's said all his words and he doesn't have to look as he pours himself through the woods toward Turtle Hole, round the big trees, onto the dirt track edging the water. If he looks the water will stop him, make him stand and try to see across, make him look at the rocks still scattered round like thick flat plates in a certain spot, the only place he can't go to or look at, the only one not part of his kingdom. And when he runs past, faster, cutting through, sometimes he can feel the angel pass by in the opposite direction, not the way he really looked behind Dad or in the water, but the way he was, faceless, like a wind, bigger than his body, trailing pieces of himself like a fog. Then the diving rock comes up beside like the flank of a wall or a tower and Buddy runs round to where the cave was, hidden now, Buddy thinks, hidden a while, anyway.

In the final days of camp he went with Lenny up and down Highest trail, last in the staggered line of girls, Cap between them and the rest to be sure there was room, like a guard. But they never talked about it, except Lenny told him once he was a brave boy, he would always be brave, and she walked with her hand on his shoulder like another boy might. Buddy put the ring back that first morning after and Lenny had waited for him just outside the door; no one ever noticed or asked. Then they all left and camp closed before August was half over; for a while it felt like they were all still there, off in the cabins and sites Buddy couldn't see from Turtle Hole. Then they were just gone and the heat was thick as soup, and he would stay near the rock in the morning while Mam worked in her garden, and he began to build over the hole of the cave. First he thought he was making a fort, then he saw it was more like a garden too, not for vegetables but for things to grow up over the opening, to look old, like it had all grown without help. He knew which logs to drag up, broken ones rotted into the heartwood in holes and crevices, ones with no bark left, the inner skin of the wood smooth and gray, etched already by worms and bugs in a near language of little forms, circles, maps, and pictograms. He used a trowel from home to dig the rich loam from underneath the shack and he brought the loam up in the bucket that's got no handle. He filled some dirt between the logs and planted in some fern and kudzu, and he watered them with the bucket, every morning all through the heat, four trips from the water, holding the bucket to his chest with both arms. He thought in a while you wouldn't be able to see the hole even if you were looking straight at it, in a year or two year; the kudzu would vine up on the pine already there and climb the rock. Kudzu could eat a town, Mam said, why, further south they had to hack it down every spring, and it never even bloomed like wisteria and redeemed itself.

Every day after school he would stand in the third-grade bus line and look in the windows of the buses pulling up. The younger girls would be at the junior high and he thought he saw Delia once. Lenny and Cap would be in high school, and a few buses loaded there and picked up at elementary when some of the older kids got off to change buses for home. But he never saw them at all, and then he got a picture postcard from Lenny, from the state of New York. It was a picture of a school building with a steeple like a church and Mam read him the words on the back a few times until Buddy knew them, and when he looked at the writing he saw it as a block of letters and knew it in one piece. *My mother and my sister live here now. We rented a house so I live at home, not at school. My mom has a job in admissions. Cap goes here too and she is going to get a car after she passes her test.* How was it anyone lived at school, Buddy wouldn't do it, it was enough Mam made him trace on his letters every night, and cut out pictures from catalogues that started with the sound. But he would want him a car, like that, as soon as he could drive. The car Dad made him drive in the woods is still there, like no one's ever seen it; maybe no one has, it's so far out in the trees, downriver of Turtle Hole past the boundary of the camp. Buddy goes there but he doesn't go in the car. The driver's side door still hangs open and Buddy can see inside, see it's empty, but he doesn't get in. The empty car sags down on one side like the ground has given way a little beneath it, and the car and the space around the car simply wait, wait to break down. The big trees Dad carried him across have rolled over and drifted farther downriver to where the water broadens out and deepens. Only the tips of the silken branches show now, the smallest, reaching ends of the branches. The riverbank there and the branches nodding in their rush of water are the farthest away of his places, each one a star on a map he walks and knows. The closed buildings of Camp Shelter are marked with the stones of their columned porches, leaves blown against their massive doors, and when Buddy climbs Highest trail he can look down and see more of the quad through the pines. The trees highest up lose their leaves first and stand near naked when the forest trees are still full flung as bouquets, yellow and fiery. Buddy sits on the platform of Lenny's tent and looks down, wishes he could stack up these platforms to make a tower for armies, and he climbs on the tarps that hold the canvas tents. There's a cache of walking sticks the girls left and he takes them home one by one, long ones sized right to be rifles, and he plays at shooting up all the trees across the road from their porch and Mam shakes her head and says to him those are the only rifles he'll have in this house, he won't go for a soldier, no sir, she didn't raise him to be sending him off to no cage, draft or no draft. We have already done enough of that from around here, she says, and Buddy shoots louder till she goes in the house and then he stops.

It's not shooting he does when he's up on top of the rock. There's no one comes near him then. He can see everywhere at once; Turtle Hole shimmers below and Mud River is an interrupted stripe through the trees, and the mashed place where Frank's tent stood is gone, nothing left but the cleared place and the low bank of rocks where he built fires, and halfway down the diving rock there's the spit of ledge people dive off, the ledge where Frank fished with his casting rod he never let Buddy touch. Buddy didn't want to fish, he doesn't like to catch fish, the way they suffocate. The way their gills work, the way they can't blink their eyes. Sometimes he sees Lenny's eyes move, very near him, like he's watching her with his eyes next to hers but she doesn't see him, and he sees the whites of her eyes and the blue rims of her irises, thin curve of color like a glass secret, and then the starred mix of blues and grays between the rim and the black point in the center. Her long hair catches in her lashes, stray white filaments like the lines of web that blow about when Mam takes a broom to the spiders under the porch.

Lenny sent him another card and Buddy keeps it with the first one; it looks like a picture from an airplane of a little town, little buildings with sidewalks between them and woods around. Mam said that's the school she goes to. *Alma is going to Delia's at Thanksgiving and I'm going with Cap to her grandparents. We're going to send you a present at Xmas so write me if there's something you want.* Now you should write back to her, Mam says, I could write down what you want to say and you could copy it out, you could do that, but he doesn't want to, he doesn't need to. He keeps the cards in a certain place and he doesn't even look at them. He knows about the writing like he has a picture of it, like he could fall into the white space between the letters, and in that white space him and Mam are at Turtle Hole like they were in August after camp closed, in the evenings after the hot days, and they would swim and then Mam would soap him off and rinse him down with the bucket, she'd make him stand out of the water in the open and she'd throw the water right over him so the suds ran off away from Turtle Hole, and she'd be using the same bucket from the shack and he'd get her to laughing, throwing the water as fast as she could, and she'd make him walk home before her so she could take her own bath in private. There is always a white space Buddy can make when he is on top of the rock, and he can put any good thing in that space. Like Mam and him collecting flowers to dry: she has herself a big jug of money tree now, the husks all taken off and the oval circles catching light like clear, skinned coins, and she keeps that jug in the middle of the table and at night a candle glow can catch a reflection and light up the undersides of each pale shape. Like parchment paper, Mam says, like glitter shell, and she slices the little tomatoes they picked, canned up with mustard seed and pickled onion, and lays them out all round on the white plates, with peeled white potatoes and white hominy, and she says to him he's got his white supper before the snow even falls, him a rich man with his money on a tree all clean and white. And she has a laugh about him liking white things, and tells him there's such a thing as white chocolate, and maybe she'll find some come Christmas.

He has the white T-shirt of Lenny's that he took last summer, the one he found in her footlocker wadded up like she wanted to throw it away. He kept it under his mattress for a while and then when school started he sat on top of the big rectangular freezer Mrs. T. gave Mam from camp, and he got Mam's kitchen scissors and cut the bottom off the T-shirt. He folded that up and put it away, and he wears the shirt now, every day; it fits him under his school clothes, under his sweatshirt on the weekend. Mam says how she got him a whole package of those undershirts and what does he do but wear just that one, worn out soft as silk and going to rip right down the middle; where did he ever get that old thing? But she washes it out for him by hand every two or three days, and dries it on a hanger over the woodstove. I don't know where your dad has gone to, she would say sometimes, back in the summer, but I reckon it's just as well. Now she says, I'm only hoping I don't hear some bad thing about him, some crazy thing he's done. You won't hear nothing, Buddy wants to tell her, but he doesn't say, he keeps his lips pressed flat against his teeth in a signal to himself to stay still. She's scared sometimes, uneasy. These weekends, the long Saturday afternoons when they're home and she's teaching Buddy to knit on the porch, she'll stand up and look out over the railing, down at the road, with the sky brilliant all round and flared near topaz over the reds and golds of the trees. Cars do pass on weekends, people from town driving out to look at the leaves now fall has peaked and the colors are rarefied, fired luminous, nodding against the evergreens. Buddy sees Mam look after cars that pass and pass again on the way back, kicking up dust on the road; she looks into the clouds of dust that stay too low to reach them, and Buddy wants to tell her. But he says to himself she'll feel safe after more time goes by, after Thanksgiving, after Christmas, and he knits at the scarf he is making, the yarn so pale a blue he's got to keep his hands washed, and Mam complains how he should be using a dark color for a scarf to wear to school, she's got some navy yarn would do just fine. He says how he likes this color and she nods and sighs, well, go right on, then, but I'm the one that'll be washing it by hand, right along with that undershirt you won't stop wearing. He will finish the scarf and he will get her to show him how to tie tassels on the ends, and he already has a box to put it in, and he can wrap the box in aluminum foil, prettier thickened with creases than any store-bought Christmas paper, and he can give it to her when they get back from church on that morning, the house all fragrant with the smell of roasting turkey. Like butter in his mouth, Buddy thinks, and clinches his jaws like he wants to hold on to something.

At night he can wake up in a sweat, gasping, thinking Dad's hand is jammed between his teeth, and he sits up straight in bed and sees where he is, and he's glad about all of it again, glad Dad can't come back, and he feels lucky for the way it went. *Lucky Devil:* the words float into his mind in pictures from the tattoo on Dad's arm. Buddy is a devil too, he knows, for what he did, and he peers through the dark and sees the God's eye Mam made him, hanging from the ceiling over his bed. Mam made it from white yarn and peeled sticks after camp closed and hung it up to watch over him because God's eye never closes. What does the eye think, he asked her, and she told him it doesn't think, it only sees and knows, and the white shape moves at night at the end of its tacked thread, turning. The blanket hangs from the ceiling too, the blanket Mam put up when Dad came. They left the blanket up to make Buddy a separate room, and the blanket stirs a little, like Dad might be behind it, but he knows Dad's not, and he listens for Mam's breathing and the sound of her comes to him, quiet and steady, the sound he listens to so he can sleep again. In the dark at night he can see the half-size bookcase against the wall beside his bed, the space so close he can reach out and touch the objects on each shelf, objects Buddy brought from the shack when the camp closed. The bones are laid out separate, and the fibrous snakeskin, and the flashlight and the piece of knife. He thought he could watch over them because winter will come and he won't go to the shack anymore then, or to Highest camp. The trails will fill with snow and the rock by Turtle Hole will be hung with ice, sheets of ice like veils, and icicles thick as a man's legs, and Buddy will walk round the snow oval of Turtle Hole and slide its frozen face on his sled, just near the edge like Mam tells him. Or maybe this year in a hard freeze he'll run right across the middle, whooping and screaming, see it all laid out hard and shining around him, gleaming. But now the water is blue, azure as the sky, and the evergreens beyond toss and stir like giant flower points in the drenched colors of the leaves, and Buddy stands up and begins to dance, slower at first and then faster, jumping like a banshee, turning and whirling, yelling out loud, and beneath his stomping feet plummets the world within the rock and the world beneath that world, the black world, escaped, vast and deep and no bigger than his mind, what he sees when he closes his eyes and watches it all from far, far above. He watches from so high, the road and the camp and the lip of the rock and the long green sward of the mountains flatten out like a picture, a picture he could send to Lenny with writing on the back.

It's when he comes down the rock, past the entrance to the cave no one can see now, and he sits down to tie his shoe, shoes like the ones he saw Lenny put on in the shack, that he sees the rabbit, a small one, a young one looks like, sitting still beside the path. He's downwind, that's what, or the rabbit is hurt maybe and can't move, but no, he sees it hop once, twice, and sniff the air. Even from here, he can see how its body moves when it breathes, its furred sides palpitating. It holds its head still and looks, no whites in the eyes but a shine like tears. Buddy sees the rabbit from one side; the surface of its visible, bright eye rounded and reflective as a little mirror. Slowly, so slowly, he stands up, begins edging away, around behind it. Still, completely still, moving on the balls of his feet, choosing steps, his body poised; in his mind he picks up the rabbit, holds it in his hands, and he moves toward that image, yearning in silence. A crow's hoarse caw rents the air, ricochets off the broad wall of the diving rock, and Buddy freezes, but the rabbit only lowers its tight round head and smells the ground. The erect ears go flat. It should be running for cover at the call of a circling crow; Buddy has seen crows drop in sprung glides to rip rabbits and chipmunks apart, fast, like tearing open a wet package. Throwing the parts around, digging for the heart. Even young squirrels, anything small enough to carry away. And rabbits, they got nothing but speed, and hearing fine-tuned as a bat's. Squirrels can bite pretty nasty, fight off birds sometimes. But rabbits got nothing but knowing, Buddy thinks. He stands behind it now, where it can't smell him, and the rabbit's bunched brown body blends into the colors of the path, the autumn reds and browns of pieweed and devil's lantern, and he knows it by the nearly imperceptible trembling of animal breath, a slow flutter in the weeds and plants of the high-grown edge of the trail. Buddy begins to creep closer, even-paced. Slowly he closes the distance and the rabbit jerks alert, ears turned, and Buddy doesn't pause, he bends down and has it in his hands, the soft body enclosed in his two palms. He picks it up smoothly, with such dexterous care, holds it chin level and looks down, afraid to bow his head and startle it; he looks down the plane of his own nose and mouth and sees the rabbit's head, the sweep of its whiskers. The animal has gone dead still, frozen, and Buddy peers farther, like looking over a cliff, he thinks. He tilts his head and sees the tender, inner curve of the ear, mauve brown like a bruise. The whiskers move, twitch involuntarily, and Buddy sees that its left eye is limned with a milky glaze. One-eyed. Big enough to be on its own but won't make first snow, all the foxes and stoats gluttonous with instinct, storing up in themselves for the long cold. Buddy can't tell if the rabbit's just blind or something maybe took that eye, but there's no wound he can see. The eye holds still, smooth orb with a skin like an egg. The rabbit blinks. Buddy holds it to his mouth, to his nose, and begins the walk home. He'll take it to Mam. She'll think it's pretty, she'll have a bottle to feed it.